IGNITING DARKNESS

IGNITING DARKNESS

By Robin LaFevers

HOUGHTON MIFFLIN HARCOURT
Boston   New York

hmhbooks.com

The text was set in Adobe Jenson Pro.
Map by Cara Llewellyn
Jacket design by Whitney Leader-Picone
Interior design by Whitney Leader-Picone

Library of Congress Cataloging-in-Publication Data
Names: LaFevers, Robin, author.
Title: Igniting darkness / by Robin LaFevers.
Description: Boston : Houghton Mifflin Harcourt, [2020] | Sequel to: Courting darkness. |
Audience: Ages 14 and up. | Audience: Grades 10–12. | Summary: Sybella locates her fellow assassin and
novitiate of the convent of Saint Mortain, only to discover that Genevieve has made a lethal mistake, and
there are far-reaching consequences for loved ones entangled in French court intrigues.
Identifiers: LCCN 2019045857 (print) | LCCN 2019045858 (ebook) |
ISBN 9780544991095 (hardcover) | ISBN 9780358335801 (ebook)
Subjects: CYAC: Courts and courtiers—Fiction. | Kings, queens, rulers, etc.—Fiction. |
France—History—Charles VIII, 1483–1498—Fiction.
Classification: LCC PZ7.L14142 Ig 2020 (print) | LCC PZ7.L14142 (ebook) |
DDC [Fic]—dc23
LC record available at https://lccn.loc.gov/2019045857
LC ebook record available at https://lccn.loc.gov/2019045858

Manufactured in the United States of America
DOC 10 9 8 7 6 5 4 3 2 1
4500796096

For Nysa and silver linings,

without which this book would not have been written

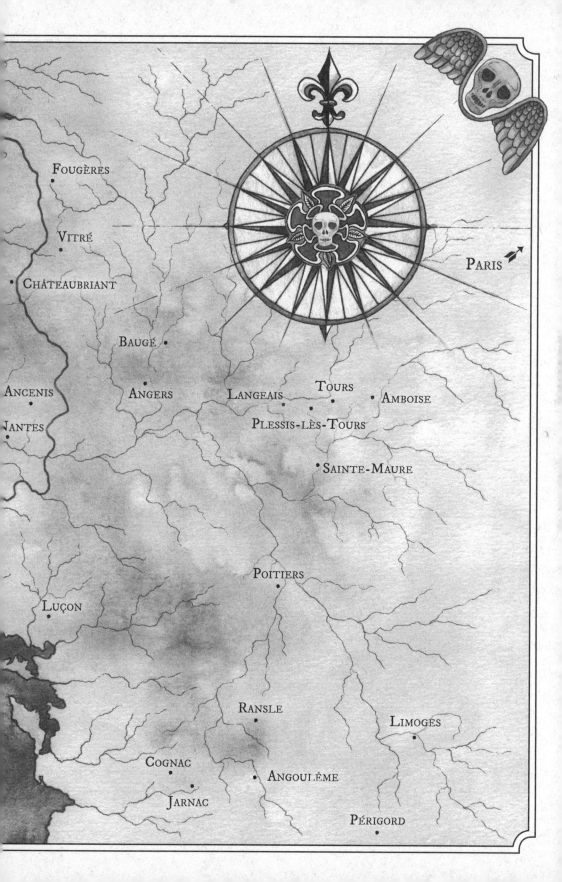

Dramatis Personae

From the Convent of Saint Mortain, Patron Saint of Death

SYBELLA D'ALBRET, Death's daughter, lady in waiting to the queen

LADY GENEVIEVE, Death's daughter, former lady in waiting to the countess of Angoulême

ISMAE RIENNE, Death's daughter, former lady in waiting to the duchess of Brittany

ANNITH, handmaiden to Death, acting abbess of the convent

BALTHAZAAR, Annith's consort

LADY MARGOT, Death's daughter, lady in waiting to the countess of Angoulême (deceased)

The French Court

CHARLES VIII, king of France

ANNE, queen of France, duchess of Brittany, countess of Nantes, Montfort, and Richmont

ANNE DE BEAUJEU, sister to the king, regent of France

PIERRE DE BEAUJEU, Duke of Bourbon, husband to Anne

LOUIS, Duke of Orléans

SIMON DE FREMIN, a lawyer

SEGUIN DE CASSEL, general in the king's army

CAPTAIN STUART, captain of the king's guard

THE BISHOP OF ALBI

THE BISHOP OF NARBONNE

FATHER EFFRAM, follower of Saint Salonius

COUNT CHARLES ANGOULÊME

The Breton Court

Gavriel Duval, a Breton noble, half brother to the queen

Isabeau, Anne's sister (deceased)

Duke Francis II, Anne's father (deceased)

Breton Nobility

Benebic de Waroch, "Beast," knight of the realm, captain of the queen's guard

Viscount Maurice Crunard, former chancellor of Brittany

Anton Crunard, last surviving son of the former chancellor

Jean de Rohan, viscount of Rohan, lord of Léon and count of Porhoët, uncle to the queen

Jean de Rieux, former marshal of Brittany

Jean de Châlons, prince of Orange

Philippe de Montauban, chancellor of Brittany

Captain Dunois, captain of the Breton army (deceased)

The d'Albret Family

Alain d'Albret, lord of Albret, viscount of Tartas, second count of Graves (deceased)

Sybella d'Albret, Death's daughter, lady in waiting to the queen

Pierre d'Albret, second son of Alain d'Albret, viscount of Périgord and Limoges

Julian d'Albret, third son of Alain d'Albret (deceased)

Charlotte, daughter of Alain d'Albret

Louise, youngest daughter of Alain d'Albret

Followers of Saint Arduinna

Aeva, Arduinnite, lady in waiting to the queen

Tola, Arduinnite, lady in waiting to the queen

Men-at-Arms

YANNIC, squire to Benebic de Waroch

LAZARE, charbonnerie, member of the queen's guard

POULET, member of the queen's guard

JASPAR, a mercenary

VALINE, a mercenary

ANDRY, a mercenary

TASSIN, a mercenary

The Nine

MORTAIN, god of death

DEA MATRONA, mother goddess

ARDUINNA, goddess of love's sharp bite, daughter of Matrona, twin sister of
   Amourna

AMOURNA, goddess of love's first blush, daughter of Matrona, twin sister of
   Arduinna

BRIGANTIA, goddess of knowledge and wisdom

CAMULOS, god of battle and war

MER, goddess of the sea

SALONIUS, god of mistakes

CISSONIUS, god of travel and crossroads

IGNITING DARKNESS

Prologue

Maraud

France 1490

araud awoke to the sound of retching — a retching so violent his own stomach clenched into a fist and tried to punch its way out of his throat.

That's when he realized the retching noises were his.

"That's right, big guy. Let it all out."

A woman's voice. "Lucinda?" he croaked.

"What kind of fool asks for the woman who just tried to poison him?"

He knew that voice.

"A straw-headed fool, that's who."

That one, too. Should be able to place them both. Saints! Why was he so disoriented? He cracked open an eye, only to find the world bobbing up and down, furthering his stomach's revolt. He shut his eye again.

"She didn't poison him," a third voice grunted.

Tassin. The name came to him so easily he almost wept.

"She most certainly did." Andry.

"Tassin's right." The woman again — Valine. "She wouldn't save him, then poison him."

"I disagree."

Maraud considered it a major victory that he recognized Jaspar's voice right away.

"Maybe she wanted the pleasure of killing him herself. She would not be the first to do so."

As he tried to sit up, Valine said something, but her words were lost as he struggled to keep from puking up his liver.

Hell. He was sitting up — more or less. On his horse. He shifted, which caused a tug around his middle. Not sitting on his horse. Tied.

"Whoa, there!" Valine drew her mount close to his. "Not so sure that's a good idea."

"I'm fine," Maraud gritted out between clenched teeth, afraid if he opened his mouth too far, he'd spew all over her.

"If you think you can stay in your saddle, I can untie you."

"In a minute." He willed the world to stop swooping around like a drunken stable boy. "On second thought, leave it. This way I can doze off again if I need to."

Valine arched one dark brow in amusement, and a strange, strangled sound came from his right, like a goose stuck in a trumpet. He turned — slowly! — to find Tassin ... laughing? Maraud hadn't seen him laugh in — Christ. Had he ever seen him laugh?

"So." Andry got back to the business at hand. "Do we follow her?"

Follow her. The woman who tried to poison him three times. And outright lied to his face ten times that. Not to mention she'd planned to trade him as if he were a pig at a fair.

"No." Lucinda made her bed, now she could lie in it. He put his heels to his horse's flanks. A good bracing gallop should clear his head.

Or cause him to dump the contents of his stomach. Only time would tell.

CHAPTER 1

Genevieve

Plessis-lès-Tours
France 1490

hether one is raised at a convent that serves Death or in a tavern room filled with whores, there is one lesson that always applies: There is no room for mistakes. The wrong amount of poison, the incorrect angle of the knife, poor aim, or a false gesture when pretending to be someone else can result in disaster, if not death.

It was the same at the tavern where I spent my earliest years. How many of my aunts would have had other lives, but for one mistake? Some, like my mother, chose their path. But for others, it was too many years of poor harvests, or crossing the tanner's guild, which was always looking for excuses to remove its female members. Being alone at the wrong moment, catching the eye of the wrong man might send one's life skidding down the slope of destiny into a midden heap.

Which is precisely where I have landed.

The shadows in my darkened room loom large as I run my fingers along the silky edges of the crow feather. The good news is the convent did not abandon me. The bad news: They might, once they learn what I have done.

And what will the king do with this knowledge of the convent I so foolishly handed him? He knew nothing about it until I spoke of its existence. Will his anger pass like a sudden summer shower, or will it fester and grow?

Far off in the distance, a cock crows. Morning comes, but no answers with it. I have spent the night trying to convince myself that, after five years of their silence, I owe them nothing. But the sick shaking that has kept me awake all night tells me my heart believes something else.

Which do I listen to?

Once before, I did not listen to my heart. *Come with us,* Maraud said. *We can help.*

Maraud. Even though he did not know what I was facing, he offered his help. His friendship. And so much more.

I have stood at only five crossroads in my life, and of all of them, that is the one I regret the most. Not trusting Maraud and accepting that help. Indeed, I have ensured he will loathe me as much as the king does. My name will be a curse upon the convent's lips and reviled for generations. Truly, the wreckage I have left in my wake is breathtaking.

Thinking of Maraud is like rubbing my heart against broken glass, so I shove all thoughts of him aside. I must find a way to fix this — to unsay those words to the king. Or at the very least, convince him they are far less important than he thinks they are. But he may not ever call for me again or may decide to have me thrown into the dungeon.

Something deep inside warns me that it is possible this cannot be fixed. Have I broken a piece of crockery that can be glued back together, or shattered a crystal goblet that is irreplaceable? As if in answer, the fine hairs at the nape of my neck lift in warning, and I realize I am not alone.

I shift my hand toward the knife I keep under my pillow.

"Good morning." It is a woman's voice, low and melodious. Surely someone sent by the convent to punish me would not use such a cheerful greeting.

I peer into the shadows for the source of the voice.

It laughs, a note of earthiness among the lilting sounds. "You do not need your knife for me, little sister. Did you not see the feather I left you?"

Keeping the knife hidden in the folds of my gown, I sit up. "I saw a crow feather." My words are as carefully measured as pennies from a beggar's purse. "But crows are a most common bird." The young woman — mayhap a year or two older than myself — sits in the room's lone chair. Even though she is cast in shadow, it is clear that she is impossibly beautiful — the contours of her face so elegantly constructed that it borders on being a weapon in its own right. While I cannot see if she is smiling, I sense her amusement, all the same.

"Who else would leave you such a thing?"

I shrug one shoulder. "The French court is a complex and devious place, my lady. Messages can be intercepted and twisted to suit any number of intentions."

"You are wise to be cautious. But have no fear, I am well and truly convent sent — and your sister, besides."

My sister. The words throw me off balance as surely as a well-placed kick. This woman. Margot. All of us at the convent are sisters. And I have betrayed them.

They betrayed me first.

I shove my hair out of my face. "If that is the case, if you are well and truly my sister . . ." Weeks — nay, months — of anger swell up, as unstoppable as the tide. "Then I have to ask, what in the *rutting hell* took you so long?"

She blinks, the only hint this might not be the greeting she was expecting. "You only just arrived, what, three — four — days ago?"

Heat rises in my gorge, making my words harsh. "I'm not talking about the last three days. I've been waiting for *five years.*"

A flash of vexation distorts her face, but her voice remains calm. "The convent has been in disarray these last few months. No one was aware you had been removed from the regent's household."

The words dangle like bait. I want to believe them, but to do so means that I fell into a trap of Count Angoulême's making. "Surely they knew of my change in residence, else why was my patron receiving letters of instructions regarding me?"

The woman grimaces — the grimace giving me more hope than any words she has spoken. "There have been many changes at the convent. The details of your and Margot's location were missing."

Missing. "We were not a pair of boots or a prayer book to be lost. We were two young girls left with no means of communication, no direction nor orders, nothing for nearly a third of our lives."

Her earlier warmth cools somewhat. "We have been rather distracted by France's invasion, the warring amongst the duchess's betrothed, and the matter of securing both her and our country's safety," she says dryly. "Surely the nature of your assignment was explained to you?"

"That was no assignment, but abandonment. We assumed you'd forgotten about us."

"You could certainly be forgiven for thinking that."

I don't want compassion, but answers. No, what I truly want is to slog back through time and unsay the words I spoke to the king. To undo my grievous mistake. But since she cannot give me that, answers I shall have. "*Had* you forgotten about us?"

She studies me, weighing how much to say. For all of her sympathetic manner, I must not underestimate this woman.

"I only learned of your existence two months ago," she says at last. "When I was assigned to accompany the duchess to France."

While her words bear the weight of truth, I also sense there is more to it than that. Frustration hums through my veins. "There are others at the convent besides yourself. Why not send someone sooner?"

Just as the convent taught us, she pivots, going on the offense. "Why?" she demands. "Are you indulging in a fit of temper, or has something happened to make timing of the essence?"

Because everything inside me wishes to avoid her question, I lean forward instead, not caring that it brings my dagger out into the open. "If you want to come back into my life after five years of nothing, you'll have to start with some explanations. Something far more satisfactory than 'we were busy.'"

She does not so much as spare my weapon a glance, but inclines her head, imbuing the movement with feline grace. "Very well. You are owed that at least." For some reason, the sympathy in her voice infuriates me. She *knows* why we were left to molder.

"The abbess who sent you and Margot to France was an impostor." Although she speaks clearly enough, the words scarcely make sense. "She was not a daughter of Mortain. Was not sired by the god of death. The person controlling all of our lives was not interested in the well-being of his daughters. Only her own."

Her words hit me like a blow, and I struggle to grasp the enormity of what she claims. "How could such a thing happen?"

For the first time, she looks away, toward the window. "Sometimes the sheer scope and daring of a plan make it impossible to see it for the lie that it is." Her gaze shifts back to me. "I am sorry that you were abandoned. Sorry that even now, you feel you must protect yourself with that knife."

The sincerity of her words permeates my fog of anger, and for a moment, I want to throw myself into the comfort she is offering. Until I remember that she would never offer such comfort if she knew what I have done. Would possibly kill me on the spot.

"Many of the decisions the abbess made were designed to keep her own secrets." The note of bitterness in her voice is personal, hiding closely held pain. She, too, has been hurt by this woman.

"Is the abbess going to be punished for what she's done?"

The woman studies me a moment before answering. "A convocation of the Nine was called. She was put on trial, stripped of her position, and is now serving the crones of Dea Matrona, making amends for those she should have mothered but failed."

I nod, but it is not enough. Not for the enormity of what her crimes have cost me. Cost Margot. Will have cost this entire convent when the truth of what I have done is laid bare. "When did that happen?"

"The abbess was removed nearly two months ago."

"What day *precisely?*" Two months was before Angoulême claimed to have received the fateful letter, but letters take time to reach their destination. Could she have sent it, or was it truly a deception on Angoulême's part?

"The convocation was called on the eighteenth of November. The abbess was relieved of her duties two days prior to that."

This answer is as helpful as a knife made of sheep's wool. It is possible that the abbess sent the letter.

"That does not explain where you have been for the last two months." Margot was still alive two months ago. Not that this woman could have saved her, but the red, angry part of my soul does not care.

"The convent records were woefully inadequate and provided nothing to help us find you."

"But I have been in Plessis for four days!" If she had found me even a single day earlier, I would not have exposed the convent to the king.

"It is a big palace with a large number of retainers. With my duties to the queen, I do not always know the moment a new person arrives. Especially if they are not formally announced." She grows still, her head cocking to one side as she studies me anew. I can practically see the rash of questions she is forming.

Since I've no wish to answer any of them, I toss another one of my own at her. "How did you learn I was here?"

"I came upon you praying in the chapel. It wasn't until you placed an offering in one of the niches on the wall that I guessed." She opens her hand. The bright red of my holly berry makes her skin look unnaturally white. "I couldn't see what it was, nor understand the significance of it, until you had already left. And then there were pressing matters I had to attend to." A cold, hard look flashes briefly across her face. A look that sends goose bumps down my spine and warns me that she would not hesitate to shove a knife in my back if my actions warranted it.

But even that knowledge doesn't temper the anger lapping along my skin like flames. *Pressing matters.* But for a hand span of hours, I would not have ruined everything. "You should have come sooner." The words are empty, those of a desperate child, but I utter them nonetheless, as if by repeating them often enough, I can make the fault hers, not mine.

"I came last night, as soon as I was certain. You weren't here. Where were *you?*"

"I was at dinner, with the rest of the court."

"It was later than that. When everyone else was abed."

As I consider what to tell her, the silence between us lengthens. Her fingers are drifting to the edge of her sleeve when a sharp rap on the door stills her hand.

"Demoiselle Genevieve?" a voice calls out.

Relief surges through me. "Coming!" I hop from the bed and straighten my skirts and bodice.

"Why are you being summoned?" The question is as sharp as I imagine her knives to be.

"We shall find out," I snap, shoving my hair into some semblance of order. When I reach the door, I am surprised to find the steward standing in the hall-way. I curtsy. "My lord, how may I serve?"

"I am sorry to disturb you, demoiselle, but the king is looking for Lady Sybella. One of the other ladies said she thought she saw her heading toward your chambers."

Sybella. I roll the name across my tongue. Grateful for this reprieve, for a chance to digest what little she has told me, I turn to her. "Apparently, you are the one being summoned."

CHAPTER 2

Sybella

 s I step out of Genevieve's room into the hallway, I wonder if she knows just how much she owes the king's steward. I was within a hair's breadth of grabbing her by the shoulders, giving her a hard shake, and ordering her to pull herself together. There are far larger problems than hurt feelings and wounded pride to deal with right now.

Perhaps that is the darkness in me — once embraced, it continues to push and prod until I do its infernal bidding. Or perhaps it is simply that between the regent's plotting, the king's indifference, my sisters' danger, and the queen's illness, I have no patience for such indulgences.

"This way, my lady." As the steward steps in front of me, I hear Genevieve slip into the hallway behind us. Not her footsteps, for they are as light as any assassin's should be. It is her heart I hear, beating the slightly too rapid rhythm it has had since she first discovered me in her room.

For so long I've held out hope of finding one of the convent's elusive moles, but instead of gaining an ally, I have found an angry and sullen girl. One who is hiding something. But what — and why — elude me. Why is nothing in this benighted court ever simple?

I resist the urge to scowl in annoyance, and keep my face carefully blank. Why does the king wish to see me? I can think of no good reason for the request — and many disastrous ones. My mind sorts through possible plans and explanations, devising lies I can tell convincingly, and truths I can share without exposing myself.

When the steward speaks to the sentries at the king's door, I fall back beside Genevieve. "Where is Margot?" I ask, my attention firmly fixed on the steward. "I fear we may need her shortly." Because of Genevieve's evasiveness, I am no longer certain she can be trusted.

"Margot will not be coming."

At the note of finality in her voice, I tear my gaze from the steward. "Why not?"

She meets my eyes coolly. "Because she is dead."

Her words barely have time to register before the steward announces me to the king. "The Lady Sybella, Your Majesty. As you requested." With my mind still reeling from Genevieve's news, I am ushered into the room. There is a faint rustle of silk as Genevieve slips in behind me and drifts — as silent and unobtrusive as a ghost — to stand among the other courtiers at the fringes of the room.

But I can spare her no more thought. The king sits on his throne with a cluster of military men and bishops behind him. Something about his manner has shifted since yesterday, although I cannot put my finger on it. The queen is not present, but the regent stands to his right. It is not until she steps away from the man she is speaking with — my brother's lawyer, Monsieur Fremin — that my worst fears are awakened.

I force a placid, bemused smile upon my face. When Fremin sees me, he takes three steps forward. Only the formality of our surroundings keeps him from launching himself at me. "What have you done with my men?"

I halt, recoiling slightly, as if his abrasive behavior is threatening to me.

"Monsieur Fremin," the king remonstrates. "I did not give you leave to assault the women of the court."

Fremin fumes like a pot on a raging boil, but clamps his mouth shut and tries to collect himself. I alter my stride, imbuing my movement with hesitation. When I am in front of the throne, I sink into a deep curtsy. "Your Majesty. How may I serve you?"

When I rise, the king's gaze rests upon me. It is far less friendly and approving than it was just two days before. "Monsieur Fremin's attendants have gone missing. He thinks you know something about their disappearance."

Unable to contain himself any longer, Fremin steps closer, attempting to tower over me. "What happened to them?" He is nearly rigid with rage.

And fear. I do not envy him having to report his failure back to Pierre. "What happened to whom?" I ask bemusedly.

He takes another step closer. "My men are missing, and you are behind it."

"Me?" I fill my voice with incredulity, trying to draw the king into the absurdity of such an accusation, but the way he studies me sends a ripple of apprehension across my shoulders. "How could I have caused your men to go missing?" I glance again at the king. He can't possibly believe Fremin. I have given him no cause to do so. "Mayhap they simply headed home early?" I suggest.

"They would never do that."

"Then mayhap they went wining and dicing, and have not yet come back? They would not be the first men to do so."

The king ignores my suggestion, and my unease grows. "When we had someone sent to your room to fetch you here, the woman told us your room was empty. Your sisters weren't there, nor your attendants."

My heart plummets like a stone. Before it has reached the bottom of my stomach, I know what I must do, and allow pure terror to show on my face. "Your Majesty, that cannot be true! They were happily playing with their nurse when I left this morning to attend upon the queen!"

"And yet we did not find you with the queen when we went looking for you," the regent points out.

I do not so much as look at her. It is the king my performance must convince. "And now you say they aren't there?" I color my voice with distress and clasp my hands together tightly — as if only just barely managing not to wring them. "Who was sent?"

The regent answers. "Martine."

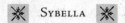

My gaze frantically searches out Martine's short figure. I take a step in her direction. "Are you certain? Could they not be outside, taking in some air?"

Martine shakes her head primly.

"We sent men to check precisely that," says the regent, "once Martine returned with her report."

Casting all conventions aside, I whirl back to face the king and throw myself onto the floor at his feet. "Please, Your Majesty! This is most alarming news. May I have leave to go see for myself? Perhaps they are playing some game or hiding from each other?"

"But of course. Your concern is understandable." At least he is not so convinced of Fremin's claims that he dismisses my request outright.

"You can't let her go alone," Fremin protests. "She might try to run."

The king casts an aggrieved look at the lawyer. "She will not run without her sisters, Monsieur Fremin. Nevertheless, she will have an escort." He waves his hand, and the regent and Martine step forward. As they take up position on either side of me, I head for the door. When the king turns to speak with his bishops, I feel Genevieve fall into step behind me. I wish that our first meeting had gone better so I could know whether she is simply curious or intends to guard my back.

As soon as we have cleared the fourth flight of stairs, I lift my skirts and break into a run. I throw the door to my room open and race inside. It is, indeed, empty. My hand flies to my mouth, as if to prevent a cry of alarm from escaping. I hurry toward the bed, yanking aside the canopies, tossing the bolsters to the floor, and pulling the counterpane from the mattress. Widening my eyes as if panicked, I call out, "Charlotte! Louise! Come out now, this is not funny!"

As the others watch, I drop to my knees and look under the bed, then rise and hurry to the window. I pull back the drapes and press my face against the glass, as if checking to see if they have fallen. It is easy enough to convey a mounting sense of alarm. I do not even have to pretend. What could have so emboldened Fremin that he would take this matter to the king?

I check the fireplace next, even looking up the chimney. "They're gone," I finally say, my voice small and hollow. "Not just them, but everything. Their clothes, their sewing, their dolls. All gone."

It is a testament to my acting abilities that both Martine and the regent look discomfited. In the awkward silence that fills the room, Genevieve steps forward to take my elbow and help me rise from the hearth. "My lady, calm yourself. You did not know your sisters were leaving?"

I cannot tell what role she is playing, but use it for my own purposes. "No. There were no plans for them to go anywhere. Both had been ill recently and were being kept to their rooms."

"Well," the regent says briskly. "You've seen for yourself that they're gone. The king has indulged you in this. Let us not make him wait any longer."

I head directly toward Fremin once we reach the audience chamber. "You!" The word is so forceful he rocks back on his heels. "*You* did this. Where have you taken my sisters?"

"What are you blathering about? It is my men who are missing."

"As are my sisters." I take another step toward him. "You were most displeased with the king's ruling. You even asked to see Charlotte and Louise afterward." Although I long to back him up against the wall, I force myself to maintain my decorum. "When you could not get what you wanted by legitimate means, you took matters into your own hands."

His face drains of some of its florid color as I publicly name the very thing he had been planning. "D-don't be absurd. You only say that to cover your own actions."

"Enough." The king's voice is as effective as a bucket of cold water on snarling dogs.

I am immediately contrite. "Forgive me, Your Majesty. My distress has caused me to forget myself."

"It is understandable, Lady Sybella. The news of your sisters complicates things a great deal." He gazes at Fremin, annoyed that the lawyer did not share this piece of the puzzle.

"Your Majesty! How was I to know the girls were not there?"

"How indeed," a male voice muses, but I dare not look to see who it is.

There are few choices available to me on how best to play this, so I plunge ahead, using the truth to bolster my lies. "Your Majesty, I saw Monsieur's attendants sitting in the antechamber the day he arrived. They are not mere attendants, or men-at-arms or even a simple escort. I know those men from the years I spent in my father's household. They are the worst cutthroats among the men that serve my family. Men the d'Albrets have used to do their most unsavory deeds.

"At the time, I thought it unusual for a lawyer to have such an escort, but I assumed it was because the war was over and they had to find something for such men to do. But now, now their purpose is made clear. He would not need those sorts of men if he intended only to escort two young girls back to their family."

The king whips his head around to spear Fremin with a look. "Who were these men who accompanied you?"

The lawyer swallows before speaking. "Their names do not matter, Your Majesty. What matters is that they are missing."

"Oh, but their names do matter," I continue, committing fully to this course of action. "I've no doubt some of your own men will have heard of Yann le Poisson." There is an audible intake of breath. "Or of Maldon the Pious." That name is followed by another susurration of whispers. "I know his exploits and strange taste for self-punishment have long been the source of rumor and gossip. And the Marquis? How many Frenchmen have been betrayed by him?"

From somewhere behind the king, a large man steps forward. "I have heard of these men." His deep rumbling voice is so very familiar that I wrench my gaze from the king to look at him. "They are precisely as she claims." He is uncommonly large — his nose, his jowls — everything but his eyes, which are small and narrow set. He has eschewed the more distinguished long robes of the king's other advisors and instead wears a shorter military style, complete with vambraces. His deep blue mantle is held in place by two gold brooches.

By his sheer size and ugliness, he can only be Beast's father, although his face has none of the charm or good humor that Beast's possesses. I drop my eyes quickly lest he see the spark of recognition in them. *Merde.* Can the gods lob any more disasters at me this morning?

A new suspicion glints in the king's eyes as he stares at Fremin. "What say you, lawyer? General Cassel has corroborated Lady Sybella's claims."

Cassel. The name goes off in my head like an alarm bell. *Look . . . to . . . cas . . . tle* were Captain Dunois's — oh, how I miss his stolid presence! — words to me. Was he warning me of this man? But I cannot think about that now. Not with the king and Cassel himself watching me with coolly assessing eyes.

Fremin swallows again — a nervous habit I am quickly learning to recognize. "The road is a dangerous place, Your Majesty. Especially with so many mercenaries recently released from service. With such valuable cargo, of course Lord d'Albret would send his most skilled men."

"There is skill, and then there is brutality," I point out.

"Are you saying your brother would put your sisters in danger by sending brutish men to accompany them, Lady Sybella?" It is the first time the regent has spoken since we returned from my room.

Yes, I want to scream at her. They will always be in danger from him and their family. "I am saying he would send brutish men to retrieve them through unofficial channels should official channels not rule in his favor."

With his eyes still on me, General Cassel leans down and speaks directly into the king's ear. A flicker of annoyance crosses the regent's face, and she leans ever so slightly closer in an attempt to hear.

When Cassel is finished, the king nods in agreement. "I must think upon this, for it is not as straightforward as first presented. Monsieur Fremin, you are excused for now. But do not leave the palace without consulting my marshal or General Cassel." Fremin starts to protest. "I have not said I am putting the matter aside. You may rest assured that I will get to the bottom of this. Unless you doubt me?"

Fremin swallows the rest of his protestation and bows. "Never, Your Majesty."

"Then leave. All of you," the king growls.

Relieved at the dismissal, I sink into another deep curtsy. But as I move to disperse with the others, he stops me. "Stay a moment, Lady Sybella." My brief hope of an easy victory crumples. He waves at the regent, Cassel, and the two bishops to stay, then studies me, mouth pursed in thought. "I am told that when they searched for you this morning, they found you in a chamber that . . . wasn't your own."

"That is true, Your Majesty."

Since he is careful not to declare Genevieve's identity, I do not either. He falls quiet again, and I can practically hear the wheels of his mind churning.

"So tell me, are you from the convent of Saint Mortain?"

The ground at my feet shifts and lurches, dread seeping into my bones. In the utter silence of the room, the regent looks sharply at the king. One of the bishops crosses himself, while the other clutches the thick gold crucifix that hangs at his neck. For a brief moment, I consider denying it, but since it is clear he knows — or suspects — lying would only make it worse.

"It is true that I was raised at the convent of Saint Mortain, Your Majesty, as are a number of the women of Brittany."

"Have you been trained in the arts of death as an assassin?"

While it is the king who speaks, the regent's eyes bore into me, hungrier for the answer than even the king. "I have been trained in the art of weaponry, Your Majesty, for protecting those I serve. I have also studied poisons so that I may detect them when the need arises. But surely you know all manner of things may be used for good or ill."

"Answer the question." Although General Cassel does not raise his voice, it cracks through the room like a whip.

"Yes. That was one of the many things we learned at the convent. We also trained in the care and anointing of the dead, the departing of souls, and how to ease the pain of the dying."

The king leans back in his chair, satisfied. "Two days ago, I would have believed everything you said here this morning unequivocally, for who would accuse such an obedient and humble demoiselle of what Monsieur Fremin suggested? But surely you can see how your true background gives much credence to his claim."

"Your Majesty, I am still precisely who I was two days ago — a woman who loves her queen and her sisters and wishes only to serve their best interests. I serve you, as her lord and husband and my king, as well."

"Even so, I must consider Monsieur Fremin's accusations carefully. Unlike most ladies, you have the wherewithal to carry them out. You, too, are dismissed. And like Fremin, you are not to leave the palace without permission. If you'd like to prove your innocence, you'd best find those men-at-arms."

It is all I can do to keep my feet firmly under me and not stumble out of the chambers.

The king knows of the convent. He knows I am an assassin. We have, all of us, been exposed to our enemies.

The question is, how?

Of a certainty the queen did not tell him.

Could Rohan have sent word? I wince, remembering how boldly I taunted the man with my connection to the convent when he first arrived in Rennes with the news that he was to replace Lord Montauban as governor of Brittany. But surely if Rohan had informed the king, his message would have arrived long ago. And the king did not know two days ago, else he would never have ruled in my favor over Fremin.

It takes but the span of two heartbeats before the answer crashes into me.

Genevieve.

CHAPTER 3

Genevieve

estled among the thick folds of a Flemish tapestry, I watch the others emerge from the audience chamber, my head reeling with all I have just witnessed. Fremin storms from the room like a bull through a field. He is not only angry, but scared. And if he works for Pierre d'Albret, he should be. I think back to Sybella's words this morning, her face as she talked about the "pressing matter," and feel certain it is related to this man and his accusations.

I am half tempted to follow him so I may report back to Sybella, but have too recently learned how awry well-intentioned interference can go. Not to mention that, if what I understood is correct, Sybella herself is a d'Albret.

I can scarcely credit it. There is no family resemblance between her and Pierre. The only point of commonality was the cold, hard look that was on her face earlier for the briefest of seconds.

And who are these sisters of hers? Are they from the convent as well? Pierre d'Albret's household?

While I do not fully understand what just transpired in that room, Sybella's ability to maintain her composure in front of the king and his court, then pivot to the role of a distressed sister with such believability that it nearly brought a tear to my own eye was a wonder to behold.

She comes striding out of the salon just then, her mask still firmly in place, her hands clenched, her face white. I wait long enough to be certain she is not followed, then slip unobtrusively behind her as she passes the tapestry. She continues in silence until she reaches the stairway. Once there, she climbs three steps, glances to either side to be certain no one is about, then looks down at me. That is when I can see that the paleness of her face is due to fury rather than fear. "What did you say to the king to sour him against me?"

"You are a d'Albret. Is that not enough?"

"He has known I was a d'Albret since I first arrived and has not held me in suspicion before." She grasps the iron railing. "Where were you last night when I came looking for you? You weren't on a mission for the convent, since you had not heard from them." She takes a step toward me. "And so I ask myself, why were you not announced, if not on an assignment? And I will tell you, I do not like the answer." She stares at me, her breathing fast and hard. I open my mouth to answer, but she talks over me. "Where. Were. You."

I have no choice but to tell her. The entire court will find out soon enough. "With the king."

She glares at me. "You were sleeping with the king."

I shrug. "Not sleeping exactly."

She grits her teeth. "So you were bedding him?"

Sleeping sounded so much better. I nod.

Quicker than an arrow released from a bowstring, she is upon me, her hand grabbing my chin and bringing it close to hers. "You betrayed us." Her voice is a low, furious hum, her anger a solid wall that has me wanting to take a step back, but her fingers are like a vise. "You aren't here hoping for a be-damned crow feather. You have some hidden agenda of your own. One that involves destroying the queen." She shoves my face away from her. "You have exposed us all to the king."

And there it is, the ugly, brutal kick I have waited for, all the more painful for being delayed long enough to allow hope to take root. As I struggle to find words to explain, she descends another step toward me. "Was it to get even with the convent for ignoring you longer than you liked? Or has your loyalty to Brittany been eroded by your years in France?"

"Disloyalty was never my intention!" Desperately needing a moment to regain my footing, I glance at the deserted landing. "Surely we do not need to discuss this where any wandering ears can hear."

In answer, she turns and strides up the stairs. Something hot and ugly uncurls inside me, filling my skin so that I fear it will burst. At first I think that it is my own temper flaring to match Sybella's, but it is more corrosive than that. Shame, I realize with a shock. This thick, suffocating feeling is shame.

When she reaches the landing, she whirls around to face me again, blocking my ascent. "Is that why Margot died? Did she discover your plans for treachery?"

Her words slam against my chest and send me reeling backwards. I grip the bannister. "No!"

"Your word is meaningless to me," she says, but something in my manner must convince her, for some of the reckless fury fades from her face. "What are you doing here, Genevieve?"

"Must we discuss this in the hallway?" It takes all my training to keep the pleading note from my voice.

She gives a brusque nod, then strides to the fourth chamber on the right and motions me inside. The door closes behind us with a click of foreboding. "Very well. We are alone. Now you can explain this treachery of yours."

That she would leap to such a conclusion hurts deeply. "Why are you so certain that I betrayed you?"

"Because the king knows I am from the convent of Saint Mortain and what we do there. He did not know that two days ago." Her expression hardens as the threads she has grabbed hold of begin to form a pattern. "You said you were with the king last night. Is that why you are poisoning the queen?"

Her accusation knocks all the air from my lungs. "No! Not the queen!"

Her eyes grow so frigid that I feel an actual chill scuttle across my arms. "But you are poisoning somebody."

"No! Not now."

She tilts her head. "But . . . ?"

"It had nothing to do with any of this. It was when I left Cognac, the only way I could escape." There. I said I had to escape. Surely she'll begin to understand now.

"Or was it the only way you could worm your way into the king's bed and betray everything the convent stands for? Do you have any idea how much you've put at risk? Any idea whose lives might be ruined?" For one heart-stopping moment, I am certain she is considering killing me where I stand. "How much danger complete innocents will be in because of you?"

Her words pour over me like acid, the burn of it mixing with the searing shame I already feel. "I was trying to save them, you rutting sow, if you would only let me explain."

She folds her arms and raises her eyebrows. "I am listening."

I force myself to draw a full breath. "I told you, we had not heard from the convent for five years. Nothing."

As I talk, she crouches down to peer at the rug, tilting her head sideways as if examining the surface. When I pause, she looks up at me. "Continue," she says curtly.

"Margot . . . Margot got tired of waiting and entered into a liaison with Count Angoulême. That is how she died."

The hand she had been running over the rug stills. "He killed her?"

"Not with his bare hands, no, but she became pregnant and died giving birth to his bastard."

"*Merde.*" She shoves to her feet, her gaze flitting briefly to me before she goes to the window. "Go on." She yanks the curtains aside.

"When the count told me that the duchess and king were to be married, I didn't believe it. France consuming Brittany was everything we'd been fighting against."

"She was out of choices," Sybella mutters as she examines the latch closely.

"That's what the count said. I took comfort in the fact that I would be in a perfect position to help her now, with all my connections at court and the knowledge I'd gathered over the years about all the courtiers, not to mention the king and the regent."

She pauses long enough to stare at me. "That was precisely the sort of aid we were hoping for." In disgust, she looks back at the window and runs her fingers over the casing, wincing at something.

"What is it?"

"A nick in the wood." She begins rubbing her finger over it, as if trying to smooth it away. "Keep talking."

"But much to my dismay, I still received no call from the convent. When Count Angoulême left for the wedding, I demanded he take me with him."

The corner of her mouth quirks. "I wager he loved that. Princes of the Blood do so enjoy being ordered about."

"I told him I needed to be somewhere the convent could find me, but he refused."

"You could have just followed him."

"I would have, but he had other news as well. News he claimed was from the convent." She stops rubbing the wood and looks at me. "The news was that, by order of the king, the convent of Saint Mortain was being disbanded." For the first time since I have begun talking, she gives me her full attention. "His followers were to be farmed out to other convents or married off to willing husbands. I was now Angoulême's legal ward, and he was to find a suitable husband for me."

"But no such thing has happened! How could you not know he was tricking you?"

"Of course that was my first thought," I snap. But how to explain the many signs that seemed to point to the same conclusion. "I considered such a possibility carefully, but he had a message bearing the wax seal of the convent. It was signed by the abbess. And he had never lied to me before. I could not discern a reason he would do so now. And believe me, I considered it thoroughly. But I could never see what he would gain, except the animosity of the convent, and he has always struck me as too self-serving to incur such wrath without good reason."

Sybella opens the windows and runs her hand carefully along the window-sill. "And so you left."

"Not right away, no." How do I explain to her the utter betrayal I felt? The sense of aloneness. "Margot had died but three days earlier," I say softly. "We had been like sisters, and I . . ." Her fingers still, and she frowns before retrieving a tiny scrap of cloth. She holds it up for closer inspection.

How to explain the enormity of what I'd lost? Not just with Margot's death, but in the year preceding it? "And there was her babe. I wanted to stay long enough to see if it lived."

Sybella shoves the scrap into the pocket of her gown. "And did it?"

"Yes. She did."

"That's good news, then," she says softly. "We must see that the babe is well cared for." She moves away from the window toward the bed, then drops to her knees to peer under it. "So then you left," she prompts.

"Eventually. I needed time to study the situation. To consider all my options carefully. I also needed to ensure they didn't come immediately after me. So I waited and I plotted, and when the time was right, I left."

She remains on the floor a few more moments before finally pushing to her feet. She looks up to meet my eyes. "Did you leave with the intention of bedding the king?"

Something in her eyes, her face — mayhap her soul — forces the truth from me. "Yes."

She looks down and concentrates on brushing off her hands. "And how was that supposed to save us? Here —" She motions toward the rich coverlet on the bed. "You grab one end, I'll take the other."

Grateful to have something to do with my hands, as well as something to look at besides her scornful countenance, I grab the corners and help her carry the entire thing over to the window. "I'm listening," she says sharply.

It is easier to talk with her attention focused on the richly embroidered coverlet rather than me. "When I was last at court, the king took a fancy to me. There was no reason to act on it at the time — the convent had not ordered me to, and there was nothing to be gained. But he did promise to grant me any favor

I should wish if I would grace his bed. In spite of my assurances to the regent that I had no intention of bedding the king, she had Margot and me sent to Cognac. When I heard that it was by the king's orders that the convent had been disbanded, I realized I did, at last, have something I truly wished from him."

I stare out the window, remembering the absolute certainty I felt in that moment, as if a long-missing piece of my life had finally clicked into place — that I had found my destiny. The memory sears my throat.

"Since he had already disbanded the convent, there was no reason for me to think he didn't know about us. And to be honest, I would have assumed the French crown's own spies would have at least caught wind of us and reported it to him. Especially with the former chancellor Crunard working so closely with both the regent and the convent."

I shift my attention from the window and raise my chin slightly. "So that was my intent, to receive clemency for the convent and prevent unwanted fates for the other girls there."

Sybella stops rubbing at a spot she's found on the quilt and lifts her eyes to mine, her brief flicker of understanding quickly shuttered. "So that was your plan. Galloping in on a destrier, fulfilling the king's carnal desires, then requesting a dispensation for the convent because of it."

Under the weight of her scorn, all of my careful considerations and deliberations seem as thin and tattered as a beggar's cloak. It was a good plan. Would have been if any of what Angoulême had told me was true.

At last she lifts one shoulder. "I have heard worse." Although her words are begrudging, they feel like a rousing approval.

I return my attention to the coverlet. "What are we looking for?"

"Any signs that Monsieur Fremin's men were in here."

"You think that they were?"

A chilling smile plays about her lips. "I know they were. This is where I killed them."

I do not think she means the explanation to be a threat, but it feels like one, all the same.

CHAPTER 4

I leave Sybella's room and begin walking. I have no idea where to go, wishing only to ward off the howling blizzard of regret and recrimination that threaten to engulf me. I had not expected the king to act so swiftly on the information I had given him, or that he would so easily identify Sybella. He would not have if she had not come to my room this morning. Had not tried to reach out to me. More than ever, I am beginning to fear there is truly no way to fix this disaster, or even lessen its impact.

I am halfway to the servants' chapel before I realize that is where I'm headed. I need the world to stand still for a moment. To quit shifting and changing so rapidly that I cannot catch my breath. Once, when I was but five years old, the tavernkeeper Sanson took me and my mother to visit the sea. It was a warm day, and they let me play in the water. Until a giant wave sucked the sand from beneath my feet and cast me backwards, end over end, so that I could no longer tell where the water ended and the sky began.

That is how I feel now, only Sanson's strong, sturdy arm is not there to lift me from the current that threatens to sweep me away.

Fortunately, the chapel is empty, its simple stone walls and small votives far more comforting than the grandeur of the palace's main chapel. My backside has barely settled onto the plain wooden bench when a voice behind me says, "So you are our missing assassin."

I leap up, my hand moving toward the knife hidden amongst my skirts. An old priest with fluffy white hair stands there, and while he looks kind enough, I cannot help but remember the vitriol in the eyes of the priests in the council room this morning. "Forgive me, Father, but I've no idea what you're talking about."

He shrugs. "I have seen you pray."

My lip curls in derision. "And that makes you think I'm an assassin?"

He tilts his head, his eyes considering. "There is something about the way you daughters of Mortain bow your heads. Not as lowly penitents, but as a dedicant ready to serve a beloved lord."

For all his fluffy hair and pink cheeks, he is no fool.

"What is a hedge priest doing at the court of France?"

"No mere hedge priest, my child, but a follower of Saint Salonius."

"The patron saint of mistakes?" My laugh echoes harshly in the small chapel. "Then I have certainly come to the right place."

"If you have made a mistake, then perhaps you have."

"What I have made is to a mistake as a mountain is to an anthill." The desolation rises up once more.

"You have spoken with Lady Sybella, I presume?"

"Oh, we've spoken."

"She has been looking for you for some time. I know she will be glad for your presence."

While his words are meant as comfort, they cut like broken glass. "I do not think she would agree with you," I mutter.

He cocks his head to the side, watching me like some little bird patiently waiting for a plump worm to emerge from the ground.

I do not know if his kind regard coaxes the next words from me or if my own self-loathing forces them out. "Let us just say my arrival did not go as planned."

"Or perhaps"—he spreads his hands in a beneficent gesture—"you are tasked with a different plan. One the gods have not seen fit to share with you."

His words are so close to the misguided reasoning that got me into this mess that I nearly snap his head off. "I do not want to hear of the gods or saints or any of their rutting plans."

My outburst does not deter him in the least. "Then what would you like to talk about?"

I am quiet for a moment, thinking. "The sisters Sybella mentioned. Who are they?"

"They are not of Mortain, but born into the family that raised Sybella. She has taken them under her wing in an effort to keep them from the wickedness of their own family."

"The d'Albrets?"

His nod is a simple gesture, but conveys a deep regret. "Yes."

This time, I truly fear I will retch. I had thought I understood the nature of the disaster I have wrought, but in this moment realize my valiant plan to save the convent has put two innocent girls in immediate danger. Not to mention all of those at the convent once the ripples of my revelations begin to reach them.

"My child, are you well?" The priest lays his hand on my arm, his touch as light as a moth's wing.

"No." The bleak word escapes before I can catch it, as if the old priest has some power to call such weaknesses from me. I have destroyed the convent's trust in me and am so far out of the king's favor I may as well be in the Low Countries. Even if I see him again, he will not listen to any explanations or exhortations I can make. "I have ruined everything," I whisper.

"You'd be surprised at how resilient the world — and yourself — can be."

Again, he is offering comfort. Comfort that is not warranted. "It is not simply my own life I have ruined, but others." So many others.

He is quiet a long moment. "Then perhaps you have come to make your confession."

I open my mouth to correct him, then stop. I am desperate to thrust some of this dark, hot misery from me. To find some way to divest myself of this guilt and shame. Perhaps this kind stranger whose eyes seem to hold three lifetimes of wisdom is the one to hear of it. "Mayhap I have, Father."

CHAPTER 5

Sybella

nce Genevieve is gone, I lean against my door, grateful for the solid wood at my back as I fight down the sour taste of panic.

What has she done?

Even though I am furious with her, I must acknowledge the part my own hand played in this. If I had not evicted Lady Katerine from the king's bed, he may not have resumed his interest in Genevieve. If I had approached her in the chapel or followed her once I guessed who she was . . . but I was consumed by my own worries and obsessions.

And what part does Count Angoulême play in all this? In spite of my anger, my heart aches for Genevieve. For the journey she has set herself on. A journey that I can only pray will lead her through her own anger and bitterness. A journey I recognize all too clearly, having made a similar one myself. I do not envy her trying to put this aright.

But the sympathy I should feel for Genevieve is overpowered by my fear of what may come of her actions. She has only the faintest inkling of what she has set in motion. Of whom she has endangered.

My sisters are gone from here, I reassure myself. Beyond Fremin's greedy grasp, beyond the king's reach, and the regent's machinations. Beast, Aeva, and the entire queen's guard are with them and have sworn by the Nine to keep them safe.

But it won't be enough, not if the king decides to act on the information Genevieve has shared with him. There is a very good chance that all of them — Annith, Ismae, the older nuns, and the youngest novitiates — could be in harm's way. I would pray for them all, but who, now, do I pray to?

I shove away from the door, cross the room to my small trunklet, and open the lid. The holly berry still appears bright red, and the leaves a vibrant green — until I bring it closer. Then I see the edges have begun to brown. Why? Why now? Is it simply the miracle of Mortain fading, much like he himself eventually will? Or is it a reflection of my own wilting faith?

Afraid I will break the sprig in its new fragile state, I place it carefully in the trunk. As I do, my fingers brush against the black pebble Yannic gave me. Bewildered, I touch it again. It is not my imagination. The pebble feels warm, as if it has been out in the sun.

I had thought it blessed by Mortain, but Yannic had indicated I was wrong. Blessed by whom, then?

It is as smooth as polished glass, and I close my fingers around it, letting the warmth comfort me. It speaks of mysteries that still exist in this world. The mysteries that have come to me before and may yet again.

I move to put the pebble back in the trunk, then pause, deciding to slip it into the pocket at my waist, savoring its gentle heat against my leg through the silk of my skirts. I will need every bit of comfort I can muster for the conversation I must have with the queen.

It is too late to disturb the queen — she has already retired for the night. I am too restless to go back to my chamber. My thoughts keep circling back to Beast and the girls, even though I know he will get them safely to the convent. But saints, I miss him already — and it has only been three days. I told Beast the girls were my heart, but that was only partly true. He is my heart as well, and it feels as if I have carved off a piece and dared rabid wolves to feast upon it.

He would be greatly insulted by my worrying. And in truth, it galls me somewhat, even though I can no more stop it than I can halt the blood flowing in my veins.

I am not surprised when I find myself standing outside the servants' chapel. There is only one person with whom I can share this disaster. Only one sworn to silence by virtue of his priest's robes.

Father Effram looks up from the brace of fresh candles he is lighting, smiling as if he's been expecting me. I head directly for the confessional booth. He slips into the other side.

"Have you heard?" I murmur as soon as his door is shut.

"The palace does seem to be in a mild uproar this afternoon."

I quickly fill him in on Genevieve's arrival and subsequent actions. "Yes," he says when I have finished. "She paid me a visit earlier. You just missed her."

Just missed her. The words poke at my memory. "You were the one who led me to the chapel that day. I had no intention of praying. You knew who she was, didn't you?"

I hear the faint whisper of fabric as he shrugs. "Let us say *suspected.*"

So he, too, played a part in all this. "Do you think she is telling the truth?"

"I do. She has asked to meet with the queen, is eager to make her apology and offer whatever aid she can to set things right."

"Or she wishes to get close enough to harm her," I mutter.

"You don't truly believe that."

His calmness scrapes on my nerves like a rasp. "She's not simply made some little mistake that is easily fixed. Monsieur Fremin has reported his missing henchmen to the king and has accused me of being responsible for it. With Genevieve's confession, he has made a shrewd guess about me and is now inclined to give serious weight to Monsieur Fremin's claims. And if anything happens to my sisters, she will pay for it with her —"

"It is not her fault." Father Effram's voice is no longer gentle, but a bracing slap.

"Of course it is her fault. It no longer matters that she meant well — she has set in motion the ruin of everything, including the lives of those I care deeply about."

"You think she is more powerful than the gods and saints?"

"No, but since you speak of them, shouldn't Mortain have foreseen this before he gave up his godhood?"

"How do you know that he didn't?"

I feel like a rabbit stunned by a hunter's club. "Are you saying he knew?"

"I'm saying that what the gods set in motion is not knowable to mere mortals. We are simply caught up in the movement of their dance and there are still eight gods, each of them more than willing to meddle in the affairs of mortals for their own purposes." The thought is terrifying. My fingers drift to the small weight resting against my leg and the faint warmth it gives off. "Does the Dark Mother meddle in the affairs of mortals?" The words bring not a chill, but a faint wash of heat along my skin. "Is she behind this?" There is a rustle of woolen cloth as he shrugs. "I would not say she meddles so much as when one thing dies and gives way to the new, it is she who guides that process. If we let her."

I am quiet a moment before saying, "The holly branch is dying."

"What holly branch?"

"The one I brought with me from Rennes. It stayed green this entire time, until this morning." A thought floats by, and I grasp at it. "Could it be that it's simply too far removed from its source? Where the remnants of Mortain's power cannot reach? Or is it simply his power withdrawing from the world, just as he has done?"

The question renews the familiar anger I have carried since that eventful battle. "Did Mortain know that by choosing life, he would leave his faith and followers to the jackals?"

"Did he know it would fade? Yes. The passing of the Nine has been coming for a long time. We have all known it. Ever since we signed the original agreement with the Church."

Agreement? What agreement? But before I can voice the question, he continues.

"Do not begrudge him love, child. That love provided him something to move toward rather than simply cease is a gift beyond measure. One I've no doubt the Dark Matrona herself had a hand in."

"So you are saying she is guiding this?"

"No, it is but one among many possibilities. We have all been given a part to play, and play it we must. Only at the end, if then, will we know if we were hero or villain."

Anger spikes through my gut. I am sick of these riddles. "I refuse to accept that."

"You are not meant to accept it. To accept it would change the outcome of the dance."

"Then what am I to do?" I spit out.

He is quiet so long that I fear I have finally gone too far and offended him. Just as I open my mouth to apologize, he speaks.

"Remember," he says simply, "you and Genevieve are not only mortal, but part god as well. It is not simply Mortain's blood that flows in your veins, but his divinity, too."

Against my thigh, the small pebble burns like a brand.

CHAPTER 6

The news I must share with the queen fills me with dread. I've no desire to drag this fresh disaster to her door, nor the possible repercussions. But I made the mistake of not telling her in the past, which proved worse. And Genevieve's actions will affect her most directly.

I wait until Elsibet steps away from the bed, then curtsy. "Good morning, Your Majesty." While the queen smiles in welcome, she is pale and her skin clammy. I snag Elsibet's elbow. "I need to speak with the queen alone. Can you make the others disappear?"

She shoots me one quick glance of concern. "But of course, my lady. Heloise? Could you assist me?"

Heloise collects a covered basin from the bedside, then hurries after Elsibet, casting a curious look my way.

When we are alone, the queen frowns. "Lady Sybella." She lowers her voice. "Is everything all right?"

I cannot help but wonder when she will ever be allowed to find the happiness — or even simply the peace — that she so deserves. "I'm afraid matters are developing faster than we would have wished."

She sits up a little higher against the pillows. "Which matters are those?"

"The men who accompanied Monsieur Fremin have gone missing." I keep my voice casual, as if merely discussing the latest gossip. "The lawyer is most overwrought and went at once to the king. He seems to think that I am behind their disappearance."

Her eyes never leave mine. "But that is ridiculous. How could a lady like yourself have had anything to do with men like that?"

"That is precisely what I pointed out, Your Majesty. Indeed, when they went looking for me this morning, they found my room empty, not just of me, but of my sisters as well."

The queen says nothing, but a small satisfied smile plays about her lips. Truly, one could not ask for a better ally.

"I told the king that it was obvious that Monsieur Fremin, not liking the king's decision, sent his men to take the girls by force."

She smiles briefly. "I am certain you are correct. Let us hope the king will now put the matter to rest."

"Unfortunately, the king is inclined to give more weight to Monsieur Fremin's words than mine."

She frowns in surprise. "Why?"

Merde, this is hard. "Because he has learned of my involvement with the convent of Saint Mortain and the nature of my service."

Her already pale face grows even whiter. "Who would have told him such a thing?" she whispers.

I close my eyes briefly. While news of my exposure alarms her, what I have to say next will hurt her. "That is the one piece of good news. It appears the convent's hidden initiate returned to court."

Her eyes harden in anger. "And blabbed your identity to the king? Surely that is not something one with your sort of training would do."

"It was an attempt to help, Your Majesty. She had been told the king already knew of the convent, and had ordered it disbanded, the novitiates farmed out to the Church or suitable husbands."

There is a long beat of silence as the queen digests this. "And how did she think confirming such revelations about the convent would help?"

"She thought she could persuade the king to reverse his decision."

Never the lackwit, the queen's interest sharpens. "Persuade him how?"

No amount of gentleness will soften the blow. "The king had expressed an interest in her once, long before you came to court. She thought to use that interest to extract a favor on behalf of the convent."

The queen's face grows as cold as marble. "Are we certain the girl is working for us? Our enemies could not have done a better job of weakening what few advantages we hold."

"I believe she is, but I have only spoken with her twice. Father Effram believes she was sincerely trying to help."

"We can do without that sort of help," she snaps.

"I agree. But there is some other plotting afoot here. She was shown a letter supposedly written by the abbess, and examined it carefully for signs of forgery. It appeared genuine. Someone wanted her to believe that it was."

"But who?"

"My assumption is Count Angoulême, the man acting as her liaison with the convent. But why he would risk making an enemy of the convent when he has long been our ally, I don't know. I intend to speak with Genevieve more about it when I can."

There is a rumble of commotion just outside her chamber and a sense of many heartbeats approaching. My eyes widen in alarm as I recognize one of them. "The king is here!"

"Fetch my chamber robe!" She throws off the covers and swings her legs out of bed.

As I help her into the robe, I talk quickly. "He will no doubt want to know if you were aware of the convent and my association with them. He has called in two of the bishops from Langeais. I tried to make the convent sound as inconspicuous as possible, but there is only so much innocence to be protested when serving death."

She nods, eyes firmly fixed on the door.

"I think . . . I think finding me here will not soothe matters. It will be best if I remain out of sight."

"I agree." She waves her hand toward the garderobe. I have only a moment to secure my hiding place — then the deep voices are inside the room.

"Your Majesty." The queen's voice drifts up from the floor where she has sunk into a deep curtsy.

"My lady wife." The king's voice is cold and polite. "I tried to visit yesterday, but you had retired early. Are you unwell?"

From the tone of his voice, it is clear that he suspects it was an excuse to avoid him.

"It is just a passing malady. Please do not trouble yourself over it."

"What if it is not some passing thing, my lady? What if it is something more diabolical than that?" This voice is deeper than the king's.

"Bishop Albi. It is good to see you again, although pray forgive my state of dishabille. If I had known you were coming, I would have dressed myself with all the honor you deserve."

"And yet you ignore his questions." It takes me a moment to recognize the voice of the Bishop of Angers, the king's confessor. "Why is that, I wonder?"

"I was not ignoring anything the good bishop said, but merely granting him full courtesy."

"Why do you not share his concern that there is something more nefarious behind your illness?" the king demands imperiously. "Could it be that you truly do not know that one of your attendants is an assassin?"

After a thick moment of silence, the queen says, "My lord husband, I assure you —"

He speaks over her. "Did you know that Lady Sybella is an assassin from the convent of Saint Mortain?"

"I know that she serves the convent of Saint Mortain, yes. But as for her being an assassin —"

"Does she serve the patron saint of death or not?" The king's voice rises.

"I just told you she did. But that is far different from being an assassin."

"So you did know!" A brief, charged silence hangs in the air.

"Of course I knew." When the queen answers, her voice is as close to deriding as I have ever heard it. "What sort of ruler would I be if I did not know all of my country's customs and religious orders?"

"But she is an assassin!" The king nearly sputters his outrage.

"She serves the patron saint of death, just as our knights serve Saint Camulos and our scholars and healers serve Saint Brigantia."

"No matter how you try to paint it with pretty words, she is an assassin, and you have brought her into your lord husband's court," General Cassel says.

"The Nine are fully sanctioned by the Church, and have been for hundreds of years." The queen's voice rings out firmly. "That they have fallen out of fashion in France does not change that."

"Maybe it should," the Bishop of Albi mutters.

"That you would think so speaks to your lack of piety, not ours," the queen says coolly.

The king interrupts their exchange. "You used these worshipers of death?"

"It was war." The queen's exasperation hardens her words to steel. "We both used what tools we had available to us. Every noble house in Europe has some kind of poisoner or assassin to serve them. The Breton court is not alone in this. Besides, none of your people were assassinated, so the point is moot."

"I have never used assassins." The king's voice is both boastful and petulant.

"That may well be true, but you had other tools in your arsenal that were no less deadly." The queen's voice shifts, as if she is in a council meeting discussing some point of philosophy. "Tell me, my lord, do you truly think it more noble to bribe my closest advisors into betraying me than to hire an assassin? How noble and fair-minded was it to capture Chancellor Crunard's last living son on the battlefield and ransom him, not for gold, but for treason and his father's honor?"

"Your Majesty," General Cassel's voice interrupts. "We are not here to recount every action taken in the long war between France and Brittany."

"Hold!" The king's voice sounds pained. "Tell me more about Chancellor Crunard, Madame."

"You didn't know." The queen's words are filled with amazement. "You didn't know Chancellor Crunard's son was held to ensure the chancellor would deliver me into the hands of France? But surely you were aware that Marshal Rieux, Madame Dinan, and Madame Hivern were all paid handsome sums of gold to betray me. My entire council was in your pocket."

"Can you prove these accusations?" The king's voice is strained.

"I do not need to prove them. They all confessed. And since it was those who served the patron saint of death who discovered their betrayal, I can see why you would resent such efficient weapons in my arsenal. But we are on the same side now." Her voice softens a bit, as if to remind him of this most relevant

fact. "Furthermore," she continues, "not one of those traitors is dead, so your fears of assassination are misplaced."

The silence that follows is so deep and wide, it feels as if a chasm has opened up in the room.

"You really didn't know?" the queen asks at last, her voice sounding younger than it has all morning. Hope, I realize. That he did not know fills her with hope.

"No." The word cracks through the silence like a stone through a window. "I did not know any of this." There are no further words, and only the clip of the king's boot heel as he leaves the room. It is followed by a rustle of fabric and a shuffling of feet as his advisors hurry to catch up to him.

The queen waits for a quarter of an hour before calling softly, "You can come out now."

I emerge from my hiding place. "I am impressed, Your Majesty. You not only neutralized his main offense, but managed to point out his own egregious tools of war."

"Tools he had no idea were even being used." Her voice is bemused. "It is hard to believe they would keep something like that from him. There is only one person who would have dared to send such orders in his name."

It is becoming clear where the seeds of his lack of trust and confidence have sprung from. "We do not know how long his displeasure with his sister will distract him from his displeasure with us, but it is a reprieve, and I will gladly take it."

The queen's face hardens. "When you can do so without rousing suspicion, bring this Genevieve to me."

CHAPTER 7

Genevieve

When I arrive in the king's apartments, I find him with his royal perfumer, bent over a tray filled with glass vials. The room is thick with the cloying scent of civet and orange blossoms. Unbidden, a memory of Maraud's face when he learned the poison I had given him was simply a ruse to force his cooperation comes to me so vividly that it takes my breath away. How will he feel after our last parting, when I had to truly poison him? I quickly hide my face with a deep curtsy. "You summoned me, Your Majesty?"

Dismissing the perfumer, he waves me forward. "So tell me, as an assassin, you stay informed of your queen's politics, do you not?"

"As much as I can, although the distance and the need for secrecy has made it difficult."

He lifts one of the small bottles to his nose and sniffs. "What do you know of her Privy Council? They were fiercely loyal to her, were they not?"

Unable to stop myself, I snort, but manage to cover it with a cough. The king's hand tightens on the thick-cut glass he is holding. "Why do you laugh?"

"Forgive me, Your Majesty. I wasn't laughing, there was something stuck in my throat. But, sire, surely you know that the majority of them were loyal to you? Do you now doubt their loyalty — loyalty you paid handsomely for?"

His face is unreadable. "And the former chancellor, Crunard? What do you know of him?"

"That he, too, betrayed the queen and pledged his loyalty to you. Although," I add, "the cost was far greater than gold."

"What do you mean?"

"Surely any man's sole surviving son is more precious than coin?" Again my mind goes to Maraud and how his father's betrayal consumed him. It is on the tip of my tongue to ask why the king is questioning me, but my own situation is too precarious.

He places the vial of scent back on the tray with such force that I fear it has shattered. He looks at the wall behind me with such thinly disguised longing and revulsion that it is all I can do not to glance over my shoulder.

"You did not know?" I am so surprised by my realization that it comes out as a whisper.

"It is my kingdom! Are you suggesting I do not know what transpires in it?"

"Of course not, Your Majesty, but the regent has been known to —"

"I am the one asking the questions. You speak at my sufferance."

The words are so out of character for him, so completely outside any way he has ever acted before, that my mouth snaps shut. I lower my eyes. "But of course. I am here to serve you."

He casts a sullen glance my way. "But are you?" His voice is low and still thrums with anger.

"Yes," I say simply. "It has always been my intent. The convent's as well."

"They sent you to my bed?"

"No, they sent me to serve you. That was my only instruction."

He takes a deep breath, nostrils flaring as he pinches the bridge of his nose. When he looks up again, there are so many emotions and conflicts seething in his gaze that I cannot identify any of them. "What am I to do with you?"

"What do you mean, Your Majesty?" I keep my voice light and innocent, as if I am not fearing punishment with every breath I take.

"I mean, I have longed for you for years, finally have you, and now I find it has been like wanting a piece of rotten fruit."

I want to bristle at the comparison, but his mood leaves no room for such indulgences. "Rotten, my lord?" I give thanks that I have had years of experience practicing my sheep's face.

"Yes." He steps closer and places a finger in the hollow of my throat, one of the most vulnerable of spots on the human body. The touch is in such contrast to his mood that it is hard not to flinch. "Since you seem to know so very much, tell me." His fingers drift upward. "What moves has your convent made against France?"

When his fingers tighten around my chin, it is all I can do not to grab him, throw him to the ground, and leave him gasping for breath. But it would not do anything to help me fix what I have broken. And while I am perfectly happy to leave him on the floor, it is not fair for others to have to clean up my mess. I will wear this mask a little longer. "None that I know of, Your Majesty."

"Then why were you sent here?"

Small truths, I remind myself. "I have asked myself that question for many years now, sire. At first, I thought we were to collect information —"

"A spy." His fingers tighten, not in threat, but in anger.

I shrug. "All kingdoms spy. However, we were also given instructions to not risk exposing ourselves by reaching out to the convent, so any information we gathered was essentially useless. It was more to educate ourselves on the leanings of the French court."

"What information did you learn here at court, Genevieve?"

What to tell him? The truth of the last three days or the lie I believed until then?

I remember the look on his face a moment ago — the gaping hole he himself cannot see. Mayhap that is a path out of this mess. The one crack in his defenses that I can slip through. "I learned that Your Majesty is honorable and chival-rous. More so than your advisors — especially your sister — would have you be. I learned that you have a formidable will and a mind of your own. You do what you think is right, no matter others' opinions."

His grip on my chin loosens to the point of a caress. "Flattery," he scoffs, but that does not hide the hunger I see there. The need he has for someone to recognize his independence and good intentions.

"Far more than flattery, Your Majesty. Did you not free the Duke of Orléans from his cruel captivity and restore his lands to him? Did you not choose peace through marriage rather than raining war down on innocent people?" His hand drops to his side, and he straightens. "Did you not rule in favor of your queen, allowing her to keep her vow to her lady and thus her honor?"

His mouth twists with bitterness. "Do not speak of the Lady Sybella to me."

"I believe it was one of your finest moments, sire." Indeed, from my new vantage point, it may be his only one.

He looks out the window. "Dammit, Genevieve, I trusted you!"

"And I you, Your Majesty. I still do."

He rounds on me. "How long have you known the Lady Sybella?"

"I have never seen her until yesterday morning when she appeared at my door and introduced herself. I left the convent long before she arrived. In truth, I have spent as much time here at court as I did at the convent. I arrived when I was seven and left when I was twelve. I've been at court for five years now. The convent is no more than a distant memory, like family one has not seen in years. And as for having taken any moves against the crown?" I laugh. "I have done nothing but serve you and Madame with every breath I have taken. Indeed, that was my order from the convent — to do precisely that. That was the only order, my lord. And I have carried it out faithfully."

"Are there more like you?"

I hesitate. But Margot has chosen her own fate and is long gone from this earth. Telling the truth will cost her nothing and could help the others. "There was one other. The Lady Margot."

He tilts his head at the name. "Have I met her?"

"Yes, my lord, when she served the regent here at court. She was sent with Louise and me to Angoulême. But it is of no matter any longer. She is dead now."

His lip curls in disgust but also, I think, to hide his fear. "Did you kill her?"

"Saints, no!" The accusation stings all the more for being the second time it has been made. "She did not die by anyone's hand, but in the most ordinary of ways. While giving birth to a man's bastard."

He looks doubtful. "What man?"

"Count Angoulême."

He draws a sharp intake of breath. "So you deceived him, too." The words are spoken softly, almost as if to comfort himself rather than extract information from me, so I remain silent. "What other actions have you taken against the crown since you've been here?"

"I have not taken any actions."

"Other than deceiving me."

"None, sire."

"You were never ordered to raise your hand against me or anyone here at court?"

"No, Your Majesty. I will swear it on the Holy Bible, on any of the Church fathers' relics, before the cross that hangs in the church. Take your pick. But I have never acted against you or Madame or anyone here in France." I do not think relieving a courtier or two of an occasional stiletto or bauble can truly be counted as acting against France.

He grows still. "Does my sister know of your involvement with the convent?"

He has not told her. Even so, the ice beneath my feet is so thin I can hear it begin to crack. "No, Your Majesty. I . . . do not know if she even knows that it exists."

He studies me a long moment, as if trying to pull the truth from my soul. "Good. Do not speak to anyone of this, not of Sybella, nor your involvement in the convent. You do not fully comprehend all that has been set in motion. If they were to learn of your involvement, I'm not sure even I could protect you."

Does he mean to protect me from whatever political repercussions the convent's presence creates? *Yes.* But not Sybella. He intends to use her as the whipping boy for my sins.

"For now," he continues, "you may return to your quarters."

Outrage and frustration at the sheer wrongness of what he is doing keep me rooted to the spot. He looks up. "Did you hear me?"

"Yes, Your Majesty. And thank you for showing me such mercy."

He says nothing, but jerks his head toward the door.

When I am halfway back to my chamber, the regent swoops down on me like a vulture on a carcass. "You were supposed to keep the king happy," she hurls at me. "Instead, he is in a foul, melancholic humor. What transpired between you?"

The sheer boldness of the question nearly causes me to blush. I look down and begin fiddling with the trimming on my skirt. "I'm not sure what you mean, Madame. The king seemed most pleased —"

"Do not play games with me," she says impatiently. "What did you discuss? Did he share any of his current thoughts or troubles? Whom has he been speaking with of late?"

"Our conversation was of a much more intimate nature."

"When did you leave? Was there time for anyone else to come to his chambers after you left?"

My head snaps up. "I . . . I'm not certain. My mind was not focused on the time."

She purses her lips, studying me. "Why was Lady Sybella in your chambers yesterday morning?"

I blink at the unwelcome change of subject. I have no idea why the king hasn't shared my association with the convent with the regent, but the longer I can hold that off, the better. I can use womanly charm to soften the king's ire, but have nothing with which to soften the regent's.

"She had heard you had a new attendant and wished to introduce herself."

"How friendly of her." The regent's voice is more acidic than verjuice. "You are to avoid her. She is too loyal to the queen and will sniff out the king's interest in you like a hound will a fox. Besides, her fortune at court is about to change. Best you are far away so that you are not caught in the undertow."

A fresh wave of anger surges over me, but all I say is, "Of course, Madame.

I am not here to make friends, but to serve both you and the king to the best of my ability."

As she disappears down the corridor, I resume my walking. The regent's warnings ring in my ears, and the king's handprint throbs upon my chin, both of them doing nothing to calm my growing outrage. The king may expect me to feel grateful for his protection, but he will quickly find that while I may be a fool, I am no coward. I will not let others take the blame for what I have done.

CHAPTER 8

Something was missing. Maraud couldn't quite put his finger on it, but its absence was palpable. It wasn't until he laid out his bedroll that it hit him. Lucinda.

And how many different kinds of fool did that make him?

"So, have you decided where we're going?"

Maraud nodded. "Flanders."

The others exchanged a glance. "General Cassel?"

He nodded again. Everyone fell silent. "What about d'Albret?" Andry asked. "You had wanted us to check on him — before you asked us to ride ahead and meet up with you. Don't you still want to know what he's up to?"

"I do. After I bring Cassel to justice."

The silence that followed was filled only by the faint crackling of the small fire and the occasional stomp of a horse's hoof. "Are you sure?" Jaspar's voice was filled with something Maraud didn't want to examine too closely.

"Saints, yes."

"But you said Lucinda needed to save someone. We all agreed to help her."

"What part of *she poisoned me* do you not understand?"

"But that's your thing, Maraud. You're the savingest mercenary I've ever met. Are you going to let a little poison come between you and —"

Maraud met his eyes across the campfire. "No. She made her wishes perfectly clear."

With a sigh, Jaspar relented.

But not Valine. "You said yourself that she was trying to save you from possible repercussions with the queen and unfair punishment."

Her words cause something hot and hard to lodge in Maraud's stomach. "She didn't trust me enough to let me help."

"Did you give her reason to?" Valine's voice is pitched low, low enough that it reaches only him. "She seemed genuinely surprised to see us when we showed up at Camulos's Cup. You didn't tell her, did you?"

"Don't you have first watch?"

"No, Andry does. You told her only half your story, and yet you're mad because she didn't trust you? I'd say she was smart not to. And you would too if your judgment wasn't so clouded."

"The poison is well out of my system."

"I wasn't talking about the poison. We call you Your Lordship for a reason, you know. You can be high-handed and arrogant, so convinced in the rightness of your decisions that you don't feel the need to include others in the process. I don't pretend to know all of what went on between you two, but what I saw of her I liked. And I know you. So I ask again, given the position she was in, and your own pigheadedness, did you give her enough reason to trust you?"

Maraud scoffed, but she was already heading for her bedroll and missed it.

Lucinda was pricklier than a thorn bush and possessed the foul temper of a maddened goose. An image she was all too eager to embrace, ensuring the entire world saw her that way.

But thorns were merely a means of self-protection.

"Bollocks," he muttered. Thoughts — and questions — about Lucinda had haunted him every night since they parted ways. Why did she come riding to his aid at Camulos's Cup, then refuse his help? It ate at him that he would likely be dead if she hadn't come back. And she refused to allow him to repay the favor. Why? What was she so afraid of that she was willing to poison him to avoid?

Valine's question was just one of the many that hounded him the entire way to Flanders.

CHAPTER 9

Genevieve

ake up!" Sybella's voice yanks me from my sleep. Certain I had locked my door, I reach for the knife under my pillow, then decide she would not wake me up if she intended to kill me. Probably.

"Why, 'tis as if the sunshine itself has appeared in my room," I mutter.

"You have precisely five minutes to get dressed, else I will take you to the queen in your undergarments."

I sit up and shove the hair out of my face. "The who?"

"The queen. You wished to speak with her. She has granted your request."

My heart hammers in my chest as I stand and reach for my gown. "I am surprised she agreed to see me."

"Our queen has never been one to shy away from facing problems head-on."

Under Sybella's cool, dispassionate gaze, I finish dressing, and quickly arrange my hair. She gives me one last second to splash water on my face before saying, "Let's go."

She eases the door open, peeks outside, then motions for me to follow. It is early yet, and the hallways are empty.

"Is our meeting a secret?"

She sends me a scathing look over her shoulder. "No. I want to sneak up on the herald before I have him announce our arrival."

I open my mouth to shoot back a retort but am cut off when she stops walking and shoves me against the wall. Seconds later, a cluster of servants bearing buckets hurries by. Sybella swears, then glances around once more before resuming. "This way."

Stepping softly, I follow her, hugging the wall like she does so that we are not immediately visible to any passersby. All too soon, we arrive at the double doors of the queen's apartments. "Stay hidden, then follow once I give the signal," Sybella whispers. As the sentries open the door to let her in, she twitches her fingers at me, and I slip in close on her heels. I barely have time to take in the sumptuousness of the queen's solar — the sunlight spilling in from the large oriel windows, the ornately carved wooden legs of the chairs, the gold and red wall hangings — before Sybella urges me along. "Hurry. The regent-appointed attendants will be here any moment."

I step smartly to keep up with Sybella. When she knocks once on the door, a short, dark-haired woman opens it. She gives me a curious look before slipping out. Sybella takes my arm and pulls me into the queen's bedchamber.

As soon as we are inside, Sybella dips a curtsy. "Genevieve is here, Your Majesty."

I sink into a curtsy as well. Sybella quietly removes herself, closing the door behind her.

The queen says nothing for a long time. When she finally speaks, her voice is low with cold fury. "How dare you? You — the convent — serve me. My interests."

Still in a curtsy, I say, "With all due respect, Your Majesty, we serve the interest of Mortain and those of Brittany."

There is a sharp intake of breath. "Are you saying I do not serve the interests of either of those?"

"Most assuredly not, Your Majesty. I am only saying that throughout the history of the country, they have not always been one and the same, which is why the convent made certain we understood the distinction."

"You may stand," she says with a sniff. "It is too hard to hear you when you talk to the floor."

I straighten, but keep my eyes downcast, catching only the faintest glimpse of her pale face and dark hair. She is small, I realize. Smaller than I had expected.

"How did bedding my lord husband serve Mortain, pray tell? Or Brittany, if that was your intent."

Slowly, I raise my gaze to hers, which is filled with deep intelligence, keen wit, and grievous displeasure. "Please know that while my reasoning will sound faulty in the retelling, it seemed solid at the time."

This causes her finely arched eyebrows to rise — whether in displeasure or surprise at my frankness, I do not know. "However," I go on to explain, "serving the interests of both Mortain and Brittany was precisely what I was trying to do. There had been rumors that you had been abducted, or perhaps forced into this union. That it was so sudden only served to make those rumors seem likely. I was making plans to come to court to offer my services to you when I was told that the convent was being disbanded. That news seemed to point to the rumors of your coercion being true, and it appeared the worst was coming to pass — you had been taken by the French crown, and they intended to crush the very things that Brittany holds most sacred. How could I not act?"

She inhales deeply and looks away to the fire for a moment. "And how was sleeping with my lord husband to help with any of that?"

"Such is the nature of men, Your Majesty. They will promise you anything once they take a fancy to you. I thought to collect on an old promise."

Her slim white fingers grip the arms of her chair. "That is not how things work in my world. Indeed, it is I who have always been promised to men as reward for their political support. Or who must make promises and concessions to them once they have shown interest in me. Or my lands."

Rutting hell. But of course she has been a pawn in men's games of politics and power. With the sort of men she was expected to marry, she could never, under any circumstances, think to exercise her own choice in any of these matters. "Forgive me. Our circumstances are very different, and my words were poorly chosen."

"It was not the only poorly chosen part of this entire enterprise."

"Knowing what I know now, I cannot help but agree with you."

She blinks, as if not expecting my quick agreement.

"I am doing everything in my power to correct my error, Your Majesty." I wince, as *error* seems such a mild word for all that I have thrown into disarray. "I have downplayed the role of the convent in Brittany's politics and told the king I did not know if you had knowledge of its existence. And while I will always serve as his loyal subject, I will no longer warm his bed. At least, not willingly." I pause. "Unless you'd like me to?" It is an unwelcome thought, and not an offer made lightly, but if it would serve her in some way, it seems the least I could do.

She stares at me, agog, her cheeks bright pink. "Whyever would I want you to do such a thing?"

I shrug. "There are many reasons. If you are not fond of the marriage bed, you can know that his needs are being met by someone who is loyal to you. Or if you would like to enjoy the marriage bed more, I can teach him better ways to please you."

The queen's hands fly to her face, which is a vivid shade of scarlet. "Demoiselle, stop!"

My stomach grows queasy. Am I destined to always misstep with her? "I did not mean to distress you! I thought only to offer my services to make amends any way I can."

"Well, you may rest assured you have offered me something no one else ever has before," she says wryly. "Nor will I require that particular service as a path to atonement."

Her words give me hope that there will be some path to atonement.

"Tell me of this letter you received."

I tell her of the letter, of how the handwriting looked right, and that the official convent seal was affixed upon it. When I have finished, she stares off into the distance, tapping her finger on her chin. "What could Count Angoulême have to gain from this?"

"I have spent hours pondering that very question and have yet to arrive at an answer."

"Well, if one occurs to you, please inform me at once."

That tiny bud of hope inside me unfurls a bit more. "But of course, Your

Majesty." It is hard to tell, but I think she holds less animosity toward me than when I first arrived. Saints, please let it be so!

I want, more than anything, to prove my loyalty to her. To prove that it is still she and the convent I serve. "Your Majesty, there is something else you should know."

She stares at me quizzically. "Yes?"

"The regent was glad that I had come back to court and thought to use me in a scheme of her own."

The queen frowns. "What sort of scheme?"

It is all I can do not to squirm, not for my own sake but because it is still so hard to believe it of the regent. "She wished to install me in her brother's bed. Only instead of asking clemency for the convent, she wished me to report everything I learned directly to her."

The queen looks as if she will be sick. "She was the one who placed you in my husband's bed?"

"No! As much as I would like to blame her for that, it was my own mistake entirely. But she was most invested in using the king's interest in me for her own ends. I refused. My loyalty was only ever to the convent and Brittany. It was never for sale."

She is quiet a long moment as she studies me, and I would give a sack of gold coins to know what she is truly thinking. "Thank you for telling me, Genevieve," she says at last.

Her words bring a flood of relief rushing through my limbs. "The regent is as cunning and devious as a fox, and twice as dangerous. Her ruthlessness in securing the interests of the crown knows no bounds."

"Oh, believe me, I am aware." She falls quiet again, and so I wait. I do not know for what — a sentence, required penance, banishment? Or mayhap some task to perform to make it up to her. Instead, she simply dismisses me. Whether that will be the end of it or I must wait for whatever ax she plans to hang over my head, I do not know.

CHAPTER 10

Sybella

It requires an enormous effort to keep from putting my ear to the door to listen to Genevieve and the queen's meeting. Instead, I try to look as if I am not waiting, but here for a purpose. I pick up someone's discarded embroidery hoop and begin stitching, my hands grateful for the small task.

Will the queen punish Genevieve? Banish her? Is that the best thing to be done with the girl? Hard to know if she can be trusted — not simply her loyalty, but her judgment. For all of Father Effram's assurances that she meant well, it is difficult to imagine giving her a second chance.

Yet how many second chances have I been given?

The outer door opens, and I brace myself for the barbs from the regent's ladies who attend the queen. My tension eases somewhat when I recognize Elsibet. At least until the look of concern on her face registers.

"My lady, they are looking for you."

"They?"

"The steward. The king has requested your presence in his chamber at once."

Merde. What new accusation can Fremin have dreamed up? "Thank you, Elsibet." I frown at the queen's door. "Would you please see that Genevieve is escorted back to her rooms when the queen is done with her? As discreetly as possible, if you please."

There are two additional faces among the king's retinue this morning. The Bishop of Albi and the Bishop of Narbonne appear to be part of his council now. This cannot bode well.

Just as he was two days ago, the king's personal confessor is perched on his left shoulder. To his right stand General Cassel and the captain of the king's personal guard, Captain Stuart. Beyond them, as if an afterthought — or a puppet master gently pulling the strings — is the regent. Foreboding unfurls inside me, sharpening my senses. Stall them, I remind myself. I must only stall them long enough that Beast can get the girls to the convent. After that, none of this will matter.

The steward escorts me to the middle of the room, then excuses himself. The king says nothing, but pins his gaze on me. "Monsieur Fremin tells me he has not found his men."

The lawyer is looking faintly smug again. "I have not."

The Bishop of Albi leans over and whispers something in the Bishop of Narbonne's ear.

"And you, demoiselle? I presume you have not managed to locate them either?"

"No, sire, but I did learn that a large group rode out three days ago. Perhaps the stable master would be able to confirm if it was Sir Fremin's men or not." Of course, those riding out were Beast and the girls, but they made sure to do that well away from the hearing of the stable master — or anyone.

The king's eyes narrow with speculation. "I will make inquiries. And what of your sisters? Have you located them, by chance?"

I do not have to fake the tension that holds my shoulders in a viselike grip. "No, Your Majesty." I make my voice tremble along the edges, just enough for him to think I am filled with distress and not considering all of them with the cold calculation of the assassin he accuses me of being. "But mayhap we should ask the stable master if they were with the group riding out."

"Your Majesty," Fremin interjects. "I must protest. My men would never take their leave without my permission."

The Bishop of Albi gives a smug nod of approval, although why he thinks he would know anything about Fremin's men and how they would behave is a mystery to me. Perhaps it is simply his faith in the orderliness of the world.

I incline my head politely. "With all due respect, Your Majesty, we have only his word that he has not granted his men permission to leave." I glance at the lawyer, hoping he will consider the out I am about to offer him. "Besides, they are not truly his men, but my brother's. Who knows what orders Pierre may have given them separate from the orders he gave his lawyer?"

There. I have given the man a chance to shift the responsibility for the men to his liege's shoulders. If he truly has no part in this, then he will be smart enough to save his own neck and grasp at the sliver of an excuse I have tossed his way. I stare at him, willing him to take it. Surely if what drove me were my d'Albret instincts, I would not do even so much as that.

"That is ridiculous! The men report to me and are mine to command."

And so he chooses. He has erased the last doubt of his complicity. I furrow my brow as if in confusion. "You are certain, monsieur?"

"Of course," he says, thrusting his head into the noose I have tried so hard to protect him from.

"In that case" — I allow my face to harden — "perhaps Monsieur Fremin can explain to us why he had one of his men scale the wall beneath my sisters' chambers and attempt to get in through the window?"

Surprised silence ripples around the room.

"Your chambers?" the king asks.

The regent speaks for the first time. "That is impossible! You are on the fourth floor overlooking the rear courtyard. There is no external access to your room."

"That is true," I agree. "But there is a wall made of stone, and stones offer the smallest of footholds and handholds. Enough for the Mouse to climb."

Fremin's nostrils flare, and his head rears back slightly. I blink innocently at him. "That is his name, is it not? Or do you know him by another?"

He swallows before speaking. "It is but a nickname, Your Majesty. Something the other men call him, for he is small and quiet, not built for combat."

"Then why bring him if the need for such a large escort was due to unsafe roads?" the king asks, and I nearly cheer at not having to draw that line for him.

A sheen of desperation appears on Fremin's forehead. "Your Majesty, she is lying! My men would never disrespect your hospitality in such a way, nor would they even know which room she and her sisters were sleeping in."

The king turns his head to me, as if watching a jousting tournament.

"I am not lying, Your Majesty. I have proof." I pull the tiny scrap of the Mouse's tunic from my pocket and hold it out for the king to see. He motions me forward, but does not take the scrap from my hand. Instead, he leans to peer closer. The small square of brown homespun sits in stark contrast to the whiteness of my palm.

Which is not nearly as white as Fremin's face. "She lies," he protests again. "That could be any speck of fabric!"

The Bishop of Narbonne reaches toward it. "May I?"

"But of course, Your Grace."

He takes it from me and examines it. "It is coarse wool, not the sort anyone here at the palace would wear, not even the servants."

"How do we know she found it where she says she did?" Fremin scoffs.

"Your Majesty, what possible reason would I have for carrying around a small square of homespun just on the off chance that I may someday present it as false proof against a future accusation I could never have foreseen?"

The Bishop of Narbonne's mouth quirks ever so slightly as he glances up at the king and nods his agreement. The king strokes his chin, eyes lingering on the scrap. "This does seem to support your claim," he agrees. "Monsieur Fremin, you are dismissed, for now. However, Lady Sybella, you will indulge me by remaining."

Fremin hesitates, glancing at the regent, but she stares straight ahead, not acknowledging him. He gives a terse bow, then takes his leave.

When the lawyer has left, the king gives me his full attention. "This does not leave you fully in the clear. I have spoken at length with my advisors. Assassins are a dishonorable, barbaric tool that I believe has no place in our — or any monarch's — court."

My hands twitch with frustration.

The Bishop of Narbonne shoots him a look that lets me know this is news to him. "Your father used them quite frequently," he gently points out.

The king's hands clench into fists. "I am not my father. And even if I were inclined to assassination as a political tool, they are far too powerful a weapon to rest in the hands of my lady wife."

"Not only that," his confessor says, "but I believe it calls into question whether or not the queen can truly serve France if she still honors the Nine and their" — he eyes me with distaste — "ways."

The Bishop of Albi frowns in thought. "What if she were to renounce them?"

"Indeed," the confessor muses. "Since the king's right to rule is derived directly from God, it is possible that belief in a saint who trains assassins for his own purposes could be considered heretical."

A murmur of discussion buzzes through the room.

The bishop nods, warming to the subject. "It is an archaic and barbaric form of worship. It is far past time the Church take this up to examine it in light of adherence to doctrine."

At his words, a chill takes root deep in my bones. It is not only our political usefulness that is at risk, but the convent's — and all the Nine's — survival as well. However, they are sorely mistaken if they think we will give up our own gods without a fight.

But your god gave you up without a fight. The realization burrows its way into my heart and will not budge.

"What say you, General Cassel?" the king asks.

The general's gaze lands on me with all the subtlety of a boulder. "I say that any assassins who do not owe their allegiance to you — and only you — are dangerous and must be rooted out like weeds."

"He is right, sire," the Bishop of Albi agrees. "If they come from the convent, or the Nine, then how are we to know whom they truly serve, let alone how to control them? At the very least, those who follow the Nine should be forbidden from practicing their arts."

I am unable to keep silent any longer. "Truly, Your Grace? And what of Saint Brigantia? Was it not her acolytes who tended King Louis in his final days, bringing him comfort and succor at the very end?"

The bishop blinks at me, no quick rejoinder at the ready.

"But the Brigantian nuns do not kill people," the king's confessor smugly points out.

I tilt my head. "What of Saint Maurice? Will you forbid his worship or the practice of his arts as well?"

"He is not one of the Nine!"

"No, but half the soldiers in France consider him their patron saint and learn their arts in his name, leaving offerings and sacrifices and prayers at his shrines. How is that any different?"

"They do not kill —" The confessor's words come to an abrupt halt as he realizes my point. "It is different," he insists tersely. "They follow the earthly orders of their liege."

"As do we at the convent of Saint Mortain," I murmur politely.

"The girl is correct. It is not heresy," the Bishop of Narbonne says.

"It should be," the confessor says darkly.

"That may well be," Narbonne says, "but the Church must declare it so. Not us."

"If you will excuse me, Your Majesty." All eyes shift to the familiar voice of Father Effram. I did not see him when I came in. The king blinks. "Who are you, and what are you doing here?"

Father Effram steps forward, hands serenely folded in his sleeves, head bowed. "I am Father Effram, Your Majesty, and the Lady Sybella's confessor."

I bite the inside of my lip, lest my own surprise give his lie away.

"It seemed important I be here to give the lady the appropriate spiritual guidance."

The other bishops are nonplussed. The Bishop of Angers actually sputters. "But you are one of them! You serve one of the Nine!"

Father Effram nods. "Yes, as I am ordained by the Church to do. You are forgetting that in Brittany, we worship Christ as well as His saints. And that the Nine are only a handful of the saints we worship. The others are the precise same ones that you yourself worship — the Magdalene, Saint Christopher, Saint Guinefort, and Saint Michael."

The regent steps out of the shadows. "This is an important matter, to be discussed at length and in private. Not, I think, in front of the Lady Sybella. Nor any of those who would be affected by such a change."

The king's eyes are cool upon her. "Tell me, dear sister, how long have you known?"

The regent blinks. "Known what, Your Majesty?"

"Known of the convent and their purpose?"

"I learned of it when you brought the matter to Lady Sybella's attention, the first day that Monsieur Fremin announced his men were missing."

I cannot tell if she speaks the truth or if she is lying. Did none of her spies ever tell her of the convent? Either way, I have so few weapons that I must take chances. "Oh, but she did know, Your Majesty," I protest. "As did your father. I do not know why they chose not to share it with you."

The king sets his teeth, a faint flush of red appearing in his pale cheeks. "We will speak of this later, you and I."

The regent whips her head toward me, her eyes full of murderous intent. Her attack, when it comes, is low and unexpected. "Your Majesty, given what we've learned of Lady Sybella, do you still think it appropriate for her to have custody of her sisters?"

He considers me, his gaze distant and assessing. "No. I do not."

And there it is. My worst fears brought to life. I allow my face to fall. "Your Majesty." My voice trembles with emotion. "I would remind you that I do not have custody of my sisters. They went missing while under the crown's protection."

"You are right, demoiselle. Matters of church doctrine aside, two young girls are missing. Two young girls who fall under the court's protection, something I take most seriously. I have sent search parties out to scour the area and look for any signs of them. Hopefully we will have news soon."

The king's announcement of his search party sets near panic aflight in my chest. How far has Beast gotten? I wonder as I leave the audience chamber, careful to keep my steps slow and even. Between Beast's need for secrecy and the two girls, he cannot be making good time.

And how far do the king's men plan to search? Four men such as Fremin's could cover a lot of ground. Much more than Beast and the girls could have.

Merde. What if he finds them? Then everything will be lost, and all that we have done will have been for nothing.

CHAPTER 11

Aeva

I smell them long before I can hear them, the stink of their iron weapons acrid in the cool, damp air. I crouch down lower in the bracken and crawl forward on my belly to look over the ridge into the valley below.

There are two, no three, columns of mounted soldiers wearing the king's colors. They are heading toward the Loire River, but bearing west, toward us. The lines ride one bowshot apart, with some of the men beating at the bush with clubs, as if trying to flush pheasant out of hiding.

A prickle of anticipation runs along my scalp, for these are not mere hunters.

We have been traveling west for two days, staying well south of the river. We did not expect pursuit. Sybella had spun plans upon plans to keep them from noticing our absence. And even if they did, they would search north of the river toward Brittany, which is why we have been heading in a southerly direction, as if traveling to Poitou. But by their formation and crosshatching, it is clear that these men are not merely in pursuit, but searching.

I back away from the ridge. When I am far enough that they will not see me, I begin to run, keeping low and matching the rhythm of my movements to the sounds of the forest, taking a step in time with the cry of a kestrel, moving forward as the wind rustles the branches.

Divona's ears prick as she hears me coming, but sensing my

urgency, she does not whinny her normal greeting. I vault onto her back, then ride hard to catch up to the rest of the group.

Beast rides behind the others, waiting for me. I warble like a thrush, and he quickly falls back. "How did you hear them?" he asks. "I pride myself on my sharp hearing, and I heard nothing."

I smile. "Nor did I. I could smell them."

He gives me an aggrieved look. "Even so, I should have gone, not you."

"Might as well send a boar crashing through the woods to announce our presence."

"I can move quietly." He sounds mildly offended. "What did you learn?"

"Three groups of men, searching in crisscross patterns between the Loire to the north and the Vienne's southward bend."

"Camulos's balls," he mutters. "How fast are they moving?"

"Faster than us, but their search pattern forces them to cover twice as much ground. They should catch up to us by nightfall."

"Any indication how far they intend to go?"

"They did not say."

"No, but since you can smell and hear things that the rest of us cannot, I thought perhaps you'd discerned it through the weight of the gear they carried or the pacing of their horses."

"Well," I concede, "they were traveling light, no pack animals. So they are likely planning to spend the night in a town or holding." I pause. "How far are we from any town or holding?"

"Not far. I had hoped to spend the night in Chinon, but it sits near one of the king's castles and is likely where they are headed. I do not want to put ourselves so directly in their path." He glances ruefully at our little party. Eight men-at-arms, two Arduinnites, one lady in waiting, a gnome, and two young girls.

"We cannot outrun them, nor are we close enough to the river to cross it before nightfall."

Beast looks wistfully at the forest around us. "A cave would be nice. But the saints only know if there is one near here or how we could find it if there was."

"I wouldn't be so certain of that, O Angry One."

He swings his gaze to me. "I only got angry once," he mutters. Or growls. I can never be certain with him.

"But it was such a deeply righteous anger. And in all fairness, Sybella deserved it for trying to slink off without telling anyone. Here."

I slip off my horse, hand Beast my reins, and move a dozen steps away from him. I kneel, spread my palms, and slowly press them into the ground, past the rich leaf mold into the deeper soil below. I close my eyes and slow my breath, allowing my pulse to match that of the earth beneath me. The rhythm is slow and steady, so profoundly comforting that my body hums with the rightness of it. I feel the pulse bounce off the roots of the trees, feel it swerve to avoid a deep boulder thrusting up from the bowels of the earth. It moves more swiftly after that, humming along until it opens up near the surface, then echoes off a small enclosed space.

I stand up and brush off my hands. "There is a cave due west, just before the forest ends. If we hurry, we can make it before they pick up our trail. But it will be close."

CHAPTER 12

Genevieve

The king stands before the east wall, studying the painting that hangs there. "Your Majesty." I curtsy deeply. I had not expected another summons so soon. If ever.

Although it is not yet dusk, all the candles are lit and the fire built high. Without taking his eyes from the painting, he motions me to my feet, then bids me come closer. "Have I told you of this painting?"

"No, sire." It is, I realize, what he was staring at the last time, when I glimpsed such longing and resentment on his face.

"My father had it made for me."

It is violent and gruesome — a soldier holds a nobleman in a blue doublet decorated with gold fleurs-de-lis by the chest, his sword raised. They are surrounded by a mob of knights and men-at-arms. Blood already pours from the nobleman's many wounds, but that does not cause the others to call off their attack, as they are poised to hack him to pieces like the two noblemen who already lie dead on the field.

"It seems a most melancholy gift."

His mouth twists in a bitter smile. "It was not a gift but a reminder of what happens to those too weak to seize and hold power. To those who lessen their stranglehold over others. It was how he ruled, how he trained my sister to rule, and how he expected me to rule."

"Does the regent have a similar painting hanging in her chambers?"

The king barks out a surprised laugh. "She needs no reminder. Unlike me."

So a reminder, then, of how lacking his father saw him. A way to reach beyond the grave and coerce him into being the man his father was instead of his own self.

He turns on me then, all the loathing and frustration he kept in check while staring at the painting unfurls, filling the space between us, the unexpected shock of it like a fist. "According to his rules, you have betrayed me, and to betray me is to betray France itself. You owe me much in the way of restitution." The way his eyes rake over my body leaves no doubt as to his motives.

I want to take him by the shoulders and shake him. To shout at him that this is not who he is. But of course, I dare not. I make no move. Not of revulsion, nor of encouragement. While I have no desire to feel his anger, neither do I wish to lie with him again. Ever. It is not simply that he cannot give me what I want, but that I have seen him more clearly for who he is. There is nothing like anger to reveal a man's true character, my aunt Fabienne always claimed. More important, the queen is not like her mother nor any of the noblewomen I have known and does not relish the idea of sharing him with a court favorite. While he is not deserving of such loyalty, the queen is, and I will honor her wish in this.

He sneers at my continued silence. "Will you not willingly give me what I want unless I shower you with fine gifts?"

"I never wished for your gifts," I remind him softly.

My words seem to anger him further. "Gifts would have cost me less than what you asked for. What you asked for goes to the heart of what makes me king."

Genuinely perplexed, and more than a little appalled at this change that has come over him, I ask, "What is it that I asked for, sire?"

"My power. You wanted to whittle away a slice of my power. In that way, you are just like all the rest."

I blink in surprise. "Power? I never wanted power, Your Majesty."

"No. Just a sweeping pardon of your fellow assassins."

"Few are truly assassins. Most simply serve the patron saint of death in some way."

"Nevertheless, to do what you asked was to impose your will — a woman's will! — over mine on matters of church and state."

"No, I thought only to ask for mercy for a group of women who raised me. Besides, you said you had never even heard of the convent."

He takes a step toward me. "That is the entire reason you came to my bed, isn't it?"

"No! I have always liked and admired you." At least until you began behaving like a maddened bull.

"Were you attracted to me?" He stares so intently into my eyes that I fear he will see the truth there — that my heart and my body long only for Maraud.

No. "Yes."

"Then come. Let us make love again. If you are attracted to me, surely you will come to my bed."

I meet his gaze steadily. "Not willingly, Your Majesty, no."

His hand snakes up and grabs my chin, forcing my head back. "Are you refusing me?"

"Not refusing, no. But I will not come willingly." Every time he speaks, memories of Maraud flood my mind — his easy confidence, his honor, his kindness — and the contrast could not be more stark. Or favor the king less. "Surely your chivalry would not demand such a thing."

He scoffs, but lets go of my chin, nonetheless. "Have you not heard? One cannot possess chivalry and honor and run a kingdom. And if ever you forget it, there will be plenty to remind you." The look he casts at the painting is so full of hatred that I'm surprised it doesn't burst into flame.

"That is not so, even though some would have you believe it. Nor, I believe, is it what you truly want."

"Do not tell me what I want," he snarls. "I am sick unto death of hearing what others think I should want."

I glance briefly back at the painting. Of course he is. Once his father died, his sister effortlessly took up that mantle and now undermines him at every opportunity.

I think back to the audience chamber and General Cassel, so quick to voice his brutal opinions. To the Church advisors, equally quick to cluck and offer up their views and judgments. So few — if any — of them ever affirming his own.

He draws close again. "What I want is you. Why is that?" A note of confusion seeps out through his anger. "And why will you not come to my bed?"

"I see no signs of the man I liked and admired. I was drawn to his honor and his chivalry, and see neither of those things in this room right now."

Not caring for my honesty, his lips grow thin. "How do you dare defy me?"

"Because I have nothing to lose."

"Your life?"

I smile, amused for the first time since I entered the room. This amusement unnerves him more than anything else I have done. "One who serves death does not fear it."

He abruptly steps away to pour himself a glass of wine. "My bishops say you and your convent reek of heresy. My general says I should execute you all for treason."

I can only pray that my own behavior has given him a taste for defiance. "I have said that I will swear on the Holy Bible or any other relics of the Church that I have never acted against you or the French crown." He does not need to know it was because I was never given the opportunity.

He falls quiet while he sips his wine. "Tell me, what do you know about the Lady Sybella?"

Not sure where this is leading, I answer cautiously. "As I told you, I left the convent before she arrived and only met her for the first time four days ago."

Even so, I have learned much about her. Things he would be most interested in knowing.

"It is too bad," he says, "because if you could shed some light on her character, it would do much to soothe my anger with you."

"In order to do that, I would need to know her character, and I do not. If I were to tell you anything, it would all be speculation."

"And what would you speculate?"

I stall for time in order to assemble my thoughts. "She is the one whose case you just decided on, no?" He inclines his head, watching me closely. "Well, I would speculate that she is a very good sister. Caring, protective —"

He seizes on that. "How would an assassin protect those she cares about?"

"In the same ways we all do. By anticipating and seeing to their needs, by placing herself between those and any who wished them harm. Much like she does for the queen."

"What do you mean?"

Small truths, I remind myself. Small truths will help us all. "I have only been here a handful of days, sire, and have already heard the gossip about the queen and the regent. That the more Madame tries to draw the queen under her influence —"

He opens his mouth to say something, thinks better of it, then motions for me to continue. But the seed is planted. He is now wondering in what ways the regent is trying to manipulate his queen just as much as she tries to manipulate him.

"— the more Sybella offers herself as a target, using distraction and redirection to shift the regent's attention away from the queen to herself."

"And thus draw her ire," the king muses.

"Yes," I say with more encouragement than warranted, but I am relieved to have pulled his attention from Sybella to the machinations of his sister. "That is a large reason the regent dislikes her so."

There is a knock on the door, and the chamberlain appears. "My lord, the Privy Council is assembled and awaiting." He gestures toward the large set of double doors at the far end of the king's salon.

"Thank you. I will be right there." To me he says, "You must leave. I have business matters to attend to."

"But of course, Your Majesty." I curtsy my farewell, but he is already headed toward the council chamber.

At the door, he stops. "And, Gen, I will remind you: Do not say anything of your true role here. While I am most displeased with you, I do not wish you to get swept up in the repercussions that may come."

No, but he will gladly feed Sybella to those same wolves.

As he enters the council room, I catch a brief glimpse of two of the bishops and the regent, then hear the deep voice of General Cassel before the door closes. I stand there, aswirl in the dregs of the king's tumultuous emotions. He still wants me but has accepted my boundaries.

He does not plan to expose my identity to the others. His father's scorn is a festering wound, one poked at constantly by his sister. A wound is a weakness, and a weakness an opportunity.

There is a way forward here. The path is narrow and twisted and surrounded by thorns, but it is a path. With that in mind, I glance over my shoulder to see if the chamberlain is still about, but he is gone. The king's suite contains four rooms altogether — a sitting room, his bedchamber, an oratory, and a private council room. I quickly dismiss the bedchamber that sits to the left of the Privy Council, as there is a good chance the king's valet awaits him in the small adjacent dressing room.

Which leaves the room on the right. I hurry over and place my ear to the door. Silence. Cautiously, I open it. When I reassure myself that it is truly empty —no minor secretaries or scribes diligently tending to the king's business — I slip inside. I head straight for the wall between this room and the council room. The outer walls of the palace are thick, but less so between rooms.

"...spoken at length with the other bishops," the king's confessor is saying. "And while it is true that the Nine were originally recognized as saints, that was hundreds of years ago. Much has changed since then, including a number of ecclesiastical positions and reforms."

"In short," someone — I think it is the Bishop of Albi — says, "it is an archaic and heathenish practice, and surely no longer orthodox."

A murmur of voices talking over each other. A lone one finally rising above the others. "Sire," the regent says, "how did you come to learn of the convent?" I hold my breath.

"A king has many spies and sources, Madame." He uses her formal title, a move I can only assume is meant to put her in her place, remind her that she does not have to know everything that he does.

But she is an expert at both deflection and manipulation. She has had years of practice, learning just where to poke and prod to elicit the behavior she wishes, and is quick to direct his attention back to the matter at hand. "Of course, Your Majesty. But this morning's meeting gives me another thought. I believe that God has placed an opportunity squarely before you."

The entire room falls silent, and I would give anything to see both the king's face and his bishops' as the regent decides to add the role of spiritual advisor to her duties.

"Continue." The king's voice is colder than iron in winter.

"You have long been troubled by your need to break the betrothal vow with the Princess Marguerite." I suck in my breath — that she would be so bold as to speak of such private matters before the entire council. "Perhaps ridding the Church of this unorthodoxy would allow you to atone for that stain on your mortal soul."

The silence in the room is nearly thicker than the wall at my ear. Again, I would give anything to know how the king is reacting to this. After a few more minutes of ominous silence, the regent speaks again. "If that does not appeal, then perhaps it would be wise to hold off on the queen's coronation."

Surprised silence fills the room. "But to what end?"

"Besides, the marriage has already been consummated," someone else points out.

The Bishop of Albi, ever political, speculates, "Won't that create more problems than it solves?"

"Only if we let it go on indefinitely. I am merely suggesting we use it as leverage to get the queen to renounce her irregular religious practices. The French crown cannot be tainted with such things."

"And if she renounces the Nine, the convent of assassins will not be a tool in her arsenal, one that could be used against you." Cassel's deep voice is easy to recognize.

I wait for one of them to point out that the queen — that *we* — would never do that — but no one does.

CHAPTER 13

Aeva

he sun is low in the sky by the time we finally reach the cave. Less than an hour until nightfall. Beast leaves me to scout out our shelter and wheels his horse around to ride back to see how close the search party is. Despite my earlier teasing, he is quick for one who is the size of a standing stone. And quiet.

"What is wrong?" The young wasp rides in front of me, her eyes nearly as sharp as her tongue. Even when alarmed, she manages to keep her voice low.

"Nothing."

"Then why are we stopping?"

"So that we and the horses may rest."

"You don't need a rest," she points out.

"No, but I am not the only one here."

"It is because of Louise, isn't it?" She glares at her younger sister, who rides comfortably nestled in the arms of the little gray dove, Tephanie, and blinks in surprise at the attack.

"Quit grumbling at Louise." My voice is clipped. "Else I will tell her that you were complaining that the saddle was making your bottom sore mere minutes ago."

The wasp's mouth snaps shut, and she glowers at me. "You just told her."

"Ah, so I did. Next time you'd best keep your grumbling to yourself so I do not slip again." I dismount, leaving her to glare at me from atop Divona, and go investigate the cave.

It is perfect for our purposes—large enough that four men can ride in abreast and deep enough that all of us—plus our mounts—can sleep in comfort. Those of us who will be getting some sleep, that is. We will need to post a watch.

I motion to Tola. "Get the others into the cave," I tell her quietly. "Far in the back. There is an opening there. Too small for horses to pass through, but large enough for us to get out with the girls if we need to."

"Something *is* wrong," the wasp says, looking smug with victory.

"I wouldn't look so pleased about it if I were you." Tola lifts the younger girl off the horse. As she lowers her to the ground, she says softly, "And be mindful of your words lest you frighten Louise unnecessarily."

"But if something is wrong, it wouldn't be unnecessary."

Boar's tits! Could this girl child be any more mulish? "Charlotte." My use of her given name catches her full attention, and I hand her Divona's reins. "I am putting you in charge of Divona, but I need to know you will give her your full attention. She does not like dark, enclosed spaces and will need your firm and guiding hand. Can you do that?"

With her eyes wide and her mouth shut for once, she nods and reverently takes the reins. She longs to ask me what I am going to do—but I look pointedly at the horse, and the question fades.

"This way," Tola says.

Long before I expect him to, Beast comes galloping back. As he swings off his horse, the wind shifts and I catch the scent of horses, sweat, and iron. They are closer.

"A quarter hour out," he mutters tersely. "Where are the girls?"

"Already in the cave, with Tephanie and Tola." I tell him about the back opening I found, in case we need to get away. I take in his considerable bulk. "I do not think you will fit through it. The other men, maybe. But not you."

He bares his teeth in what he thinks is a grin but is more like a rictus of death. "I do not plan to. If it comes to that, the men and I will make a stand here at the entrance while you and the others slip out. Our posted rear scouts can pick off any who try to follow you." The weight of his resolve is as unmovable as the cave beside us.

"What should I do with them?"

"Get them to the convent." I barely recognize the note of bleakness in his voice before he swings around and begins issuing orders to the men.

That bleakness has me kissing my fingers and pressing them against the wall of the cave, begging Dea Matrona and Arduinna to hold us in their protection.

By the time I reach Tola and the others, the coil of tension that permeates the air is unmistakable. The little one huddles in the dove's lap. The dove's hand trembles as she calmly strokes the child's back, murmuring words of comfort.

The wasp is gripping Divona's reins in her left hand, so tightly that her knuckles are white. In her right she holds the knife that Sybella gave her. It is pointless to tell them everything will be fine when we can hear the search party's hooves thudding on the forest floor, shaking the very ground beneath our feet. I give the wasp a nod of approval instead.

One of the men near the front of the cave spits, another coughs, and the hooves grow louder, closer, accompanied now by the squeak of leather and the jingle of tack.

A voice, sounding far away because of the thickness of the cave walls, calls out, "Over there! A cave!"

Another voice calls back. "This will be the last one for the day. We're almost out of light."

The direction of the horses shifts so that they head directly for us, then come to a stop. The cave rings with the silence that follows, broken by a creak of leather as someone hoists himself out of a saddle.

Tola looks at me. I point at her, then the opening, then hold my palm out flat. She is to go first, but not until I give the signal.

My heart beats faster in both anticipation and excitement. If not for the girls and Tephanie, I would relish this skirmish. After weeks cooped up at the French court, I am hungry for a fight.

In the fading light that just reaches the cave, Beast looks at me over his shoulder and nods.

I lift my bow and draw an arrow, calculating a path that will allow me to pick off the first men in without hitting Beast or the queen's guard. Before I can give Tola the signal, a hunting horn sounds, and a new rider comes galloping into the clearing, eliciting curses and mutters from the French.

"Where's your captain?" a voice shouts over the others.

"I am here," a deep voice answers.

"The search has been called off," the messenger calls out. "They've found something."

The men whoop, and the captain says, "You heard him! Mount up and ride out."

It is not until I hear the last of them ride away that I finally lower my bow.

CHAPTER 14

Sybella

s I prepare the queen's morning tonic, I try to decide how much I should share with her from yesterday's audience with the king. If they are truly considering appealing to the Church to have the Nine declared heretical, she will need to be informed. And while she should know their claims that following the Nine divides her loyalty, I'm not sure that would do more than make her angry.

"Well, are you going to ask me?"

I glance up from the pestle I'm using to grind the cardamom to find her watching me, amusement dancing in her eyes. "Ask you what?"

"How my meeting with Genevieve went."

Merde. News of the search party had driven all of that from my mind. "Of course I am curious, Your Majesty, but it also struck me as a somewhat personal conversation."

She waves her hand. "I have no privacy. You know that."

As if to prove her point, there is a sharp pounding on the door before it is thrust open and Captain Stuart strides in, followed by a half dozen soldiers.

"What is the meaning of this?" the queen demands.

Captain Stuart bows. "I beseech Your Majesty's forgiveness, but I am here on orders of the king." The queen stares at him, disbelief writ plain on her face. Ignoring her, he motions his men forward. "Lady Sybella, you are to come with us."

My heart sinks. I do not know what this means, but surely something dire. Have they found Beast and the girls?

"All seven of you are needed to escort her?" the queen asks waspishly.

He bows at her politely, but does not answer the question. I carefully set the mortar and pestle down. "Heloise? Would you mind finishing this? It is almost ready to steep." Then I step out from behind the table. "By all means, please take me to the king."

To my surprise, we do not head for the king's audience chamber but back toward the kitchen and a small room that stands off to the side. The first thing I notice is the mud-splattered soldiers standing at attention. The second thing I notice is the stink of death that permeates everything, explaining why the king and his advisors have not entered, but stand cramped in the hallway.

Upon my arrival, the king turns to me. "My search party has found something, Lady Sybella. Or has found someone, I should say."

Every fiber of my being grows as taut as a bowstring. I arrange my face in what I hope is mild confusion. "I am glad of it, Your Majesty."

The king gestures to the mud-splattered captain, giving me a moment to compose myself. *Do not let it be Beast. Do not let it be Beast.* "Report, Sir Reynaud."

"We found a man's body southeast of here, washed up on the banks of the river."

I am so relieved it is not Beast that I hardly hear the rest of his report.

"Is it one of my men?" Monsieur Fremin has arrived, only he is not under armed guard.

"I don't know, sir. He had nothing to identify him."

General Cassel steps out from behind the king, his eyes boring into mine. "We have reason to believe it was you who killed him."

The hallway grows as silent as a crypt. "And what reason would that be?" I ask.

The Bishop of Albi answers. "What more reason do we need than the fact that he is dead and you are a known assassin?"

"Even an assassin needs a motive," I point out.

"Do they?" The king's confessor's eyes are alight with something both gleeful and terrifying. "When they serve the god of death, do they truly need a motive?"

"Yes. For political expediency, to protect others under their charge, in self-protection. The list is long. But those of us at the convent not only need a motive, but Mortain's blessing, and I have neither."

"That is not proof that you didn't kill him," the Bishop of Albi says.

Are they truly this stupid? This blinded by their own prejudgment?

"Does your list of motives include strange and unholy rites?" I jerk my head around to stare at the regent. The self-satisfied look on her face warns me I will not like what comes next. "There have been many reports of your tending to Captain Dunois when he fell from his horse. I am not convinced that it wasn't you who killed him."

"Those were not unholy rites," I say tightly, "but earthly ones. Checking for wounds I might stanch, an arrow I might pluck from his chest, a puncture where poison might have entered so that I might draw it from him. That is all, my lords. That and praying."

"Praying to the god of death," Albi mutters.

"Praying to Saint Mortain, the patron saint of death," I correct him sharply. "He is recognized by the Church."

"Lady Sybella is correct." The Bishop of Narbonne's voice rings as clear as a bell among all the muttering. "What she, what all of Brittany, practices is not heresy."

The look on the Bishop of Albi's face all but screams, *Not yet*.

General Cassel takes a step closer, his gaze never leaving my face. "Could this man have been sent to kill the queen, and you killed him instead?"

"He could have, and I would most assuredly have stepped in to save the queen. But I'm afraid I was not given a chance to show off my skills, for that is not what happened here. Besides" — I tilt my head — "if I had, would I still be accused of murder? For daring to save our queen from an assassin?"

There is a satisfying pause as they all realize just how deep a thicket their single-minded focus has led them into. The king recovers first. "Of course not. In such a case we would thank you for saving my lady wife. Although we would prefer that any such malfeasance be brought before the king's justice for punishment."

"As would I. But as you no doubt know from your own experience on the battlefield, sometimes we are allowed only the briefest moment of time in which to save a life. Your Majesty, those very skills also allow me to identify the means of death. If I stand accused, I would ask to be allowed to examine the body."

As I expected, this generates another round of outraged muttering, but again, Bishop Narbonne comes to my aid. "Of all of us, she is the best trained to make these determinations. And whether you like it or not, her worship is not heresy. Let her examine the body so that we may all learn something."

"What if she lies?" General Cassel asks.

"The king's physician is with the body now. Surely he will know if she is lying."

The smell is stronger inside the small room, where the body is laid out on a thick stone table used for butchering deer and boars. The king's physician peers up at me as I draw closer, looking in perplexity from me to the king.

"She has trained in the arts of death," the king explains.

The physician merely nods before resuming his work.

The body is swollen and bluish white, bloated from river water. I glance up at the king. "He has been dead far longer than Monsieur Fremin's men have been missing." I step closer to the table, right next to the physician, who casts me one annoyed look before continuing to probe at the man's throat. "What have you found there?" I ask as if it were not I who inflicted the wound.

"A hole," he says.

"Like that of an arrow?" General Cassel asks.

"No," the physician says, and I breathe a sigh of relief. "It is too ragged for that. The best I can piece together is that he fell from his horse, breaking his neck. He then had the misfortune to land on a small branch poking out of the bracken."

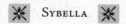
"Let me see." Monsieur Fremin shoulders his way through the small gathering so he, too, can examine the body.

I keep my face focused on what the physician is doing, but my gaze follows the lawyer closely, watching to see if there is any spark of recognition. There! His pupils dilate, and his eyes start to widen before he catches himself, pulling the collar of his shirt up to cover the movement.

"Is he one of your men, Monsieur Fremin?" the king asks.

"No," he tells the king, but it is a lie. I don't know if he recognizes the horribly distorted face or the man's clothing or his boots. But recognize him he does. Fremin looks from the body to me and smiles, like a man who has unexpectedly caught a hare in an old, forgotten trap.

CHAPTER 15

Fremin knows. The look he sent me fair trumpeted his awareness clear across the room.

Thank the saints everybody else was too busy looking at the body to notice.

But that will not last long. I've no doubt Fremin will find some way to use this knowledge to his advantage. Except, then he would have to admit he knew the man — which would raise new questions, and the king has not cleared him of all suspicion.

Well, not yet. But after this newest revelation, it is hard to say if that will hold. Clearly Fremin's best hope is that I will be found guilty of this crime, but if not, he will no doubt take matters into his own hands.

A knock sounds on my door, and I scowl, wondering what new catastrophe waits on the other side. I consider not answering, but everyone saw me escorted back to my rooms. Besides, only a coward hides. I check the knives at my wrists, school my features, then head for the door, stopping as it opens and Genevieve slips in.

At the sight of her, the ugly tangle of fear that fills my belly coalesces into something hotter and far more satisfying. "What are you doing here?" I spit out. If not for her . . . I do not even let myself finish the thought lest I do something I regret. "I see that *you* are not confined to your chambers."

It is hard to tell, but I think she winces slightly before her face resumes its normal impassive mask. "I have not been accused of killing four men," she points out as she closes the door behind her.

My arm is raised, fingers curled, before I catch myself and wrap my hands around my arms instead of punching her. I storm over to the window and stare the long way down into the courtyard. The room is quiet except for the shifting of the dying embers in the grate.

"Is this newest body one of yours?"

I shoot her a scornful glance. "I am not so foolish as to hand you my secrets so you may take them back to the king."

This time it is her fists that clench as she takes a step farther into the room. "I would not do that."

The anger burbling through my veins does not want to believe her, but all my training and instincts fair shout at me that she is telling the truth. Even so, I owe her nothing. "You betrayed us once before."

Her soft mouth grows hard. "I was wrong — but that does not make my actions a betrayal. Knowing the king's own ambitions and devotion to the Church, it made complete sense that he would shut down the worship of the Nine."

I cannot argue, because that seems to be precisely what he is doing now that he has learned of it.

"So yes, I believed it. And I wanted to fix it. I could not accept that I had been sired by Mortain for no other reason than to molder in an obscure castle under the leering eye of a debauched lord."

Although her face is carefully arranged, it is clear how very young she is, for all that I am only a year older than she. And like me, from twelve on, she lived in a hostile household, where she needed to conceal her every thought and true action from everyone around her.

She begins to pace. "I only hoped to gain clemency for the convent. Instead" — her voice grows rough with emotion —"I exposed everyone and put you all in even more danger." She falls quiet a moment, then stops pacing to face me, chin held high. "However, I am not here so you can throw my past sins in my face."

Impressed in spite of myself, I lean against the window. "Then why are you here?"

"I heard the king talking with his advisors."

"When?" I ask sharply.

She glances away for the briefest of seconds. "Last night in the king's privy chamber."

"Why were you there?"

She shrugs. "The king enjoys railing at me at the moment. It is easy enough to endure, and I can learn much. Things we may be able to use to our advantage. Or at least protect ourselves against. The king had dismissed me to attend the meeting. But I did not leave."

She takes a step closer. "Sybella —" The urgency in her voice shoves aside my anger. "His council — with the regent leading the charge — is urging him to petition the Church to have worship of the Nine declared unorthodox. They are trying to convince him that the queen cannot honor both the Nine and her marriage vows. I do not think any of them, with the possible exception of General Cassel, believe such a thing, only that it provides a political advantage."

"What did Cassel say?"

"He wants the convent eliminated because it is a weapon the king does not control. But it is the regent who is more dangerous. She is urging him to do this as penance for breaking his betrothal vow."

"A vow she encouraged him to break!"

She plucks at her skirt in frustration. "It doesn't matter. She is happy to jerk her brother around like a dog on a leash as long as it allows her to do what she thinks best for France. She is also proposing to hold off on the coronation until the queen has agreed."

Merde. The regent's brain has more twists than a labyrinth. "You must tell the queen."

"What? No! She is not fond of me. It is better if you tell her. She does not need to be reminded that I have private access to her husband."

It is a considerate gesture. "Normally, I would agree with you, but with guards at my door, I don't know when I will be allowed to see her."

After a moment, Gen nods her head, then takes a step toward the door. "The body they found?" I say.

She stops. "Yes?"

"He was an assassin my brother sent to kill me at Christmas."

When Father Effram looks up from putting away the altar cloth and sees my face, he immediately heads for the confessional booth. Fortunately, my two guards do not invade the sanctuary of the chapel and linger outside in the hall.

As soon as he slides the grill open, I tell him, "There has been a new development."

"By your voice, it is not a happy one."

"The search party has found a body. The body of the assassin Pierre sent."

"That is a shame it didn't stay put, but surely they cannot connect it to you?"

"Fremin suspects I killed him. He might tell the king."

"Would that not also implicate him and your brother, since they are the ones who sent the assassin?"

"They would not say the man was an assassin. They would claim he was a messenger."

There is silence as Father Effram digests this. "What will you do?"

"I have considered how I might neutralize Fremin without killing him. Now that the king knows I am an assassin, any death will immediately call his attention to me."

"That is true."

"I could cut out Fremin's tongue, then he could not speak, but he has hands and knows how to write. I could cut off his hands as well, but would it not be kinder to kill him outright? In Pierre's world, a man with no voice and no hands will not last long." A silent burble of laughter threatens to crawl its way up my throat. "In truth, Father, I killed him the moment I removed my sisters from his reach. My brother does not tolerate failure."

"What do you wish to do?" Father Effram's voice is gentle and coaxing.

The dark ribbon of rage unfurls inside me. "I want to kill him," I whisper, the longing in my heart causing my voice to tremble. "I want to slip my hands around his throat and squeeze the life from him. I want to squelch any threat he may now — or ever — present to those I love." As the wave of fury subsides, an icy fear replaces it. "But surely it is one thing to kill the henchmen as they came to our room to kidnap my sisters, or to throw a knife at Pierre and the men who think to grab them from my arms. But to kill a man for something he might do in the future feels as if I am crossing a dangerous moral line. And yet no matter how I look at it, the only solution I can see is his death."

"What happens if you don't kill him?"

"He tells the king, or the regent. They believe him. I am tried and hanged for murder. My sisters will have no one to see to their safety. Worse, who is to say that Pierre won't find them now that it is known I serve the convent? Eventually, he will look there, and he will find them."

"The convent would not hand them over."

"Not without a fight, no. But how can they withstand the thousands of troops Pierre commands? Must they all die, too, because of my blighted family?"

In the silence that follows, I can hear the cogs of his mind turning. At last he says, "The solution is obvious, child. You are acting out of love, not embracing darkness for its own sake. You must follow your heart."

"Even if my heart says to kill him?"

He is quiet so long, I wonder if he is going to leave me to answer my own question.

"You — all his daughters — have only touched the surface of your power. You must stop being afraid to use it. Being small and hiding yourself does not serve anyone. It may have once, but no longer."

His words fill me with both trepidation and exhilaration. It is the exhilaration that scares me the most. "But then I become what I am trying to protect my sisters from."

"The Dark Mother takes life in order to make room for new life. But every time she does, she creates an opening for rebirth."

For some reason, his words create a flutter of panic deep within me. "I am not the Dark Mother," I rush to point out.

"Perhaps not, but that does not mean we cannot learn from her. Even when death looks us in the face, we can still choose life. If we do, we are reborn into something new. If not, death claims us for eternity."

"Are you saying that if I threaten Fremin with death, he may change his ways?" I snort. "He is too afraid of Pierre to do that."

"Fear is a powerful thing," Father Effram agrees. "And goes to the crux of what I am asking you. Is your fear of the darkness greater than your love of your sisters?"

His words feel like a slap in the face, even as they pluck the chords of my own memory: *Hate cannot be fought with hate. Evil cannot be conquered by darkness. Only love has the power to conquer them both.*

And as soon as I remember those words, I realize there is no choice but to kill Fremin.

CHAPTER 16

Genevieve

hile not pleased with the news I carried, the queen was most grateful to have it. Indeed, she treated me with every courtesy and did not make me grovel. She is one of the rare nobles who dip into the well of power only to do what must be done rather than to feed her own gnawing hunger.

However, I am not allowed to bask for long in the queen's beneficence. One of the understewards appears in the hall before me with a summons from the king.

He is not in his apartments when I arrive. Uncertain what to do, I perch on the velvet-covered bench and wait. Moments later, I hear his voice and that of his valet from inside his bedchamber. As he draws nearer the door, he calls back, "And burn the clothes. You will never be able to remove the stink of death from them."

His words capture my attention as surely as a hook snags a fish.

When he enters the salon, his cheeks are flushed and his hair still faintly damp, as if he has just come from a bath. Giving no greeting, he goes to stand directly in front of the fire. Still not looking at me, he asks, "From your training at the convent, is it possible to hasten the putrefaction of a body?"

"What, Your Majesty?"

"Is there any way to speed up . . ." He waves his hand, unwilling to ask the gruesome question again.

"What has happened?"

"Answer the question!"

"The only way to do such a thing is to leave the corpse out in the hot sun. That is known to speed such . . . processes up."

The king strokes his chin, staring into the fire. "But it is winter. We've had but a handful of sunny days and none of them warm."

I wait, hoping he will give me some explanation. Instead he asks another question. "Would someone of your size and skill be able to overpower a much larger man?"

This must have something to do with Sybella. "It depends. In a face-to-face conflict, likely not. But if stealth is used, yes. It is possible to sneak up on a man and render him helpless." *Render him helpless* seems a safer choice of words than *kill him*.

"What if he was on a horse?"

"A horse?" I echo, willing him to tell me more, but again, he does not. "That would present a number of difficulties." I have no doubt anyone with their full training from the convent could do such a thing, but that was not his question. "Being mounted would give the man great advantage in height, as well as the added protection of his horse's formidable legs and hooves. So no, I do not know how one could use stealth on someone astride a horse." Unless one dropped out of a tree or from a roof, but I do not share that with him. He views women so narrowly, sees us as so incapable, that I have only to encourage his belief in that lie.

Unexpectedly, he looks up from the fire, his eyes unnaturally bright. "Would Sybella kill to protect the queen?"

"Yes," I answer without hesitation. "Or you, if you were threatened."

He makes a sound of disgust and looks back at the fire.

"Why does that answer displease you?"

With the toe of his boot, he reaches out to nudge a log. "A body has been found. All signs point to Sybella being the killer."

"And you wished to see if my answers matched hers."

"Not her answers, but the evidence. As king, I must judge and weigh the evidence."

"And have you?"

He shoves away from the mantel and lifts a flagon of wine from a small table by the fireplace. "My bishops say that this is a sign from God that, if not the Nine, then certainly those who worship Mortain have gone too far. The knowledge and familiarity with death that she demonstrates belong only in the hands of God. They think that Mortain is encroaching on His power, eroding His position as the one true God."

Much as the king's advisors and sister have been doing with him. No wonder he holds natural sympathy for such a position — and what a ruthlessly clever approach to take. I wonder which one of them thought of it.

"But, sire, surely Mortain's power, and that of those who follow him, is derived from God Himself. Is it not equally unorthodox to question how God chooses to manifest His power in the world?"

He pauses in his pouring of the wine. "I did not know you were a philosopher."

"No philosopher, Your Majesty. Only someone who has tried to reconcile this very issue since I was old enough to understand it."

"But of course you would have been taught logic that supported your convent's position." He sets the decanter down. "General Cassel says that the entire issue is moot. That she is an assassin, a weapon trained to kill." His words cause a thrum of pride deep in my own chest. "If not this man, someone else. If not now, then in the future. Best to neutralize her before harm is done."

"But what if her purpose is to protect someone? Yourself or the queen?"

He swirls the wine in his glass, staring at it. "That is precisely what she claimed. Have you been speaking to her again?"

"It is our convent's mission and not unusual we would both suggest such a thing."

He says nothing, but shifts his gaze to the fire. After a moment, I cannot help but ask, "Will you take your advisors' suggestions?"

He tosses back his wine, taking half of it in one gulp. "You have nothing to fear."

"I am not worried about myself."

"Ah, yes," he says. "You already have me wrapped around your finger. It is your convent sister you are worried about."

I cannot help it, I laugh, even though it is unwise. "Wrapped around my finger! Every time I am with you, I must fear your wrath, some punishment, or the further erosion of trust between us. If that is wrapping a man around one's finger, then I am glad that is not ever something I aspired to."

His face shifts, and his eyes look faintly bruised, as if I have wounded him in some way. He glances at the painting on the wall behind me, his grip on the goblet growing more pronounced. I hold my breath, wondering if he will succumb to the demands of his father, reaching out from the grave. "I have never hurt you."

"No, you haven't. As I have told you before, your honor and chivalry are the things I admire most about you." It is not meant to be flattering, but an appeal to his better nature. The one I know he possesses. The one everybody else is fighting to destroy.

And in that moment, I recognize that he and I are fighting the same war. I was so hungry for the world's respect that I forced myself onto a path that robbed me of my own. I would spare him from making that same mistake — especially with the lives of so many hanging in the balance.

CHAPTER 17

I arrive at Sybella's chamber dressed in the clothes of one of the maids — Saria, who is sleeping off a night of too much drink. Her cap is drawn close around my hair so that it shadows my face, and my eyes are cast down at the heavy bucket I carry rather than on the guards at the door. "May I take my lady her wash water?" I ask.

Tired and bored from a long night of tedious duty, they nod and step forward to open the door without knocking.

Sybella whirls from the path she was pacing in front of the hearth. When she sees it is me, she gives a brusque nod.

Things must be worse than I thought if she does not try to chase me away.

Once I hear the door closed firmly behind me, I carry the bucket to the hearth and set it down.

"Were you able to get an audience with the queen?" Sybella all but pounces. In truth, she looks as if her bones are trying to gnaw their way out of her skin.

"Yes, and she was glad for the information, if distressed to learn of it."

She studies my appearance. "Are you finally to suffer consequences for your role in deceiving the king and the regent and be relegated to the position of scullery maid?"

"The king is decidedly not happy with me and lets me know in small ways. And, surely having to put up with his inept sexual threats counts as some punishment. I would not wish that on anyone."

Her mouth quirks in one corner ever so slightly, but it feels like a victory. A moment later, she takes two steps toward me. "Has he forced himself on you? Harmed you in any way?"

It takes me a moment to recognize her concern for me. "Other than berating me for my heartless treachery, no. He is wroth with me, but still willing to listen. Still wanting . . . to recapture what he thought we had." Oddly, I find myself blushing at this, embarrassed at this strange infatuation the king has acquired for me. I lift the bucket and carry it to the washstand. "He is still coming to grips with all that he has just learned. Torn between what he wants and hopes for and what his bishops and General Cassel are whispering in his ear."

"You would do well to steer well clear of General Cassel," Sybella says, an unaccustomed weight to her words.

I set the bucket down. "Why? What do you know of him?"

Sybella blinks in surprise. "What do *you* know of him?"

I curse myself and the curiosity that led me into this trap. I've no wish to tell Sybella of Maraud, but by the look she gives me, if I choose not to, I will be giving up all chance of earning her trust. "I learned of him when I was at Cognac. There was a prisoner in the dungeon. We came to be acquainted, and he spoke often of General Cassel's brutality and lack of honor on the battlefield."

Sybella raises her eyebrows in mild surprise. "A prisoner told you all this?"

I lift the bucket and fill the ewer with fresh water. "As I said, he was in a dungeon — an oubliette — and left to die. He had no one else to talk to, and it seemed important to learn what I could."

"And did you?"

"Yes." How much to tell her? I do not know how the queen feels about the Crunard family and will not risk exposing Maraud. At least not until I better understand the political implications. "I learned he was hidden away in the dungeon by order of the regent."

"Why?"

I stare down at the washstand and try to hold off the nearly suffocating sense of loss thinking of Maraud always brings. "Something both he and I would like to know."

"Where is he now?"

"I may have taken pity on him and freed him when I left."

Sybella folds her arms and studies me as if I have just sprouted two small goat horns atop my head. "I can't decide if that was honorable or stupid. Did you know why he was in prison? What if you released a murderous outlaw?"

"I told you, he was a soldier and, from his story, wrongfully imprisoned." I remove a linen cloth from my belt and wipe at a drop of water that spilled. "It was becoming clear that the regent was no ally, and surely our enemies' enemy is our friend." I do not tell her that I was also irked at Count Angoulême and this seemed a way to muddy his life as much as he'd muddied mine.

"That is true sometimes, but you have no idea what his crimes were or who he will harm."

"He will not harm anyone, except Cassel if they meet. Now, if you've finished interrogating me, I've come to offer my help. Father Effram told me what has happened."

Her eyes burn with ire, as if she cannot believe Father Effram's audacity, but bleakness lurks there as well.

"Let me help."

"Very well." She forces the words between her lips as if they were thorns.

"Surely it does not have to hurt so very much to accept it."

She reaches out and grabs my arm, nearly causing my elbow to knock over the bucket. "I do not have time to coat my words in sugar and honey so they are easier for you to swallow. Two young girls' lives hang in the balance. Will you help me or not?"

I do not pull away, but stare into her eyes, which are dark with fear, but not for herself. "Do you know where your sisters are?"

"No."

"You're lying."

She lifts one slender shoulder. "I may be willing to trust you with my life, but not with theirs. Not yet, anyway."

Fair enough. "It doesn't matter. What needs to be done?"

"There is someone I must kill."

At her words, a faint thrill runs through me. The convent's work. "Who?"

"The lawyer Simon de Fremin. But it cannot look as if I have done so, for they know I am an assassin. And I do not have the king's protection."

"So you want me to kill him for you?" I try not to let my excitement show in my voice.

The look she gives me is one she might give a besotted fool. "To be clear, I will do the killing. I would not ask that of you. But I need help with access, supplies. A plan."

I nod, waiting for her to continue.

"Fremin was sent by my brother to abduct my sisters. He has been given orders to take possession of them by fair means or foul. He is desperate. Furthermore, since the king knows you are an assassin too, we should avoid implicating you in the death as well. His fondness will only protect you so much."

"*Fondness* is not the word you are looking for," I mutter. "Fondness was booted out the palace door once I told him of the convent and my involvement with it."

"Then why is he still summoning you?"

"Punishment. Humiliation. Loneliness. He wishes for us to go back to the way we were before I told him. So, tell me of this brother of yours who would kill a lawyer for acceding to an order from the king."

Her face grows stark and drawn. "If you cross a d'Albret, you pay with your life."

I take in her delicate features, her beauty. Even with her apparent lethalness I cannot believe she is related. "Is your brother named Pierre, by any chance?"

She grows unnaturally still. "Do you know him?"

I grimace. "Unfortunately, I have had occasion to meet him." I remember his horses nearly running down the children in the road, the test he put Maraud through before we left the city of Angoulême, and the small army he sent after us. "The good news is that I believe every word that you say. You do not need to convince me. You said your sisters were safely gone. What power does the lawyer still have over them?"

Her hands ball in her skirts. "He has deduced that I had them removed from the palace. Since only he and I are interested in them, it was inevitable that he would figure it out. This recently discovered body hands him one more weapon in making his case to the king."

I hold my tongue, afraid that if I speak, she will stop sharing her secrets.

"If I am absolved of this murder, I am certain Fremin will tell the king the man was sent by my brother and that I killed him. It will be too much proof for the king to ignore. He will have to act."

"What can I do to help?"

"Why?" She tilts her head. "Why would you risk the king's favor to help?"

"Because if not for me, they — you — would not be in danger now. Besides, it is Mortain's work, after all."

She is silent a long moment. "No." She returns to the window. "It is not."

Disbelief scuttles along my spine. "You wish to kill outside Mortain's grace?"

A smile that feels more like despair flashes briefly, then it is gone. "Mortain's marques do not align so conveniently with our own wishes."

And of course, that is true.

She looks away, staring at something outside. "Actually, that is not the whole truth. The nature of Mortain's marques has changed some —"

A sharp rap on the door interrupts her words. We barely have time to stop our tongues from moving before the regent herself strides in, head held at an imperious angle, face white with anger.

I am much quicker to curtsy than Sybella, desperately wishing to hide my face. "Madame Regent," Sybella drawls. Her voice holds a note of challenge I do not understand — until I realize that she is doing it for me. To keep the regent's attention on herself. "To what do I owe this pleasure?"

The regent lifts her hand to shoo me out of the room. Even though my head is down and she normally acts as if servants are invisible, as I scuttle to the door, her haughty gaze flicks over me. Her hand freezes in midair. "Genevieve?"

Sybella momentarily forgotten, she takes three steps closer to where I hover by the door. "What are you doing here?" Her voice is a low thrum of anger. "You were told — warned — to stay away from this woman."

I bob another curtsy and keep my eyes downcast. "Madame, she is not a leper. There is no —"

"You know nothing."

I open my mouth even as my brain scrambles for some clever excuse. Behind the regent, Sybella gives a sharp shake of her head, and my mouth snaps shut.

"Go," the regent says. "Wait for me in your chambers."

"Very well, Madame." Her gaze sweeps from my head down to my feet, taking in my maid's garb. Desperate to remove myself before her clever brain can catch up, I quit the room.

In the hallway, I force my movements to a casualness I do not feel, as if I am naught but a servant on her rounds. I saunter past the two guards at Sybella's door and into the room next to hers. Once inside, I hurry to the adjoining wall.

"How do you know each other?" the regent asks.

"I introduced myself shortly after she arrived at court, nearly a week ago. She had not seen me in a few days and came to see if I was ill or in need of anything."

"How kind of her." Even through the thick stone, the regent's voice is as tart as an unripe quince. "Although that does not quite explain why she is in servant's garb."

Rutting hell. She has begun to piece the puzzle together. Sybella diverts her. "You wished to see me?"

"Not really, but I bring you a message. The king has declared that the cause of death for the body that was found was accidental. You have been absolved of all charges."

For a moment, elation fills me. The king followed the evidence. It quickly fades when I realize that Sybella will have no choice but to kill Fremin now.

But she will not have to do it alone.

Moments later, when my door bursts open without so much as a knock, I am sitting by the fire, stitching my embroidery. The regent wastes no time with preamble. "What were you doing in Lady Sybella's room?"

"I hadn't seen her since the first day she introduced herself and worried she was unwell. The queen has been ill, after all."

"You went to check on her even after I forbade you to?"

I raise my eyebrows in surprise. "Forbade, Madame? I had thought it was a warning not to socialize with her, not a command to ignore simple Christian courtesy."

She takes a step closer. "You were dressed as a maidservant."

I stare at her, wide-eyed. "I have only two gowns, including the one you secured for me. I did not want to risk ruining either of those if she was ill."

"Only two gowns? I wonder if that is true." She strides abruptly from me to my travel bag and begins rifling through the contents. I try to tamp down my racing pulse and force myself to watch her calmly. Not finding anything of interest there, she goes to the bed to toss back the covers, then throws aside the pillows. When that yields up nothing, she casts her gimlet gaze on the rest of the room.

"May I ask what you are looking for, Madame? I assure you I have not stolen anything."

"Only my trust."

I carefully set the embroidery hoop down in my lap to give her my full attention. "That was never my intent, my lady."

"Let me make myself clear. You will not associate with Lady Sybella. She has been accused of serious crimes. Crimes that can taint those around them. Crimes that may still lead to a most unpleasant punishment." Her face softens unexpectedly. "I would not want that for you, Genevieve. Besides, you have a far more important task before you than Sybella's poor health. The king needs you now more than ever, as there are heavy decisions weighing upon him. Tend to those needs as you have been instructed. As you have promised. Else I will make certain you wish that you had."

CHAPTER 18

Sybella

wait a quarter hour after the regent leaves, then make my way to the queen. My two guards still follow, but from a greater distance than before. When I slip into the room, Heloise looks up from the posset she is preparing.

I keep my voice low. "How is the queen doing?"

Heloise glances over at the bed. "Not much better." The cheerful note in her voice is at odds with her words as she takes a pinch of cloves and adds it to the cup.

"Does her illness no longer concern you?" Or is she snubbing me for not doing a better job of fulfilling my duties?

Heloise opens a second small jar and takes another pinch, this time of ginger. "I think I will let her tell you." She drops the spices into the hot posset, shoves it into my hand with a smile, then shoos me toward the queen.

Unable to make sense of her manner, I feel my hands grow damp, and foreboding settles in my belly. Elsibet is just securing a thick blue velvet shawl around the queen's shoulders as I reach the bed. The queen's face is still pale, but there is no clamminess or greenish tinge to it.

With a final plump of the pillow, Elsibet retreats to the window next to Heloise and takes up her stitching.

"Your Majesty." I curtsy deeply.

As I hand the queen her posset, she says, "Genevieve told me what has happened."

"About the regent and the Bishop of Albi working together?"

"Yes." She sips her posset. "But also about the accusation being made against you."

I grimace. "I am sor —"

"I believe I have ordered you not to apologize for such things before, and you dare not disobey a direct order from your sovereign."

Her words fill me with both warmth and humor, removing some of the chill that had beset me. "But of course. I dare not."

She lowers her voice. "So did you kill him?"

As I look into the queen's sweet young face, I am filled with despair. No matter how hard I try to break free of this darkness, it always pulls me back. "Yes. Pierre sent him to kill me."

The queen settles back against her pillows. "I thought as much. That's why I didn't ask you before the trial — in case they called me to testify."

Clever queen! "You don't seem perturbed by it at all."

"Perturbed? No! I am glad that you have the skills and the strength that allow you to survive. That allow us all to survive."

"The good news is the death has been ruled an accident. I am absolved."

"Oh, that is good news!"

"Unfortunately, I do not think that means they will give up on their hope to position our worship as heresy."

The queen stares glumly into her posset. "If they succeed, then all who worship the Nine will be declared heretics."

To try a queen for heresy would be a shocking scandal — but one that might suit the regent's aspirations perfectly. "I do not think they will go that far," I tell her, but I no longer pretend to understand just how far these people will go.

"Not only have the Nine been sanctioned by the Church," she grumbles, "they have lent me their aid when I needed it most." She sets her chin stubbornly. "I will not renounce them." She looks up at me then, her eyes suddenly sparkling.

"But I forget. You have not heard the news. We may yet have one more arrow in our quiver." She smiles shyly. In truth, she appears to be blushing faintly.

"What news?" For some inexplicable reason, I grow chilled.

Her blush deepens, and she looks down at her fingers, playing with the rim of her goblet. "I am pregnant."

My body feels as if it has turned to stone, and my vision narrows until small black spots begin dancing before my eyes. "Pregnant?" My voice is steady. Normal, even. I clap my hands together to keep them from drifting to my belly. No matter how deeply the mind tries to hide it, no matter how thick the heart builds the walls, the body remembers. "You are certain?"

She tilts her head, perplexed. "Is this not good news?"

"Of course, Your Majesty! This is a most joyous and welcome event!"

"Then why do you look as if you are attending a funeral?"

"I am just stunned. I did not think enough time had passed." It has just been over five weeks since the wedding.

The queen wrinkles her nose. "It was too early to tell before now, but this is the second monthly course I have missed. The first one was right after the wedding, and we thought it was due to the travel and excitement. But now, with the second one . . ." She shrugs gracefully.

"And there are other signs, as well." Heloise appears beside me and takes the half-drunk posset from the queen. "Her breasts are tender. She cannot keep food down. And she is sleeping nearly all the time."

My own breasts tighten in painful remembrance. "Those are the signs. And may I just say again, Your Majesty, how happy I am for you. There is nothing that could tip the scales in our favor more than this news." That is when the first glimmer of happiness finally gets through — not only because she will be having a child, but because the political implications are so far-reaching. She now holds an entire handful of cards she did not have before.

She smiles, joy and relief writ plain on her face. In spite of the wretched trembling of my body, I *am* happy for her.

"Surely our new position" — her hand waves awkwardly at her middle — "will make the king think twice before making any such decisions."

Her words are a vicious reminder of how unfair the world is. That only her potential to produce a dauphin can assure her of the king's favor. "Surely he will, for he won't wish so much as a whiff of illegitimacy on the dauphin. Even so, I think it best to wait for the right moment to share this news with him." What I do not say is that between the regent and the bishop, there is a chance things could get even worse, and we do not want to use up all our arrows before the true fight has even begun.

The walk through the palace halls back to my own room lasts a lifetime. Nay, a thousand lifetimes if counting my baby's lifespan. She is long grown cold now, but I held her tiny, warm body for a handful of minutes, each one of them more precious than any jewel. The wound should be long healed, but my body — my stubborn, obstinate body — will not forget.

Nor my heart. Both tremble and flutter as if it were still holding that small bundle in my arms.

When at last I reach my door, I thrust it open and stumble inside. Desperately in need of air, I rush to the window and throw it open, lifting my face to the cold bite of winter that pours in, welcoming its bracing slap. When my lungs no longer feel as if they are bound in iron, I lean against the stone wall next to the window. Of all the locked doors in my heart, this one has the most chains wrapped around it. More than any of the others, it has the power to rob me of what little peace I've managed to eke out.

I do not begrudge the queen her growing babe. Indeed, I am happy for her. I only wish her happiness did not feel as if it were ripping my own heart wide open.

I press myself more firmly against the hard stone at my back and pretend it is Beast's solid presence that holds me until the wave of pain and desolation has passed.

CHAPTER 19

Reva

After our near miss with the search party, the rest of our trip is uneventful. The cities and larger holdings are crawling with soldiers, but we evade them easily. Tonight, there are barely two hours of daylight left when we decide to halt for the day. Once I have seen to our horses, I make my way toward the camp Tola and Tephanie are setting up for the girls. Tola looks up as I approach the campfire. "There you are." She stands up and brushes off her hands. "It's your turn to help set up, and I have promised to show one of the queen's guards the secret of how we shoot a bow so accurately."

I scowl at her. "You're going to tell him our sacred secrets?"

She rolls her eyes at me. "No, cranky goose. I'm going to pretend I am, then use the opportunity to teach him how to shoot better." As she brushes past me, she says in a lower voice, "Besides, I think it is high time you put the girls to bed for a change. I have had my fill of Charlotte for today."

"Liar," I mutter. She laughs and disappears toward the other end of camp.

When I look down at the others, the little wasp is watching me, her eyes unreadable in the deepening shadows. Sometimes when a mare throws a foal, even though we begin training it in its earliest days, it will never accept a saddle or rider. I wonder if the wasp is like one of those wilding foals that cannot be tamed no matter what, or if she has just not found the right trainer yet.

I reach out and ruffle her hair. She ducks away in annoyance. "If you're waiting for us to make your bed, you will be stuck sleeping on the bare ground," I tell her.

Her head snaps up. "Tephanie and Tola always make our beds for us."

"For Louise, yes. But you are of an age where you can do things for yourself."

She thrusts out her pointed chin. "I am a lady, and ladies do not do such things for themselves."

I laugh outright. "And that is something you are proud of?" I squat down so that I am eye to eye with her. "You have it wrong, waspling. There is no pride in not knowing how to do things, in having to be waited on like a small child."

"Why should I want to do servants' work?" The scorn in her voice could peel the bark off a tree.

"Why would you want to be dependent on others? Why would you — who are so filled with pride — not relish doing things for yourself? Being competent. Having skills."

She scoffs. "There is no skill in making a camp bed."

"Oho!" I lift a brow. "You think not? Perhaps we should wager on that."

"There is nothing that you have that I want." Her mouth twists into an irritated little bow.

"And here I thought you enjoyed our knife lessons."

At last — a reaction! She gapes at me. "That's not fair! You're already doing that."

"True, but it is something you want from me."

She considers another minute, then rolls her eyes. "Very well."

I must work to keep the smile off my face. "We have a deal," I agree solemnly.

We collect the bedding from the packs and move closer to the fire that one of the men has started. She looks around at the ground. "Where do we place it?"

"Now, see? That is the art of bed making — knowing where to put it. If I were to tell you, you wouldn't be doing it by yourself." From across the fire, I can feel the dove's eyes on me, observing.

The wasp sighs and flounces six arrow lengths away. "Well, I don't have to sleep beside you, do I?"

"No, just within the circle, like we do every night."

While she busies herself kicking the largest stones out of the way, the dove rises and comes to stand beside me, her eyes on Charlotte. "She likes you, you know."

I blink at her in surprise. "I would not wager my life on that."

Her eyes are still on the younger girl. "Oh, she would never show such a thing, but she does. You are the only one who treats her as if she is your equal." Her gaze is warm and soft, and reflects her nature.

"It is how we raise young girls when they find their way to us. When they come to us from a world that sucks the very marrow from their bones, rebuilding from the ground up helps them reclaim their own selves."

"I think it is the right approach. She needs things to do, to occupy her hands and especially her mind, else it goes to places it's better she not visit."

CHAPTER 20

Sybella

 do not know how much time passes before I claw my way out of the past back into my body. Perhaps it is the growing heat from the black pebble I still carry, or perhaps it is the voice I hear outside my door that pulls me from my grief.

Fremin's voice.

He has come. And sooner than I would have thought. Too soon for me to have a plan in place. Guided by sheer instinct, I surge to my feet and reach for my trunklet to retrieve le Poisson's knife. It is an instinct forged in the same d'Albret household that sent Fremin to Plessis, but honed far more sharply through the convent's training.

I have just finished tucking the knife into my belt when the door opens. I leap back against the long curtain to shield myself from view. It is not the guards, come to announce Fremin's arrival, but Fremin himself.

He looks around the room as he shuts the door behind him, his heart beating rapidly, as if he's been running. Or was poised to fight.

He takes three steps toward the bed, then pauses to glance around the room. He frowns in annoyance, a question forms on his lips. Before he can give voice to that question, I step up behind him and place the sharp edge of le Poisson's knife at his throat. "To what do I owe this most delightful surprise?"

Beneath the blade, his pulse begins to race. "The king may have exonerated you, but we both know you are guilty of this murder."

"Oh, not just this murder, but a few others besides. Remove your weapon."

He swallows once, his throat working against the edge of my blade, then slowly draws a knife from his sleeve and drops it onto the floor. I kick it out of the way. "That still does not explain why you are here. I assumed you would report your suspicions to the king."

"I am here to encourage your cooperation should you have qualms."

I laugh. "I have many qualms, Monsieur Fremin, but you are not on that list." At least, not any longer. By coming to my room, unannounced, with a knife, he has reignited that white flame of anger and seared any doubt from my mind.

"You realize if you harm me, it will only support my assertion that you are behind the disappearance of my men as well as your sisters."

"Will it? To me it supports that this was your plan all along. Once you'd gained possession of my sisters, you had no intention of remaining behind to face the consequences. And surely no one can question my need for self-defense. Turn around. Slowly."

If I am to step so fully out of whatever of Mortain's grace still exists in this world, I will not hide from it. I will look into the eyes of the man who has brought me to this crossroads. For assuredly, it is a crossroads. I will not hide from that either.

Against my leg, the pebble burns like a brand.

Fremin does what I order, the tip of my knife staying in contact with his neck the entire time. This does not feel like a choice rooted in love. Or fear. With the full, visceral memory of the depravity of the d'Albret family still pulsing though my limbs, it feels more like a burning need for justice.

For vengeance. For righting a scale that has been tipped too long in darkness's favor.

"Why?" I whisper when I can see his face. "Why did you not take the chance to claim your men acted without your knowledge when I gave it to you? We could both have walked away then."

He barks out a harsh laugh. "Walking away was never an option for me." His heart beats fast with fear, his pupils are wide with it. "Why could you and your sisters not just have come with me when I asked? Returned to your brother's side, where you belong?"

There it is. The reason he deserves to die. He would trade innocents' safety for his own. I press my knife closer. "For the same reason you are too afraid to return to him empty-handed."

"He will send others."

"And I will kill them, too."

"Then he will come himself, with an army at his back."

I raise my eyebrows in surprise. "He would stand his army against the crown of France? I think not."

"You assume the crown will still support you after I tell them you are responsible for the corpse they found."

I lean in closer. "What makes you think that you will be allowed to have that conversation?"

He looks down at me and smirks. "I am bigger and stronger than you, even with that knife."

"That may well be true, but I am more ruthless." I silently place one foot behind his, then shove hard against his chest, knocking him backwards. Unbalanced, he falls. A grunt escapes him as he catches his head on the hearthstone.

His eyes flutter once, but he does not move. It is done. The line crossed. The decision made. Although it never truly felt like a decision. More like the satisfaction of pulling a thorn out of one's heart.

I consider — briefly — offering a prayer to Mortain. Of thanks? Of forgiveness? But instead, my mind goes to the Dark Mother. While Mortain's divinity may still flow in my veins, it is through the Dark Mother's grace that I have been reborn through the ashes of my own pain and heartache. Mayhap I should pray to her instead.

I wait a moment longer to be certain he will not move, then shove my knife into my belt, bend over to grab the edge of the rug, and drag him to the window. Praise the Nine he is not bleeding.

He is heavy, but the rug moves smoothly across the stone floor. At the window, I pause. How best to disguise what I've done? The guards saw him come in, but they did not see me. I peer down into the empty courtyard, which is as deserted as it ever is. I go to my trunklet and retrieve the Marquis's rope, then hoist and tug and shove until he is braced on the ledge. After confirming the courtyard is still empty, I give a final push.

A second later, there is a heavy thud, then a silent pop as his soul bursts from his body like the flesh from an overripe plum. As I stare down, I feel the ashes of my faith in Mortain scatter with the wind, and a new, tentative faith is born. I have not only ended a life, but created a space, a pocket of safety, for two young lives to come to fruition. Fremin's death creates security for my sisters.

I glance down once more before tucking my skirts up into my belt. The Mouse was able to climb the wall, and he is not any smaller or lighter than I am. And if the be-damned Mouse can do it, so can I. I toss a leg over the sill, then begin the long, treacherous climb down into the courtyard.

CHAPTER 21

By the time my feet make contact with the flagstones, my toes and fingers are cramping and my arms are as weak as wet straw. Ignoring the irate flapping of Fremin's livid soul, I stay pressed against the wall until I am certain no one has seen my descent.

When I am sure, I hurry over to check the body. The soul follows closely, as if it still had a physical body and could intimidate me. His neck is broken. Keeping an ear out for approaching heartbeats, I place le Poisson's knife in Fremin's hand, then remove the length of rope from my belt and tuck it into his. It will look as if he came armed for an abduction.

Outraged by my actions, his soul crashes against the barriers I have erected.

"Begone," I hiss.

It retreats enough that I can examine my handiwork. That is when I feel another heartbeat. As my hand reaches for my dagger, a voice calls softly through the darkness, "Don't need your knife. It's only me." Lazare steps through the narrow gateway that leads toward the stable yard.

"Well, if this isn't a most pleasant surprise," I say, and mean it. "What are you doing here?"

"Beast said to watch your back. You don't ignore an order from Beast."

My heart warms. Of course Beast would have left someone to have a care to my well-being. Lazare cranes his neck to gaze up at the window. "That was a bit of a climb."

Reflexively, I stretch my cramping toes, then shrug. "How much did you see?"

"I saw the clumsy ox reach out too far to close the window and lose his balance." Whatever else can be said about Lazare, one cannot fault his sharp wit.

"It was a true tragedy."

"Why d'you think he's carrying the rope?"

"Because he meant to abduct me, of course. Like he had my sisters." Our eyes meet, and silent understanding — and admiration — passes between us.

The shared moment is interrupted by the sound of another heartbeat coming. Fast, by the sound of it. I grab Lazare's arm and pull him back into the shadows near the wall just as Genevieve appears. When she reaches the bottom of the stairs, Fremin's soul rushes her, and she begins swiping and ducking in an attempt to avoid it.

"*Merde*," I mutter.

"Who is she, and what is she doing?"

"That is our five-year-missing assassin from the convent. And I don't know if she has had any experience with the souls of the dead." I step from my hiding place, calling out softly, "Genevieve."

She glances briefly at me, her face relaxing somewhat. She was worried. For me. "Close your mind to it," I tell her. "As you would a shutter."

"I'm trying!" she says. With one final swipe of her arm, she seems to be able to repel Fremin's soul, who moves to squat above his body, glowering at us.

When I reach her side, I study her to see if she is unnerved. "That was a soul."

"I know." She doesn't quite snap, but her words are clipped. "I've seen them before. Once before. But I was unprepared for this one."

"I don't know that we are ever truly prepared for any of them," I murmur. "Is anyone with you?"

"No. I was summoned to the king's chamber when I heard the beating of a heart."

"You mean you heard it stop?"

"No." She examines my face in the darkness. "I mean I first heard the heartbeat. I hear them just before they die. Don't you?"

"No. I hear the heartbeats of the living."

"A far more useful skill," she mutters. "You decided to act without my help?" A faint note of hurt seeps into her voice, but is quickly chased away when the angry soul swoops down upon her again.

"No." I bat at the thing. "Fremin came to my room. An opportunity presented itself, and so I took it."

Lazare steps out of the shadows. "Seems to me we have some cleanup to do before the two of you get out your stitching and settle in for a nice cozy chat."

At the sound of his voice, Genevieve whirls around, her hand going to the dagger hidden at her waist. I am pleased to see that her reflexes are good. I give Lazare a shove to get him out of range of Genevieve's knife. "The only stitching I've got in mind is to shut your sneering lips. Genevieve, this is Lazare, one of the charbonnerie who accompanied us to France. Lazare, this is Genevieve."

"A charbonnerie?" She gapes slightly.

"It's a long story, one the charbonnerie in question has reminded me we do not have time for."

Lazare smirks. "So what's your plan, my lady?"

I gaze up at the night sky, at the darkened windows and the empty staircase. "I think we will leave him here until morning and let others find him."

"How will you explain that to the guards who let him into your room?"

I tap my finger on my chin, thinking. "I will not be in my room." I look back at Genevieve. "I was never in my room. The queen requested I attend her the entire night."

Lazare whistles through his teeth. "Got to admire a queen as accommodating as that," he says. "I bet this fellow had a horse and a spare saddle in the stables, since he was planning on abducting you."

"I am sure you're right."

Lazare hooks his thumbs in his belt. "I'd best go get to the stables and arrange for such horses to be found."

"Very well. And you —" As I turn to tell Genevieve what she should do, I see her dodging the soul again. Wondering if she is incompetent or the soul is especially enraged, I let down my own shields and am immediately accosted by a sense of malevolence and a thirst for vengeance so profound it leaves my own throat dry. "We cannot leave this here," I mutter.

"What?" Genevieve says.

"I said you are to hurry to answer the king's summons. We can't risk raising any extra questions tonight. Go back to the palace and continue your evening as if nothing has happened."

"Of course," she says, relishing, I think, this chance to be involved even in a small way.

I kneel beside Fremin's body and take out my knife. "What are you doing?" she asks.

"I can't leave a soul this angered to flit about, hoping to attach itself to any susceptible passersby. Especially with the queen being with child. It is far too risky."

"The queen is with child?"

"Yes. One bit of good news."

"What part of the not having time for stitching and chatting did you not understand?"

I glare at Lazare. "I thought you'd left. Surely you'd best be on your way."

"Depends on what you're going to do next."

What I do next is swipe the edge of my dagger across the pad of my littlest finger. I close my eyes and try to remember exactly how I did it with the murdered sentry back in Rennes, which seems a lifetime ago. Then I reach out and smear the faintest bit of blood across Fremin's brow. His face is bloody from the fall — cobblestones are not kind to soft human flesh — and one more smear will not draw undue attention. I hate to grant him anything remotely like grace, but it would be worse to leave his soul to turn into a vengeful ghost.

The moment my blood touches his skin, Fremin's soul comes rushing back to his body, but is caught up, as if in some great, invisible bird's beak. And then it is gone.

"What was that?" Gen asks.

"I don't have time to explain," I tell her, not certain that I can. "Now go.

Hurry back to the king. See if you can keep him distracted for the entire evening."

She shoots me a look filled with disappointment. "No! Not like that." I wave my hand. "Some other way."

Mollified, she picks up her skirts, casts one lingering glance at Fremin's empty body, then hurries toward the stairs. Lazare stares at me with a bemused expression.

"What?"

He shakes his head. "You are just a never-ending source of tricks, aren't you? You sure it's Mortain you serve?" And with that, he saunters off to the stables.

No, I want to call after him. I am not sure at all any longer.

CHAPTER 22

Genevieve

y heart races in my chest as I calmly stroll back through the halls. My head is full of all I have seen —not only the realities of dealing with a dead body and the wonder of its soul—but the skills Sybella commands. I had never imagined powers that great, and questions crowd my head like a hungry flock of doves.

But I have no time for them now. I have not delayed the king's summons that long—surely no more than a quarter of an hour—but he will wonder why. Tonight more than ever, all must appear ordinary.

When I reach the king's rooms, the guard bows, opens the door, and motions me in. I am relieved to find the king staring into the fire and not at the rutting painting his father gave him. That always portends an ill humor.

At my entrance he looks up. "Ah. There you are." He swirls the wine in his goblet. "I thought I would have to send out a search party."

"I beg your pardon, Your Majesty." I sink into an extra-low curtsy. "Something came up on the way here." I allow some of the breathlessness to escape.

His eyes widen, not in surprise so much as challenge. "I am all aflutter to hear what warranted you ignoring your king."

I do not rise, but simply lift my head. "I wasn't ignoring you, sire, but serving you."

Some of the mocking gleam leaves his eyes. "Now I must know," he murmurs into his cup before taking a drink. "Rise and tell me, dear Genevieve."

I stand and hold myself as demurely as possible. "On my way here, I passed by one of the corridors and heard voices. Voices that made no sense to me."

All the derision is gone from his face now. "Whose voices were they?"

"The regent's and the Bishop of Albi's."

I need say nothing more, his own suspicious nature does the rest. "What were they talking about?"

"About the queen. And the Nine. And the holding the regent would sign over to the bishop if he continued to raise questions about the queen's faith and pursue them with the pope."

There is a brief moment of outraged silence, followed by a crash as the king hurls his goblet into the fire, the wine hissing as it hits the hot embers. "I have not indicated I wish to pursue that course of action yet."

I dip a respectful curtsy. "That is why I thought it worth mentioning."

"Did you hear any more?"

"No, after that their voices started moving in my direction, and it seemed wise to be discreet. I came directly here."

"You have done well. Thank you." Agitated, he puts his hands behind his back and begins pacing in front of the fire. "I am sick unto death of my wishes being overruled or argued with. Not just by the regent, but by the entire council. I am king, dammit, not some weak fop." His gaze slides to the painting on the wall behind me.

"My lord, perhaps they challenge you not because they see you as weak, but out of their own self-interest. Perhaps it is not even challenge so much as manipulation. Surely if the regent's meeting with the bishop tells us anything, it is that."

"And that makes it better?"

"No, but it makes their motives different."

He falls quiet, thinking. "What you say makes sense. Especially with regards to my sister. She is ever trying to steer me to her wishes. The queen, as well."

As hard as it is to let the latter one go, I do.

"But what earthly reason would the bishops have for such manipulation?"

"I have found that bishops are as fond of wealth and power as any man."

He pours a fresh glass of wine. "I do not believe that is the case with General Cassel. He has served my father well and loyally since he came to the throne. Longer! He not only has the crown's interest at heart, he has shown his loyalty honorably throughout the years."

"Your Majesty, was your valet not your father's also?"

"Yes. What of it?"

"Does he dress you in the same chamber robes and somber colors that your father preferred?"

"No!"

"And yet he continues to serve you nonetheless, loyally and faithfully. But he does not insist you adopt your father's fashions. He allows you to have your own. I think General Cassel is of similar intent, although poorer execution. While he has served the crown well, his temperament, his tactics, and his approach are more suited to the France of twenty years ago when it was beset by rebellious dukes on all sides. They have gotten fewer and fewer, my lord, with the vast majority of them now falling to the crown's rule through death or marriage."

"Brittany rebelled," he points out, watching me closely.

"They did. Nearly the last of the independent duchies. And it was gracefully handled. When you hold all the power, there is rarely any reason to exercise it. The threat is often enough."

"General Cassel would say that the threat is empty without the will to see it through. He thinks I was wrong to offer marriage. Thinks I should have simply continued the siege and invasion."

"Of course he thinks that. He is old and set in his ways. Unwilling to learn new tactics and strategies that the exciting new France presents. What purpose would it have served to conquer Brittany in such a way? To acquire a broken, defeated holding whose population had been decimated by war and hunger? Who would always see you as the conqueror and never as a beloved or admired king? Who gains by that, Your Majesty?"

He stares into the fire.

"I'll tell you who gains — men who like to make war. Who thrive on battles and conflict and conquest. Men who have no other skills or talents or values. General Cassel is a man with one weapon and one weapon only. He does not understand the man who has an array from which to choose. And you, Your Majesty, have precisely such an array."

He glances at my empty hands. "Here, let us get you some wine."

That is when I know that I have not only lightened his mood, but have given him good counsel as well. Now all I must do is manage to get him to invite me to spend the night without warming his bed, and this evening will be a rousing success.

CHAPTER 23

Sybella

s I lie on a thin pallet on the floor of the queen's chambers, I am not flooded with shame and regret at what I had to do. Relief, yes, for it took naught but a glimpse of Fremin's soul to leave no doubt in my mind as to what he deserved, but I am also filled with wonder. Unable to resist, I rub the tender cut on my littlest finger.

Have I always possessed such powers, precisely as Father Effram has claimed? Or is it a byproduct of Mortain's death? As if by leaving the world, he has left an empty space or void that pulls such power from me, much as the sun pulls the plant from the seed.

To waste such a miraculous gift on someone like Fremin sours my stomach. But it could not be helped. The risk of his soul never passing on was too great, the queen and her unborn child were too vulnerable.

Thoughts of the queen's unborn child have my hand drifting to my belly and my heart yearning for Beast. For the comfort he always gives me, for his easy acceptance of who and what I am and all the scars that accompany that.

I take out the memory of him offering to marry me, handling it like a fragile sculpture of spun sugar. I was lying to him — and myself — when I said I could not bear the idea of ever belonging to any man. Beast would never think to own me. He considers *his horse* as a creature entrusted to his care rather than a possession.

The idea of being joined to him for the rest of our lives — for eternity — is nearly irresistible. To love openly and freely, and not care who sees or knows. To be at each other's side, always.

But it is complicated, too. Not only in the obvious ways — my brother must give his permission for us to legally wed, which he would never do — but in subtler ones. The hand on my belly is one of those. I do not know that I can bring myself to ever have another child. This wound and scar run so deep, I cannot even hear of another woman's pregnancy without suffering all over again. But if ever a man should be a father, Beast is that man. There should be legions of hulking young babes swaggering around on their toddling legs with laughing blue eyes and small lumpy noses.

I do not think I can do that. My heart is not strong enough to travel that road again.

In the morning, the servants arrive at the queen's apartments and light the fires. I rise to my feet and slip out of the room. When my door comes into view, I take a deep breath. The next five minutes will determine whether or not I can wrestle Fortune's wheel in my favor.

Are the two guards standing lazily on duty the ones who did not bother to announce Fremin's visit before letting him inside? Did he bribe them?

At my approach, one of them looks up, his mouth falling open at the sight of me. He nudges the other guard to attention. "My lady." He frowns. "How did you get out here?"

"I walked. I believe that is how most people move about from room to room."

"I mean" — his voice grows more gruff — "we did not see you come out."

I study them more closely, then shake my head. "I don't believe you are the guards who were on duty when I left."

"When was that?"

"Midday yesterday. I have been attending the queen ever since."

"No one mentioned you weren't inside."

"You will have to take that up with your fellow guards, won't you?"

The sentry looks over his shoulder at the door. "We thought you were in your chamber. We allowed Monsieur Fremin in to speak with you." He reaches up to scratch his ear. "Although I guess wait for you is more accurate."

"Hours ago," the second guard adds.

My face shifts from mild boredom to simmering anger. "You allowed Monsieur Fremin into my chambers without my permission? And allowed him to pass the entire night? When you thought I was inside?" Righteous anger fills my voice. "Did you think to check on my safety? Or did you just stand here snickering at my loose morals?"

By their chagrinned expressions, I see that is precisely what they did. I press my advantage. "He and his men-at-arms have abducted my sisters and threatened my personal safety, and you granted him access to my rooms?" My voice rises slightly with each word.

"My lady, surely he meant you no harm. Not with us just outside the door."

"If he meant me no harm, why did he not come out immediately and tell you that I was not inside?"

They exchange glances again, then one of them raps on the door. Nothing. His face shifts into hard lines as he lifts the latch and steps inside. The other guard and I follow.

The first man stops in the middle of the room. "He's not here." His voice holds a note of confusion.

"No," I say slowly. "At least not where we can see. Could you please check under the bed?"

The guard shoots me an exasperated look. "I'm sure he —"

"Did you see him leave?" I demand.

The man gets down on his knees to look under the bed. "He is not there, my lady," he says, then stands with as much dignity as he can muster.

"Could he be hiding in the garderobe?"

Not bothering to argue, he goes to check. "It is empty."

I wrap my arms around myself, as if trying to get warm. The second guard notices the window standing open. Clearly wanting to appease my roused temper, he asks, "Would my lady like me to close her window?"

"Yes. Thank you." I hold my breath as he crosses over to the window and grabs the latch. "Sweet Jesu!" he breathes.

"What?" The other guard nearly bumps into me as we hurry over to see. Fremin's body is exactly where we left it, the entire courtyard glistening with a faint wash of morning dew.

I cross myself. "We should send for a physician. He is likely gravely injured."

The guards exchange a glance. "He is likely dead, my lady," one of them says gently.

I do my best to look shocked.

CHAPTER 24

eloise?" I whisper softly, not wanting to disturb the queen.

The Brigantian looks up, alert but not startled. "Lady Sybella. I did not realize you'd left."

Good. Then none of the other less loyal attendants will have noticed either. "Are the others still breaking their fast?"

"Yes." Her mouth twists in derision. "Saints forbid they should go hungry while attending to their queen."

"That's not fair, Heloise." The queen's voice comes from the bed. "We do not want them any more than they wish to be here, and we encourage them to leave at every opportunity."

"That may well be," Heloise concedes. "And if their service to you at other times were in any way commendable, I would not be burdened with such uncharitable thoughts."

I leave her smirking at the queen's garments she is laying out and approach the bed. "How is Your Majesty feeling this morning?"

"Better," she says with a smile. "Your tincture is working."

For the dozenth time, I wish I could leave her out of all this. Wish I could keep her in the dark. But experience has already proved that an uninformed queen is both vulnerable and righteously angry.

"I am glad. I will prepare this morning's for you in a moment, but first" — I lower my voice — "I must apprise you of some recent events."

She hears something in my tone and glances up at me warily. "I am listening."

"I'm afraid Monsieur Fremin has met with a most unfortunate accident. Last night, while I was attending upon you, he was waiting in my room to speak with me and managed to lean too far out the window. He fell to his death."

A single note of exquisite silence follows my news.

"How clumsy of him," the queen murmurs dryly, nearly echoing Lazare's response.

Surely the equanimity with which she greets all the tumult that surrounds me is as beneficent as that of any saint. I likely should not accept it as easily as I do, but it is one of the few grace notes in my life.

"Well, it is good that you were here attending upon me, so you did not have to witness such a tragedy." She is quiet a long moment, a veritable tempest of questions she'd like to ask gleaming in her eyes. "Did Fremin's soul linger?"

I feel my face harden. "Yes. And such a despicable thing it was. We were right all along. He had always planned to return for the girls and myself, regardless of the king's decision."

"Well, good riddance, then," she mutters.

I fold my hands demurely. "I will be sure to pray for him, Your Majesty."

"As will I. Now, I think it would be a good time for my tonic, if you don't mind? I find my stomach unsettled somewhat."

I curtsy. "I am deeply sorry, Your Majesty." My voice is low with remorse.

"No," she says quietly. "It is not you who have disturbed my digestion."

Yet another moment of grace I do not deserve, but I take it gladly. "Thank you." I cross over to the sideboard beside the far wall and retrieve the mortar and pestle. As I grind the ginger down to a fine powder, the act of making something that will aid new life helps to chase away the dregs of my earlier encounter.

I am just pouring the spice into a goblet when I sense a clamor of heartbeats outside the queen's door. "Leave!" The deep command is followed by a flurry of gasps and squeals as the queen's attendants who have just come back from breakfast are chased away. The door bursts open, and the king steps over the threshold, followed closely by General Cassel and Captain Stuart.

The king's gaze sweeps around the room. When it lands on me, he shouts, "Seize her!"

General Cassel twitches and for one moment I think he is going to grab me himself, then four guards step around him and pour into the room.

"Hold!" The queen's command halts the men as thoroughly as any sword. She stands beside the bed at her full height, cheeks aflame with matching fury. "Why are you seizing my attendants?"

"She is a murderess." The king's voice is low and thrums with anger. "Even now, she tries to poison you."

The queen throws back her head and laughs, a move I cannot help but admire, given our circumstance. "Poison me?" She shakes her head as she would at a foolish child. "She is preparing my daily tonic. If it were poison, I would have been dead long before now."

The king frowns. "But your illness —"

"Ill is not the same thing as poisoned. Truly, my lord." Her voice is softer now, soothing. "What brings you here in such a state?"

"The lawyer Monsieur Fremin has been found dead. Pushed to his death by this woman." It is all he can do to keep from pointing at me.

"I am sure you are mistaken." The queen gives me an opening. "My lady? What say you to these accusations?"

I carefully set the mortar down. "Your Majesty, I was distressed when I learned of Monsieur Fremin's death this morning, but it was not my doing. You have only to ask the guards — I was with them when they discovered his body."

One of the same guards stands just behind General Cassel. He nods. "It is true, sire. She was not in the room with Monsieur Fremin."

The king rounds on him. "Why was she not in her chambers?"

The queen answers. "Because she was here, attending to me."

He ignores her and continues speaking to the guard. "She was supposed to be under close supervision." His voice is deceptively smooth.

Looking acutely uncomfortable, the guard glances at his companion, then shrugs. "She left the room before we came on duty."

"Find who was on watch then!" A flurry of movement follows the king's command. "And remove her." This time, he does point at me.

The guards take two steps forward before the queen interferes again. "No! You will not seize my lady in waiting and accuse her of such vile things with no more proof than that. The guard has said she was not in her room. I have confirmed that she spent the night attending upon me. What possible reason do you have to suspect her?"

Hands clenched at his side, the king takes a step forward. "She is an assassin." He and the queen stare at each other for a long, uncomfortable moment. Finally, the queen speaks, her words deceptively soft and pitched so that only the king can hear, like a knife sheathed in velvet. "She is not the only assassin at court though, is she?"

The king looks as if he has been struck with a pole. His eyes and mouth are open with surprise, but the deep scowl carved into his forehead bespeaks his displeasure at having this information revealed. "Why are you so convinced this woman is not guilty? We have been awash in bodies since her arrival."

"On the contrary, sire, it has only been the last week."

"How can you be so certain she has your best interests at heart?"

She smiles. "I have many reasons, but the news I will share should help convince you, although it is for your ears only at present."

The king's eyes gleam with both curiosity and suspicion, and he orders his men from the room. When they are gone, the queen takes a deep breath. "I am certain she is not poisoning me, because I am not dead or even ill."

"But you have been —"

"No, my lord husband. I am not ill. I am pregnant." Her hands drift to her belly, not yet round. "I carry the future dauphin of France, and like many women before me, suffer only from pregnancy sickness."

This time, the king looks as if he has taken a jousting lance to his gut. Pleasure, pride, and disbelief battle for dominance on his face.

The queen ventures a step closer. "Are you not pleased, my lord?" she asks in a small voice.

The scowl clears, and he tentatively takes her hand. "I am most pleased that God has granted us such an early blessing. I only wish to have received such news under happier circumstances."

"But what could be happier than a baby, Your Majesty?"

"Nothing, my lady. I only wish that the joy be untainted by politics."

"It is for me."

His face grows serious. "This is even more reason to have only the most trustworthy companions around you right now. There are two lives whose protection are of paramount importance to me."

I am glad at least he included the queen in his magnanimous sweep of protection.

With her delicate stature, pale complexion, and enormous brown eyes liquid with emotion, she is the very picture of wifely perfection. She grips his hand, then bends to kiss it, before standing once more. "That is what I've been trying to tell you, my lord. It is only because of Lady Sybella that I am not wretchedly ill all the time. It is her skill with herbs and tinctures that allows me to take any nourishment at all for the babe, else I would have lost it by now."

My hand on the pestle tightens, impressed at how easily the small lie slides off her tongue.

The king's head rears back. "Truly?"

"Truly, my lord. As I told you earlier, she has attended to me since before dinnertime yesterday. It was only when she went to her room for supplies this morning that she learned about Monsieur Fremin. She had just returned to tell me the news herself and to fix my morning tincture."

The king squeezes her hand. "Very well. I will speak with her before I make any judgments."

"Thank you, my lord."

"Now." He gestures to Heloise and Elsibet, who have been waiting silently all this time. Fortunately, enough time has passed that they are no longer gaping. "Let's have your women get you back to bed. It would not do to take a chill."

As Heloise and Elsibet help her into bed, the king comes to where I am grinding herbs with the pestle. He peers down into the mortar. "What is that?"

"Naught but chamomile, my lord."

"And what will you do with it?"

"Add it to a goblet of heated wine, along with some spices, including ginger, which shall calm the queen's stomach." I look up and meet his gaze for the first time. "I would be happy to take a sip while you watch."

"That is not necessary." He lowers his voice so that it will not carry across the room. "But know this. In spite of my lady wife's words, I cannot help but feel you are involved in Fremin's death in some way."

"Only as a victim, Your Majesty." I hold his gaze a moment longer before returning my attention to my work. "I heard a rumor that the lawyer carried a length of rope on him. Is not the simplest explanation the most likely? He meant to abduct me like he did my sisters."

"Abduct an assassin?" His voice is incredulous.

"The lawyer — indeed, my brother — did not know that it was the convent of Saint Mortain that I was sent to. Only that I was convent trained."

The king is quiet, observing my every movement like a hawk watches the grass next to a rabbit warren. "I do not trust your theology any more than I trust you. When she is in a less vulnerable state —"

It is all I can do not to scoff. She just lied to him as coolly as any assassin and played him like a minstrel does his mandolin.

"— I intend to remove you from the queen's circle."

His words settle over me like a noose. Perhaps that is what makes me so bold. I look up from my work. "Do you dare?" I ask softly. "Are you so certain that you and your bishops know better than the Church itself? What if it is due to honoring the Nine that she is with child so quickly? What if I am the only reason this babe thrives instead of shrivels?" I lean closer to him. "I told you once that we trained not only in matters of death, but how to protect against it. How can you be so sure that I am not precisely what the queen needs right now, in her most vulnerable moment?"

"Are you threatening her?"

"Far from it, Your Majesty. I am serving her with all my skill and devotion, ensuring both her and the babe's health. I know more about the nature of life and death than all of your bishops and philosophers and executioners combined." I do not know where the words come from, but they pour out of me, like water from a spout. "I am an initiate of the saint God placed in charge of such

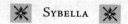

matters. Is it wise to question the gifts He has given me, especially when the life of your wife and child are concerned?"

When I have finished, the king stares as if he has never seen me before, and perhaps he has not. He has only seen the palest reflection of me as I work in the shadows to dodge and spar with the queen's enemies. But seeing the faint glimmer of awe mixed in with the fear and shock in his eyes, perhaps it is time to leave that pale reflection behind.

CHAPTER 25

Aeva

The wasp is grumbling again. "I don't think you're taking us anywhere. You're just going to force us to ride on horses until we die."

"Would you rather walk?" She shoots me an exasperated look, but I did not mean it in jest. "Sometimes our legs need to move."

"I would rather ride in a litter like the grand ladies do."

I laugh. "You wish to be carried? And what does that prove to the world? That you can be carted about like a sack of grain? That you are a burden to be borne on the shoulders of others?"

Her mouth clamps down into a flat line, a sure sign that although she is mad, the point of my words has gotten through to her. "However," I say in a more conciliatory tone, "you will be happy to learn we will be reaching our destination soon."

"What destination?" She glances around at the rocky soil and pebble-lined beaches. "There is nothing here but the sea. Whenever I ask where we are going, you say, 'West,' but now we are west, and there is nothing here."

"And which way is west?"

She hesitates, then points in the correct direction.

"And east?"

She points correctly again. I have been teaching her some small navigation skills along with how to use her knife so she can care for

herself in the most rudimentary ways. It gives her sharp-toothed mind something to chew on other than my ear, and while she does not yet realize it, the
more skills she has, the more confident she becomes. Both the confidence and
skills will make her a little safer in the world.

And prepare her for the lessons at the convent.

"And north?" I ask. It always takes her a moment to get her bearings, but she
points to the right. "Correct."

"What is north of here?" she asks.

"Not much, now that we are this far west. Brest, then east from there —"

"You mean back the way we came?"

"Yes. Is Morlaix, then Guingamp, then Saint-Brieuc." She falls quiet, thinking, and I am pleased that I have managed to redirect her thoughts. Then, just as
if the gods had planned it, Beast, who had ridden on ahead to check for armed
sorties, comes trotting down the road toward us.

"All clear," he says. He gives the wasp a smile, but as usual, she ignores him.

The road curves just then, and we find we have come nearly to the end of it,
the sea spreads out before us.

"Who are those people?" the wasp asks, her voice wary.

Three figures stand on the shore, a small boat pulled up on the beach behind
them. The tallest, in the middle, is wearing a black cloak, and her long blond hair
is braided in the style of Arduinna.

"It is Annith, your aunt," Beast says. "We have arrived."

CHAPTER 26

Genevieve

S tay, the king ordered me, when he was called from his morning toilette by an urgent summons. As if I were some trained hound. I had feigned too much wine last night and acted as if I had fallen asleep on his couch. Out of tenderness or optimism, or possibly even embarrassment, he did not order me carried back to my own room. It is precisely what Sybella wished — for me to stay with the king the entire night. And given what the urgent summons was likely about, this is the best place for me to be.

The faintest click comes from next to the fireplace. A servant bearing a load of firewood comes through a small door hidden by the paneling. He blinks in surprise when he sees me, then quickly looks away to tend the fire. When he has finished, he departs through the same door.

I have only a moment to ponder this discovery of hidden doors and servant passages before I hear the sound of voices — many voices — approaching. Alarm drives me to my feet. Even though the king may not feel the need to be discreet, I do not wish to proclaim my presence in his chamber quite so boldly. I hurry into the bedchamber and reach the valet's closet just as the main door opens.

"What brings you here, Madame?" I hear the king ask.

"Clearly there is much afoot." While the regent's voice comes from outside the room in the hallway, it is as cool and possessed as ever. "I thought to offer my help in some way." She thought to slip in with the others. Interesting that she was not invited.

"Thank you for your kind offer." The king is stiff and formal. "Arrangements need to be made for Monsieur Fremin's body. That would prove most helpful."

A long moment of sour disappointment hangs in the air as she grapples with the king's clear rejection of her participation. Finally, the regent says, "As you wish, sire."

"Come in, gentlemen." The king's order is followed by heavy footsteps. I count six in addition to the king. He leads them straight through the elegant drawing room into the private council chamber that sits beyond it, their voices growing indistinct.

I hurry over to the wall that abuts the council chamber and place my ear against it.

"You don't truly believe the woman is innocent, do you?" It is the traitorous Albi.

"According to the queen, Lady Sybella was with her the entire night," the king reminds them.

"But, Your Majesty," Albi continues, "she is an assassin. Well-schooled in the unholy arts of Saint Mortain. Surely such evil is not bound by the same rules of the physical world as we are."

The silence that follows is not truly silent at all, but filled with unease that rifles through the men like a cold winter breeze.

"What are you saying?" the king finally asks, his voice holding both warning and the curling edges of fear.

"I'm saying their ways are shadowed and closed to the eyes of man. Just because no one saw her there at the time should not be enough to clear someone of her skills from suspicion."

"And she did have a motive." I recognize General Cassel's voice. "She and Fremin have been at each other like cockerels ever since he arrived."

"Not to mention that is two bodies she has left in her wake," Captain Stuart says.

"Six." General Cassel's deep voice rasps over the others. "If you count the men Fremin claimed were missing."

"We cannot forget that she is an assassin trained who does not serve us — you, Your Majesty — and is thus suspect," the Bishop of Albi presses.

"What sort of saint trains assassins, anyway?" Stuart mutters.

"A heretical one." It is the first time the king's confessor has spoken.

"We have been over this," the Bishop of Narbonne says. "The Nine are within Church canon."

"They shouldn't be," the confessor mutters darkly.

"This does shed new light on Fremin's missing men," Cassel points out. "It could well be his claims were true."

"But if his claims were true, what has happened to the girls?" The king's voice is tired and strained. "For all of her strange ways, I cannot believe that she did them any harm."

"Perhaps she and the queen are counting on your honor and chivalry to blind you to her crimes, as if you were some poor hapless fool who couldn't see past such subterfuge."

Silence follows, and I can only marvel at how skillfully the general has thrown his spear.

When the king speaks again, his voice is harder than iron. "Very well. You have convinced me. This matter is resolved. General Cassel," he barks, "search the Lady Sybella's room. Let us see if she is hiding something."

CHAPTER 27

Sybella

am standing in front of the fire, considering my options, when the door bursts open. Only years of hard discipline keep me from startling, but I do not wish to give them the satisfaction. Instead, I turn calmly around.

Six of them storm into the room, General Cassel at the fore, his cold, brutal eyes on me. For one heart-clenching moment I fear they intend to grab me and drag me from the room.

"Search the chambers!" he orders.

The men fan out, dividing the room with practiced precision, each taking a section. The window, the bed, the chest. Cassel comes to stand in front of me, too close, hoping I will cower before him. I smile sweetly. "To what do I owe this pleasure?"

"We are looking for the murder weapon."

I ignore the sound of the men churning through my things and cock my head to the side, considering. "The guards said he had broken his neck. What sort of weapon do you expect to find?" It is all I can do not to flex my hands, which have indeed broken many a neck. But Cassel does not know that and hopefully, like all men, will not consider that a possibility.

"Rope," he says grimly. "A noose."

"Ah," I say, grateful that the rope I used to strangle Fremin's henchman is now looped through his belt.

His gaze drops down to my waist, to my belt of gold chain from which a small knife hangs. Anger begins to bloom deep inside my gut, but I hold it firmly in check. "That could not break a neck," I helpfully point out.

His gaze shifts to my face.

"Sir!"

Reluctantly, Cassel looks back at the guard. "What?"

"Knives, sir. Lots of 'em."

A sense of violation squeezes me by the throat when I see that one of the soldiers has lifted the mattress from the bed frame, exposing four of my longest knives.

Cassel swings his shaggy head back to me. "No weapons, eh?"

"I never said I had no weapons, only none that were capable of breaking a neck."

He crosses over to the bed and lifts my anlace from its hiding place. "This is not something a lady in waiting would have."

I curl my fingers into fists so I will not grab it from his meaty hands. "We have already established I am no ordinary lady in waiting. I cannot protect the queen with naught but my bare hands."

At his gesture, his men collect my knives. For a brief moment, I indulge in the vision of me leaping forward, taking back my knives, and killing the four of them before the other two can blink. Instead, I move to the window, where one of the men is still fumbling with the drapes. "Here, let me give you more light." I yank one of the drapes aside. The soldier startles, dropping the curtain, his hand going for his knife as light spills into the room. I cluck my tongue at him. "It is only a drape, monsieur, and a dusty one at that." His cheeks flush dull red as two of the others snicker.

Another shout goes up, and we all look to the soldier kneeling beside the chest, his hand gingerly holding out a glass vial filled with amber liquid. "We've found her poisons, sir!"

I laugh. "Poison? I imagine the queen would beg to differ. Those are the very physics I give her daily. Here. Let me show you." As I reach for the vial, the man flinches as if he expects me to throw it on him and turn him to stone. I take it

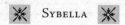

gently from his hand, put the vial to my lips, and swallow. "See? Nothing even remotely harmful."

Cassel stares at them impassively. "Take them anyway."

I shove the vial at the soldier and glare at the general. "You'd best check with the queen. She will not look kindly on one who destroys the only tisane that has brought her any relief."

He hesitates then. "Take the vials to the queen and ask if she recognizes them," he orders. "But be careful — do not risk her touching them or drawing too close."

For all of his brutishness, the general is not an idiot. As we stare at each other a moment, I try not to see all the physical similarities to Beast. It is too painful to see them in this man — one who embraces brutality, savors raw power, mistakes violations for strength. He could not be more different from Beast had they been born on opposite ends of the world.

I focus on that, will myself to discern the differences. They are there — the eyes that feel wolfish and feral in Beast's face are darker and more piggish in Cassel's. Beast's nose has been broken more often, but his mouth holds humor and kindness rather than cruelty.

Cassel breaks our gaze, looking to something behind me atop the cupboard. I see my small casket, then bite back an oath as he heads toward it. It is a good thing Beast is not here, I realize, else they would come to blows. While there is no doubt in my mind that Beast would prevail, it would cost him dearly. It would not just wound his soul, but the repercussions for killing the king's favorite general could easily cost him his life.

CHAPTER 28

Genevieve

hen I deem it safe to emerge from the valet's closet and make my way to the sitting room, the king looks up from the fireplace, his eyes troubled and distant. He blinks at me, as if he'd forgotten I was here. "Thank you for your discretion."

"But of course, Your Majesty. I have no desire to bring any more trouble to your door. It is my hope to ease your burdens."

He nods vaguely and turns his attention back to the fire.

I try to keep quiet, to wait for a moment that I can choose once it is ripe, but my anger and my fear for Sybella are too great. The memory of the regent searching my rooms, the sense of violation it filled me with. It will only be worse for Sybella, with the brute Cassel taking pleasure in such a show of raw power.

"They are wrong, you know." I curse myself for my own artlessness. Recklessness will not aid me here.

He lifts his head and scowls in disapproval. "Were you eavesdropping?"

"Not intentionally, but there were few enough places for me to hide. Would you rather I pretend I hadn't heard, even though we both know I have?"

"I'd rather you mind your own business and not insert yourself," he says coldly. "These matters do not concern you. Not if you are, as you say, loyal to me. In truth, it's getting harder and harder to know if your loyalty is to me or the queen." He shoves away from the mantel and stalks toward me. "You don't work for the queen, do you?" While his voice is deceptively soft, the menace in it is unmistakable. "She hasn't placed you under my nose? To spy on me and influence me to do her bidding?"

No, I want to shout, *your rutting sister has.* "No, Your Majesty. But you do remember what I told you last night? That the regent and the Bishop of Albi are working together. You would do well to keep a mind to what his motives are."

"And you would do well to tend to your own affairs," he says curtly.

My subtlety falls on deaf ears. Very well. Subtlety be damned. "It is my business. I am from the convent. I honor the Nine. Their accusations affect me as well."

He waves a hand. "Not if you don't tell anybody, they won't."

"I don't mean in terms of repercussions, but when they disparage my faith and dishonor my saints." For all that I don't consider myself particularly devout, the bishop's words fester in my soul. I take a step closer to him. "They are wrong," I repeat, willing him to hear me.

"So you are a theological expert now?"

"No," I admit, "I am Sybella's sister, and what they say about her and our faith is untrue."

"You should refrain from reminding me of your relationship with her just now."

I stare at him a long moment, unable to keep from shaking my head.

He glares at me. "What?"

"I have never seen a man work so hard to ignore the parts of the world that are inconvenient to him."

"Careful," he growls. "My affection for you is not infinite. And it certainly isn't something you can use to sway me from impartial judgments I must make."

Impartial. I nearly laugh. Why are the bishops' and Cassel's counsel considered impartial while mine is not?

"Sybella has multiple marks against her, from her undue influence with the queen, to her unorthodox faith, not to mention that she is an assassin — reportedly of some unnatural order."

"She is not guilty of the crimes you accuse her of." At least, not all of them.

"As you said, you are her sister, of course you would defend her." That is when I realize he is hurt. Hurt that I have taken her side against his, adding one more mark against her.

Desperation fills me. I had so hoped I was beginning to help him see more clearly, but he won't believe me. He certainly won't believe her. Not even if she told the full, unpolished truth about her vile brother. It is too easy — too convenient — for him to place all the blame squarely on her, someone he doesn't like and who threatens the natural order of his world.

I close my eyes for a moment as my despair flares into hot, bitter remorse. I will never be able to unring that bell. To fix things.

I study his profile as he broods into the flames. *Not if you don't tell anybody, they won't*, he said.

While I cannot fix the whole, mayhap I can fix some of it.

The room is empty, the king leaning on the council table in front of him. The blue velvet of his doublet is stretched tight across his bunched shoulders. "Your Majesty."

He holds up one hand. "Not now, Genevieve. I have no wish to hear a defense of your friend. This was exactly the reason I ordered you not to consort with her. Her scandal threatens to drag you down with it, merely by your association."

It is not her association with me that has caused this problem, but my own actions. Without the knowledge of the convent I provided, his suspicions would never have fallen on her.

Every word he has uttered crystallizes my resolve. "But, sire," I say softly. "What if it is not Sybella's scandal?"

He twists his head to look over his shoulder at me. "What are you saying?"

For days I have wondered how I could fix this, but no answer has presented itself. Very well. Perhaps it cannot be fixed, but I can at least soften the most painful edges of the blow. "I am saying that I killed Monsieur Fremin, not Sybella."

CHAPTER 29

The king shakes his head. "No."

"Yes."

His arms fall to his sides, his fists clenching. "You committed murder under my roof?" He looks at the couch where I passed the night. "Under my very nose?"

"It was more a matter of protection than murder."

"He threatened you?"

"He threatened Sybella's life and the safety of her sisters. No one would listen."

"You have betrayed me. Betrayed my trust in you." As he talks, the note of hurt in his voice is quickly overrun with anger. "You spit on the protection I offer. Why?"

"I will not cower in safety behind your robes while those who are dear to me are cast to the wolves. You judged her guilty before you even knew all the facts."

"I had heard the facts and had determined her claims to be false."

"You were closing ranks and shutting your ears to an outsider who rubs you the wrong way."

His nostrils flare. "I do not believe your claim. Why would she not kill him herself? She is an assassin as well."

"Because she knew that you did not trust her, that you would not believe her."

"And why should I believe you?"

I shrug. "What have I to gain by lying? In truth, I have everything to lose — your protection, your good opinion, my life."

He grinds his teeth and slams his palms against the table. "Dammit, I trusted you!"

"Indeed, sire. And still you may."

"I cannot trust someone who murders my guests at will! Who treats my favor with so little regard. Who casts aside everything I have done to help her."

For once, prudence takes hold of my tongue, and I do not point out that I have received no favors, not one, nor have I benefitted much from his protection. "It was not at whim. He entered her chambers with the intention of doing her harm."

He whirls back to me. "How can you know that?"

"Because I was there."

"The sentries did not report that they saw you."

I lift one shoulder and allow a smile of satisfaction to play about my lips. "I am an assassin. Shadows are my friend. They were right about that much."

He stares, his breath growing more rapid. Whether from anger or shock or dismay — or all three at once — I do not know. He strides closer. He is not a tall man, but his anger makes it feel as if he is looming over me. My heart wants to race in apprehension, but I will not let it. I deserve his wrath, not Sybella. It is I who have upset his neatly ordered world with my revelations; Sybella has only tried to protect her sisters. Indeed, this is the only way to tip the scales of justice back into balance.

"I could have you put to death for this." The anger that colors his voice does not completely hide a faint thread of distress. I grasp on to that thread as a drowning man would a rope.

"You could," I agree. "But is there not some legal argument to be made for protecting someone? Is that not at the very core of chivalry and honor?"

"That is for knights," he says, "not demoiselles who cannot mind their own business. Besides, you would have a hard time making that case when she is an assassin."

"Do you intend to put me on trial?" I ask, trying not to hold my breath.

When he does not answer, I continue. "Sybella is well aware of the suspicions you harbor against her, and would never hand you a rope with which to hang her."

"Then why are you?"

Because I am the only person he seems willing to protect. But will he for something this serious? "I made sure it looked like an accident, and Sybella was nowhere nearby when it occurred. I did not realize your dislike of her would blind you to the evidence."

"You just told me that shadows are an assassin's friend — why would that not apply to her as well?"

"It would, and does. But your own guards saw her arrive and discover the body alongside them. Why do you not believe their account?"

"Perhaps she bewitched them. I don't know what assassins who serve the god of death are capable of."

That is when I get my first full taste of the fear that lurks behind his feelings for Sybella. It is not merely that she is an assassin, but that she feels otherworldly to him.

"If she had bewitched them, would they have allowed him into her chambers, unescorted and unchaperoned? I think you should ask them what *their* motives were."

His eyes widen at the implications of my words, and for the first time since I stepped over this cliff's edge, I feel that I have forced a crack into his thick, closed skull. Now if only some light can get through it.

He glances at the painting on the far wall. "Who else knows that you have been in contact with Sybella?"

"The regent saw me coming out of her room yesterday. I told her I was concerned about her health, as way of explanation."

"She demanded an explanation of you? What business is it of hers?"

Ah, she is rubbing him raw with her interference. Good. I will toss a little salt into that wound. "Madame Regent believes that all matters that affect the crown of France are her business."

His mouth tightens. "So you've told no one? What of the queen?"

I shake my head. "I've told only you."

He stares into the fire for a moment, thinking, then barks for the guard. When the man hurriedly appears, the king gives him an order. "Fetch General Cassel from the Lady Sybella's chambers. At once."

CHAPTER 30

Sybella

assel sweeps the trunklet up, cradling it against his chest with one arm while he uses the other to flip open the lid. The force of the movement nearly breaks the small brass hinges.

The fury inside me coils tighter as his meaty hand rifles through the contents, this violation of my things reminding me of every other violation I have suffered. But I fold my arms and wait patiently.

He lifts my golden bracelet, then tosses it to the floor, dismissing it as a woman's bauble. When he finds the handkerchief that Tephanie embroidered for me, I must bite back a stream of curses. I hold my breath, hoping he will ignore the rest of what is in there. None of it is even remotely weaponlike — he simply enjoys the violation.

When he plucks the twig of holly from the bottom of the casket, my heart clenches, but I force my face into a bored expression. He gives a snort of contempt, then flings the holly sprig onto the ground. I must give myself away somehow, for he pauses, glances at me, then grinds it under the heel of his boot. The act causes all the air to flee from my lungs. It takes every ounce of will I possess to refrain from snatching up the holly and cradling it in my hands.

"Feel better now?" I ask, making certain the faint mocking tone hides my distress.

He tosses the trunklet to the ground and comes to stand before me, closer, closer, until our chests are nearly touching and I must tip my head back to meet his eyes. "We should search you, as well."

Hot fury writhes inside me, but my voice is colder than the deepest crypt. "If you lay so much as a finger on me, I will kill you. I don't care whose father you are."

His face shifts, going from hard anger to something closer to bewilderment. "What did you say?"

Merde. Before I can answer, one of the soldiers returns and sticks his head in the door. "Sir! The king wishes to see you at once."

Cassel does not look away. "I'll be right —"

"The king said to come at once, sir," the man says unhappily.

Reluctantly, Cassel pulls his gaze from mine. "This is not over," he says under his breath.

"Oh, but it is," I say just as softly to his retreating back.

When I am alone at last, I grab my skirts to give my hands something to do besides tremble. It is not fear that has me shaking, but rage. I make myself draw a deep breath, then another, using the air to cool my anger.

As my mind clears, my gaze falls on the trampled holly twig, the broken leaves and smashed berries as bruised as my heart. I kneel down, and fury explodes inside me again, although this time it is accompanied by a hollow sense of desolation. It is just a twig, I remind myself. Just a stupid piece of a branch that fools liked to call miraculous.

It was also my last remaining piece of Mortain. The desolation that fills me is so complete that I cannot breathe. I fumble for my pocket, my fingers closing around the pebble, welcoming the bite of pain as it presses against my palm. I stare down at the ruined remains of Mortain's last miracle, the heat of unshed tears searing my eyes. But one escapes, landing on the holly. I stare at it, the last mingling of his essence and mine.

I blink, trying to clear my vision. The crushed edges of the leaves are not torn, merely sharply bent. And the berries are not crushed, but simply misshapen. As I watch, the holly shifts, so slowly my eye cannot truly see it, but within a hand span of minutes, it is whole again. Not quite new — there are creases where it was torn and scars along the berries' surfaces. But it is whole and remade. A miracle, for all that it is a small one. I gently scoop up the sprig and cradle it to my breast.

CHAPTER 31

The next day, when it has grown dark, the door to the king's chambers finally opens. It is not the king, but two young boys — apprentices, I realize — jostling a large wooden trunk between them. On their heels comes an older man of middle years. He is not a servant, and certainly not a courtier. His clothes are of good quality, but serviceable. He does not so much as glance at me. "Careful with that, you despicable turnips! Set it down in the far corner near the fire. Carefully!"

The boys hurry to do what he asks. With quick, practiced movements, they open the top of the traveling case, which folds out to create a table.

The man crosses to the fire and stokes it, motioning at one of the boys to add fresh logs until it is burning hotly.

When he is satisfied with the fire, he tells the boys, "Enough! If that table is not set up by now, then I've wasted these last seven years on you." There is no malice in his words, and the boys ignore his scolding as a tree ignores the wind. "Now begone. And stay out of everyone's way. I'll send for you when I'm done."

As they clamber to the door, one of them shoots a curious look my way — the first one of them to make eye contact. I smile, but he ducks his head and scurries out. A faint swell of understanding begins forming in my chest. The king was very happy to remind me that he had a variety of punishments at his disposal. Clearly he has put some thought and planning into this one.

The man has tied on a leather apron and is muttering over a set of tools — a hammer, pliers, tongs. I think of Maraud, nearly broken in the dungeon at Cognac: the iron chains, the manacles, the oubliette.

The king would not have me tortured, would he? I square my shoulders. Just because that is what they have in mind does not mean I must submit to it. I run my hand down my skirts — a seemingly nervous gesture — to assure myself of my knife's solid presence.

The man begins hammering. Before I can investigate, the door opens and the king strides in, moving with confidence and purpose, the dregs of last night's anger still lurking in his eyes. He does not look at me as he crosses the room to the worktable. "How is it coming?"

The man drops his tools and bows deeply. "It is almost done, Your Majesty. I must simply take a measurement before adding the final link."

The king waves his hand in my direction. "But of course."

The man approaches me like a horse that might bolt, and with dawning recognition, I understand what is happening.

He holds an elegant necklace of finely worked silver. It is long, longer than I am tall. Almost as long as a . . . chain.

I jerk my head around to stare at the king. He is pouring a generous glass of wine. I think he means it to be a careless gesture, but I can feel his attention on me. The man — a silversmith, I now realize — grunts. "This way, if you please." His words are brusque and impersonal.

Before I can ask a question or register a protest, his arm snakes out and the cool silver is around my neck. He loops the chain once around the base of my throat, a second time so that it rests just below my collarbone, then a third time so that it spans across my chest, like a livery collar.

"Like this?" the silversmith asks the king.

He studies me from across the room, head tilted, eyes narrowed. "Yes. Although a little longer, I think, to trail halfway down her back."

The silversmith adjusts the length, then glances once more to the king, who nods in approval.

A part of me wishes to yank the rutting thing from my neck, throw it in the smith's face, then ask the king to explain what he thinks he is doing. But the other part, the part that chose to protect Sybella from the king's version of justice, is genuinely curious as to what game is being played here.

Besides, penance is not meant to be easy. I am lucky his idea of punishment does not extend to scourges or hair shirts, as many in the Church prefer.

Behind me there is a tug and a twist, followed by the sound of a tool snipping, then the entire thing comes to rest against my neck. It is surprisingly heavy. Carcanets are the height of fashion, the sheer weight of the precious metal involved adding to their prestige.

I slip my hand behind me to grasp the loose end of the necklace, smiling at how sturdy it is. It is truly a chain, which means it is also a weapon if I so wish.

At the look in my eye, the silversmith steps away and packs up his tools, not bothering to call for his assistants. When he has quit the room, the king comes over to study me appraisingly. It is so plainly a move to gain control and make me squirm that it loses any power to do so. But there is more than one way to play with power, so I remain silent, forcing him to speak first. Truthfully, serving in Angoulême's home has trained me well for these stupid games.

"Why are you smiling?"

"I am admiring your gift. It is remarkably generous and an undeserved sign of your favor."

"It is not a gift," he snaps, "but a punishment."

"You have given me a necklace a third of my weight in silver as a punishment?"

He grits his teeth. "It is a chain. A chain to keep you in your place." He takes a deep breath, trying to regain his composure. "I told you to avoid Sybella, and you didn't listen. Three times you snuck to her room, and during the last of those visits, you killed someone." He folds his hands behind his back and nods his head in a grave manner. "I can no longer trust you, Gen. I cannot let you run free anymore." The words please him more than they ought.

"You should feel grateful," he continues. "I thought about branding you — we do that to some criminals, you know."

"I do know, Your Majesty." My words work to calm his ruffled feathers, and his features relax somewhat. I move to stand in front of the mirror. "It will show."

The king drinks heavily from his goblet before answering. Another move intended to intimidate. "Not if you keep the back of it underneath your gown. To everyone else it will simply appear as if I have given you a most generous gift."

My eyes meet his in the mirror. "So what am I to be chained to, Your Majesty?"

His smile is filled with pride. "That is where I have chosen to show you mercy. I will not chain you to anything yet. But if you cross me again, I will do it — and gladly." His voice holds a note of eagerness that is faintly unsettling. Then, so quick that I do not see it coming, he hurls his goblet into the fire, where it shatters loudly, the wine hissing as it is consumed by the flames. "Do not look at me like that." His cheeks are flushed, the true depths of his anger rising to the surface at last. "Not when I have had to stand before my council and declare Fremin's death an accident even as they howled for Sybella's head. Not when I have hidden your crimes from my closest advisors. Spared you from a trial that would cost you your life. Do not dare to look disappointed in me." As he speaks, I realize that some small part of his own self — the hidden part I had been reaching — is also disappointed in him. That is all the spark of hope I need.

"I wasn't disappointed in you, Your Majesty, but that I have ruined the trust between us."

"Trust can be rebuilt," he says, sounding like a priest beginning a Sunday mass. "But it takes time, and much effort on the part of the one who has broken it. Because I care for you, I am giving you that chance." With that pompous proclamation, he nods once, then leaves the room.

Because I care for you, I am not strangling you with this rutting chain, I want to say to his retreating back, but of course I do not. The entire point of willingly submitting to this farce is to make him feel powerful and less threatened by me. The less threatened he is, the greater the chance he will continue to confide in me so that I may in turn try to sway him from the influence of his late father and General Cassel.

I grip the silver chain and tug on it in disgust, wincing at the memory of how I forced Maraud to wear a chain of his own, only his was made of thick iron and held no pretense of fashion or favor. And yet he bore it good-naturedly, and I can as well. Besides, I am a far better target for the king's wrath than Sybella. Not only is he willing to indulge me more than her, I am fairly certain she would have killed him by now, and that would only complicate everything.

CHAPTER 32

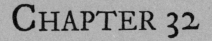

Saints, Maraud hated the mud. Slimy, gritty, soul-sucking sludge that threatened to pull them down to the very gates of the Underworld itself. It was so deep in some places, they'd had to dismount and squelch alongside their horses, their boots disappearing into the foul stuff.

And it was everywhere: In his hair, his eyes. Even in his damn teeth.

The others were no doubt regretting their decision to come with him.

They finally managed to slog their way to the crest of a small hillock — more of a pile of mud, really — the only one they'd passed in the last four days. Below them, like a child's wooden blocks cast down in a fit of temper, lay Flanders.

"It's probably nicer than it looks," Jaspar said.

Tassin grunted. "Probably worse."

Andry reached up and scratched his beard. "You know they're going to overcharge us."

Jaspar's voice was glum as he pointed out, "That's if we're lucky enough to find a room."

In spite of the drizzle, in spite of his friend's melancholy, Maraud felt a sense of triumph deep in his chest, his heart nearly swelling with it. He'd waited for this moment for over a year now. Dreamed of it, plotted it, fed off of it. The idea of confronting Cassel had sustained him through those first awful days after Ives was killed. It kept his resolve firm during his initial captivity and imprisonment. It had fed him during the long, bleak months in the oubliette — the sustenance provided by this need for vengeance filled him even when his hunger was gnawing its way out of his belly.

Lucinda had been right about one thing. It was long past time he saw to justice for his family.

CHAPTER 33

Sybella

It has taken three days, but finally the castle feels quiet once more, as if things have returned to normal. I dress with care, wearing a somber, modest gown. I kneel down to lift the corner of the feather mattress, then huff in annoyance as I remember. I loved those knives. We were old friends. I will have to see about retrieving them somehow.

I head for the thick tapestry against the wall and pull it back, revealing a half dozen other knives, hastily stitched into the backside of the fabric. I slip them into the sheaths hidden under my gown. Since they did not search me bodily that night, I will have to hope that they will not today either. If they do, the fact that Cassel missed these will make him look foolish before the king.

And I would very much like to make Cassel look foolish. I would very much like to hold one of these knives at his throat and press—slowly—until his eyes bulge with fear, blood trickling down his neck and piss down his leg.

That thought puts a faint smile on my lips so that I will not have to fake the pleasant greeting I intend to give my guards.

Except there are no guards in sight. Surprised, I step all the way into the hall, expecting to hear them call out to me to stop, but they do not. The guards at the queen's apartment do not make any move to stop me either. They simply nod a greeting, then step aside to open the door.

But the queen is not in her room. Instead, I find Heloise, overseeing the airing of the queen's mattress. "Where is she?" I ask.

Heloise glances over her shoulder. "Since the sun decided to come out today, the king invited her for a short stroll in the garden. We all thought the fresh air would do her and the babe some good."

"That is pleasant news."

Heloise nods. "The king has visited every day and is most solicitous."

"Have they announced the pregnancy yet?"

"Not yet. They have decided to announce it at the coronation." Heloise tilts her head. "You have not heard, have you?"

Startled birds take flight in my stomach. "Heard what?"

"The king has decided Fremin's death was an accident."

I stare at her a moment, the fullness of her words not penetrating.

"A most tragic one," I finally say.

"Indeed."

I head directly for Gen's chambers. Around me, everyone is busy readying the household to make the great trek to Paris for the coronation. I am glad that it appears to be proceeding as planned and wonder how the regent lost that battle.

When I reach Genevieve's room, I knock, but there is no answer. There is no heartbeat, either. Puzzled, I open the door and slip inside. Her room is empty, the bed not slept in. I frown, remembering my last words to her to distract the king. *Merde.* I told her not to do anything other than distract him. But that was naïve of me. I have seen the guilt and remorse she drags behind her like a millstone. She would have done whatever it took. If she is not here, nor in the ladies' solar, then there is only one place she could be.

And fortunately for me, the king is outside with the queen.

Using the small servants' corridor, I count the doors until I reach the one that leads to the king's private apartments. I put my ear to the door and hear only one heartbeat — too steady, strong, and familiar to be the king's elderly valet. I silently lift the latch and peek into the room.

In the dim light I see a slim figure lying on the couch, covered in a blanket. While I do not like that the curtains have not been drawn back from the windows, I am glad she is at least on the couch and not in the king's bed.

As I step fully into the room, Gen stirs and sits up, pushing her hair out of her eyes.

"Good morning, sleepyhead," I say cheerfully.

"Sybella?" She quickly grabs the corner of the blanket and pulls it close.

"'Tis I. Come to thank you for distracting the king long enough that reason could prevail and" — my voice gentles — "to be certain you did not force yourself to cross any lines you did not wish to."

"Of course not," she says, appearing discomfited by my words.

"Well and good, then. He has declared Fremin's death an accident, and the queen is back in his favor. If that was all thanks to you, it is no wonder you are still abed."

Genevieve smiles, but it does not quite reach her eyes. "I am glad." While there is no doubting the sincerity of her words, something is off. Something I cannot yet put my finger on.

I glance around at the sitting room that, for all of its opulence, feels dim and dour. "Why is he keeping you shut up in here?"

"He is the king. Does he need a reason?" Her answer furthers my unease. It was meant to be a jest.

"Is it because of your association with me?"

"No."

"Then why?"

She sighs heavily, as if annoyed. Since it is a ploy I am well familiar with, I ignore it. "Because it suits him. He is . . . less than happy with me at the moment and finds it amusing to keep me under his thumb."

I come farther into the room, examining her face closely, trying to discern what her words are hiding. "What did you do that has him so wroth with you?" And yet so at peace with the rest of the court. Including me.

She looks down to fiddle with the corner of the blanket. "It is a private matter. There is no need to discuss it. Now I have a question for you," she says in a rush, blocking any attempt I might make at arguing. "How — what — did you do with your blood? What trick was that — to make souls disappear in such a way? Is that another of your gifts from Mortain?" Her voice holds a faint note of bitterness.

"That is a fair question — with a complicated answer." I sigh. "In truth, we must have a long conversation about the convent and Mortain himself. But not here, where any approaching servant can hear us. And not until you have told me what is going on."

"What if it is not any of your business?"

"Would you rather I ask the king?"

"You wouldn't."

I smile grimly. "You have no idea the things I would do. Shall we fight for it? Test our skills against each other? I win, you tell me. You win, you don't."

The look she sends me is so full of exasperation that it reminds me of Charlotte and nearly makes me laugh. "We both know that you would win any contest between the two of us."

"I don't know that."

She shakes her head. "You will not like it any better than the king."

My uneasiness returns, but I keep my voice light. "At least I cannot order you confined to my chambers."

She looks to the window, then the fireplace, anywhere but at me before she finally speaks. "It's about Monsieur Fremin. I . . . I may have confessed to killing him."

CHAPTER 34

er words are so unexpected that it feels as if she is speaking some strange language I have never heard. Except that with these inconceivable words, everything falls into place. Guilt and anger wash over me. "I asked you to distract the king, not confess to a crime you didn't commit! That was not your sin to bear. You had nothing to do with it." Indeed, my mind is still struggling to grasp the enormity her — of anyone — taking the blame and punishment for something I did.

"It was a sin I contributed to, no matter how unknowingly." She tightens the blanket around her shoulders and leans forward. "It feels good to be able to do this."

I feel my mouth snap shut. "Good to take the blame for someone else's killing?"

"No." She huffs in frustration, then looks over at the sideboard. "Do you remember the jars of toad livers Sister Serafina kept in the poisons room?"

I blink at this change of subject. "The ones that stank like rotten feet? How could I forget."

"When I was finally allowed to begin helping at the convent, I was sent to her workroom. But on my third day there, I accidentally dropped the crock full of toad livers." Her gaze shifts from the crystal goblets on the sideboard back to me. "She did not yell or get mad. Nor even punish me with quiet satisfaction like some of the other nuns did. She simply told me to collect the broken pieces of crockery and bring them to the table. When I had, she plunked down a pot of glue and a brush, then told me to take whatever time I needed to put it back together.

"Sybella, she allowed me to fix it. To take the pieces of what I had broken and make them whole again." The sheer wonder in her voice makes me realize how rare a thing that is — to be given such an opportunity. I can so clearly see the nine-year-old she must have been, bent over all the broken pieces, painstakingly working to fit them together. "Doing this feels as if I am being given that chance again. The king will not hurt or punish me. Not over this. And if he does —"

"I will not let him."

She gives an emphatic shake of her head. "He won't. Oh, he's posturing and strutting and will bark at me for a while, but he is not a cruel man. Not like General Cassel or Pierre. He is —" She waves her hand as she searches for the right word, the blanket slipping down her shoulder.

A glint of silver shines at her throat. I scowl. "Why has the king given you an expensive bauble if you just confessed to murder?"

She pulls the blanket back into place, making sure to cover her neck. "I told you, he wouldn't punish me as he would you."

"A generous gift is no one's definition of punishment."

She looks away. "It is a power game he plays. Nothing more."

"If it is nothing more, then let me see it."

"No," she says mulishly. "You will only grow jealous."

I laugh outright at that, then stride over to the couch and yank the blanket from her. She stares up at me, both startled and dismayed. Three coils of thick silver links are wrapped around her slender neck and drape gracefully down her chest. And while it is a necklace, one in the style favored by the Germans and the English, it also bears remarkable resemblance to —

"A chain? I thought you said he was not cruel."

She shrugs the blanket back into place. "He's not. But he is feeling threatened —"

"By you?"

"By everyone. He feels harried on all sides. He is tired of having his authority questioned by the regent and of the pressure from his spiritual advisors, and afraid any kindnesses to the queen will be perceived as weaknesses by his council, especially Cassel. Every time the king learns something he didn't know before, it is like rubbing salt into a festering wound."

I stare at her in silence, weighing her words. Remembering the carefully decorated reception at the wedding, the extreme kindness he shows occasionally. His belief in honor and chivalry. How hard the regent works to keep her hand unseen as she stirs the pot. It all fits exactly as Gen says.

"Perhaps," I concede grudgingly. "But forcing you to wear a chain comes dangerously close to cruel."

"It is as much to punish himself for being weak enough to want me, even though we have not shared a bed except that one time. But since then he has begun to talk to me in a way that he doesn't let himself talk to others. Reveals to me, often without knowing it, parts of himself that he can't share with anyone else."

"That is charming," I say dryly, "but you are not his confessor, nor his prisoner, or even a willing favorite. You don't owe him or the convent or even me this servitude you are performing for him."

"You are right. This is something I want to give, rather than what is owed. This chain around my neck makes him feel as if I have no power. It is not true, and I suspect even he knows it on some level. But it allows him to feel as if he has punished me and granted me mercy. Or as if in wearing it, I have agreed to the terms of the punishment. Which I have." She grins at me. "For the time being."

That mollifies me somewhat. "Does he intend to chain you to something?"

She shakes her head. "Only if I step out of line." Her face creases. "Will you explain it to the queen? In case she notices the necklace. I don't want her to think I am acting as his favorite for baubles."

"I will, but I do not like any of this, and I will be watching him carefully. If I feel he has gone too far, or you are in any danger, I will intervene."

She smiles at me, a jaunty curve of her lips. "Since when do I report to you?"

"I am your older sister, and that grants me a certain authority over you, whether you like it or not."

CHAPTER 35

Genevieve

t a loss for words, I stare at Sybella, realizing she has just given me what I have been missing for the last five years — this sense of someone having my back. Of seeing to my safety when I am too caught up in the moment to care.

Of being a sister. A true sister. Not one who undercuts me at every opportunity. Who sends sly, subtle barbs my way only to claim it was a jest later. Who laughs at my attempts to fix things or improve them or even adjust to them.

It feels as precious as a newly formed pearl. Before I can find my tongue and say something — anything — Sybella glances around the room, cocking her ear.

"Do you hear something?" I ask.

"A heartbeat. The servants, most like. I must go. I should not be discovered here. But I will be watching the king. Know that."

As she heads for the servants' passage, I call after her. "Do not forget that talk you promised me."

She tosses a nod of agreement over her shoulder, then opens the door. She does not gasp, but I feel her breath catch in her throat.

It is not a serving maid, or even the valet that stands there, but the regent.

A moment of utter silence captures us all. Sybella recovers first, inclining her head at the regent as if they have merely passed each other in the hallway, then slips out of the room.

As the regent emerges from the narrow passageway into the king's apartments, a shiver of deep apprehension racks my body. "Madame Regent?" I drop into a curtsy.

Her gaze moves from my face to roam over my body, as if appraising a mare she has purchased only to find it is lacking. "You and Sybella know each other. You are from the convent as well."

My entire body grows cold. "I never met Sybella until ten days ago. That was not a lie."

She studies me with the intensity of a mason looking for a flaw in his stone. "What did she want with you?"

The faintest scrap of hope moves inside my chest. She did not hear us talking. "She was only asking if I would put in a good word for her with the king. She knows he does not care for her."

She looks at the painting behind me and smiles, then gives me another appraising look. "While your good fortune seems high at the moment, you'd best hope he doesn't tire of you any time soon, my dear, for who will protect you then?"

The night before we leave for Paris, the king allows me to return to my own chambers. He has many demands on his time before we leave in the morning, and I have a few things I must do to get ready as well.

Sybella finds me there, packing up my few possessions. One eyebrow arches, in mockery or amusement, I can never be certain with her. "The king has allowed you out of your cage?"

I throw one of the old riding boots I am holding at her, then shove the other one into my pack. "He is convinced that I mean to accede to his punishment."

"And what of you? Are you convinced this charade still has merit?"

"Yes."

She nods, then hands me my boot and peers down at my small pile of possessions. I shove the boot into the pack and reach for my jerkin.

She picks up a small leather packet — it is all I can do not to grab it from her — and asks, "What is this?"

"My sewing needles."

The eyebrow quirks again. "You plan to have time to stitch on our way to Paris?"

I grab the case from her hands. "Spoken like someone who has never had to mend her own clothes."

A faintly startled look crosses her face. "You have?"

"Yes."

"But surely now . . ." She waves her hand at the gaudy chain around my neck. "You no longer need to do such things."

I look down at the soft leather case I hold in my hand, feeling both proud and shy. "These are not ordinary needles," I say. "But ones I made for myself."

At her inquiring look, I continue. "The convent gave us very little to work with when they sent us out. When I felt vulnerable, I would fashion something for my needs."

"Let me see."

I hesitate briefly before opening the case and showing her.

"Why do some have red thread and others white?"

"The red have been dipped in poison. Probably not enough to kill a man, but enough to put him down for a while."

She whistles appreciatively, and I am embarrassed at the warm glow of pride her approval brings. "That is ingenious. Truly."

"Thank you." I only just resist pulling out the leather cuff I made to conceal them in and showing it to her as well. Instead, I tuck the needles into my pack. "What?" I ask as she continues to stare at me.

"You said the other night that your gift from Mortain was that you are able to sense heartbeats when someone dies. That is the only time?"

I shrug. "For the most part. As I told you, it is a useless gift."

"For the most part?"

I pause in my packing. "Once I heard a heartbeat. It was the one that led me to the dungeons in Cognac when I first discovered the prisoner. It was the strongest I had ever felt." I pause, remembering the way the heartbeat reverberated through my body, up through the very ground itself. "But the prisoner wasn't dead, and I never learned the source of the heartbeat." I shrug again. "Other than that one time —"

"Wait!" Sybella's eyes are narrowed. "When was that?"

"Around Saint Martin's day."

"No, when *precisely*?"

I stop packing and count back in my head. "It was four days after Saint Martin's day."

Sybella's intrigue becomes awe. "You felt it. You felt *him*."

"What are you talking about?"

She picks up one of my shifts from the bed and smooths it. "Remember when you offered to help me with Monsieur Fremin, I told you that the nature of Mortain's marques had changed?"

"Yes. Then we were interrupted, and you never did explain to me how."

"Well, what I did not get the chance to tell you was that the nature of Mortain himself has changed."

I frown, not understanding.

"You said you were so surprised to learn of the marriage agreement between the duchess and the king. You were not alone. That was not expected by anyone, least of all the king."

"But the duchess knew to expect it?"

Sybella shrugs. "She did not know to expect it so much as hope. It was a final, desperate effort to prevent Brittany from being engulfed by yet another war. It was an opportunity born of the Nine."

"The Nine?"

She looks at me then, spearing me with the intensity of her gaze. "It was Arduinna's last arrow. Hidden away at the convent of Saint Mortain for centuries. Guaranteed to ensure the love of whomever it struck. And the duchess had one shot. Or rather, one person who could make such a shot."

"You?" My voice sounds breathless to my ears.

"No. Our convent sister Annith."

"Annith. The perfect one. Of course."

"Don't say that!" Sybella snaps. "There is far more to her story than you can even guess at."

"Then tell me."

"It is not my story to tell. But on this day — four days after Saint Martin's day, with the armies of France encamped before Rennes, the Nine came to the duchess's aid. The Arduinnites, the convent, the hellequin —"

"They are real?"

"Even the trickster god Salonius had a hand in that day." Her voice grows distant with remembering. "But in order for Annith to take that shot, the king had to be lured onto the battlefield where she could reach him. That is where the others came in."

She sets my carefully folded shift back on the bed. "And so, with the Arduinnites on the battlements to cover them with their arrows, they rode out of the gates of Rennes, the hellequin and the Breton armies, led by Mortain himself."

My mouth drops open, and every word I know leaves my head.

"We were victorious, else we would not be here with the duchess, now the queen, but our losses were great. Including Mortain."

"But he is a god. Surely he cannot die."

"He can if he inserts himself into the affairs of man. And so he did. While he did it because it was what was best for his people, I think it was also because of Annith."

"He did it for one of his daughters?"

She cuts me a sideways glance. "That is one of the things about Annith you do not know. She is not one of Death's daughters. That was a subterfuge her mother pulled in order to find a safe home for her."

So many questions crowd onto my tongue that I do not know where to begin. "How did they not find out? Surely the nuns would know. The abbess?"

"Ah, well, you see. That was the clever part. Her mother *was* the abbess."

My head is well and truly spinning now. I sit down on the bed.

"But that is not the point of what I am telling you. The point is that Mortain died on the battlefield that day. The *god* Mortain," she corrects herself. "For as we learned then, the gods' first death results in them becoming human, their second is when they truly die."

My head cannot contain the enormity of what she has just said. I close my eyes, willing the world to make sense again.

"So you see, your mistake was just one in a long line of mistakes and random turns of events. If the abbess had been a true abbess and not someone focused on keeping her own daughter safe, she would likely have not let you and Margot slip from her memory. If the Arduinnites had not offered up their last arrow to avert war, you would not have been surprised by a marriage you believed would never take place. If Mortain had not altered the very warp of his existence, he might have better answered your prayers."

My body is so full — full of surprise and anger and disappointment. I've been trying to honor a convent whose god no longer even exists. "Why didn't you tell me sooner?"

"I had to know if I could trust you first. Besides, it wasn't a scrap of news I could just toss in your lap and be done with. If you are at all like me, the news will shift your entire world and there needed to be the time and space for that sort of telling."

My sense of despair, of utter futility, must show on my face, for she suddenly leans close. "None of that, now. You believed in yourself long before the convent came along."

"That was easier when I thought I was special, sired by Mortain."

"You still are. Because *he* has changed, does not mean that we have. As Father Effram pointed out to me, the blood of gods still flows in our veins."

"Is that why you were able to do that with Fremin's body? Make his soul disappear like that?"

She tilts her head, thinking. "I don't know. I don't know if that is a power I've always had or something new now that he is gone from this world. But no matter the king's opinion or the regent's or that of the other lickspittles of the court, you are the daughter of a god, and no one can take that away from you.

"Remember that when you feel close to despair. It is what I am trying to do."

Those are not words I expected to hear from her. She is so skilled, so artful, so coolly competent. "Does it work?"

She slides me a glance. "I'll let you know."

CHAPTER 36

Maraud

They'd been in Flanders for three days and had spent every waking hour tramping through the mud-clogged streets — some with water still running up over their boots. At first they'd thought they would simply follow the flow of French soldiers, but that proved harder than expected. The constant rain didn't help, but neither did the overall confusion and lack of organization. French soldiers mingled with Flemish soldiers, along with a heap of Germans. The Flemish claimed the Germans were in charge — often with a snicker — and the Germans were distrustful of anything even remotely French, no matter how many times they explained they were simply mercenaries.

It took three days to find out where the frontline was. They'd had to stop in every tavern. Ply untold soldiers with gallons of wine, and eavesdrop until their ears shriveled. They'd finally found a sergeant who was so thoroughly disgusted by everyone that he no longer took sides. And now this.

Maraud shook his head, trying to dislodge some of the rain from his ears. "What did you say?"

"I said he ain't 'ere. Was called back to court by 'is king."

Before he knew what he was doing, Maraud's hand snaked out and grabbed the sergeant by the throat. He felt a hand on his shoulder. Heard Jaspar's voice. "Steady there, Your Lordship."

Slowly, Maraud let go of the man, but the mud was slippery. The man wind-milled his arms to try to keep his balance, but the mud won.

They all watched as he scrambled back to his feet, then retreated, tossing insults at them over his shoulder. Realizing that was the only satisfaction he was going to get, Maraud turned on his heel and walked away.

"That'll cost us," Andry muttered.

"How many of his friends d'you think he'll come back with?"

"Half dozen at least. Maybe twice that."

"They'll still end up on their asses in the mud."

"Yeah, but we'll have to go to a lot of work to get them there."

"Since when are you afraid of a little work?"

"Unpaid work always terrifies me."

Maraud ignored Andry and Tassin's bickering. Frustration seethed through him, lengthening his stride and making his fists clench. So close! Only to have it snatched away. Jaspar fell into place beside him. "It's not like you — to not have a plan. To not have a plan within a plan within yet another plan."

"Saints," Valine said from his other side, giving this the distinct feel of an ambush. "Maraud's plans have plans, who then go off and have little plan babes, until before you know it, we're knee-deep in plans. Your judgment is clouded."

He glared at her. "Like hell it is." Though maybe he should have spent a little less time thinking about Lucinda on the way here. "I told you I was going to get justice for my family. I also told you that you didn't need to come."

"It's not your need for justice or vengeance that's causing your judgment to be off. Or at least, it's not the only thing clouding your judgment." Valine's voice grew gentle, and a gentle Valine unnerved him. Maraud hunched his shoulders and kept walking.

"It's your grief."

He stopped walking so suddenly that Andry and Tassin bumped into him. "My *what?*"

"You heard me."

He shook his head and resumed walking. "You're daft. I'm not feeling grief, just a hunger for vengeance."

"You're still mourning your brother."

Saints take her! Why did she have to go and say it? Because now the pain was back, throbbing as if his arm had been hacked off. Only worse. Deeper. "Ives has been dead over a year," he said woodenly.

"It's not just your brother, but your father as well."

Maraud kept his gaze determinedly forward, anger sizzling deep in his belly. "Why would I grieve that traitorous bastard?"

Valine's voice was soft with understanding. "You're mourning the man you thought he was."

Sometimes the death of those we hate is harder to bear than that of those we love.

His own words, spoken to someone whose grief was fresh and raw came rushing back at him. "You're daft," he said again, but the words lacked conviction.

After a few moments of awkward silence, Jaspar said, "So, where to now?"

"To the French court," Maraud replied without hesitation.

"Court," Tassin grunted. "Isn't that where Lucinda said she was going?"

Maraud tried to make his shrug as indifferent as possible. "She's probably long gone by now." But if not, he could kill two birds with one stone. Because once he was done with Cassel, he was going to find Lucinda. The two of them weren't done. Not even close.

CHAPTER 37

Genevieve

uring our travels toward Paris, my mind is consumed with what Sybella has told me — both about the convent and Mortain. Some days it feels as if the knowledge of the abbess's betrayal and Mortain's abdication have lifted a veil from my eyes, making the world both brighter and more stark, but clearer at least.

On other days, like today, the knowledge presses down on me, making it difficult to not slouch in the saddle during the long day's slow ride to the next village. So much of how I saw myself, so much of what gave me value and strength, purpose and conviction, no longer applies. And while Sybella claims that the blood of a god still flows in our veins, what does that mean — or matter — if the god no longer exists?

When not even the clear joy of the villagers who greet our processional at every village we pass manages to lift my spirits, my two guards begin casting me worried glances. Whether they have been assigned to ensure that I do not run away or that I am not attacked and robbed of my expensive necklace, I do not know. It could feed three villages for a year, I've no doubt.

Fortunately it is winter and the days are short. Darkness comes quickly, and we are all parceled off to whatever accommodations can be found. Tonight, we are in luck. There is a castle nearby. Other nights we must make do with whatever inn, tavern, townhouse, or stable is available.

Although this castle is large, the royal traveling party is larger still, and the lord of the keep is hard-pressed to find places for us all. Many of the lower servants and all but a handful of our guards are lodged in the stables and cow byre.

I, however, have been given the luxury of my own room. Of course, it is a small, cramped storeroom just off the kitchen, and my two guards are posted outside. But it is warm and private, which is a great luxury.

When a dark, stooped figure appears in the doorway, my hand reaches for the hem of my skirt and the knife that hides there. The king had not thought to have me searched for weapons. Truly, he is bad at this. The figure stops — it is a woman — and raises her slim fingers to her lips. The hood slips back enough for me to recognize Sybella. She carries something in her left hand, something round and heavy.

"What did you do to the guards?" I whisper.

She raises an eyebrow, and even in the dim light, I can see the wicked gleam in her eye. "You mean those two boys with their fresh-scrubbed faces and newly sprouted whiskers, who look as if they should have gone into the clergy rather than soldiering?"

"Yes. What did you do?"

"A bit of sleep draft mixed in with their dinners. Only enough to make them mortified when they wake in the morning and realize they fell asleep while on duty."

She weaves a path between sacks of wheaten flour and barrels of oats toward me. After nudging two sacks of dried peas out of the way, she settles onto the floor. The small pop of a cork is followed by the sharp scent of wine. She lifts the jug that she has been carrying and takes a healthy swig, then holds it out to me.

"Well, sit down," she says. "I don't want to get a crick in my neck. Or are you mad at me for not telling you about Mortain sooner?"

The question surprises me. "No." Of course she would have to ensure both my trust and loyalty before sharing something of that magnitude. Besides, it's not as if I've told her all of my secrets yet, either. I do as she orders.

That settled, she takes another drink. "I was afraid I was going to stab someone if I had to endure another moment of pompous speeches, ceremonial presentations, or unctuous praying on behalf of our beloved queen, as if they hadn't all been trying to bring her down for the last two months. How the queen can bear it, I've no idea." She stretches her legs out so that one of them presses against mine.

"I'd wager she's used to it by now. Maybe not the hypocrisy, but she's no doubt had an entourage like that since birth." I take a gulp of wine, welcoming the pleasant warmth of it against my throat. It isn't watered.

Sybella leans her head back against the wall. "True enough. Although that would have sent me running years ago."

"It is a good thing you are not the duchess, then."

She smirks and holds her hand out for the jug. "I think we can all agree on that."

It is such a small thing, I realize, to share a feeble joke, but it warms me more deeply than the wine. "How is the queen?" I ask.

"Away from the palace, surrounded by ceremony and celebration rather than intrigue and backstabbing, she blossoms — her cheeks have taken on a healthier color, her eyes are less shadowed and tinged more with, if not happiness, a relief of sorts."

"That is good news. I was also worried about traveling in her condition. Especially since it is still a secret."

"We travel so slowly and for such short distances that it won't be an issue. In truth, I find it hard to believe we'll reach Paris before August at this rate."

"It is still only January," I point out.

Her mouth quirks. "Precisely." She shoves the cask at me. "Here. Maybe this will help you better appreciate my jests."

I roll my eyes and take it from her. Mayhap I will drink it all and then we can talk about jests.

"How are you doing?"

Her question causes me to choke on the mouthful of wine I've just swallowed. No, not her question — the genuine concern and compassion it holds.

"I am fine. The king has not visited me since we left Plessis, although he has set others to watching me. They are not very good at being subtle."

"In addition to the two men currently napping?"

When I nod, her lips curl in amusement. "You will have a parade at your back before you know it." Then she sobers, her glance drifting to my neck. The weight of the silver collar feels heavier under her gaze. "I still cannot believe you are letting him force you to wear that."

I blush at the faint scorn in her eyes, but she leans forward and catches my chin gently between her fingers. "My scorn is not for you, but for the pompous kingling." She gives my chin a squeeze — one could almost call it affectionate — before letting go to lean back against the wall.

"There is no harm in it for me — I can remove the chain whenever I choose. But it allows him to feel in control of something right now, and I think that aids us all, in the long run."

"How did you get so wise?" The faint mocking tone of her voice does not hide the admiration it holds.

I look down at the jug, as if contemplating my next sip. "My mother and aunts were knowledgeable in the ways of men and their foibles. They shared that knowledge with me."

She cocks her head, curious. "Tell me of this family of yours."

I lift the wine to my mouth, taking a moment to collect my thoughts. There is no reason not to tell her the truth of my upbringing — except she is noble and lovely and has such scorn for men and their appetites that I fear those feelings will carry over to my family, and they do not deserve her scorn. "They — we — are not nobly born like you. My father ran a tavern, my mother helped him in his work. My aunts all lived in the same . . . village . . . and they too would lend a hand."

"And how did your father take to being surrounded by so many helpful women?"

Her question surprises me. "He welcomed their help and helped them in turn. Everyone benefitted."

"And where did you fit in?"

I smile in memory. "I was the lone child, always underfoot, asking questions, trying my hand at any little kitchen or garden task they would entrust me with."

Her lips curve upward. "They sound charming." There is no hint of mockery in her voice. "I would think it hard to leave a family like that. For me the convent was a refuge, but I imagine for you it was something else."

The memory of that loss is as sudden as a fist to my gut. I look down at the earthenware jug in my hands. "It was."

"How old were you?"

"Seven." I take a generous swig of the wine, then shove the jug at her. "And you?"

She looks out the window. "Fourteen."

"Fourteen! Why did they wait so long to send you?"

She barks out a bitter laugh. "*They* did not send me at all." Her finger drifts up to caress the base of her neck. "My old nurse did. When she feared I was at the end of my rope. Ha!" She nudges me with her knee. "That's a good one."

I tilt my head. The jest escapes me, and I furtively weigh the cask in my hand, wondering how much she had before she came to fetch me.

She lets her head fall back against the wall and closes her eyes with a sigh.

I do not know what she is thinking, but it is like watching someone be pulled down into dark, murky depths. I search for something to say that will call her back. "Do you want to hear what the regent had to say when she caught us together?" There. Talking about the regent ought to cheer her right up.

Her eyes fly open. "Go on," she says.

I tell her of the regent's disturbing visit and my concern as to how much she might have heard. When I have finished, Sybella swears and holds her hand out for the jug. We fall silent, thinking of all the ways this could have gone horribly wrong.

As if discerning the direction of my thoughts, Sybella nudges me with her foot again. "This is not solely your fault."

I open my mouth to argue, but she reaches across our legs and puts a finger on my lips, its warm firmness startling me into silence.

"Even your decision to trade favors with the king to gain mercy for the convent does not rest solely on your shoulders."

Hearing my foolish actions fall from her lips causes my body to grow warm with embarrassment. "Of course it was! It was my idea, my plan, my lips that shared with him the convent secrets."

"What else were you to do? How were you to know the letter was a lie? That Angoulême had betrayed both you and the convent?" A deep frown creases her brow. "I still cannot guess what game he plays. After the Duke of Orléans, he is next in line for the throne. Could this be some way of trying to block the marriage or prevent it from producing an heir?"

"I have not been able to see how such a scheme would play out. Besides, as you say, the Duke of Orléans is next in line. Surely it is he and his heirs who would benefit. But either way, isn't that what they trained us to look for? This sort of scheming and lying?"

She is quiet, considering. "Mayhap. But it is not a skill one can fully master by twelve years of age. Besides, were any of your decisions made out of malice?"

"No!"

"Revenge?"

"No."

"Then it was not your fault. You did what any number of us would have done in your place. What you were trained to do. Used your judgment and Mortain's guidance — if he bothered to offer any, which he did far too infrequently. The gods seem to amuse themselves by using us at their whim to achieve their own ends."

As she speaks, it feels like an invisible bucket of warm water is being gently poured over my head, sending rivulets of gentle heat down my limbs, across my skin, seeping, somehow, into my very bones. My body feels heavy with relaxation, and I want to laugh with relief and cry from the sheer magnitude of it.

Grace. It is one of Father Effram's words and reminds me of that moment when I first experienced the souls of the dead. First experienced the fullness of Mortain's gifts.

Except the fullness of this moment is wholly human.

Unsettled by how quickly my body accepts the forgiveness she is giving, how hungry I am for it, I grumble, "Easy for you to say, when you've never made such a monstrous mistake."

A gale of laughter bursts from her, so sudden that she slaps a hand across her mouth lest others should hear. As she laughs mirthlessly into her palm, I cannot help but feel I have just made yet another blunder. In trying to push away the comfort she offered, I have caused her pain, which has never been my intention. And yet, I realize glumly, it is what I do with everyone.

"If you only knew the sheer number and horror of the mistakes I have made," she finally says, the shadows back in her eyes and darker than before. "The lives I have cost." She looks bleakly at the wall above my head.

"Surely if my mistakes are not my fault, then neither were yours?" I offer.

Her gaze snaps back down to mine. "You don't know what you're talking about."

"Mayhap," I concede. "It would not be the first time. But surely if I am absolved of my crimes for having made the best choice I could with limited knowledge, then that would also apply to you."

She opens her mouth to argue, and I long to put my fingers to her lips to shush her. But am not quite that brave. I hold up my hand instead. "How old were you?"

"For which mistake?"

"Let's start with the first one."

She looks down at the jug in her hand "Ten."

"So younger even than when I was sent from the convent. And, according to your earlier story, not even aware that you were one of Mortain's daughters. Was your decision made out of malice?"

She blinks slowly, as if trying to orient her mind to what I am saying. "No."

"Revenge?" I ask, more softly.

She glares at me, and I am struck again by her beauty. "No."

"Were you trying to prove yourself?"

"Protection. I was looking for protection."

The word reminds me of my mother and my aunts, so many of whom spent their early lives looking for that very thing. "Well," I say crisply. "I cannot think of a single decision a ten-year-old could make while looking for safe harbor that would be anything other than innocent."

"But —"

"While a child may be able to burn down a farm, if he has not learned the power of flames, how can it truly be his fault?"

"I *was* playing with fire," she mutters, not to me, but to whatever ghosts lurk inside her. "But what of when I was old enough to understand its power?"

I stare at her, only barely able to imagine how many horrors she's endured. "If no one showed you where the bucket was kept, or even how to use it to douse the flames, how can you be expected to simply know such things?"

"I was trying to use the bucket," she whispers. "I wanted so badly to put out the fire that ravaged our lives."

"What happened to . . . the bucket?"

"It was consumed by the flames." Her words fall softly into the silence, but fill it almost beyond bearing.

"Not your fault," I say firmly. "A tragedy that was simply playing itself out."

She holds my gaze, before finally closing her eyes. For a moment, I imagine I hear her heart beating. *Tha-bump, tha-bump.* A tendril of panic tries to rise up, but she is so clearly not dead that I beat it back down. Then, just as quickly, the sound is gone, and I can see the rigidness of her body melt away. When she opens her eyes, the darkness is only shadows, the sort found in any darkened room, and her face is younger somehow, yet older as well. As if she has gained both wisdom as well as her lost innocence.

She sighs noisily. "Very well. You win. It is neither of our faults. It is both or nothing."

Feeling as if I am holding something more fragile than a spider's web, I whisper, "Agreed."

ugly crown of France that is too large for her does not mar the import of the moment. Indeed, it adds to it as the Duke of Orléans silently holds it in place for her, even going so far as to lower it when she kneels. It adds greatly to the charm of the child queen, and no amount of gold the regent wears will detract from that.

Even so, my body is tensed, and I keep expecting the regent to step forward and call a halt to the ceremony. The weight of my knives is heavy against my wrists as I wonder what I would do if that happened.

Since it is not wise to stare too long, I resume contemplating the murder of the Bishop of Albi and the king's confessor. They continue to whisper poison in the king's ear. We must find some way to neutralize their influence before any of their plans come to fruition. I long to look among the lesser court for Gen, but refrain. For all that I hate that be-damned chain she is wearing, she is our best access to the king. Even though the queen is back in his good graces, he greatly limits the scope of their interaction.

When at last the cardinal daubs the queen's brow with oil, places the scepter of France in her right hand, and pronounces her the queen of France, something deep inside me finally eases. The queen looks up just then, and our gazes meet. She is queen — in the eyes of the Church and France. It is a holy anointing of her rights and duties under the auspices of the Church, and therefore no longer something political, but an authority derived from God Himself. She will be far harder to cast aside now. If that is what the regent was planning.

When we finally step outside the basilica, every street, every corner, every doorway of the city is packed with people, and every one of them lifts their voice to cheer the new queen of France.

The regent looks as if she has just taken a bite from a wormy apple. That is when I indulge in my first smile of the day.

CHAPTER 38

Sybella

 fter two long weeks of ambling through every village, town, and city between Plessis and Paris, we reach Saint-Denis, just outside Paris, where the coronation is to take place. At long last the day has come, and as I stand on the platform erected in the choir of the basilica, I study the twenty-two bishops in attendance, contemplating the ones I would like to kill. It is the most unholy of thoughts to have in such a place, but it is also the only thing I can do to keep myself from pointedly glaring at the regent.

She is holding the long satin train of the queen's gown while the cardinal archbishop of Bordeaux says the coronation mass. It is supposed to be a gesture of honor and support, but that is not how the regent means it. Rather than a sign of her fealty, it is one meant to intimidate and crowd. It is the same tactic used by my father and Pierre when silent intimidation was called for. If I had possessed any doubt, it disappeared when Madame appeared beside the queen dressed in cloth of gold, an attempt to overshadow the queen's modest white gown.

It does not work. The light pouring in from the high-arched beams of the cathedral cast the queen in a nearly ethereal light. She is dressed simply, although elegantly. Her long mink-colored hair falls in two braids at her shoulders, and her face shines with youthful beauty, deep devotion, and the solemnity of the occasion. Even the somewhat

CHAPTER 39

Maraud

By the time they drew near Paris, four weeks of rain had finally cooled Maraud's temper. That and being out of the mud. He'd decided he was no longer mad about the poisoning incidents. Indignant, yes. Mad, no. Especially as the first time was in self-defense, when he'd tried to overpower her, and the second time had been a farce all along. And the third, well, it had been her misdirected effort to save him from himself.

Most of the other things that had angered him were about wounded pride. That she'd got the jump on him — twice. That she'd saved his life — twice. The last time in particular didn't sit well. He'd told her to leave, but she'd ignored him and come back, giving him the precious minutes he needed for the others to arrive.

He had needed her help.

All of these occasions had one thing in common: Maraud not seeing her as an equal. He'd told himself that he knew better — knew what was best.

And he'd been wrong.

His hand clenched around the glass vial as he realized how rutting stupid he was. Why would she trust him? A prisoner, who tried to overpower her. A man whose family had betrayed the duchess. And then he'd gone and tried to make her fit into his plan — essentially telling her that his needs were more important than hers. Saints, he was an idiot. Three times an idiot.

Would she still be at court? Or would she have concluded her business and be long gone?

Had she managed to save the innocents she'd been so worried about? He hoped so.

Up ahead, Jaspar whistled, and reined in his horse. Maraud shoved the vial into the leather pouch at his waist, then pulled alongside him to survey the city ahead — Saint-Denis.

Even from their vantage point he could hear the music of celebration and the cheers of the solid mass of people filling the streets. A small cluster of figures stood on the steps of the basilica. Maraud could make out the king and queen, but only because of the crowns on their heads. Everyone else was so far away as to be indistinguishable from one another. Even Cassel's bulk was disguised by the distance. But he was here. Maraud felt it in his bones.

"The watch captain said the royal party will ride to Paris first thing in the morning," Jaspar reported. "A processional to introduce the new queen to her people. She'll be accompanied by the entire court. If Cassel is with her, you'll have a chance to see him then."

Maraud sighed and eyed the crowd of revelers still gamboling through the narrow streets. "Do you think there is any lodging to be had for the night?"

Andry snorted. "Probably not. We'll be lucky to find a stable to sleep in."

"Better'n mud," Tassin muttered.

CHAPTER 40

The hardest part was getting across the damned bridge. There were more people clogging the streets of Paris than there were fish in the sea. Boats filled the river, all clustering near the island like piglets sucking on teats. They perched on top of the rooftops of the houses that lined both sides of the bridge that led to Notre Dame, leaning out of the windows and gathering in the doorways, spilling out onto the bridge and blocking the way. The nobler families that lived in the elegant storied houses were all likely waiting at the cathedral, although a few seemed to be having parties and were perched on windowsills to watch. Even the servants seemed to have abandoned their duties and puddled around the houses like voluminous skirts.

"There's no way a royal procession can get through this crowd," Jaspar muttered.

"Maybe they'll part like the Red Sea when they get here," Maraud said. It was one big field of people, none of them with the sense God gave a sheep. They just stood there, milling and gawking. How they expected the royal party to get through was anyone's guess. He tried to use his elbows to force a path, but the crowd was implacable, and they were stuck in it as it slowly oozed toward Notre Dame. Maraud felt swallowed by the whole of it, almost like being swallowed by the mummer's dance.

Only this time with more stinking and shoving.

They finally popped through the final throng of bystanders on the bridge, only to find the streets of the island itself just as crowded.

"Just keep moving toward the spire," Andry said.

When they drew nearer the cathedral, Maraud used his elbows

again to work to the edges, then broke free at last. The others followed in his wake, stumbling out behind him.

The square was bursting with so much color and life that it momentarily dazzled his eyes. Vibrant tapestries, boughs of greenery, and cartloads of flowers — even in winter! — filled every available space not taken up by the stone cathedral. Maraud had seen the cathedral only once before, and it seemed even more impressive now with its tall spires reaching toward the heavens for what seemed like miles.

"We going to stand here like rocks in a stream?" Tassin barely spared the cathedral a glance.

"Never realized how much I hated crowds," Jaspar muttered.

"I prefer the mud," Andry said. "It smelled better."

People lined both sides of the street, sitting in the gutters and hanging from windows and ledges. A wooden platform had been built near the cathedral — a stage of sorts, with a tall mechanical contrivance nearby. "We can sit at the base of that tower and see the entire square." Even better, the legs would offer some cover if Maraud needed to hide his face.

Nearly two hours later, a roar started up on the bridge. Maraud hopped up and climbed a few feet on the wooden tower. The banners on the bridge were unfurling, and voices cheered. His heart beat faster. The carefully banked ember that lurked deep in his belly flared to life, and his jaw tightened with anticipation.

"They're coming," he called down to the others.

Valine shielded her eyes and looked up at him. "Aren't you worried Cassel will spot you?"

"He's too arrogant to pay attention to the crowd. And if he does, I have this." He thumped the wooden beam he was clinging to.

Valine nudged his boot with her elbow and pointed to his right. "He might not bother with the crowd, but will he stop to watch the play?"

Maraud looked to the right of the platform, where costumed players scrambled in a flurry of last-minute preparations. He half expected to see Rollo or

Jacquette grinning at him, but these men were town fathers and guild members rather than mummers. "We won't be onstage."

The crowd around the cathedral erupted in a deafening cheer. The procession had arrived. Serving as the queen's honor guard, officers of the city and members of parliament rode their mounts as if they were royalty and not she, but the crowd's noise was so loud he couldn't even hear their horses' hooves on the cobbles. Across the square, an older woman collapsed dramatically into the arms of her friends.

Maraud cocked an eyebrow at Valine and leaned in close so she could hear. "You going to faint when you see her?"

She shoved her elbow into his ribs so hard that he grunted. By the time he was upright again, the queen's litter had rounded the corner. Maraud studied her escort, searching out the big ones with a military bearing.

Maraud saw General Cassel the moment he emerged in the square, as if his need for justice was so great that it could sniff the man out like a hound.

Jaspar nudged his shoulder. Maraud nodded without taking his eyes from the general. He hadn't changed. Still the same ugly, arrogant bastard. Still surveying the world around him as if he were a wolf trying to decide which sheep to eat next. No, not a wolf. They killed only out of need. Cassel was more like one of the big hunting cats that chose quarry just to maim and torture for their own amusement.

The memory of the general's face, his arm as it swung toward Ives flashed brightly. *Found you, you great big hairy bastard. I'm coming for you.*

The tower he was leaning against began to rumble — so close and deep that he felt it in his gut — as great gears and chains began to move within it. He leapt back, head tilted upward. A man dressed as Peace began descending from the sky — as if from heaven itself. On the stage below waited a man dressed as War. The crowd watched in awed silence. Once low enough that he could leap from the contrivance onto the stage, Peace seized War by the throat and drove a sword through his heart, killing him on the spot.

The crowd roared its approval, and the queen smiled prettily. Maraud was the only one not smiling. He was too busy planning the moment when he could do the same to Cassel.

As the actors playing France and Brittany embraced, trumpets blared and the crowd in the square erupted into renewed cheers. Even the queen — *his* queen — clapped her hands in delight.

When the cheering finally subsided, she waved once more, then the procession moved across the square to the palace. The crowd surged forward, nearly cutting her off from her own attendants, who followed along behind her. Close to twenty ladies in waiting rode behind the queen's litter, their brightly colored gowns brilliant in the sun. A shaft of sunlight sparkled off a woman's silver necklace, nearly blinding him. As he blinked the dark spots from his vision, she turned to stare at the tower that had so miraculously lowered Peace. Her eyes were wide with wonder. Golden brown eyes that made his breath catch in his throat.

Lucinda. She *was* still at court.

Maraud waited until she, reluctantly it seemed to him, hurried to catch up to the others, then fell into step beside Valine, and allowed the dispersing crowd to separate them from the others. Not so much that they'd never find each other, but enough that they couldn't hear every word he said to Valine. "I need you to do something for me."

"What?"

"It would be best if you could do it without asking questions."

She raised one eyebrow. "It would be best if Tassin would quit picking his teeth after he eats, but that doesn't seem likely."

Maraud sighed. "I need you to get a message to someone."

"There's a reason you can't go?"

Maraud looked over at the queen's departing procession. "Because the person is in residence at the palace."

Valine gave a low whistle. "Good reason. Now for the important question. Who am I to get this message to? Do they have information on Cassel?"

Maraud grabbed on to that. "Yes, I think they do."

"Okay, then. Who and when?"

Maraud casually looked up as if admiring the cathedral. "Lucinda," he told the spires that towered above them.

When the quiet stretched out so far he thought she hadn't heard, he risked glancing back at her. She was smirking. "Jaspar owes me. I knew things weren't over between you two."

"You placed a wager?"

She ignored his offended pride. "What makes you think she's at the palace?"

"I saw her just now. She was riding with the queen's attendants and courtiers."

Valine whistled again. "Coming up in the world is our Lucinda. I wonder who she's planning to poison this time."

Maraud sighed. "And if you don't say anything to the others, I'll pay you twice whatever Jaspar owes you."

CHAPTER 41

e do not stay at the royal palace in the old city but cross the river to the Louvre, which sits on the right bank of the Seine. It is the moment I've come to hate the most — this arriving at a new place for the night. The long moments of awkwardness strung out like pearls on a chain, each one plump with dread and embarrassment at the last-minute scramble to decide where to put me.

But this time, it seems to all have been decided beforehand, and an understeward escorts me past the queen's apartments on the ground floor to a chamber on the first floor, where the king's rooms are. It is a large, well-appointed room, the sort that would be assigned to a court favorite. It is less heavy feeling than most of the palace rooms. Perhaps because the rich curtains and wall hangings are of a softer blue, shot through with yellow. A large canopied bed dominates one wall, and an equally large fireplace the other. The third wall holds an oriel window — a true luxury.

The understeward's gaze lingers briefly on my necklace before he bows out of the room. I have gotten somewhat used to the opulence of the French court after the last five years, but have never had it lavished on me. Not wishing to dwell on what it might mean, I cross to the window. It looks down into the palace courtyard, the stables and barns to the north, the armory and smithy to the south. The courtyard itself is full of vendor stalls — indeed, it is nearly a small market — set up to take advantage of the arrival of all the nobles with their easy coin. My stomach twists in hunger — not for what they are selling, but for the freedom of being outside wandering in a crowd, unwatched.

At the door I pause, trying to decide the best approach. In the end, I decide to brazen it out. I have not been forbidden to go anywhere. Yet.

I open the door and step into the hallway, smiling brightly at the guards. "I'm going to visit the market stalls," I say as I begin walking. Gilbert gapes at me, then looks to Roland, unsure what to do. Before they can decide to stop me, I call out over my shoulder, "Well, are you coming?" I flutter my lashes. As always, Gilbert grows flustered and blushes, but it diverts his mind from protesting.

Outside in the courtyard, rubbing shoulders with pie sellers and ribbon vendors, fruit mongers and wine merchants, my skin pulls less tightly over my bones, and it is easier to breathe.

Gilbert and Roland are uneasy in the crowd. Not for fear of me wandering away, but simply because they are as out of place as a two-headed cat. Ignoring them, I peruse the bright silken ribbons fluttering gaily in the breeze.

A woman examining a length of green cord brushes against my skirts, then murmurs an apology. "I beg pardon, my lady. No offense."

My hand on the ribbon stills. The voice is familiar and a jolt of recognition flares through me. While she now wears the gown and the headscarf of a serving woman, it is Valine.

As she slowly drifts over to the fruit seller's stall, a hundred different possibilities run through my head, none of them pleasant.

With a quick glance at my constant shadows, I stroll after her, as if she is a serving woman I am familiar with. When I am close enough, I murmur, "What are you doing here? Is Maraud hurt?"

She shoots me a sideways look before directing her attention back to the fruit. "And why, I wonder, is that your first worry?"

I open my mouth, then realize I have no explanation. "Mercenaries lead dangerous lives, and he is not one to shy away from impossible odds. It is not so strange an assumption."

She runs her finger along the skin of a golden late-winter pear. "No," she agrees amiably. "But one could also conclude you had reason to think he might be injured." Her gaze rakes over me, taking in my gown, my necklace. Her lip curls faintly.

She knows. She knows Maraud was not overcome with wine sickness, but that I had something to do with it. Mayhap he could not be bothered to exact vengeance himself and has sent her in his stead.

I, too, study the pears. "Do not play coy. It does not suit you any more than it suits me. I gave him a draft so he would not follow me and do something foolish. I am not trying to hide it from you."

She looks up, weighing and assessing my words as surely as her fingers weigh and assess the pear in her hand. She lightly drops it back into the basket. "Now, that does sound like him. And no, he is not dead or injured or even fighting a chill."

"Then why are you here? And how did you find me?"

"He saw you in the procession this morning. He was most . . . surprised." The sideways glance she casts confirms my suspicion that that word was not her first choice. "He wishes to speak with you."

My heart lifts even as my stomach drops, and a dozen different thoughts and possibilities crowd into my head. I resist the urge to check over my shoulders for my guards. "Why?"

An amused smile plays about her lips. As much as I like her, my hand itches to smack it off her face. I pick up an apple instead.

"He wishes to learn about General Cassel before he approaches the court."

Of course. Understanding is followed closely by an inexplicable disappointment. "It is a wise move. The general is in the deep confidences of the king."

Valine swears softly. "Which makes this twice a fool's errand, then."

"You do not approve of his desire for justice?"

"I highly approve of his desire for justice. It is his belief that he can find it at court that causes me to think he has exchanged his brains for a turnip."

"It will not be easy," I agree. "Cassel counsels the king in many things, not simply battle strategy."

Valine sighs down at the pear, as if it is too poor a quality to purchase. "Well, he will not believe it from my lips — they have said as much a dozen times already. Perhaps he will believe it from yours. He suggested meeting tonight. There is to be a coronation ball, yes?"

"Yes, but —"

"He thinks that will provide the best opportunity for him to get onto the palace grounds and allow you to slip away from your . . . duties. Where shall I tell him to meet you?"

"There is no good place." Nowhere that is safe from the king and his spies. Or the regent and hers.

"He said you might balk. If you did, I was to remind you that you owe him at least this much."

"Do I? Even after I saved his life — four times — at Camulos's Cup?"

She nods her head, conceding the point. "Sometimes anger makes us forget how the scales of justice are weighed."

What should I tell her? To slip out and meet him risks destroying the fragile trust I am trying to build with the king.

As if that is not already lying shattered at my feet.

The king has not visited me in over two weeks. It is possible that, having punished me, he is done with the matter.

"Although he would gut me if he knew I told you, Maraud thinks of you constantly." Valine's voice is soft with the affection she holds for him.

And I him, I want to say, but do not. However, my capacity for hope is larger than my ability to learn from my mistakes. "Very well. Tell him to meet me at —" My mind scrambles, trying to come up with a likely location where we won't be discovered. "The smithy. And for the love of the saints, tell him to wear a disguise lest he be recognized."

Valine turns her face to mine, all the amusement and humor gone. "And you, Lucinda? How are you faring?" Her genuine concern unnerves me.

I laugh, pleased that it does not sound forced. I feel Gilbert and Roland look at me. "How can you ask? I am settled in the richest court in the land, with every luxury at my fingertips."

Her gaze seeks out the silver necklace at my throat. "That is no answer." Then she disappears into the crowd, and I am left standing there, wondering if I am being given a chance to put things right or will make yet another foolish blunder.

CHAPTER 42

My guards murmuring, "Your Majesty," is all the announcement I receive before the king arrives. My heart beats painfully against my ribs as I curtsy. Was I spotted in the courtyard talking to Valine? Surely, that would not be cause for remark.

When he waves me to my feet, I stand. "I am surprised to see you here, sire, but glad." The entire point of this exercise is to encourage his company.

"I came to see how you find your room. Do you like it?"

I take in the enormous room and rich furnishings. "It is luxury far beyond any I have ever experienced, let alone expected."

He clasps his hands behind his back. "I chose it myself," he says with an almost shy pride. He wants me to like it. Cares what I think of his choice. "It is but a few doors down from my own chamber. With the queen and the coming babe, I thought it best if we met somewhere other than my apartments."

A giddy little beat of hope thumps against my chest. The bond between us has held, in spite of my confession.

"Your discretion is most kind, sire."

He smiles, then looks away, his gaze landing on the apple I hold in my hand. "Where did you get that?"

I motion to the window. "The courtyard is full of vendors and stalls. It felt good to stretch my legs after so many days of riding." I hesitate. "I hope that does not displease you, that I visited the court-yard? My guards were with me the entire time."

He saunters toward the window. "But of course you may have free rein of the palace and its grounds. Just remain within the palace walls." To his credit, he does not even look at the necklace to warn me of our agreement.

I smile brightly, then follow him to the window. "There." I point. "That is the woman with these honey sweet apples. And did you see the man with the little monkey in the silk doublet?" I am not flirting with him but trying to extend the moment of simple companionship a little longer. "There is a Flemish wine seller, silk ribbons of all colors, songbirds in little wicker cages, and even a dancing bear!"

He looks at me, glancing from my eyes to my cheeks, which grow pink under his perusal, and I realize I must present the very picture of pastoral, maidenly allure. He smiles wistfully. "I wish I could see it as you do," he says. "The Princess Marguerite also took great delight in the world around her."

He still misses her. Mayhap not as a betrothed, but as someone who had been his cheerful companion for nearly eight years.

"You can," I say gently. "Come." I tilt my head toward the door. "Let me show you all the simple delights your own courtyard holds."

He smiles. "I would like that."

CHAPTER 43

Sybella

onight is a crowning achievement, the queen's shining face far brighter than any of the hundreds of candles they have brought in to light the grand salon. The king is at her side, polite and attentive. The two of them are surrounded by dignitaries and the highest nobles in France. The regent is not nearly far enough away for my liking, but at least she is not hovering like a macabre crow.

That role is reserved for the bishops and the king's confessor, whom I do my best to ignore. They will not steal this victory from us, from her, for all that they have tried. The Bishop of Albi looks up just then, his gaze finding me across the room and narrowing in distaste. He whispers something to the confessor.

Refusing to let them dampen my spirits, I ignore them and examine the rest of the crowd, looking for Genevieve. Although I spend a few minutes searching, I see no signs of her. Surely the king has not confined her to her room. Just as I decide I will go check, Father Effram sidles up next to me.

"Lady Sybella." His bright blue eyes focus on mine with such intensity that I am momentarily nonplussed.

"Good evening, Father. Have you seen Genevieve this evening?"

"Not yet. Perhaps she is in the chapel?"

"Gen? In the chapel?" I nearly laugh.

He shrugs. "I *did* say 'perhaps,' my lady. You have had good fortune finding those you seek there."

I stare at his lively face a moment before his meaning becomes clear. "Oh!" I say, then hurry out of the room, trying with all my might to not break into a run.

The chapel is lit by flickering candlelight that reflects off the stained-glass windows and casts everything in jewel-toned shadows. In the front a lone man kneels in prayer, the width of his shoulders leaving little room for anyone else to join him there.

At my arrival, his head lifts, but he does not turn around until I am standing behind him. Slowly, he rises to face me, my heart nearly bursting from my chest at the sight of him. "You're back," I whisper, afraid to say it too loudly, lest I wake up and find it a dream.

"And you are well." Beast's pale blue eyes glow like the colored glass of the windows as he takes my hand. It fits inside his enormous callused one as neatly as a glove.

"I told you I would be."

"You did." His gaze does not leave mine. "But I have learned the world often has other plans for you than the ones you make."

"I cannot be blamed for that." I laugh as I draw him away from the nave toward a small room that opens up off the rostrum. I do not think anyone will be visiting this chapel tonight, but there is no reason to be careless.

"I make you laugh, do I?" he growls.

"Always."

He peers down at me. "You are different. Lighter. As if you've clouds inside your skin instead of bones and blood."

I rise up on my toes. "It is simply my joy that you are back."

"It is infectious," he murmurs, capturing my lips, as if he, too, wishes to be filled with clouds.

It is a heady thing, this moment, this kiss. For nearly six weeks, I have longed for this moment, even as I feared it might never come.

He pulls away just enough so that our eyes meet. "You missed me."

I close the door behind us. "What makes you think that?"

"You did not even ask if the girls were safe."

I snort and place my hands on his shoulders, savoring the rock-solid feel of him. "That is not because I missed you, but because I knew you wouldn't be here if they were not." It is truly a miracle to trust someone so very much. I pull his mouth back toward mine. "You are as dependable as the plague," I murmur.

His hands move up to cradle my face. I close my eyes, savoring the roughness of his palms against my cheek. Savoring this sense of being cherished, of being precious.

Then his lips are on mine, and I revel in the feel of them, warm and soft, with hunger lurking just beneath the surface. Hunger that is far more than simply the time apart, but speaks to the danger we have both been in, the desperate need to believe we would be safe until we could be with each other again.

"I love you," I whisper. "I love the way you kiss and the way you touch me and the way you always, always see me. And accept whatever I am. Whoever I am in that moment. Truly, you are the gods' greatest gift."

He looks as if I have taken a poleax to his head. As if he has never expected such words from me. And perhaps he hasn't. His face grows serious with the weight of his own emotions, his mouth parting slightly in surprise.

Before he has time to respond, I reach out, grab his head with my hands, and bring his lips to mine. He does not resist, his mouth hungry and warm, his wide hands coming around my waist, sliding upward and drawing me closer. My fingers relish the solid, implacable feel of his muscles beneath his linen shirt. Savor the hard planes of his stomach, the faint traces of the myriad scars that he wears as easily as that shirt. And heat. The man is like a smelting furnace. I gently nip his bottom lip and angle my head to deepen the kiss, swallowing the groan that escapes him.

It is like a dam breaking, and all that I have been feeling in the last hours, days, weeks, rushes at me in one giant wave that leaves me lightheaded, dizzy, wanting. Beast has seen me, at my worst and my best, and in those moments when I am both at once.

He not only welcomes those parts of me, but rejoices in them.

He pulls his mouth from mine, his lips working their way to my ear, nibbling and tasting. "Sybella."

We want to take our time, to enjoy all the kisses we feared we would not have, to slowly welcome each other home — for wherever we both are is home — I know that now. But everything that I feel in that moment is so big and overwhelming that it cannot be contained in one body. I slip my hands around to his back, bringing him closer. He groans, then presses his entire body against mine so that I am engulfed by him, awash in sensation that licks at my skin like flames until I am utterly consumed.

With exquisite tenderness, he lays me down on the floor and then the time for tenderness is gone. "I will not break," I murmur against the hard line of his jaw.

"No." He grins. "But I might." And then he is on top of me, covering me, warming me, loving me, and I give myself over to the magic that only he is able to work upon my body.

When we have taken our pleasure, we lie together with my arm draped over his chest, feeling the steady — if somewhat rapid — thudding of his heart against my ribs. His hand runs lazily through my hair, stopping to rub strands of it between his fingers. He shifts so that he can look down at me. "Do you think that we will ever manage to do this in a bed?"

"A bed," I scoff. "Where is the fun in that?" But, oh, how I long for such simple meetings. Not wishing to think of that right now, I let the questions that have simmered inside me for weeks come tumbling out. "How did things go at the convent?"

He shifts under me, making himself comfortable. "Annith was not as surprised to see us as you might think."

"What do you mean?" I murmur, kissing the rough misshapen shell of his ear, wondering if anyone has ever done that.

He flinches and reaches up to rub it, so I'm guessing not. "She said Sister Vereda had seen us coming."

"So the old woman is still alive."

"And thriving, according to Annith. Balthazaar's arrival has breathed new life into her."

Is it just my imagination, or does he hesitate ever so slightly over that name? "And Balthazaar?" He is not Mortain any longer, but it is still hard to separate the two.

He shrugs, making it feel as if the earth beneath us is moving. "Ah, he seems to be well. I think he's still adjusting to the wonders of being human."

"And the girls?"

Beast puts his free arm around me, pulling me closer. "They will do fine there." His voice is filled with absolute surety, but the vise of my worry will not let go.

"What makes you say that?"

"Because Annith and the others have had years of experience taking in frightened, wounded girls. Because all the nuns were kind and welcoming. Sister . . . the older, fussy one who loves clothes?"

"Beatriz. That is Sister Beatriz."

"She took Louise under her wing immediately, petting and coddling her like a small dog. Louise enjoyed it for a grand total of one day before whispering to Annith that she really didn't want to spend her entire day being fitted for new gowns."

I laugh with relief and joy that Louise felt comfortable enough to state her desires so plainly. "And what of Charlotte?"

"She took longer to warm up to any of them. Insisted on sleeping outside with the Arduinnites for the first two nights. But Sister Thomine arranged with

Aeva to have her come watch as they were training in the yard, and that got her attention. They told her if she trained with them, she would be allowed into the armory to see the weapons. After that, she moved into the dormitory bed next to her sister."

"Does Louise partake in the training?"

"No, she is enamored of the horses and has attached herself to Sister Widona."

My mind reels back through time, to my own arrival at the convent. I arrived damaged and broken, nearly feral with grief and anger. "Widona and Thomine were the ones who calmed me when I first showed up on their doorstep. Louise and Charlotte will be naught but a breeze for them after what I put them through."

He gently takes my hand, covering it with his blunt, warm fingers. "I have met them, Sybella, and I know they would take issue with the suggestion that you had put them through anything. Indeed, I think they would say instead 'after what you had suffered.'"

His words are meant to comfort me and challenge the way I see myself. They succeed at both. "Did Balthazaar seem to mind them being there?"

"No." Beast grins. "Especially once he was reassured they were not yet more of his daughters."

I snort. "Won't Annith love that — never knowing if her consort's unnumbered children will be showing up on her door."

"She seems to take everything in stride."

"I'm sure she does," I murmur, remembering how comfortable she's always been at the convent. How strong she's always been in her faith. How she was the one who oversaw the younger girls' happiness, ever since I'd first arrived.

I allow the knowledge that my sisters are safe to soak in. Feel it ease the gnawing at my heart that I have endured for months. "Is that what took you so long? Waiting to get the girls settled?"

"No." The word is almost gruff, and something inside him shifts. "There is more to the story, I'm afraid. None of it good."

I pull back to better see his face, but it is mostly hidden by shadow. "What is it?"

"Rohan is gearing up for something."

"What do you mean? I thought that was the entire point of overriding the queen's counsel and installing the king's man as governor of Brittany?"

"One would think, but we could not get through to Rennes. All the roads to and from the city were patrolled by Rohan's men. We sent scouts and learned that everyone had to check in with the city watch and state their business. We could not take the risk. Not with my face being so recognizable. It also seemed too great a risk to try to contact Ismae or Duval if Rohan had the entire city under that close a watch. We left the next morning for the convent."

Beneath me, his heartbeat shifts, increasing ever so slightly. "Our path to the convent took us through Rohan's lands, which slowed us down considerably, as we did not wish to be seen. But worse than that was that every one of his strongholds was fully garrisoned, with additional soldiers encamped outside the keeps. We had the devil's own time evading them without being seen. Fortunately, we had the Arduinnites' help in that."

He squints down at me. "Is it possible that word of our absence reached the king and he sent word to Rohan to intercept us?"

"No. The king did send a search party the second day you'd been gone, but he was looking for Fremin's henchmen, not you."

"Did they find them?"

I meet Beast's steady gaze. "No."

He nods. "Good."

"And what of your return trip?" I ask. "Did you try to contact Ismae or Duval then?"

"I had hoped to, but in the few days I was at the convent, even more troops had amassed. I decided it was more important to report this situation to the queen rather than pursue Duval."

"And here you are."

He pauses. "And here I am. Lingering with you when I should be making my report." He sits up and begins to pull on his shirt.

"You couldn't have very well stormed into the coronation ball and made your announcement. It would not have been well received. Besides," I add softly, "things have not gotten smoother while you were gone."

He sighs. "I would have been surprised if they did."

There is so very much to tell him that I hardly know where to begin. "I suppose there is a piece of good news," I say lightly. "I found the missing initiate." And then I tell him of Genevieve, trying to smooth over some of the rougher edges of her story.

Beast swears. "Are you certain she is not working for France?"

"I was not at first," I admit, "but now I am certain." I sigh deeply, then tell him of Fremin coming to my room, killing him, and how Genevieve took the blame.

He is quiet a long moment. "You have been busy while I was gone," he says lightly, even as he pulls me closer, as if he would protect me from all the ills the world has to offer.

"As have you," I remind him. "There is more. Your father is here."

His entire body grows so still it is as if he has been turned to stone. "I have no father."

"Your sire, then. You know who I mean, Beast."

He pulls away from me to lie down on his back. The chill I feel has nothing to do with the removal of his body heat. "Captain Dunois spoke true. The resemblance between the two of you will be unmistakable if you are in the same room together. People are sure to notice and comment. I have already warned the queen."

He turns his head to me, a wounded look in his eye. Needing to touch him, I place my hand on his cheek. "We cannot let her go stumbling into quagmires if we can help it, and she thought nothing less of you for it."

"I think less of me for it," he mumbles.

"That is because you are a turnip brain. Besides, you cannot tell me the d'Albret blood holds no influence over me, yet also claim your father's blood holds sway over you."

He moves swiftly, rising up on his elbow and towering over me. "Have you forgotten the battle lust? The savageness that comes over me?"

"How can I forget that which has saved countless lives, yours and mine included, countless times?"

He closes his eyes, as if steeling himself against the comfort I offer. "It is just as savage as he is."

"No. It is a gift — however much a cursed one — from your saint. His is born of his own brutality and crudeness. Yours is something that comes over you when your saint bids you act. They are entirely different things, Beast."

His arms tighten almost painfully around me, sending a faint whoosh of air from my lungs. He eases his hold, but does not let go of me.

CHAPTER 44

Genevieve

t is easy enough to slip away. Even with three hundred nobles, church officers, and foreign dignitaries standing between me and the door that leads out of the grand salon where the coronation ball is being held. When I am certain both the king and regent cannot see me, I allow the ebb and flow of the crowd to carry me toward the exit, no different than a small boat bobbing on a turbulent sea.

Along with granting me his permission to roam the palace grounds, the king bid me to enjoy tonight's ball as well. While he has made my meeting with Maraud easier by granting such freedoms, I am certain that was not his intent. If he learns of it, it could set everything back.

So I will make certain he does not learn of it.

The sentries at the door barely notice me. They are not posted to keep anyone inside, nor out, for that matter. They are merely part of the pomp of the occasion.

The hallways and galleries are lit only by torches, which provide enough shadows for me to cling to in order to disguise my passage through the sparsely populated galleries and corridors. When I reach the ground floor, I clutch the shadows more firmly, then step outside into the night.

I hurry past the armory to the blacksmith's shop on the far side of it, every nerve in my body ajumble. I am both hot and cold, excited and terrified. I do not allow myself to think of how my carefully built trust with the king will crumble if he learns of our meeting, and focus instead on the debt I owe Maraud.

But of course, that debt is not the only reason.

I wish to see him with my own eyes. To know that he is unharmed. That he is the same as when I left him. And I am hungry to know why he thinks of me often.

I know why he *should* think of me often — to curse my name to the heavens. But the nature of Valine's words did not suggest that was the case.

Hope wriggles in my chest, a frail young chick trying to break free of its egg.

We danced well together, whether in a mummer's parade, a daring escape, a lover's embrace, or a sparring match. Looking back, without my fears clawing at my throat, I cannot help but wonder how things might be different at court if I had allowed him to help me.

If I had allowed myself to trust him. My hand reaches up to ensure the dangling silver chain of my necklace is completely concealed in the back of my gown. Of a certainty, it would have been better than the current mess I've made of everything.

CHAPTER 45

Maraud

Maraud had no trouble slipping into the palace grounds. All of Paris was out tonight celebrating the new queen, and crowds of people milled everywhere. There were even a few stalls — wine sellers mostly — set up, calling out their wares. Now, that would have made a fine disguise, he thought, tugging his leather jerkin into place. He'd come dressed as a tradesman — a stonemason — carrying the chain from his old mummer's costume on his belt as an excuse to visit the smithy. And if that didn't work, one of the heavy hammers or sharp chisels in his belt would.

Out of the corner of his eye, he saw a brief flicker in the shadows, then the flash of a jewel-toned gown before it disappeared into the smithy. Something lurking near his heart unclenched. She came.

The smithy was deserted, the fire banked low for the night. At first look, it appeared empty, until he stepped fully inside. She was there, toward the back.

He'd thought, once he saw her again, that he'd want to wrap his hands around her lovely neck and wring it until she felt just how angry he'd been. How betrayed he felt. How much frustration had consumed him.

He must have made some noise, for she whirled around, and their eyes met, and all he wanted to do was to touch her. To cup her cheek in his hand and rub his fingers on the skin that he knew was as delicate as a flower petal.

She looked away first, down at the chain in his hands. Her eyes widened, and her mouth twisted. "Well, you've not strangled me with it, so I guess that's something."

She'd grown thinner, he realized, the line of her jaw sharper, her eyes larger. She was also dressed in the fine silks and elaborate jewelry befitting a lady of the royal household. A deep spike of loss jabbed at him. He missed the rough-and-tumble, earthy Lucinda. Her eyes had seemed more alive, her face more vibrant then.

"Considering you haven't gone for your poisoned needles, I feel safe keeping my weapon sheathed."

Her cheeks pinkened slightly at his unintended double entendre, and oh-so-briefly, it was the old Lucinda standing before him.

"I've missed that about you." Her dark honey voice was exactly how he'd remembered it. "Your ability to turn everything into a jest."

His looby of a heart wanted to soar out of his chest. She'd missed him. "And here I thought it was one of my most annoying habits."

She frowned slightly, as if puzzled. "It was."

He wanted to place his thumb right there — on the faint crease between her brows — and smooth it away. He wanted to touch her so badly that he clenched his hands to tamp down the urge.

Her eyes darted briefly to his hands, then back to his face. "You are angry still," she said softly.

"No." Was he ever angry? At her? Or simply himself? "You've grown thin."

She gave an impatient shake of her head. "It is only the shadows." But he'd seen her in the bright light of full day, and she still looked thin. He should look away, it was probably rude staring at her so, but he could not get his fill. Before he could stop himself, he closed the distance between them. "Lucinda." It came out as a whisper.

She looked up at him, her eyes shining with what he would swear were tears. His hands clenched again with the need to touch her. To wipe away the sadness on her face.

"My name is Genevieve." It was nothing. A name. But it was everything. She was trusting him with her name.

He shouldn't touch her. It would be wrong to answer that trust by touching her, but his body didn't care about such rules of engagement. He placed one finger on her full lower lip, felt the faint trembling. When she did not pull away, he brought his other hand up and gently brushed a stray hair from her cheek. Smooth and flawless, just as he'd remembered. She drew in a ragged breath. Or maybe it was his own ragged breath. "Genevieve."

Her gaze grew dark, and she drew another trembling breath before leaning — ever so lightly — into his touch.

Inside him, need tried to claw its way out, but he ignored it. Instead, he cupped her face, relishing the shape of her jaw against his palm, the feather-light touch of her cheeks against his fingertips.

"It is not too late," he whispered. "If something is wrong, I can still help."

Her eyes flew open, wide with wonder and disbelief, and for a moment, he feared she would unravel before him.

CHAPTER 46

ith the force of an ax coming down on a rope, I am undone. My remorse is like a boulder barreling downhill, flattening everything in its path. Every twig gives way in resistance, every blade of grass is crushed beneath the onslaught. He is, once again that voice in the dark, wholly understanding, withholding all judgment. It is too much. It is far more than I have earned, and yet I am helpless before it. I want to lean into the comfort he is offering. To accept the grace he is extending. And even though a small part of my heart knows he could be setting some ghastly trap for revenge, I decide I do not care. Not if — for these few moments — I am able to believe that he is so large-hearted.

And so I let myself believe his words. Believe him. And if they or him are false, it is no more than the debt he is owed.

"I'm sorry I did not trust you before," I tell him.

"I'm sorry I didn't do a better job of earning your trust."

I shake my head. "You did, though. All the times you could have overpowered me and didn't."

"But the time I did overpower you overshadowed that. You didn't know me. I had given you only the barest scraps of the truth you had asked for. Saints! You had only my word that I was not imprisoned for the wanton murder of innocent people.

"You were alone, venturing into a dungeon cell, with few weapons at hand. Which" — he gives my shoulders a little shake — "you should never do again. Why *should* you have trusted me?"

I close my eyes. "There are many things I would never do again."

He rubs my cheek with his thumb, the faint roughness of it as sensual as any embrace. "For all that my intentions were good, they were mine and not something I shared with you. In doing so, I all but told you that my own justice, my own revenge, was more important than yours. The same when I did not trust you enough to tell you that I was sending the others on ahead to meet us in case of an ambush."

I am awash in the unexpectedness of his words. That he recognizes my concerns, sees them as valid, feels as if some invisible weight has been removed from my side of the scale.

No. From my heart.

"I took advantage of someone who I knew was grieving, and seized an opportunity for my own freedom. It was wrong, but if I am truthful, and I will be with you, I cannot say I wouldn't do it again. I could not die in that place."

His face shifts so that it is as stark and gaunt as when I first came upon him. And of course he is right — for who can turn away the only chance they are likely to come upon to secure their freedom? To continue to live. This feels like the most honest thing he's said.

"The truth is," he continues, "we both did the only thing we could under such circumstances."

"We did," I whisper, pressing my cheek into his hand. My heart pounds with want. I want him to move closer, to press his lips to mine. When another moment passes, I realize that he is waiting for me. To decide if I can trust him again. To give him permission. To say yes.

In answer, I bring my lips to his. He pauses for the briefest of seconds, then utters my name again, his voice low and gravelly and full of the same desire. Then his lips are where I've dreamed of them being since the last time we met. Since the first time we kissed — on the road out of the city nearly three months ago. He is every bit as warm and skilled as I remember, his impressive strength bound by a gentleness that both arouses and reassures. His lips demand, even as they caress. Demand my secrets, my surrender, my trust. And in this, I do trust him. Wholly and completely. I trust my body, and how it reacts to him. That has never been a question between us.

I give myself over to the kiss, to the press of our bodies. He moves one hand to the small of my back, pulling me closer. As his hand begins to slide up my back, caressing the curve of my spine, I remember the chain and jerk away.

He frowns down at me, his face a tangle of confusion. "What's wrong?"

I have but a moment to decide what to do. I do not wish to lie to him, but when he discovers the chain attached to my necklace, he will have questions. Questions I am not ready to answer.

"We do not have much time," I remind him as I remove his hand. "Valine said you wished to know about General Cassel, and I must warn you about him."

He blinks for a moment, like a bear who has discovered bees in the honeycomb. "Warn me about what?"

"How thoroughly he has the king's ear. The king's confidence. In all things, not just battles and tactics." For all of the progress I have made, I've not been able to make a dent in that.

Maraud frowns. "But why? He is only a general. He has not been a close advisor to the king before."

"That is the gall of it. The king is feeling . . . surrounded by opinions that are fighting for his attention. Needing to weigh such decisions makes him feel weak. It is a fear others exploit. The general in particular. He is harsh and brutal and calculating, without an ounce of humanity in him. But he is decisive, and the king is drawn to that. He is also, I think, the sort of man the king was never allowed to be around as a child. He admires all that virility, all that brutal strength, and thinks to fashion himself after it. He sees General Cassel as the man his own father wished him to be."

Maraud is quiet a long moment, and I cannot help but wonder if his thoughts go to his own tumultuous relationship with his father. "That is most unwelcome news," he says at last.

"In so very many ways," I mutter. "The king does not piss without consulting him first. You must tread warily. The king will need to know and trust you before you make any accusations against the general."

Maraud smiles humorlessly. "And how am I to do such a thing without Cassel recognizing me?"

"That I do not know, but I fear to do otherwise is a loser's game." Reluctantly, I take a step away, then another. I do not want our time to end. I should be grateful, I know, that we have been able to reach a greater understanding of each other, but I am greedy and want more.

"When will I see you again?"

My heart skitters at Maraud's question, as if he somehow snagged the very wish from my head. "It isn't safe for us to meet."

He grins, a quick white flash in the dark that is as familiar and welcome as the sun. "And when has that ever stopped us?"

He is back, my heart sings, even as my skin still hums from his touch. He is back, and holds no grudge nor expects restitution for the wrong between us. Truly, my feet feel as if they are dancing over the gray flagstones of the courtyard.

The giddy feeling stays with me all the way to the palace and through the long galleries toward the grand salon. It does not leave until I see a man standing with his back to me, the set of his shoulders, the lazy tilt of his head both familiar yet so unexpected that it takes me longer than it should to recognize him.

Count Angoulême.

CHAPTER 47

Angoulême is so busy flirting with a bored-looking noblewoman that he doesn't see me.

Keeping my movements silent as a shadow, I draw the single knife I carry from its sheath. The noblewoman, growing less bored as Angoulême pays her compliments, does not notice me either. It is not until I stand right behind the count with the point of my knife pressed against his kidney that he becomes aware of my presence. To his credit, though his body grows still, he continues speaking with the woman, suggesting a meeting place for later.

When she has left, he does not move, but simply says, "I thought I spotted you earlier in the crush, but convinced myself I was mistaken. Surely the clever Genevieve, last seen cavorting with a troupe of mummers, would not have the audacity and poor sense to show up at court."

"Turn around," I order. When he does, he stands too close, as is his wont. "What are you doing here?"

His sardonic gaze sweeps over me, taking in the fine gown and the even finer necklace. "Attending the coronation ball, as ordered by the king. A more intriguing question is what are you doing here? Last I remember"—he reaches up with a hand and gently probes the back of his head—"you were running away to be a mummer. It seems you have risen much farther in the world than that." There is no amusement in his face now, only grim intensity.

I set the knifepoint against the green brocade covering his belly. "I am the one asking questions tonight."

He eyes my blade. "So you are."

"Why did you lie to me about the convent? Why would you do

such a thing? I have spent weeks thinking on it and have yet to find an answer that makes sense."

"Must it make sense?"

I press the knife closer. "Yes."

He stares at me a long time before muttering, "Sweet Jesu, you are so very young." He leans closer to me then, close enough that I can smell the wine on his breath. "To. Free. You."

"Free me from what?"

"The intolerable limbo you had been living in for at least a year, probably more than that. The convent never contacted me after your initial placement. Never wrote to check on you, to pass on any assignments, or to advocate for any specific training. They ignored every letter I sent, until I stopped sending them."

"Why would they trust you with such things?"

"They'd trusted me with you and Margot." His voice, this foolish, foppish, self-indulgent man's voice, holds true reverence. "I truly believed — still believe — that they had forgotten about you. It was too cruel to keep you on their leash any longer — especially when you were so miserable."

It is too much. I want to put my hands over my ears and walk away from him. "Then why not just tell me I was free to go?"

"Your own stubbornness would not have let you take such an option had I presented it."

I feel like a pawn who has been dropped onto a chessboard, not even realizing there was a game in progress.

"If I had said you were free to go, would you have considered it?" I open my mouth to lie, to refuse to give him the satisfaction of being right, but he talks over me. "With the scorn and contempt you felt for me, can you honestly say you would have believed me?"

I nearly squirm in discomfort that my feelings were far less hidden than I had thought. "Probably not," I admit grudgingly.

"You would have assumed it a trap and refused."

"I said you were right," I grind out.

"You were miserable and angry, and needed somebody to fight with. I was an easy focal point for that anger."

While I recognize the words coming out of his mouth, they do not make any sense. "Are you saying you did all that as a service to me? To give me someone to be mad at?"

He looks at me, all his artifice falling away, and I feel as if I am finally looking upon his true face for the first time.

"Tell me that anger didn't sustain you those long first months at Cognac." There is no mocking note in his voice, no faint drawl of amusement. He is . . . It's true, damn his rutting eyes. I clench my teeth, not willing to admit that to him.

His voice softens with something that sounds surprisingly close to affection. "I always said you were different than the other women. I wasn't wrong. They wanted reassurances and safety. Attention, and to be loved or cosseted." He shrugs. "I gave them what they needed. You needed something else. So I gave you that."

I feel as if I have been chained to a water wheel and given a hard spin. "But why?"

"It is what makes me a good guardian. I enjoy keeping those around me happy. Even churlish, angry people."

No. I do not believe that. It is yet some game he is playing. "And what of Margot?" We both grow still, her memory sitting between us as palpable as the marble column Count Angoulême leans against.

He eyes me warily. "What of her?"

"How was seducing her keeping her happy?"

A look of annoyance distorts his face. "Sweet Jesu, you are blind. She initiated the flirtation with me."

"Because the convent ordered her to!"

He outright laughs at that. "Is that what she told you?" He shakes his head, then glances down at his hands, his face growing somber. "She was as unhappy as you were, but for a different reason. She was lonely. Missed her old life. Not the one at the convent that you missed, but the one before that. Before her father found out his wife had been unfaithful — with a god, no less! — and insisted her mother send her away. She missed the luxury of that life. It suited her. She wanted to be a lady, with all the privilege that came with it. She never saw the convent as an opportunity, but a punishment. And for her, it was."

My heart feels stripped bare as he exposes the depths of Margot's unhappiness, taking the bones of what I knew and dressing them with all the confidences she'd shared with him. That she never shared with me.

"Being my favorite was as close as she could get to that dream — and I would have let her keep it as long as she liked."

No. My fists clench. He will not try to paint himself over with kindness. Not when I know how heinous a betrayal he has committed.

"You intimidated her, you know. For all that Margot looked down her nose at you, you made her feel lacking and inferior."

His words not only rip open the faint scab that has formed over that wound, but pour salt into it. "How?" I whisper.

"Your sense of purpose, duty, your fierce commitment and loyalty. In contrast, she felt none of those things."

"But she could have felt those things, too, if she chose!"

"That's where you're wrong, Gen. She was never going to feel that way about anything. When you set a vine to a trellis, it becomes so entwined that the two cannot be separated. So it was with her and her earliest dreams. They could not be removed and replaced with new ones."

His words make me want to burrow into the earth like a worm and hide from the world. "I do not know any other way to be," I whisper, stricken.

"Of course you don't. You were set to a different trellis when you were planted. But that trellis was better suited to the convent's purpose."

No, I realize. That trellis *was* the convent's purpose. My mother encouraged my own wants and desires to grow along that framework rather than the foundation she could offer me.

Perhaps to pull me from my despairing thoughts, Angoulême looks to the grand salon. "Where is the prisoner?"

His words are so unexpected that it is all I can do not to gape at him.

"Do not look so surprised."

I scowl and increase the pressure on the knife. "Why do you care what has happened to him? You left him for dead."

His eyes shift to the ballroom behind me. "I had orders."

When still I say nothing, he ignores the knife pressed against him and leans closer. "Tell me what has happened to him."

"So you can report to the regent and she can set new men after him? I think not."

"Do not be an idiot. She is why I couldn't act. She was having me watched. Closely. But not you. I knew that her spies would follow me when I left. Why do you think there were no guards on the lower floor?"

"B-because he was in an oubliette that was impossible to escape from." Heat rushes along my skin, as if my body understands before my mind does.

"Did you truly think I didn't know where you disappeared to, all those times? In my own holding? I wanted you to free him. That was the plan all along."

"Why?" I whisper, still not sure I believe what I am hearing.

"Because what they did was wrong. There are codes of conduct that were broken. And if that code does not mean anything, then we are all at the mercy of their whims and tempers."

"Some of us already are," I point out. "Why would the regent not honor her agreement with Chancellor Crunard? He did her a great service."

"Because she was protecting General Cassel. He has long been loyal to her father and the crown, and she did not want to see the king's displeasure fall on him. He has been too good at being France's brutal fist for too long." He pauses to study me. "What did you do with the prisoner?" he asks again.

I shrug my shoulders. "Freed him, like you planned." Oh, how that galls me! I lean closer, nearly putting my nose against his. "I do not think you comprehend what you have set in motion by forging that letter from the convent. Weren't you afraid they would come after you?"

"Let them," he says. "They chose to ignore you — and my own letters — for *five years*. They ignored every letter I sent. I am half convinced they *have* disbanded."

My eyes narrow. "They haven't, and if I were you, I would watch my back and have a better excuse at the ready when they come for you."

Chapter 48

Sybella

y steps are light as I head back to the palace. While it is true that Beast's safe return and news of the girls has lifted my spirits, that is not the entire reason. Nor is it that being with Beast makes me feel whole again. We are always stronger with each other at our backs.

Something else has changed. Something deeper and older. Gingerly, with the memory of Beast's arms wrapped around me, I allow myself to pull that sliver of burgeoning awareness from its dark hiding place.

It is Charlotte, I realize. Somehow, getting her to safety feels inexplicably as if I have reached back through time and gotten my *own* self to safety. As if I have somehow managed to unravel the tapestry of fate and rewoven it with the ending I had wished for.

There is no longer a sharp barbed splinter residing there, only scar tissue, newly formed. It is as if from the ashes of my own innocence, I have created safety for Charlotte. Given her a childhood that will not have to end like mine.

The small black pebble that I carry with me grows warm, the first time it has done so since I made the decision to kill Fremin. Although I do not understand what causes the warmth — my thoughts, the heat from my own blood, the flush of pleasure that still purrs along my skin where Beast has touched it, or something else I cannot fathom

—I welcome that heat. I have missed it. Mayhap it is simply yet another small miracle Mortain has left in his wake.

I nod to the sentries at the door. With all the festivities, there are many people coming and going, so my presence does not raise any questions.

Once inside the inner courtyard, I head for the queen's wing of the palace. I want to savor what Beast and I have just shared. As I come around the corner, the pebble burns hotter. I frown down toward my pocket, then stop and begin to reach for it. But as my footsteps' echo fades, I hear the faint sound of heartbeats. It could be two more guards, but one of the beats is familiar to me—both, I realize. I cock my head, trying to discern the direction. There. They are coming from the guard room at the base of the old donjon.

Moving silently, I use the shadows to cover my approach. As I draw near, I hear a voice, and recognition slams into me like a fist. It is Pierre's voice.

"My men were not the problem," he is saying. "You promised me my sisters —all of them—and still I have none. Surely those men of yours were the most inept soldiers in all of France."

"You cannot be here. It is not safe for us to meet," the woman hisses. The regent. A chill runs down my spine, then simply disappears. No familiar fear follows in its wake.

"You are ignoring my letters."

"Letters you should not be sending. Besides, I gave you what you asked for —the ambush went off as planned. It is not my fault your men could not follow through on the opening we gave them. We are done here." I hear two footsteps before she comes to a stop. "Get out of my way."

"There was more to our agreement."

"No there wasn't. Brittany belongs to France now."

"It was rightfully promised to my father."

I keep expecting the old fear to come rushing at me, but it does not. I am genuinely curious who will win this battle of wills.

When the regent speaks, her tone is more conciliatory. "Would one hundred thousand gold crowns help ease the pain of that broken promise?"

I can practically hear the wheels of Pierre's brain calculating his options. "If it must," he finally says.

"It must. Now leave. And do not approach me directly again."

The door opens just then, the light from their lantern bright amongst all the darkness. It takes them a moment to see me. When they do, an intricate moment of silence follows.

The regent speaks first, her voice tinged with relish. "Are you not going to greet your brother, who has come all this way for the festivities?"

Beside her, Pierre watches me, his face hidden by the shadows thrown off by the lantern.

"No," I say simply. "I do not think I will. I would rather he wasn't here at all."

She clicks her tongue. "Such unwelcoming words from a sister."

I fold my arms, considering her. "Has it ever occurred to you there's a reason I wish to avoid him? Wished for my sisters to avoid him?"

"What possible reason could justify the ways you have cast aside your familial duty?"

At first I think she is simply prevaricating, but as I study her more closely, I realize she is deeply serious.

Pierre chooses that moment to intervene. "Thank you, Madame, but I do not wish to pull you into our family's disputes."

I nearly laugh. He has pulled her in as thoroughly as a snake swallowing a lizard.

"Of course not," the regent says. "I must get back to the festivities anyway." She crosses the long vestibule and disappears up the staircase.

As Pierre walks toward me, I savor the heat of the pebble against my thigh and realize I am no longer afraid of him. When he is close enough, he takes my arm in his. The scar across the back of his hand has not healed well. "If you'd wanted to see me so badly, you need only have written. It wasn't necessary to kill five — no six — of my men to summon me. If you want my attention, you have only to ask for it." He has changed, I realize. Grown more subtle. He lifts his hand, as if intending to touch my cheek. Curious, I let him.

His fingers are cool and dry, and I feel no fear, no revulsion, no doubt. Only fury. But a quiet fury that burns as hotly as the pebble at my leg. "My goal was not to rouse your interest, but to keep our sisters safe from the men you sent for them."

His hand falls from my face. "They are no more ruthless than you. Indeed, that is why I sent them. I needed men who could get past you. But once again, I underestimated your cunning." He leans forward and brings his mouth closer to my ear. "You have been in France for what — two months now? — and have killed six men." He pauses as a thought occurs to him. "That I know of." He shakes his head in true admiration, something I have never seen on his face. "The d'Albret blood has never flowed stronger than it does in you. Surely you recognize that now."

Once, those words would have grated on me like a rasp on soft wood. All my life my family, my brothers, the entire be-damned French court, have tried to define my darkness for me.

"Come home," he whispers. "To your rightful place. If we combine our forces, we will be unstoppable. Your dark talents are wasted here."

Definitely more subtle. This is no threat, but him offering me the most advantageous of opportunities. "I could even let you raise our sisters and have a say in their marriage arrangements."

As I stare into Pierre's eyes, I finally understand that I am not as dark and ruthless as he is. I am far darker and more powerful than he could ever be.

A knowledge both primitive and true rises up from deep within me, and I feel the power of the Dark Mother fill me. Understand in my bones that while I have been broken and beaten and beyond despair, I have also rebuilt myself and have risen from the ashes of my own funeral pyre.

"You are mistaken. Not a single drop of d'Albret blood flows in my veins. I was sired by the god of death, not your puling father. For the last six years, I have trained in Mortain's arts. So while I know more ways to kill a man than you, it has nothing to do with being a d'Albret and everything to do with being the daughter of Death."

Pierre stares at me a long moment, his face blank with incomprehension before it grows pale. "You lie."

I smile, genuinely amused. "That is what children tell themselves to avoid an unpleasant truth. Ask how I was able to disarm you and your two soldiers in the garden alone. How was I able to kill four of your most ruthless men? Or the assassin you sent for me? Or lure Fremin to his death in such a way that all have accepted it as an accident?"

His heart beats fast with fear. "I was there when you were born — sitting right outside the chamber. I heard your first mewling cries, saw your wrinkled red face."

"Ah, but were you in my mother's bedchamber nine months before? No, of course you weren't." I lean closer, as if whispering a confidence. "I know it is upsetting to think of your father being cuckolded, for if it can happen to him, it can certainly happen to you. But at least take comfort in the knowledge that he was cuckolded by Death and not some simpering courtier."

It is only when I see the truth of my words finally sink in, see the fear that widens his eyes, that I turn and walk away.

CHAPTER 49

The sense of power I feel does not leave me, not even when, the next day, I find myself before the king.

His audience chamber is an enormous room with towering ceilings, meant to hold crowds of petitioners and courtiers as they watch the king of France hear their pleas, hand down his proclamations, and mete out justice. But this morning, the room is empty of all but a small handful of the king's closest advisors, the ones I have come to know all too well. General Cassel stands behind the king on his left, while his confessor is to his right. The regent, I am happy to note, has been relegated to a position farther down, standing with the bishops. From the corner of my eye I glimpse the humble brown of Father Effram's robes among all the snowy white and scarlet, and wonder how he gained a seat at this table.

"Sister, dearest!" Pierre breaks away from the others, coming forward to greet me when I am only halfway to the dais. He takes my hands in his, and I stare pointedly at the cut on the back of his hand and smile.

His pulse quickens in anger.

"When your brother heard of what had befallen his men, he became most worried on your behalf, Lady Sybella," the king says. "He wished to assure himself of your safety." The king looks both pleased and relieved, as if the world has once more been reordered to his liking.

"Indeed." Pierre squeezes my hands in what looks like an affectionate gesture, but the grip grinds my bones together painfully. "I had to see for myself that you were alive and well."

I tilt my head, as if perplexed. "But, brother, we saw each other

last night, at the coronation ball. Right after you had spoken with the regent."
Something flickers in Pierre's eyes — fear? Unease?

Before he can say anything, the Bishop of Albi speaks. "Your Majesty, surely
Viscount d'Albret's concern for his sister can ease all the misgivings she expressed
regarding Monsieur Fremin and his men before they disappeared."

With his back still to the others, Pierre asks, "And what misgivings would
those be?" His voice is normal, controlled, but his gaze is hot with fury.

"She thought your men afraid to bring you ill news," the king explains,
watching us both closely.

"Ah, in that she may have been correct. I do not tolerate failure, not when
my sisters' safety is concerned."

"If you are so concerned for our safety, why have you not asked after our
younger sisters?"

In the beat of silence that follows, he realizes his mistake even as my words
renew the others' uncertainty. He recovers quickly. "Because I have already heard
of it." He shifts to face the king and his council. "Imagine my surprise to arrive in
Paris and learn most disturbing rumors regarding my sisters. Rumors Madame
Regent has confirmed are true. I am not inclined to allow even one sister to
remain in royal custody."

The king shifts on his throne, face grown thunderous, and the entire room
pauses in stunned silence. "We believe Monsieur Fremin's men took the girls."

"And I believe my sister is behind this," Pierre says quietly.

I laugh, surprising everyone. "How, brother dear? I have been here the entire
time. I have never left." Before he can answer, I take a step toward him, serious
once more. "Tell me. Did you know which men Monsieur Fremin had chosen to
travel with him on this business of yours?"

Unease flickers across Pierre's face. "It was a task I delegated to him. I did
not need a list of his traveling companions and supplies."

"So you did not know he had chosen four of your most foul, vicious men to
escort us home? Men no true brother would ever want his sisters near?"

"I already said that I did not."

I shake my head, as if amused. "Come now, brother. You are among friends." I glance pointedly at the regent. "You may tell everyone why you are really here."

Pierre's eyes widen in faint alarm as he realizes I heard the conversation last night. The room falls silent with anticipation. I turn to the king. "Madame Regent and Pierre are old friends, Your Majesty. They have been since he betrayed the queen and handed the city of Nantes over to your sister." The king's jaw flexes. Gen is right. He hates that she did so without consulting him. Allowed him to think they had been cheering him as their rightful king rather than through an act of betrayal.

"In fact," I continue, "she is so very fond of him that she agreed to pay him one hundred thousand gold crowns."

"Why?" The words explode from the king as his gaze flies to his sister.

"To compensate him for the loss of Brittany, something my brother still believes rightfully belonged to his father." I do not know whose face has grown paler — the regent's or Pierre's.

"Your Majesty." Interesting that General Cassel decides to step into the fray. "These actions the girl speaks of are the tactics of war."

"We were not at war." The king's voice is cool. "The betrothal agreement had been signed. The marriage taken place. The house d'Albret is owed nothing. It is not our fault the late duke handed out false promises like alms."

I make no attempt to hide my scorn for the general. "I am surprised to learn that is how you prefer to win wars. By throwing gold at them. Perhaps you are not as fine a tactician as your reputation would have others believe. Surely anyone can throw gold at an enemy to make him go away. Indeed, I have always thought it more of a woman's tactic." I glance at the regent.

The thundering of Cassel's enraged heart is so loud it's a wonder not everyone can hear it.

The king shifts in his chair, his distaste plain on his face. "I have to agree. There is little honor in that."

"Easy to say now, when you now sit atop the throne that we secured for you," the regent says.

Another silence, this one a clash between the resentments of the two siblings. That is when I step in for the killing blow. "But the gold is not the whole of it, Your Majesty. According to their agreement, she is in his debt for failing to provide the successful ambush she'd promised him."

The king's face is awash in incomprehension — until it is not. His head whips back to his sister. "You were behind that?" he asks at the exact same moment that Pierre proclaims, "I had nothing to do with that. Nothing!"

In the deafening silence, I can hear all their hearts beating — rapid with excitement or anger or apprehension. The king clenches the arms of his throne and leans forward. "Is this true, Madame?"

"Of course not," she says lightly. "Why would I set up such an elaborate scheme to return his sisters with no gain for myself or the crown?"

Why indeed? I think, and the king's eyes narrow at the word *crown*.

"Well, then, you are either lying to Pierre or you are lying to the king. I would think long and hard on which it is," I tell her. Then I address Pierre. "And, brother, I have to wonder why you would have reason to ambush the queen's traveling party. Was it to insist she marry our father? Insist she marry you?"

"No!" Pierre's face is white — he is terrified the king will believe me. Before the king can speak, the regent whirls on me, even now working in tandem with my brother. "I could have you hanged for such falsehoods."

The king does not take his eyes from her. "Not when I have asked for her testimony."

I feel the regent's heartbeat stutter in panic as she shifts her gaze back to the king. "She is trying to distract you from her own crimes."

"What crimes are those?"

She flings her hand out. "Fremin's men, Fremin himself, the body that the search party found."

At the mention of Fremin's death, the king's face hardens. "We have already adjudicated those claims and found her innocent. It seems to me that you are trying to distract us from yours." My heart nearly sings in pure joy at having the king begin to see her clearly.

"Your Majesty." Cassel steps forward, but the king rounds on him.

"She was under our protection, traveling to our wedding," he says.

Cassel remains silent.

"There is no proof I was involved in the ambush," the regent practically spits out.

"I recognized two of our attackers." That is not precisely true, but I saw their souls, and the proof that they were associated with the house d'Albret. "They have worked for my brother before."

"Then why not say so sooner?" the regent demands.

"Because I had assumed that they left his service and became mercenaries."

"Of course that is what happened," the regent scoffs.

"And so I would have continued to think — until I heard you admit in your conversation last night with Pierre that you were involved."

Her head rears back as if she has been slapped. "I admitted no such thing."

"Let us say revealed, then."

To others, the regent's pale face and pinched nostrils will look like anger, but I know them for fear. "Are you going to let her besmirch your own sister's honor?"

It is only the fact that the king sits with his chin in his hand that keeps him from gaping at her. "The sort of honor that you have mocked me for valuing? That you claim has no place on the throne? No. I am going to adjourn so I may think upon all that I have learned and pray for the wisdom to find the truth in this mess."

CHAPTER 50

Genevieve

hat did you learn?" Even though the queen's attention is on the stitches she embroiders, she studies me from beneath her lashes.

To my embarrassment, I find myself tongue-tied before her, still unable to get over my shock at being summoned earlier this morning and asked to serve as one of her attendants. I would never have imagined receiving such an honor after our history together. "You were right. The meeting was called on behalf of Pierre d'Albret," I tell her.

Sybella enters the room just then, coming to a stop when she sees me with the queen. Her look of astonishment is so great that I must bite my cheek to keep from laughing.

"Lady Sybella!" The queen waves her forward. "We've been waiting for you. Come, tell us how the meeting went."

She stares from the queen back to me. "You knew of the hearing?"

"Genevieve told me."

The glance Sybella sends me chases all thoughts of laughter from my mind. "You were spying on me?"

"She was there on my orders," the queen says crisply.

An almost hurt expression flits across Sybella's face, then is quickly gone. The queen's voice softens. "When I heard Pierre was here, I wanted someone near you at all times. It is not a matter of trust."

Sybella looks as if she has been punched — albeit with a velvet-covered fist. "Your Majesty, while I am humbled and grateful for your concern, I am sorry that you felt you had to do such —"

The queen holds up her hand. "Spare me your unnecessary apologies, else I will be forced to apologize for my husband's stupidity every five minutes. We have been over this many times, and while I am willing to repeat it until I am blue in the face, I would rather not have to." I bite back a smile. "You are not responsible for your family's actions. Now, how did it go?"

Sybella pauses a moment to collect herself. "It was not what anyone expected," she says with a curious smile. Then she tells us what transpired, both in the meeting and during her confrontation with Pierre and the regent the night of the coronation ball.

The queen clasps her hands together and grins. "You essentially fired warning shots at both of them. I cannot help but be glad. I am tired of them backing us into corners. Let us see how they like it for a change."

"Well," Sybella reminds her, "cornered dogs do tend to bite."

"We are prepared for that."

Sybella pauses, as if undergoing some internal struggle. "I have more news. Some of it good, some of it less so."

The queen wrinkles her nose. "Let us start with the bad."

"Before we left Brittany, Captain Dunois confided in me that Beast's father still lived. Not his mother's husband, but the man who raped her and got her with child. That man is General Cassel."

The name causes me to gasp. "But of course," the queen murmurs. "Now that you point it out, I wonder that I did not see the similarities before."

"That is one of the reasons the captain told me. He said the resemblance would be undeniable. Which brings me to the good news. Beast is back."

The queen's eyes widen with pleasure. "Oh, that is the best news, Lady Sybella!"

"I think so, too, Your Majesty." Sybella's smile holds far more than simply being the bearer of good news.

Understanding dawns. "You and the Beast of Waroch?"

"You have heard of him?"

"Everyone has heard of him. Even here in France. If I had a coin for every time some young boastful knight at court bragged that he could take down the Beast of Waroch, well, I would be very rich indeed."

A small flame of pride flares briefly in Sybella's eyes, then is hurriedly dampened. She is in love with him, I realize.

"He brings news from Brittany, as well. Viscount Rohan is up to something. He is amassing troops, but Beast could not find out why. He was too busy trying to escape detection."

The queen purses her lips in thought. "We must hear this news."

"I agree. But once Beast reappears, people will ask where he has been. And there is no doubt that his resemblance to Cassel will be noted and commented upon."

Her embroidery forgotten, the queen drums her fingers on the edge of her chair. "We will wait a day or two. Look for an opportunity to present itself. Besides, we do not want to do anything to detract from the king's anger at the regent before it comes to full flower."

There is a knock on the door just then. Elsibet rises to answer it. When she returns, her cheeks are faintly pink, and she does not meet my eye. "The king's chamberlain is at the door, Your Majesty. He is requesting the Lady Genevieve attend upon him at once."

Mortification curdles around me like souring milk, but I keep my head high. "I am more than prepared to refuse."

The queen waves away the suggestion. "Don't be ridiculous. Now more than ever we need to know what he is thinking. Go. And with my blessing."

I blink in surprise. "As you wish, Your Majesty."

She turns to Sybella. "You will no doubt want to be dismissed as well, as I imagine you have others you would like to discuss this morning's events with." Her eyes sparkle a bit, then grow serious. "I do not want you to be alone any more than you have to, Lady Sybella. Not with Pierre here in the castle. Look to your own safety as dearly as if it were my own. If you don't, I will have to tell Beast, and you would not like that."

CHAPTER 51

he king is dressed more casually than I have ever seen him, in a shirt, breeches, and a leather vest. He wears deerskin gloves — the kind more suited for riding a horse than something one might do inside. The room we stand in is large and vaulted, its ceiling towering two floors above. Some of the walls are stone, and others are lined with small boxes — viewing boxes, I realize. It is only when he begins tossing the small ball in his hand up into the air and catching it that I realize where we are.

He throws the ball against the wall, then catches it when it bounces back. "What were you doing in the queen's chamber?" His brown eyes study me intently.

"Answering her summons, Your Majesty."

He advances down the court toward me — for that is where we are, a *jeu de paume* court. "Why did she summon you? Have you been reporting our conversations to her?"

"Saints, no!" The true shock in my voice seems to convince him somewhat.

"Then why?"

My fingers drift up to play with the silver necklace around my throat. "She wished to become better acquainted."

His brows rise in surprise at this. "Does she know you're from the convent?"

"She does now."

He says nothing, but pivots to the wall and throws the ball against it once more. It rebounds quickly, but he is quick as well and slaps at it with his palm. Keeping his full attention on the ball, he asks, "Why would you tell her such a thing?"

"Because she asked. Because I have served her since I was twelve years old. Because she is my liege, just as you are. Because I did not see that I had any choice."

He seems appeased by this, and his palm makes contact with the ball so that it ricochets off the wall toward him. He is damp with sweat, and there is an intensity I have not seen in him before.

Perhaps it is because his attention is so focused elsewhere, but I find myself saying, "They say it was a love match, you and the queen." I do not pose it as a question, but it is one, nonetheless.

"Do they?" His palm makes contact with the ball with a loud *thwap*.

"Wasn't it?" I no longer watch him, but the ball's hypnotic trajectory between the wall and the king.

"What sort of man would allow himself to fall in love with one lady when he had pledged betrothal vows to another?" *Thwap.*

"Our hearts are not always ours to command," I say softly. He does care for her, I realize, my heart softening in relief. As long as he cares, whatever is between them can be mended.

The thudding stops, and he holds the ball trapped in his hand as he looks at me. "I am king. Everything is mine to command."

I bow my head. "As you say, sire."

He bounces the ball off the floor twice, then on the third bounce, reaches out and slams it against the wall, concentrating on nothing but that small hard object, hitting at it until more beads of sweat form at his temple. "My sister," he finally says, although it is more of a sneer. "My sister has summoned your sister's brother to court." *Thwap.* "My sister has agreed to pay him a ludicrous amount of money." *Thwap.* "My sister has gone too far." *Thwap. Thwap. Thwap.*

I want to reach out and grab the ball from him so we may have an actual conversation, but I dare not. He is too angry, and it is far better the ball be the recipient of that anger than I. Even so, it makes talking difficult.

"The regent is working with Pierre d'Albret?" I ask.

"Yes." *Thwap.* "He and the regent stand on one side of the argument. Your sister, the Lady Sybella, on the other." This time when the ball returns to him, he catches it and faces me. "I do not trust or believe Sybella's account. She has too many reasons to lie to me."

"And you believe Pierre d'Albret does not?" I allow a touch of disbelief into my voice.

"What reason would he have?"

"What reason does your sister have? Power, of course." With the ball momentarily stilled, I risk taking a step closer. "My lord, what do you know of the house d'Albret?"

"They have extensive lands in both France and Brittany. The eldest son is the king of Navarre. Count d'Albret is — was — a powerful baron until he fell ill. And they threw their luck in with the late duke of Brittany when he rose up against me, and the count likes to claim he was betrothed to the duchess."

"All of that is true enough, but what do you know of them? Their honor, their character, how others see them?"

He frowns. "I do not engage in gossip. But I will admit that having met Pierre, I do not much care for him."

"What if it is not gossip?"

"What do you mean?"

I stare at the wall for a minute, collecting my thoughts. "At the convent, we study all the noble houses of Europe, although we focus most on those of France and Brittany, for obvious reasons." I shift my regard back to the king. "You know that he had thrown his support behind the late duke and promised him troops to guard his flank in battle. But did you know that when he saw how the battle was going, instead of providing those troops that could have shifted the tide, he let his sworn allies be slaughtered?"

The king's face grows pale. "If so, that would mean . . ."

"That the family has no honor? Yes, that is precisely what it means. The same way that handing Nantes over to the duchess's enemies, when he was her sworn ally — shows a striking lack of honor. Count Angoulême thought the entire family cruel and cunning and not to be trusted." The king now holds the little ball tightly in his hand, his game forgotten. I take another step toward him.

"I, myself, saw with my own eyes as he nearly rode over a group of children who could not get off the road fast enough. I saw him order six of his men to attack a single knight — from behind — with no warning or challenge. The man is completely without honor and possesses a cruel streak that is truly frightening. Your instincts are correct," I add softly. "He is not to be trusted. And maybe now you might understand why Sybella has fought so hard to keep her sisters from having to return to his custody."

I have his full attention now.

"When you look at her behavior from that angle, it all makes sense, does it not? Would you want someone you cared for, the Princess Marguerite, for example, to be in the custody of someone like that?"

I can see from his eyes that it does make sense, although he does not go so far as to say so. Not wishing to push the point, I change the subject. "As for the regent, she has consistently — and in large ways — gone against your express wishes. She has undermined you, made alliances without your permission, and emptied the coffers, bribing otherwise honest men. Why would you trust her?"

He stares at me, his breath coming hard, then slams the ball into the wall. "Why indeed."

CHAPTER 52

uilt chases at my heels all the way to the smithy. I long to glance over my shoulder to see that I am not being followed, but that would only call attention to myself. I consider not going — if I am caught, the repercussions will be huge. It is a foolish chance to take — especially with the king's most current demonstration of trust. But I told Maraud I would, and I will not abandon him again. Besides, he must know that General Cassel has the regent's full support before he attempts to bring his cause before the king.

When I slip into the smithy, it takes my eyes a moment to adjust to the room, the banked furnace giving off a faint red glow as well as heat. Maraud steps away from the wall. "I wasn't certain you would come."

"I should not have. There are palace intrigues everywhere I turn, but since some of them may affect you, I decided to risk it." That and my silly heart defies all reason where he is concerned.

"Come." He takes my hand and pulls me nearer the furnace. "Sit and tell me of these palace intrigues." He does not look perturbed at all, as if he doesn't believe such machinations can touch him. Irritation flares — irritation that he would hold his own safety so lightly.

"Count Angoulême is here in Paris."

His hand around mine tightens briefly. "Does he know you're here?"

Remembering the knife, I smile. "Oh, yes. We've spoken. One of the things we spoke about was you."

"Me?"

"Yes. He holds no ill will against you for your escape."

"Well, that's noble of him. Too bad I hold great ill will against him for imprisoning me."

I watch him closely as I say the next words. "It turns out, he wanted me to free you."

He lets go of my hand. "What?"

"It made no sense to me either." I have spent hours running Angoulême's revelations through my mind, feeling the heft and weight and fullness of them. I would never have expected him to play such a deep game. I have been studied, analyzed, and prodded along a path I thought was of my own choosing and feel like a game piece on a board. "But more important than whether or not you two decide to kiss and reconcile, he divulged that the regent ordered you imprisoned —"

"We knew that."

I shoot him an annoyed look. "In order to hide General Cassel's actions and protect him from the king's wrath. She is as fiercely loyal to the general as he was to her father." Maraud's mouth flattens into a hard line. "So you will have twice the battle to make your case, with the regent fighting tooth and claw to shield not only her involvement, but Cassel's as well."

Maraud swears. "Does the man have no weak spots?"

"He has a son."

Maraud's eyes narrow. "Then mayhap I will begin by aiming my revenge at him."

I watch him closely. "Do you know the Beast of Waroch?"

Maraud's entire face breaks into a wide grin. "Yes. I count him among my closest —" He scowls. "You don't mean . . ."

"He is Cassel's son."

He looks as if he has taken a club to the head. "Beast always claimed he did not know who his fath —"

"He doesn't know. Not yet. He has been on business in Brittany for the queen and left before Cassel arrived at court."

Maraud grows quiet, looking into the red glow of the embers. Finally he says, "If there is one man who is owed vengeance upon Cassel even more than I, it is Beast."

"I thought you could work together. He could be an ally in this. As could Angoulême. He can explain who gave him the order and why. And speak on your behalf. He is a Prince of the Blood. Furthermore, I believe the tide is turning against the regent."

"Why?"

"Pierre d'Albret is here in Paris."

His entire body stiffens. "Has he seen you? Recognized you?"

"No. But I wanted to warn you, all the same."

He reaches out and takes both my hands in his, gripping them firmly. "You need to be careful. He saw through my disguise, he could easily see through yours."

I purse my lips, weighing the risk. "Our paths have not crossed. I only learned it when someone else informed the queen. I will be cautious. But the more dire news is that Pierre and the regent are working together."

"To what end?"

"We don't know yet, but they have conspired in many ways against the queen, as far back as when she was duchess, and have not abandoned their alliance. However, it has begun to come to light, and the king is now mistrustful of them both."

Maraud grins. "Then now would be a good time to add to the regent's sins by revealing her role in my imprisonment."

"And would remove one of Cassel's most loyal supporters. And with Angoulême to speak on your behalf, you may well have a solid enough case to lay before the king."

Maraud strokes his chin, thinking. "But would the count speak on my behalf?"

"Yes," I say grimly. "He owes me that much at least."

"Won't that expose him to the regent's ire?"

"Not if she is out of favor."

To my surprise, he leans forward and plants a quick kiss upon my mouth.

"Such a brilliant girl you are." Something inside my chest feels light and frothy, like the foam on the ocean's waves. After all that I have endured these last weeks, his words are a much welcome balm to my ragged soul.

Then his face creases in thought as he studies me so intently that I nearly blush. "What is your role in all this?" His gaze flickers briefly to the necklace before returning to my face.

"I wish to help you."

At my words, his hands come up to cup my face, his thumb rubbing gently against my chin. "Why?" he whispers. "What has changed?"

"Everything."

His gaze moves down to my lips. "Good," he murmurs, pulling my head closer. He sets his mouth against mine, savoring the feel of my lips, brushing his against them once, twice, before he slants his mouth over mine, giving rein to the urgency that fills both of us.

I allow my own hands to touch his shoulders, savoring the sleekly muscled shape of him. For a brief moment, a memory of the king on the tennis courts barges into my thoughts. Guilt, quick and hot, causes me to pull away, and then Maraud steps closer, wrapping his arms around my waist, drawing the entire length of our bodies together, and all thoughts of the king scatter.

"Genevieve," he murmurs, then moves his mouth to the line of my jaw, kissing along it until he reaches the sensitive place where it meets my neck.

I raise my head to give him better access and let my fingers play with the edges of his hair. My entire body aches for his touch, and I want him both to linger where he is and to hurry on to other places.

As if hearing my thoughts, one hand strokes its way up the curve of my waist, brushing teasingly against the underside of my breast. Of its own accord, my body arches into him. He groans and runs his hands up along my back, his fingers pausing at the feel of the silver chain along my spine.

I grow still, letting his fingers explore the silver links through the thick fabric of my gown as I curse the way my body responds to him, curse that such feelings can drive all caution from my mind.

He pulls just far enough away that he can look into my face. "What is that?"

I reach around and remove his hand from it. "'Tis a necklace, that is all."

"That runs down your back?" While he does not raise his voice, neither does he try to hide his disbelief. "That feels far more like a chain to me, and I would know."

I think of all the jests he could make, all the ways he could crow about who is wearing a chain now. But he says none of those things. He simply pulls me closer to the light of the furnace so he can examine the links.

"It is not a chain, but fancy court jewelry in the style that Germans or the English favor." My heart beating too fast, I pull out of his reach.

He lifts an unwavering gaze to my face. "What is going on, Genevieve?"

"Nothing is going on. And I have stayed overlong already. I must go."

He reaches out and grabs my wrist, but gently. "You're talking fast, and your voice is high. You're lying. Why are you wearing a necklace with a chain?"

I force myself to meet his eyes. "It is part of my work for the convent," I tell him. "Truly. I can take it off and walk away any time I choose."

"I would hear of this assignment, then." Slowly, his movements achingly tender, he pulls the chain from beneath my gown and lays it across his palm. The orange light from the fire sparkles off the silver surface. Even though the late-night air is warmed by the furnace, I shiver. "Tell me, Gen."

How do I tell him of the magnitude of the mistake I've made? The narrowest of paths I must tread to make things right?

"You said you trusted me." His words do not feel as if they are meant to shame, but to remind me in case I had forgotten.

I close my eyes, and the impossibility of my situation hits me. I was a fool to come here. A fool to think I could reach for such a gift and not have to pay in some way. "I do," I whisper.

"I do not know what your assignment is, but with what you have told me, things are clearly getting dangerous at court." It takes great effort, but I watch as he pulls his mind back from all the possibilities it is constructing, all the dark scenarios he can imagine, all the disasters I might find myself in. He closes his eyes for a moment, and when he opens them, they are clear and unshadowed. He reaches for my shoulders, the heat of his hands warming something that has grown cold inside me. "I will admit that I do not like this, but I trust that you are doing what you need to do and that you will do it well."

It feels as if all my life I've been pushing on a heavy door, trying to get it to open. With his words, it has suddenly given way, and I am thrown off balance.

"You do?" But I do not have to ask. Not really, for that trust shines in his eyes.

"However" — those eyes darken slightly — "I am also trusting that if you need help, or things go awry, you will tell me."

Trust for trust, that is the trade he demands of me.

"I want to meet again. Tomorrow," he says.

The reasons I should not agree have increased tenfold, but agree I do. "Not here. The smithy will be open then, and we could be seen. We need to find some-place else."

"The fletcher's hut, near the armory," he says at once.

"Very well. The fletcher's hut, then. And during the council meeting will be the safest time."

I start to move away, but he grabs my hand, pulls me close. "You are not alone in this, Gen. And if the danger becomes too great, you can find refuge with us." Then he presses one last kiss upon my lips and lets me go.

This is harder than I had imagined — although what I had imagined I cannot say. Bouncing between the king and Maraud like one of those little leather balls against the wall? If I continue to see Maraud, my resolve will crumble faster than a sandy cliff before a winter storm — and my work here is not finished. The catastrophe I set in motion not resolved. The regent's plans are unraveling. The king is beginning to see her — and her allies — more closely than he has before. Sybella has been removed from the king's wrath, now I must simply find a way to remove her from her brother's. Maraud is a gift I have given myself, but one I have not yet earned.

Should I kill Pierre? Sybella said the lines of Mortain's grace are blurred now with his death. Do any of the rules of the convent still apply?

And surely Pierre presents as great a threat to her and her sisters as Monsieur Fremin did? More.

Why would she not have done this already? Is it some sense of obligation because she once thought him her brother? Or is she unable to get close enough to him to do the deed?

He doesn't know me. Would not recognize me. Especially if I came to him at night. I could get close enough to strike. I even have my poisoned needles left. If I used all of them, it would be enough to kill him. And Sybella and her sisters would be free. It is not saving the entire convent, but it is a start. It will save the ones I have come to care the most for.

This new plan puts purpose back in my steps as I climb the staircase to my chambers. It will be easy enough to discern which rooms Pierre uses. The hardest part will be ensuring suspicion does not fall once again on Sybella.

Or myself. Because of course the king will suspect me. I have already confessed to Fremin's murder, and told the king the ugly truths about the d'Albret family. He will think I am merely carrying out the next logical step. I will have to find a way to arrange this so that both Sybella and I are far away when the poison takes effect. The needles are small enough that no one will notice their puncture wounds on his skin.

When I reach the hallway that leads to my room, I see Gilbert and Roland standing rigidly at attention. They have not guarded my room since the day we arrived. My heart skips a beat. Has the king guessed where I've been? Had me followed?

Painting a cheerful smile upon my face and a ready excuse upon my tongue, I greet them. In response, they give me nothing but stiff nods. Gilbert steps forward to open my door for me. Before I can thank him, the regent pulls away from the window where she's been waiting.

"There you are."

CHAPTER 53

I have not been face-to-face with the regent since we last spoke at Plessis. Have not seen for myself how she's grown bitter-looking, like a too-thin blade before it is broken. While she stands composed, arrogant even, a faint desperation taints her features. Perhaps she senses her carefully spun web beginning to unravel. Desperate people begin to make mistakes, as I should know, and their mistakes might grant us further leverage.

"Madame Regent." I sink into a curtsy.

Her gaze scans me from head to toe, and for a moment, I fear she will sense traces of Maraud clinging to me. "The king has set you up well. Where were you?"

"This morning I was attending upon the queen. This afternoon, I met with the king. He is quite good at *jeu de paume*."

Her brows arch in surprise. "You serve the queen now?"

"She is my queen, and she sent for me. I answered her summons."

The regent crosses the room to examine the blue brocade of my bed curtains. "We have not seen each other since Plessis," she says pleasantly.

"I did not think it wise to seek you out."

She twists her lips in a pale imitation of a smile. "There is that notable wit of yours. Tell me, do you remember the last time we spoke?"

"But of course." My heart begins to beat faster. I could hardly forget — Sybella and I were arguing over this necklace when the regent came upon us.

She lets go of the curtain to face me. "You are from the convent."

It is not a question. She takes a step toward me. "I trusted you." Her voice is like the thinnest of whips, lashing across the room, meant to draw blood.

But her trust is not what I am worried about. I do not like the faint gleam of victory in her eyes. Whatever this is about, it is not injured trust. "We are even, then, for you broke my trust first." The moment the words are out, the truth of them punches me low in the belly.

She scowls. "What do you mean?"

"I mean, I trusted you to act as a mentor, and instead you acted as the procuress for your brother to feed your own political hunger."

"You were no innocent, but an assassin."

"But you did not know that!" We are silent, staring at each other, the weight of tangled betrayals filling the room.

"This only proves how correct I was to try to place someone in the king's confidence. His relationship with you, his handling of this entire matter, only proves he cannot be trusted to rule on his own. His judgment is flawed and lacking."

And there it is. The thing that will ultimately destroy her relationship with the king. Whether it will happen in time to do me any good is the question. "The king has now reached his majority. The crown is his, Madame, not yours."

Her head rears back as if I have slapped her. There is nothing I could have said that she less wished to hear. "You know nothing." Her pale face is now white with rage. "I have ruled this country for eight years. I have expanded our borders, put down rebellions, negotiated treaties so complex that your feeble brain could not fathom them." She takes a step toward me, but I give no ground. "I was charged by my father to act as steward to the crown, and I will not abandon that responsibility. Unlike my brother, I have a distinct talent for politics. My father even declared me the least foolish woman in France."

I want to shout at her that that is no compliment, but bite my tongue.

"He charged me with a sacred duty to continue to consolidate power to France, and I will allow no one, *no one*, to interfere with that duty." She recovers her equilibrium somewhat, and an oily smile shimmers across her face. "While trusting you was clearly a mistake — one I will not make again — you have served some purpose. You have provided me with a new weapon." Her eyes burn bright. "The time has once again come for you to remember who you truly serve. I have a task for you. One of utmost importance. You must ensure that the king grants Pierre full custody of Sybella in these hearings. I do not care what else happens, I do not care what else you hear. But Sybella will be in Pierre's custody within a week's time, or I will expose your secrets." My heart begins hammering against my ribs like a rabbit caught in a snare.

She takes a step closer. "And I do not mean that I will simply expose *your* secrets, Genevieve. I mean I will tell the entire council that the king has knowingly harbored an assassin and a murderer under his wing. How far do you think the king will go to protect you from that truth getting out? What would his Privy Council and bishops have to say about that revelation? Once they hear that, once they see how badly his judgment has gone, they will be inclined to look to me for leadership once more. Do you understand?"

"Madame Regent, I understand, but what you ask is —"

"I am not asking, I am ordering you. If that is too difficult for you to manage, there is one other option."

I wait, knowing I will not like what she is about to say.

"If you cannot convince the king to hand Sybella over to Pierre, then you may kill her yourself. Either way, I wish her removed for good."

Why? Why does she harbor such hatred for Sybella? It is one thing that they cross political swords, but to arrange her murder? "Madame, you must understand it takes time to arrange to kill someone."

"I do. That is why you have a week. No more talk. Simply nod if you understand me."

It feels as if this woman has just grabbed a spoon and scooped out my heart. She has taken one of the most selfless things I have ever done and turned it into a weapon to be used against the king. With no other choice before me, I nod. She sends me one last scornful glance and disappears through the door.

I force my body to breathe. My head grows light, and I stumble over to sit on the bed. My carefully crafted and painstakingly built progress toward fixing this catastrophe has been hacked from under my feet.

Of course, there is no decision to be made. I will not hurt Sybella, not for any price, and certainly not for the king's power struggle. But, oh, the innocents who will be caught up in this wake!

The queen, who has so graciously opened her doors to me, in spite of everything. The king's budding confidence, which could allow him to grow into a decent ruler. All for want of the regent's rutting schemes. I want to explode into action to begin escaping this carefully laid trap, yet I remain motionless, fearing what I may step into next.

If I choose to stay or warn the king, he will likely think he can simply overcome the regent's claims, bargain it out, no matter that the Bishop of Albi is already in her pocket, his confessor is likely shocked, and General Cassel will sneer at his weaknesses.

What little remnants of his decency that remain will shrivel before that onslaught.

And his advisors? The majority of them will not trust his judgment again, allowing the regent to create a power vacuum into which she can readily slip once more. She will have robbed him of the one thing that mattered most to him — their respect. As well as robbing me of any chance I had of righting the scales.

A new horror occurs to me. If I stay, if the king resists, the regent could easily claim that I was working for her, gaining his trust in service of her ambitions rather than for my own reasons. And he will, of course, believe her.

The thought has me leaping to my feet and rushing over to the basin, where I retch into it, trying not to make a sound. Even worse, Sybella might feel as if she needs to come forward and confess to Fremin's murder in order to neutralize this weapon the regent now holds. It will all come crumbling down on her undeserving shoulders. I retch again.

As I rest my head on the small table, waiting for my stomach to stop roiling, my eyes fall on the pitcher of fresh water. I'd almost been able to fix things — but the glue was too thin.

But, I slowly realize, even thin glue requires a hammer in order to break it. And the regent can only make use of a weapon if she holds it. Without me, there is no leverage over the king. No one Sybella or the queen will feel they need to protect.

CHAPTER 54

Your Majesty,

If you are reading this, then I have had to make a most difficult decision, and you will not like the news I am about to share with you.

Back in Plessis, the night of Monsieur Fremin's death, Madame Regent overheard our conversation. She has recently confronted me with what she learned that night and is planning to use it to force you to bend to her political will. I cannot allow that to happen. As I have always told you, my first duty is to serve, and I cannot do that if I am to be used as a weapon against you.

The only way forward is for me to leave and, after I am gone, for you to announce that you have discovered my role in the matter and have banished me as punishment. That way, the information she holds cannot be used against you in any way.

Your Most Humble Servant,

G

I carefully place the letter on my pillow. Either the maidservant or one of the guards will take it directly to the king. I leave a second letter for Sybella, but this one under my mattress, knowing she will search to see if there are any signs of why I have left.

I fetch the maid's gown that I carried all the way from Plessis, and begin to undress. When I have stripped down to naught but my shift, I reach around to the back of my neck and fumble with the clasp of the necklace until it releases. As I remove it, I marvel at the heaviness of the silver links that spill though my fingers.

Setting it on the foot of the bed, I am reminded of the tales my mother told of the followers of Saint Mer. How they could slip out of the skin that allowed them to move so freely in the ocean in order to walk among men unremarked. But woe to the one whose skin was found by humans, for once it was taken from her, she would never have the same freedom of movement in the sea again. With luck, everyone who has seen me has noticed only the necklace and will not recognize me without it.

The king will never forgive me. In spite of my note and my careful explanation, he will never forget that I did not trust him to protect us against the regent's schemes. He will believe I thought him too weak. But this is not about me, it's about his standing with his advisors, and his continued ability to rule. The more that is undermined, the greater the threat to the queen, the convent — and Sybella.

How does one even shield oneself against a creature like the regent? I wonder as I step into the humble servant's gown. Mayhap I will find answers to that question out there. Something is going on in Brittany, according to the Beast of Waroch. Surely Maraud and his crew — including me — could help there. We could even send reports back to Sybella and the queen.

If I can convince Maraud that is where we should go next. And, oh, how Andry and Tassin will like that — the woman who poisoned their friend returning to tell them what to do and where to go. Oddly, I relish the prospect of arguing with them about it.

I have little enough left to call my own — I take even less. My few weapons, the poisoned needles, my handful of possessions I've carried with me since Cognac. They hardly fill a small sack, but still, they are the pieces of my life that I have not — yet — had to leave behind.

Fortunately, no one looks at servants, especially not those hurrying by with chamber pots or pails of dirty water. It is easy enough to find the scullery, then slip through the servants' door into the palace yard. Once outside, I keep walking, half afraid someone will call me back, but no one does.

I hurry from the main area of the courtyard toward the outbuildings, where I will not be so visible from the palace windows. Once I am well hidden among the scores of other bodies going about their palace business, I begin making my way to the fletcher's hut.

With hindsight, I can only wonder why his original offer of help terrified me so very much.

No, not his offer, my reaction to it. That was what scared me so.

My mind — my pride — wants to shy away from this truth. Pretend I have not seen it, but pride is how I ended up on this path, and I do not wish to learn the same lesson twice.

So I take out that moment between us, that memory of when he looked at me with those laughing brown eyes of his, so solemn and sincere. "Let us help you."

That he would set aside his plans for vengeance to help still stuns me.

Before that, no one in all my life had offered to stand by my side. Not Margot, not Angoulême, not the convent. Not even my mother, who left me to face the convent alone. He was the first, and it was so foreign to me, I did not know what to do with it.

And in that moment, his offer made me realize how hungry I was for that. How starved, just as he was starving when we first met. Only I was starving for . . . what? I cannot even put a name to it. Companionship is too weak. Support does not do it justice.

That deep hunger that terrified me. Like a starving man who will do anything to fill his belly, I feared what I would do to fill that hole in my heart. I feared I would turn my back on the convent, on everything I'd worked toward. On those I'd sworn to help.

I feared that I was weaker than I had ever imagined. And since I could not pull that weakness from me, could not yank it from my breast and cast it aside like the weed it was, I struck out at him instead.

The fletcher's hut sits nestled between the armory and the artillery buildings. No one lingers outside. Inside is a lone fletcher seated at a table, carefully attaching gray feathers to an arrow shaft.

When I reach the far side of the hut, I pause. My pulse, already erratic, grows even more so. Was his invitation to join him sincere? He could easily have made it in the heat of the moment, with our kisses still warm upon our lips and the unexpected discovery of the chain.

No. I recall his steady, imploring gaze, and his insistence that I could take refuge with him should I need to. He was not simply polite.

Forcing aside my doubts, I pass the fletcher's hut once more, walking slowly to give Maraud time to see me should he be watching out of view. Still nothing, other than a curious glance from the fletcher himself.

Am I early? Or is he late? Or has something caused a delay? Mayhap the others did not want me to join them. Or he has been detained by the guards. Or recognized.

My heart thuds into my stomach. No. There would be more of a hue and cry, a bustle of some activity if that were the case.

But perhaps someone lingered near the fletcher's hut who could recognize him. Angoulême. Pierre d'Albret. Even General Cassel himself. The list is long. In case that is what happened, I make my way over to the smithy to see if he is waiting there.

The smith's hammers clang loudly throughout the crisp morning air. And while a half dozen apprentices and journeymen scurry about their work, Maraud is nowhere in sight.

CHAPTER 55

Sybella

 heed the queen's warning and spend the rest of the afternoon in her solar, then pass the night in her apartments along with the rest of her attendants. In the morning, however, I am required once more to present myself before the king to further discuss "certain matters," as the understeward puts it.

Although I do not plan it so, I am the last to arrive. All but one.

"Where is he?" The king does not try to hide his exasperation.

"I am sure he is on his way, Your Majesty," the Bishop of Albi soothes.

"One would think he would understand the folly of being late for a hearing he requested," the king points out.

"He should be here, my lord. I am certain there is a good reason why he is not." The faint smugness on the regent's face disappears when she notices my arrival, replaced instead with a vague uncertainty. I cannot help but wonder what new scheme she and Pierre have devised.

"Whatever it is, I do not care." The king turns to Captain Stuart. "Have someone fetch him at once." Captain Stuart bows, then strides off to find my errant brother.

The regent's face resettles into its normal inscrutable mask as she studies me. "Perhaps she had something to do with it."

I lift one shoulder in calculated unconcern. "Or perhaps he is not here because he cannot defend his actions to the king."

The regent smiles thinly. "Perhaps you murdered him," she says.

That surprises a huff of laughter from me. "If I were inclined to murder him, do you not think I would have done it before he presented his claims to the king? Besides, who is to say that you are not behind his disappearance? Perhaps you wished to save yourself one hundred thousand gold crowns." I brace myself, expecting the king to jump in and order us to stop, but he does not. When I risk a glance in his direction, he is staring thoughtfully at the regent.

Unaware of his scrutiny, she says, "Your Majesty, if he is not here, he cannot defend himself against the Lady Sybella's accusations."

"Perhaps not, but you can."

His words surprise her into stillness. "I did not realize I had to," she says at last.

"The accusations the lady made involved both of you. So while we are waiting for Lord d'Albret, I will ask you. Why are you working with him against the crown?"

Her face grows white. "Never against the crown, Your Majesty. *For* the crown. Always for the betterment of the crown."

"How does paying him such a large sum of money for a false claim better the crown? From where I sit, it seems more like robbing it."

Before she can answer, Captain Stuart returns, somewhat breathless. "He is gone, Your Majesty. Viscount d'Albret is gone."

The regent scowls at me, as if perhaps I have murdered him after all.

"One of my men checked with the stable master. He and his entire party left early this morning, just before dawn."

"So not murdered, then," I murmur. The regent shoots me a look that is sharper than the point of a spear.

The king's jaw tightens, his entire face pinched with the anger he is trying not to show. "If he is not here, his claim is forf—"

"But, Your Majesty," the regent interjects. "Surely after all that has transpired you cannot believe that the Lady Sybella is in any way fit to serve as guardian to her sisters? Or should be left free to roam among us?"

He studies her for a long moment. "She, at least, is here. And for now, that is more than can be said of her brother."

Deciding it is better to take the loss, the regent curtsies. "Very well, Your Majesty."

He leans forward. "But you and I have much to discuss, because I dearly wish to hear the reasons behind both your involvement in the ambush and the reason for that payment."

I am careful not to let a whiff of the victory humming through my veins show. I keep my face downcast and sober, taking measured steps as I leave the audience chamber. Pierre is gone. He walked away from his claim. Is that all that was ever needed — telling the truth? Or is it something more?

The regent could be behind it, I suppose. Setting him up in some way to take the fall for their conspiracies. And I did not like the way she was looking at me. But for now, the king's wrath at her is greater than his dislike of me, and that is a true victory. I cannot wait to tell Gen and the queen. And Beast.

As I reach the foyer, General Cassel falls into step alongside me. "What have you done with your brother?"

The force of his full attention is as solid as a rock. "Nothing. It is his own poor judgment that kept him from the meeting." Even though my face and body are relaxed, every fiber of my being is attuned to him, the rhythm of his heart, the intake of his breath, even how often he blinks. Too many times, the unconscious change in those vitals is the only warning I have gotten. If Beast's presence is like a cheerful mountain, the general's is all serrated edges and menacing heights. His cool, predatory gaze makes me glad of the knives hidden in my sleeves.

"I do not like or trust you." The deep timbre of his voice holds no craggy comfort like Beast's, only the deep rumble of threat.

My mouth twists in amusement. "Nor I you." I do not look at him, but I feel his brief flicker of surprise. If he had hoped to intimidate me, he will have to try harder.

"Women who do not know their place and are disloyal to their families are both unpredictable and useless. That is your one duty — fealty to your family, and you cannot even manage that."

This time I laugh outright. "And here I thought our one duty was as brood-mare."

"Once you are handed over to your husband, yes. Until then, you owe fealty to your family. To do otherwise is to be without honor."

I look at him then, allowing my disbelief to show plainly on my face. "Honor? This from a man who prefers to win wars by throwing gold at the enemy or their potential ally."

He stops walking, shifting the mass of his body so that it partly blocks my path. I could keep going, but I would have to brush past him to do so. "You are either remarkably foolish or dangerously overconfident."

"Or neither."

He leans closer. I do not back away, which also surprises him. "What you are is a rogue assassin with allegiance to no one. Not even the Nine, whom you profess to hold dear," he spits out.

"You know me that well, do you?"

"I know that you lie."

"Of course I lie! I am neck deep in a court full of intrigue, advisors who wish my queen ill, power plays behind every corner, and political plots hatching like spring eggs. To not lie would be a fatal mistake."

His eyes blink, holding something akin to admiration — or it would be, if I were not a mere woman. No, I realize with disgust. That is interest. The interest of a man who thinks he has just found a new enemy he must conquer. "We will find your brother and learn what has happened. You may rest assured."

I resume walking. "You hold such scorn for the Nine. I must say I am surprised, as I would have taken you for an admirer of Saint Camulos."

"I am an admirer of skill in war and battle. I have no need of saints."

I smile. "Careful, they might hear you."

He snorts in derision.

"Have you ever been to Brittany, my lord? I don't recall your name among the generals we fought against in any of the campaigns." If he thinks my change of subject odd, he does not say so.

"I was there once, a long time ago." No hint of memory of his black deeds or remorse crosses his face. "The recent conflict was not important enough to pull me from my command in Flanders."

I tilt my head. "And yet, here you are, with no skirmishes on the horizon."

"There have been skirmishes aplenty since I arrived."

"Touché. But surely none that require your military expertise."

"Our king is young. He needs guidance. I will help him become the man his father wished him to be."

"Not if I — or Gen — can help it," I mutter to his retreating back.

CHAPTER 56

After my confrontation with the general, I attempt to speak with the queen and inform her of Pierre's departure, but she is receiving one of the many illuminators who have flocked to court to ask for her patronage. I decide to seek out Gen, surprised that I did not see her in the meeting. With Pierre gone and the king now aware of the regent's perfidy, mayhap we can finally gain ground with him. Or, more accurately, Gen can, so that we may all benefit.

But when I knock on her door, there is no answer. Surely she is not in with the queen and her illuminators? "Gen?" I call out. She has looked tired of late. Mayhap she is still abed. Finding the door unlocked, I let myself in.

The bed is empty — empty of all but the heavy silver necklace that glitters in the morning sunlight like a malevolent serpent. I cast a quick glance around the room. It feels abandoned, though when I check her cupboard, her gowns are there.

But not, I notice, her travel bag. As I survey the room, my eye lands on a small, white square nestled against her pillows. It is addressed to the king. "Gen, what have you done?" I pick the letter up and consider opening it, but decide not to in case I must deliver it to him untampered. I slip the note inside my pocket. Perhaps Father Effram will know where she is.

In the chapel, I do not find Gen, but Father Effram administering a blessing to a man kneeling at his feet. The man looks up at my arrival, a wide smile breaking across his face. Yannic.

My heart hitches in my chest — is there some dire news? — until the little man wobbles his head, then scampers away, glancing over his shoulder to be sure I am following him.

Before I do, I pause long enough to ask Father Effram, "Have you seen Gen this morning?"

"No, is something amiss?"

I run my hand along my skirt where the letter to the king hides. "I don't know yet. Keep an eye out for her if you would."

Once he agrees, Yannic leads me through the courtyard past the wine vendors and pie sellers and fruit stalls, past the old lady selling birds in wicker cages and an old, tired man with an equally old, tired dancing bear, toward the pungent scent of the palace stables and barns. Of course Beast would find his way to the animals.

Yannic grins, then bows as if presenting me to the queen. I have missed this man's humor. I murmur my thanks, then, before he can scamper away, call out, "Wait."

He pauses, sidling back to stand beside me. I fish in my pocket to look as if I am giving him a coin for his trouble. "That pebble you gave me, before I left for France."

Yannic slides his gaze up to mine, then quickly drops it back to the ground as he nods.

"You indicated it was not from Mortain. Did it come from the Dark Mother?"

His head swings up, a wide grin on his face, and he bobs his head up and down enthusiastically. Well and so. "Thank you," I say, meaning more than the answer he gave me.

His face sobers, and he bows, this time grasping one of my hands in his old gnarled ones and bringing his forehead to touch it, as if receiving a benediction. It makes me profoundly uncomfortable, but I do not pull away for fear of insulting him.

He smiles once more, then scuttles away like a crab toward the cow barn.

I find Beast wearing the traditional homespun tunic and hood of a peasant, mucking out one of the stalls. Although I move silently, he looks up as I reach for the latch to let myself in. He does not pause in his shoveling, but the horse — an enormous chestnut gelding — swings his head around to study me.

I glance back at Beast. "A friend of yours?"

He grins. "Animals like me." He reaches out to scratch the gelding, his big fingers calm and soothing along the creature's nose. It is wrong to be jealous of a horse, I remind myself.

The gelding seems to sense my thoughts and stamps his hind leg, ears twitching. "Stop that, now," Beast tells him, and he does.

Beast returns to his shoveling. "With so many guests and nobles gathered at court, there is always need of help mucking out the stables."

Keeping my eyes warily on the horse, I edge around the stall until I am close enough that Beast and I can speak without being overheard. He glances up, his blue eyes piercing even in the dim light of the stables. "More news?"

"Are there fish in the sea?"

"Last time I checked." The gelding nickers impatiently, and Beast resumes his shoveling. "Best if I don't stop. It will help cover our voices."

"I learned who was behind the ambush."

"Who?" His arms do not stop their work, even as his eyes bore into mine.

"Pierre and the regent. I heard them with my own ears. The regent was most irate with Pierre for even risking meeting with her. And that is the other piece of bad news. Pierre is here."

Beast keeps his attention on his work "Is he?" It is one of his most admirable qualities — the ability to remain focused and on task no matter what else is going on around him.

"Well, he was. He did not appear before the king today, and the regent seemed most surprised. I do not know what to make of it all."

"Well, then, that is good." Beast seems remarkably unperturbed by this news. Else he is trying to hide the full force of his anger from me.

I fold my arms and begin to pace. "It was most unexpected. Even the regent was surprised. It is hard to believe my exposure of his dealings with the regent would have spooked him that badly." Beast is still focused on his shoveling. "Have you heard any rumors among the grooms or stable workers?"

He shakes his head. "None. But I will be grateful for it, all the same."

"As will I. Truly, it is as if a great weight has been lifted from my shoulders. And the king is still most irked at the regent."

Beast grunts. "As well he should be."

The scrape of a boot on flagstone draws my attention. That is when I realize that a cluster of heartbeats has drawn closer. Much closer.

I step away from Beast just as the stall door bursts open, surprising the gelding. He neighs and rears. Calm as a mountain, Beast gracefully avoids the flailing hooves and grabs the rope. As soon as he has the creature under control, he calls to the intruder. "Mind the horse, you fool."

No longer needing to dodge the startled horse, I look toward the stall door.

General Cassel's enormous bulk and glowering countenance have my heart slamming into my ribs. At Beast's words, he draws himself up taller, making his shoulders even broader, like a bear rising up on two legs. In contrast, Beast does not need to make himself bigger, he is already larger than Cassel. Two men of the same blood and bone, so much alike and yet so wildly different. While Beast appears calm, I can feel the furious pounding of his heart as if it were inside my own chest.

Cassel takes a step closer to Beast, the group of men at his back moving with him. "How dare you speak to me thus? Who are you?" As his savage blue gaze meets Beast's lighter, feral one, I marvel that it is not obvious to him. I cannot decide if I am grateful for or resentful of the peasant hood that cloaks Beast's face and casts it in shadow.

"I am captain of the queen's guard, and I speak to anyone thus if they do not know enough to not barge in and startle a high-strung horse."

Cassel's nostrils flare. "There is no queen's guard."

"In truth, there is." At my challenge, Cassel swings toward me like a battering ram to a new target. "The queen's guard came with her from Brittany," I continue. "The queen had sent them on a mission, and now they have returned. She asked me to ascertain how they fared and how quickly they could meet with her."

"What mission is that?"

"That is the queen's business. You shall have to ask her, as I do not have permission to speak of it, my lord."

He studies me a long moment before turning back to Beast. "The king has said nothing of such a guard. Until he has sanctioned your presence here, you are either an intruder, a soldier who has abandoned his post, or a traitor. Seize him! Take them to the guard tower until I send further word."

"No!"

The general's eyes widen in surprise at my protest. He is not accustomed to being naysaid by a mere woman. "He is the queen's man and answers to her."

"All answer to the king." He glowers.

"Unless you have looked at the marriage contract with your own eyes, you cannot presume to know that."

The air in the room grows thick. At first I think it is tension, until I realize it is rage. Rage that I have dared to defy him. Rage that I have plucked at a thread of uncertainty. But I do not look away. Slowly, my eyes on his the entire time, I cross my hands to my wrists and let them rest closer to my knives, reminding him that I am not some hapless courtier he can intimidate.

His eyes sharpen with understanding, and a thirst for vengeance. "Take them to the king's audience room. He is in attendance there."

I give a brusque nod and drop my hands back to my side. "That is all we wished for."

I bite back a humorless smile of triumph when his jaw clenches in irritation at the thought that he is doing precisely what we wanted.

CHAPTER 57

Genevieve

Alarm snakes along my shoulders. I have made a bold move, but the door I thought open is not. With no other choice, I begin heading back to the castle, my heart thudding as loudly as the blacksmith's hammer.

Maraud did not come. Only something dire would keep him from his word. Unless — my steps slow — he had planned this from the beginning, a setup to even the score between us.

I try the idea on much as I might a hair shirt, and though it itches and scratches painfully, I find myself hoping that it is the case. Better that this be some well-thought-out retaliation rather than some new misfortune that has befallen him.

I am halfway across the courtyard when my dismay at Maraud's failure to appear shifts to panic. The note!

I must get back to my room and get the letter to the king before others find it. I look up at the sky. I have not been gone that long. Surely their meeting has not adjourned.

I have just resumed walking when a loud commotion erupts over by the stables. I stop near one of the wells and glance up. A cluster of a half dozen king's guard, led by General Cassel, strides toward the castle. The guard's bodies block my view of who they have in custody. The crowd rapidly parts for them, and it is not until they veer around one of the wine stalls that I catch a glimpse of a deep red gown and a woman's black hair. Sybella.

A fresh wave of panic slams into my chest. What is Cassel doing with her? Why is she under guard? I take two steps in their direction before I realize there is nothing I can do to help her. Not like this. I whirl back around, intending to enter the palace through the servants' entrance near the chapel, but am stopped by something hard pressing into my back.

"What have you done with Maraud?"

I recognize Valine's voice immediately. Is that who the man with Sybella was?

"I've done nothing to Maraud. I've been out here looking for him for over an hour."

The knife against my back eases. "Why are you looking for him?"

"Because we had planned to meet. Over at the fletcher's hut. But when I got there, he was nowhere to be found. I've waited, thinking he'd been delayed or something had come up." I do not tell her my fear that it was his plan all along to humiliate me. The fact that she is here does much to allay that concern.

"He left to meet you over three hours ago, wanting to arrive early to ensure the fletcher's hut was safe. I have not seen him since."

I shift my gaze to the general, who has almost reached the palace. "Do you think General Cassel saw him? Is that who he is escorting?"

She glances over her shoulder. "That is not Maraud."

The guards step back just then, to make room for the others to pass over the causeway. The man with Sybella is taller than Maraud, nearly half again as broad, and dressed in a peasant costume. Beast.

"I must go," I tell Valine. "Send word if you learn anything of Maraud."

Slipping back into the palace is nearly as easy as it was to slip out, although this time I take the back stairs to my chamber. I open my door, step into the room, and toss my small sack onto the bed, then freeze. My note to the king is gone. But there is no time to think upon that now. I cross to my cupboard, toss my traveling bag inside and strip out of my servant's garb. Once I am dressed in my court finery, I lift the silver necklace from the bed and wind it around my neck. It is not the same as getting the note back, but it is as close to normal as I can make myself.

I take a moment to steady my breathing, then head to the king's audience chamber to see if there is anything I can do to help Sybella.

CHAPTER 58

Sybella

he king's audience chamber is only half full. With the exception of the regent, all my least favorite advisors are here. The king looks up as we enter the room. When we are close enough, Cassel gives a deep bow, as do we all.

"What is this?"

"Your Majesty, I found this man lurking in the stable. Trespasser at best, traitor at worst."

The king's gaze lands on Beast. "That is no traitor or trespasser, but the captain of the queen's guard. Although I am uncertain why he is dressed as a peasant."

I want to chortle in victory when annoyance spasms across the general's face.

"If that is the case, why have I not seen him before now? Why has he not been guarding the queen?"

The king waves his hand. "It was what was agreed upon. The captain and his guard would attend the queen only when she and I were not traveling together."

"Yes," Cassel says patiently, as if to a small child. "But where has he been all this time? Why has he not been training in the yard with the other men? I have not seen him riding with the rest of the guard. Indeed, he claims to have only just returned. Did you know they were gone?"

The king frowns at this, and I want to shake him for shifting faster than a weathervane in a storm. "No. I did not." He looks at Beast. "Where have you been?"

Beast bows deeply before speaking. "The queen sent me on her business, sire. I would not do her dishonor and speak of it without her permission."

Cassel's chest puffs even larger with belligerence, and the king's nostrils flare in irritation before he speaks. "Well, then," he drawls, his voice laced with barely concealed vexation. "We had best send for the queen."

The queen arrives escorted by four of her ladies. She does not look in my direction or Beast's but goes directly to the smaller throne that sits to the king's right. She curtsies deeply — "Your Majesty" — then takes her seat.

"My lady." He returns the greeting amicably enough, but whether it is for show or his quicksilver temperament is once again at peace with her, I cannot begin to guess. "Did you know your captain had been gone from court?"

"Why of course, my lord. I sent him."

The king's cordiality slips from his face like wine from a drunkard's cup. "Without informing me?"

The queen's forehead creases in confusion. "He is captain of my queen's guard, sent on my own business. I did not know I needed permission."

The king shifts in his chair, unsure of whether she should need his permission or not.

"Your Majesty." General Cassel's deep voice calls everyone's attention. "What personal business would a new bride have that required such an absence?" As quickly as a serpent injects venom into its victim, so does the general undermine the queen's authority.

"Where did you send him?" The king's tone is carefully neutral, as if he is working to keep his irritation in check.

The queen meets his gaze squarely. "To Brittany."

A long, charged moment of silence greets the queen's words.

"You did what?"

General Cassel places his arms behind his back, lifting his chin in victory. The queen does not so much as flinch. "I sent him to Brittany. I had reason to believe that all might not be as it seemed there, and wished to have a firsthand account."

"That is not personal business, Your Majesty," General Cassel points out, "but the crown's."

Anger pinches the corners of the king's eyes as he stares at the queen. "We have talked about this," he says in a low voice.

"No, actually." Her words ring out loud and clear. "We have not. I have tried, mind you, but you have been too busy to have the conversation. Besides, I would not risk giving you false information, so I needed to send someone to ascertain what was true before bringing it to your attention."

"And what did you learn?"

"The motives of Viscount Rohan."

The king grips the arms of his throne. "You are questioning my choice for governor?"

"Sire, may I remind you that before you left Brittany, we had already decided upon a governor."

"I changed my mind." His words are those of a defiant child who knows he has cheated.

"And I have learned from painful experience that Viscount Rohan cannot be trusted and sent the captain to report back on his activities. It is a good thing, too. It appears I was right."

The king's face flushes with anger. "I did not give you leave to do so."

To her credit, the queen merely meets his gaze steadily. "Our marriage contract did."

The silence in the room crystallizes into something brittle. "That same contract binds you to me as wife, binds you to my orders, my decisions. It gives you no power to act as your own sovereign power."

"Then tell me, Your Majesty, what was I to do? Every time I tried to speak to you of Brittany, you turned your back. You did not want to discuss politics or governing with your wife, a wife who has been involved in politics since she was four. A wife who has governed since she was twelve. A wife who brought one of the most valuable dowries in Europe. I could not sit by and risk that some pompous noble's scheming would take that from us. So I sent someone I trusted to scout out the situation and report back. And here he is."

The king shakes his head, still trying to dislodge his disbelief. "I gave you no leave."

"Sire, if I suspected a noble to be working against his king, how could I not act? What loyal subject could stand by and let such a thing happen?"

This, finally, gets through, and the king's face grows less fraught. I want to cheer for the queen's wit at finding this one small crack to slip inside.

"Your Majesty." General Cassel's voice rumbles into the silence of the room, breaking the fragile truce the queen's words have wrought. "While it is true that the queen, being a woman, did not know the enormous disservice she did you by overruling your wishes, of a certainty, her captain did." His cold blue eyes fix upon Beast as he slowly walks toward him. "You knew you did not have the king's permission, else you would not have snuck into the stables like a thief in the night."

Beast keeps his stony gaze affixed to the wall, refusing to look into the face of the man — his father — who is accusing him of treason. "I am captain of the queen's guard and serve at her pleasure, by permission of His Majesty himself."

General Cassel whips his head back around to the king. "You gave him such permission?"

The king is scowling in memory. "I gave him permission to lead the queen's guard, but only when my own was not available."

"And they were not available for this." Beast's voice is deeper than Cassel's, and even though it has a rougher edge, his words are more polished.

Cassel's face grows red. "You are playing word games. You know your authority comes direct from the king, not his lady wife."

Beast does look at Cassel then. "My lord," he rumbles, the threat in his voice clear to all. "You will address our queen with respect."

Cassel takes a step closer. "Or what?"

Beast doesn't move, but somehow seems to grow even larger, taking up more space in the room. "Or you will dishonor both her and our king and be forced to make amends."

Cassel clenches his jaw so tightly that I feel my hand begin to drift to my knives, unsure what he intends to do. Unsure if the king will — or can — stop him, I take a step forward. "Your Majesty, mayhap it would help the queen understand what is happening in Brittany if you would share with her your reasons for appointing Viscount Rohan as governor."

General Cassel shifts his attention from Beast to me. "Are you suggesting the king needs to *explain* himself to anyone?"

"Not anyone. His queen, who was granted a certain amount of autonomy in overseeing her former duchy." I smile playfully. "Are you married, general? If so, you would understand that the surest way to a harmonious marriage is trust."

"No," he grinds out. "I am not married."

"Oh?" I ask, feigning coyness. "Is that why you followed me into the stable, then?"

Beast grows rigid even as the general looks discomfited.

"How did you come to choose Viscount Rohan, my lord?" The queen's question is perfectly timed to reduce the tension in the room.

"He was suggested to me."

"By whom?"

"Your Majesty." The regent's voice comes from the edge of the room as if she has only just arrived.

"Ah, there she is now," the king mutters.

She is smiling like a barn cat who found the cream, Captain Stuart trailing behind her. As she draws closer to Beast, her eyes sweep over him. "Don't you see?" Her voice is light, almost gay. "Here is the answer to all the mysteries that have plagued us."

Panic begins hammering against my ribs as I discern where she is going with this. She raises a finger and points to Beast. "It was he, not Fremin's men, who stole the girls from their room in the dead of night!"

CHAPTER 59

The king frowns, his irritation not inclining him to humor her. "Whatever you are trying to say, just say it. Do not force us to tease it out of you."

Resentment flashes briefly in her eyes. "I am only remarking that his disappearance coincided with that of the two d'Albret girls. If ever a man appeared capable of vile acts, it is he."

The stricken look in Beast's eyes is so brief and fleeting that even I almost miss it. Or mayhap it never shows on his face and I simply feel the twist of pain in his heart. I imagine a lifetime of being accused of misdeeds simply because of his looks.

"Impossible." The queen's clear voice rings out. "I sent him out myself three days before Monsieur Fremin made his claims."

My knees weaken with relief, but Beast's rigidness does not leave him. Nor his fury. It emanates from him like steam from a bubbling pot.

It is there on the tip of the regent's tongue — her wish to accuse the queen of colluding with Beast in this, except that even she cannot imagine what the motive might be. Madame whirls back to face the king. "Of course he would not announce his true intention to the queen. But the rebellion can only be an excuse to cover his unexplained trip to Brittany."

The queen leans forward in her chair, bright spots of anger on her cheeks. "That is untrue."

The regent raises a delicate brow. "If so, then the only other explanation is that this entire incident is a way for you to insert yourself into the king's prerogative to rule. Is that what you are doing?" She tightens the jaws of the trap she has set, forcing the queen to choose between her own reputation or Beast's.

The queen stares at her frostily. "Madame, are you suggesting that I am lying?"

"Either you are or he is."

"Neither of us is lying about this."

The king stares at his wife as if he has never seen her before. "Is this true? Did he abduct the girls?"

"No," the queen answers forcefully. "He did no such thing."

"You cannot believe her, Your Majesty." The regent's words are as smooth as glass. "What else would he be doing? How would she have even known such activity was afoot?"

"Answer," the king orders.

"I received letters from my loyal advisors who still reside in Brittany." Satisfaction glints in the queen's eye as she sets a trap of her own.

The regent scoffs. "I have seen no such letters." It is not until the words are out of her mouth that the regent realizes her mistake.

The queen tilts her head. "Have you been reading my letters?"

Even the king seems shocked. "You've done what?"

Madame shrugs, but she is not as indifferent as she would like to appear. "We had to know if she was loyal to her new husband or her old one." The queen's breath comes hard and fast at this affront to her honor.

"Enough!" The king's voice lashes out like a whip. His face is stony, his heartbeat rapid. He turns to Beast. "When I agreed to have you serve as queen's guard, I made it clear that it was to accompany her when I or my guard was not available. I did not authorize you to meddle in affairs of state on her behalf."

"Your Majesty," the queen tries again. "Surely you should hear what he has to say before you dismiss my concerns and his report out of hand! I believe he carries vital information."

But it is too late. The king's power has been threatened. "And what did you see that was so concerning?" The king's scorn is so thick I am surprised it doesn't choke him.

"Viscount Rohan appears to have called all his men-at-arms from his holdings in France to Brittany. Rennes is fully guarded, allowing no one into the city or out of it without the viscount's permission. Every one of his holdings in Brittany is fully garrisoned, including the western and southern coasts."

The queen looks at the king, any victory she feels at being right chased away by her concern. "There is no reason for his troops to be there," she points out.

"There are no reasons for his troops to be there that the king has chosen to share with you," General Cassel answers for the king, and he allows it. "There are many reasons he would take up such positions."

"Such as?" the queen asks.

"Such as guarding against possible retaliation from the English for having secured Brittany against their effort to maintain its independence."

"Then he should have told Her Majesty of such, surely," I point out.

"Perhaps he did."

The queen rears, as if struck. She turns to the king, who leans back in his throne, arms folded, watching the general. He does not look at her.

Finding no answer to her unspoken question, she asks Cassel. "But why seal off Rennes?"

"In a city that has recently been besieged, with mercenaries and remnants of opposing troops roaming the countryside, why wouldn't a responsible leader secure his city in such a manner?"

"That may be so, but it doesn't explain why he has hundreds of his troops encamped within miles of each of the queen's advisors' holdings." Beast speaks again, his eyes fixed on Cassel.

Cassel takes a step toward him. "Perhaps he has reason to believe they hold conflicting loyalties. After all, the truce was sudden, the marriage recent. It is not unwise to ensure everyone's loyalty."

"Those men, those most honorable men," the queen says, "witnessed the contract themselves. They would never betray me or their honor in such a manner."

"But, Your Majesty," the regent coos. "Can you truly be so very certain of your advisors?" She may as well have picked up a knife and stabbed the queen in the heart with it.

"You mean the very men and women you bribed with France's gold? No, I do not trust those people anymore. They are your creatures now."

The king glowers at his sister, reminded of the dishonorable victory she secured in his name. But the regent is an expert in diversion tactics. "Your Majesty, this is a waste of time and effort. The captain is making this up to cover for his depraved abduction of those girls."

I can stand it no more. I glance first to the queen, who gives an imperceptible nod, then at Beast—to ask for permission or give warning—but his burning gaze is fixed on General Cassel.

"What if both are true?" I say.

All eyes turn toward me, but it is Beast's that I feel the most. "Your Majesty, it is true that Captain Waroch took the girls—not to abduct them, but to get them to safety."

At the name *Waroch*, General Cassel takes another step toward Beast and yanks the peasant hood from his head. His nostrils flare, the recognition instantaneous. "Who are you?"

"Benebic de Waroch," Beast says softly. Then, softer still, "Your judgment day."

"Your Majesty," I say in desperation. "This man, Sir Waroch, would have no reason to harm those girls. Indeed, one of them was his own sister's daughter. He simply went searching for them. And once he found them, he took them to safety."

"Where did you take them?" Cassel demands.

"Where they will be safe."

"How dare you suggest the king cannot be trusted."

"It is not the king I am concerned with. As I understand it, the regent is working closely with Pierre d'Albret."

The regent steps toward Beast. "The girls are his property."

Beast does not back down. "They are not safe in his custody."

"And you think we will believe they are safe in yours?" Cassel's eyes sweep over him, taking in every muscle, every scar, every bit of ugliness that adorns Beast's face.

Beast does not look away. "In this case, the apple has fallen far from the tree. I do not rape women. Especially not little —"

General Cassel strikes him across the mouth, the loud crack halting his words as Beast's head snaps back. A lesser man would have been felled like a tree, but Beast simply shakes it off and stares silently at the general, blood pouring from his nose and mouth.

The king glances briefly at the queen's pale hand on his arm, then says, "Enough, General. Captain Waroch, explain this accusation."

His eyes never leaving the general, Beast begins. "General Cassel raped my mother during the War of the Public Good. He occupied the holding, then raped her, using her for the entire length of his stay — a fortnight — then rode away leaving her weeping and praying for death. God did not grant her wish. He gave her me instead."

Silence permeates the chamber. Shaken, the king looks to the general. "Is this true?"

General Cassel starts to deny it, but the king cuts him off. "Do not lie to me. All the proof I need is in the face of the man who stands next to you."

Cassel shrugs his heavy shoulders. "It was war, sire. It was twenty-four years ago, and I was young. The fighting heated my blood. It was a youthful indiscretion. I would never do anything so dishonorable now. Do we all not temper and mellow with age?"

The king studies him, his disgust plain on his face. But he is torn as well, eager to accept the justification the general has offered that will allow him to dismiss the entire abhorrent situation. That will allow him to avoid having to examine his own choice of advisors. He nods briefly. When he speaks to Beast, his voice less cold and more polite.

"I am sorry for the injustices suffered by your mother. As you can see, General Cassel is remorseful and has given his word that it did not happen again. Now I will ask you to tell us where the girls are so we may fetch them."

"No, Your Majesty. Not until I have ensured they will not be returned to their brother."

The king's hands grasp the arms of his chair. "They belong to him."

"Perhaps they should not."

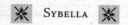

Any sympathy the king felt toward Beast disappears. "Then you leave me no choice but to imprison you until you trust us with this information."

Cassel steps forward, eyes gleaming. "I will get the truth from him."

"No!" The king's voice rings out. "No coercion. I feel certain Sir Waroch will come to trust us soon enough."

The general's rationale has not worked as well as he'd hoped, for there is still faint revulsion in the king's eyes as he looks at Cassel. It is the faintest spark of hope in an otherwise disastrous meeting.

Chapter 60

Geneviève

s the meeting breaks up, I slip out of the audience chamber and head back to my room. Sybella and the queen have enough disasters to wrestle with at the moment. They do not need my additional problem added to their load. I will find a solution myself.

Somehow.

But answers remain elusive, and I ache with the sense of an impending disaster like old Solange's joints used to ache before a storm.

I let myself into my room, relieved there are no longer guards to watch my every step. As I move to shut the door behind me, a hand reaches out to stop it.

"You're back." Sybella's eyes are unreadable as they search my face.

"I didn't realize you knew I had left." She holds the note to the king in her hand. "Have you read it?"

"No, I've not had time. It has been a most eventful morning." Her entire face is drawn tight, her eyes clouded with agitation.

"I left one for you as well. It's under the mattress."

She fully enters the room and closes the door behind her. "Where were you going?"

"The letter explains it."

She folds her arms. "Well, you are here now, so why don't you explain it and save me the trouble of heaving your furniture around."

When I hesitate, she says, "Am I to assume you still want this delivered to the king?"

"No!" I reach to snag it from her, but as fast and unexpected as I am, she is faster. We stare at each other a long moment. "You don't have time for this," I tell her. "Surely Beast is a higher priority."

Her casual shrug is one of the more artful lies I have ever seen told, as I know what she must be feeling right now. "He is not going anywhere. And I will not be able to sneak in to see him until they have gotten him properly settled in whatever section of the dungeon they choose." A note of bleakness creeps into her voice. "So actually, this is a welcome distraction."

"You won't think so for long," I mutter.

"Come." She sits on the edge of the bed and pats the space beside her. "Tell me what has happened."

"The regent approached me last night. Apparently when she came upon you and me talking just before we left Plessis, she heard our entire conversation."

Sybella closes her eyes. "Of course she did. And of course she would hold such a card close until it could do the most damage."

"It was foolish of me to think otherwise. Anyway, she has given me an ulti-matum. I must do as she asks or she will expose not just me to the council, but the king's knowledge of what I've done and who I am. She will use it to under-mine his ability to rule and force him to give back some of the power she had as regent."

Sybella swears colorfully. "What does she want in exchange?" She speaks softly, and I cannot tell if it is in sympathy or carefully banked anger.

"You. She wants me to ensure the king hands you over to Pierre's custody."

Her eyes widen in surprise. "I did not realize I had gotten quite so deeply under her skin," she murmurs.

"And if that does not work, she suggests I kill you. Either way, you must be Pierre's by the end of the week or she will expose the king."

"When did she speak to you?"

"Late last night. After midnight. Why?"

She begins tapping the note on her chin. "Because Pierre did not appear at

the hearing this morning. When the king sent someone to check, it was discovered that he and his party had left before dawn. It was as much a surprise to the
regent as any of us."

"He is gone?"

She nods, still thinking.

"Well, that is welcome news, but I am not certain it solves my problem."

Her lips curve in a faint smile. "You do not wish to kill me?"

"Not at the moment, no."

She laughs, then grows sober. "Were you just going to run away? Into the
city? Hide yourself among the masses? Alone?"

"I had a plan."

She arches a brow. "Given how your plans have gone in the past, you will
forgive me if I ask you to elaborate."

Even though it is deserved, I wince. "I've done it before."

"Yes, but according to you, there was an imposing prisoner traveling at your
side."

It is all I can do not to squirm. "Odd that you should mention that. He was
going to accompany me this time as well."

"He followed you to the palace?"

"No. He has other business here."

Her eyes narrow. "What other business? I think it is time you tell me all that
you know about this prisoner of yours."

Of yours. The words pinch at my heart. With no other options before me,
I tell her about Maraud. The reason he was in the dungeon, Cassel's killing of
his brother, and his vow of vengeance against the general as well as his desire to
make his crimes known to the king. In truth, it feels good to free myself of these
secrets. I did not intend or wish to keep them from her, but there has been no
time to speak of it since I knew she could be trusted. By the time I am finished,
Sybella is staring at me with an odd expression on her face.

"Does this prisoner have a name, by any chance?"

"His name is Anton Crunard. He is the son of the former chancellor of
Brittany."

Sybella stares at me, then closes her eyes before muttering, "*Merde.*"

"Has the queen been looking for him? She needs to know that none of this was his fault. He had no idea that his father would betray the country for him. Indeed, they are estranged and have been for years."

Sybella's eyes fly open. "Estranged, you say?"

"Yes. He was the prodigal son."

The letter begins tapping furiously at her chin again so that I want to jump up, snatch it from her hand, and toss it into the fireplace. "What? What are you thinking?"

"Not so much thinking as remembering. Just before the queen left for France, Crunard senior attempted to escape his imprisonment. He told us the reason was to go look for his son. He did not trust the queen to do it, even though she had promised she would. When we arrived in France, we received word that he had made a second attempt to escape and succeeded."

"Why would she promise a traitor she would look for his son?"

"The promise was not made to the father, but to Maraud's half sister."

I gape at her. "A half sister he does not yet know that he has," she amends.

I can scarce wrap my mind around this. Know that Maraud will scarcely be able to wrap his mind around this. He is not the sole remaining child, after all.

"I think that will come as a great relief to him," I say softly.

She runs her fingers along the edge of the letter. "There is something else you should know about this half sister of his. Her name is Annith. From the convent."

This revelation leaves me well and truly speechless. "Annith?"

"Remember I told you she was the abbess's daughter and not one of Mortain's? Well, Crunard was her father."

My mind churns as all the implications of this spread out before me like a giant web.

"That is the hold that he had over her as abbess," Sybella continues. "The chancellors of Brittany have often acted as liaisons with the convent on behalf of the sovereign, so this was no different. Except that when he wished her to look the other way or apply pressure here instead of there, as he wove the rope he was hoping to hang us with, she had no choice but to agree lest he expose her secret."

"My heart holds no forgiveness for her. She had a choice."

"I agree, and she chose poorly. But I am gathering that you and Anton were — are — close, and I want you to know how he came to have a sister."

"Well," I say, unwilling to address the question in her voice. "What am I to do regarding the regent's demands?"

"You are to remain calm and stay in your chamber as much as possible."

"What if the king summons me?"

"You will have to go. And say nothing of the ultimatum. Not yet anyway. We have a week. That is enough time to come up with a countermove."

"While you're thinking on it, may I please have the letter to throw in the fire and burn before somebody else sees it?"

As she hands me the letter, she tilts her head to stare at the fire in the hearth, her eyes taking on a faraway look. "Why did you not tell me about the regent's ultimatum before deciding to leave?"

There were so many reasons. "I was afraid you would try to protect me rather than stay focused on the longer view of the king and his struggle against the regent. I was afraid you might confront the regent. Or go after Pierre. Or confess to Fremin's murder. Every option I saw you choosing might ease the pressure on me, but would make things worse for yourself."

"So you did not trust me."

"I trusted you too much. I have seen how you thrust yourself between those you care about and the troubles that plague them."

She arches one of her elegant brows. "You think I care about you?"

I shrug, embarrassed now. "You had seemed determined to act the older sister before we left Plessis. I didn't know how long that impulse would last."

"You will be happy to know that I still have that impulse. Which is why I will not let you leave like you want to. We are the daughters of a god, Genevieve. We were not meant to move in this world as pale reflections of ourselves. It is not how we serve the gods who made us."

"But Mortain is no longer."

"He is not the only god." Her eyes gleam faintly. "It is time for you to meet the Dark Mother."

I draw in a sharp breath. The Dark Matrona is rarely spoken of, a dark goddess of death and destruction. "But only the charbonnerie worship her."

Her hand slips inside her pocket, and she smiles faintly. "They are not the only ones." For some reason, a shiver goes down my spine.

When Sybella speaks again, her voice is firm. "You have wallowed in the ashes of your remorse long enough. It is time to rise."

Even though her words make no sense, they spark a small ember of hope — of anticipation — inside my chest. "And how am I to do that?"

Her eyes never leave mine. "You simply choose. When it feels like there is no other alternative before you, you decide to rise." She stands, then reaches for my hand.

"You don't understand," I whisper. "That is how I came to be in this mess in the first place. I allowed myself to believe I was an instrument of the gods."

"That was your mistake."

"But now you are telling me to do that very thing again!"

"This time I'm reminding you that you are already part god. The time for hiding from that is over. You have been stripped bare of your pretenses." Her gaze dips down to my neck. "You gave up any thoughts of grandeur or glory long ago, else you would never have allowed that collar around your neck. You are no longer acting because you feel a need within yourself, but because it needs to be done. I do not know how the Dark Mother works, only that when she offers us hope, we do well to take it." Her eyes glow with both ferocity and love, and it is like nothing I have ever seen.

Still not fully understanding, I take hold of her hand and rise to my feet.

CHAPTER 61

ou sent for me, Your Majesty?" He is as agitated as I have ever seen him, pacing back and forth before the enormous fireplace. In truth, it is so large he could pace inside it.

He whirls on me then, nearly shaking with rage. "Have you learned what happened yesterday? Do you know that your queen has been operating behind my back? Lying to me? All of them — the queen, Lady Sybella, my sister, even General Cassel — lying to me."

I open my mouth to answer, but he has no interest in hearing whatever I have to say.

"My council was right. The queen cannot serve two masters. As long as the queen honors the Nine, her devotion to them puts her at odds with me. We must be rid of them. Not just have the queen renounce them, but eliminate them all." He pins me with a scathing glare, wanting the words to hurt, as well as shock. I say nothing and allow his anger to wash over me like a sudden storm. Once it passes, I can hope to restore order.

"Do the other Nine have convents like yours? Are they all fostering traitors and rebels inside their walls?"

"Not to my knowledge, Your Majesty. There are the Brigantian convents, with which France is already intimately acquainted. Indeed, I believe there are one or two here, as well as in Brittany. And the convent of Saint Mortain, of which there is only one, and our numbers are small. Saint Amourna and Saint Camulos are removed from this world, their followers simply honoring them, as they do the Church's other saints. Saint Salonius and Saint Cissonius have few followers, all of them old men."

"That is only six," he says.

"There is one other small convent, the convent of Saint Mer, but they are concerned only with the sea. Those who serve Arduinna have no convent, choosing instead to live in the forest in small groups. As for the followers of Dea Matrona . . ." I frown. "There are no convents, but crones, I believe, who live at the edges of the forest and villages. But other than blessing the fields before planting, I do not know what they do."

The king gives a noncommittal grunt.

"As you can see, sire, not much of a threat to anyone, let alone the power of the Church. Or yourself."

"The power does not lie in them, but in what your queen will do in their name."

"Do you not see that most of the queen's actions would not have been needed if not for the regent and her scheming? Can you not see how hard your sister has worked to discredit the queen? Drive a wedge between the two of you?"

"The regent didn't force the queen to go behind my back and send men to Brittany."

"Are you so very certain of that? Who intercepted all her correspondence, leaving her no choice but to use messengers? Who brought d'Albret's lawyer to court and allowed him immediate access to you? If you look closely enough, every time the queen has moved in a way you didn't like, it is because Madame — and occasionally yourself — gave her no other choice."

"How do you know all this?"

I shrug. "I have spoken with both the queen and Sybella, Your Majesty. That is no secret."

"They lie."

"While it is possible they may lie to you — out of fear — they would have no reason to lie to me."

He is quiet then, pondering my words. "The regent did not force Sybella to lie to me about her sisters." He takes a step toward me. "Did you know she had them sent away from here? That they were not abducted?"

"She did not tell me that, no. But it is good news. Surely you think so as well. Better to have them safe, even if a lie was required to keep them so."

"I would have protected them."

"I know you would have, if you had believed there was a threat against them. But you did not believe Sybella until I revealed that Monsieur Fremin appeared in her room carrying a blade and a length of rope."

My words discomfit him, and he turns to face the fire. Pressing my advantage, I ask, "Why are you not equally outraged by the lies General Cassel has told you?"

He waves his hand, dismissing them. "It was an indiscretion of his youth. He swore he would never do such a thing now."

"Such a thing as rape Sir Waroch's mother?"

"A youthful indiscretion," the king insists stubbornly.

"He was older than you when it happened. Would you commit such a youthful indiscretion?"

"Never!" I see the moment he remembers laying his hands on me roughly.

"No," I say softly. "You didn't. You stopped yourself. Why should General Cassel be held to lesser standards? Besides, who knows how many times Cassel has done such a thing?"

"He was young," the king repeats mulishly, and I want to reach out and shake his rutting shoulders.

"He was older than the queen is now, when she acted out of true concern for her countrymen. Why are you so willing to forgive him, but not her?" When he says nothing, I step out onto the thinnest of ice and continue. "It cannot be because you think she took something from you, while Cassel's transgression hurt another."

It is exactly that, of course, but in so asking, it forces him to see that truth, and he does not like it.

"If General Cassel holds no honor in how he treats women, where else is his honor lacking?" I want so desperately to tell him of Maraud's brother, Ives, but it is not my story to tell. Instead, "I have heard rumors," I say.

The king's head snaps up. "What rumors?"

"Among the men at Cognac, those who served with Angoulême. They said

General Cassel did not observe the custom of ransom. That he coldly butchered those who had laid down their swords in surrender."

The king grows pale. "I have never heard such claims. That goes against all constraints of honor."

What he means is, it is one thing to show dishonor to a mere woman, and something else entirely to show dishonor to a man of his own rank.

"Everyone knows how you favor General Cassel, Your Majesty. Mayhap they did not have the courage to tell you.

"What will you do?" My voice is soft, hopefully naught but an echo of the very question he is asking himself.

"I don't know." He faces me then. No, not me, but the wall behind me. I turn to look, my eyes landing on the painting his father gave him. I did not realize he had it brought with the other household items from Plessis.

Something inside me snaps. "Do not look at that be-damned painting," I all but shout. "It is as much a chain around your neck as this silver one is around mine."

His eyes widen, and at first I think it is because he recognizes the truth in my words. But when he raises his gaze to me, it is shuttered and tight. "You go too far. Get out," he says.

In that moment, all his smallness and narrow-mindedness is as vivid as the painting, and I would happily leave him to the political machinations of his devious sister — if it were not for all the other lives that hang in the balance.

CHAPTER 62

Maraud

When Pierre d'Albret and his men had surrounded Maraud on his way to the fletcher's hut and said, "You are coming with me," Maraud had laughed.

Until Pierre had said, "We have someone who is very much counting on your cooperation." Then he was terrified. Terrified that somehow, Pierre d'Albret had seen him and Genevieve together. Terrified that she was the someone d'Albret was so confident he would want to see.

"As I told you back in Angoulême," Pierre had continued, "I have a proposition that will hold great personal interest for you, and I will not take no for an answer. Unless you do not care if you ever see that person alive again."

Maraud's mind kept trying to imagine what d'Albret's men might be doing to Gen even as he reassured himself Pierre couldn't have strided into the palace, past all the king's guards and men-at-arms, and abducted her.

Except Pierre was also a guest at the palace and likely was not given a second glance. Or, worse, his every whim was seen to.

There was a second option that was less terrifying, but just as bleak. That she would have no choice but to think he'd begged and pleaded with her to come with him, only to abandon her. Knowing her, she'd assume he'd planned that since he first came to her in Paris, set her up for the fall she no doubt thought she deserved. That thought was a twist of a knife in his vital organs rather than a full disemboweling.

But at least that meant she was safe. By the horns of Camulos, he prayed it was so.

CHAPTER 63

Sybella

hy am I always the one in the servant's gown?" Gen mutters. Because I do not know what I will find or whether I will need a diversion, I have brought her with me to the donjon.

That and to keep the regent from pouncing on her unawares again.

"Because I am visiting the prisoner on behalf of the queen, who wishes her loyal knight to have this book of hours to sustain him through his time in captivity. There are just enough who are aware that Beast and I have a connection that if I were to be seen dressed as a servant, it would immediately raise suspicion."

Gen nudges me to silence then. We have reached the donjon. The central tower is the oldest part of the palace and surrounded by a ditch. A guardhouse — holding four heartbeats — sits next to the only entrance. I nod at Gen, and we use the shadows to move along the edge of the guardhouse to the stairway beyond. As we creep down the steps, I listen carefully for heartbeats below, but hear none. However, the stone walls are twelve feet thick, so we remain cautious.

When we reach the deepest level, I step off the stairs. The donjon may be old, but it is well maintained. Iron lanterns, rather than torches, hang from hooks in the wall, and full suits of armor stand at regular intervals. Whether it is intended to trick others into believing there are more guards than there are or simply a testament to France's sense of grandeur, I do not know. I listen again. I am able to feel Beast's heart, as steady and familiar as my own, but that is all.

Gen remains behind at the foot of the stairs to keep watch as I follow the curving wall past a half dozen empty rooms — some with iron bars and others with thick, iron-banded oak doors with naught but tiny, barred windows — and a small table underneath one of the iron lanterns on the wall. They have stripped Beast of all his possessions and laid them here upon this table. My hand twitches, wishing to retrieve at least some of them for safekeeping, but I do not know how thorough an inventory they took.

The moment I approach Beast's door, he lifts his head. One of his eyes is swollen shut, and there is a cut on his lip. When I drop the shadows from me as I would a cloak, he surges to his feet and comes to the door. The hardened resignation on his face melts away like smoke and is replaced by a lopsided grin that causes his lip to start bleeding.

"This brings back fond memories." His voice is the rasp of a sharpening stone on dull iron.

I shake my head. He is as resilient as gristle. "You are fond of dungeons?"

He places his hand upon his chest. "But of course. I first met you in a dungeon."

The foolish man will have my heart melt into a useless puddle at my feet. "The queen sent me." I do not tell him of the regent's ultimatum. There is nothing he can do about it from here, and worrying on it might cause him to do something truly witless.

His face sobers. "I was hoping she would."

"You are to tell me everything so I may make a full report to her."

He nods, all signs of my lover gone, and naught but a soldier stands before me. "What I dared not say in front of the king was that as we traveled farther west, we continued to find his holdings fully manned. On our return trip, the marches were crowded with Rohan's troops as well. We were not able to get through unseen and were chased from Ancenis to Baugé before we managed to evade them."

My next words are carefully chosen. "Will they carry the tale of your presence back to Rohan?"

"No."

I nod in approval. "Likely no more than a simple defensive maneuver, then. What counsel would you give the queen?"

He scrubs his face with his hand, wincing as it brushes against his swollen eye. "To get word to her councilors so they are not caught unaware."

"Do you think Duval would be allowed to receive a message from the queen?"

"Possibly not, but we must try."

The next part is the hardest, but he may have some insight I do not. "I am sorry," I say softly. "Sorry that I spoke out about your connection to the general, but I could not keep silent in the face of the vile accusations made by the regent."

"I would rather be imprisoned for defiance than have anyone think me capable of such an act. But now you will have drawn his attention and need to be alert. He is every bit as dangerous as Lord d'Albret was and will poke and prod at us for weaknesses."

"You do not have to tell me that," I mutter. "Why is he so set against believing anything you have reported?"

Beast's entire face hardens, and his heart quickens. "Because he thrives on war and discord and does not care what lives are lost, as long as there is the opportunity for glory and power."

"But how does that serve the king?"

"The king is only the second most important thing to men like Cassel. The first is his own self-interest or else he would at least have entertained the report. Mayhap he wishes it to come to a head so he can ride into the fray and declare himself the savior."

"Surely the king would see through such raw self-interest?"

"You saw the way he watched the man. A noxious mix of fascination and admiration, tempered by only a sliver of doubt. That is what makes the general so dangerous — the sheer power of his will pulls others into its path."

"How will we ever get the king to listen, let alone act?"

"I don't know that you can" is Beast's stark reply.

As I consider his words, Gen appears, her eyes wide. "He is coming!" she hisses.

"Who is that?" Beast asks.

"Genevieve. Who is coming?" I ask her. "The guard?"

"No! The general!"

Merde. "We have to go," I tell Beast as Gen grabs my elbow and begins pulling me away from his cell door.

"In here," she whispers, tugging me into the cell next to Beast's. This one does not have a solid wooden door, but iron bars. However, if we press ourselves into the corner and draw the shadows around us, he will not be able to see us unless he has reason to enter the cell. We hide not a moment too soon — the heels of Cassel's boots echoing off the stone walls. Gen nudges me, then points to the suit of armor against the wall behind us and to the right. Cassel is reflected back in its polished surface.

He is not rushing, but strolling, as if he has all the time in the world. He glances at the small table holding all of Beast's possessions before continuing to Beast's cell.

"Prove to me you are who you say you are, else I will believe you are merely some charlatan sent by my enemies."

Beast's voice rumbles out of his dark prison. "Have you never looked in a mirror?"

"That merely tells me there is more than one ugly man of exceptional size in France. You have no proof that I was in Brittany as you claim."

"There were and are a dozen witnesses who heard you boast of your occupation of that holding during the war. It was one of the moves that brought you so quickly to the attention of King Louis."

"Present your witnesses. Let us see how their stories hold up under my questioning."

"I'm not interested in proving anything to you."

"Then I will have no choice but to believe you are making all this up and have been planted by my enemies." His voice drops. "The queen perhaps."

"What would you accept as proof?" Beasts wonders. "The great welts and bruises that never faded from my mother's throat and reminded her daily of how you held her down as you dishonored her?"

Cassel's heartbeat, which has been steady until now, comes more rapidly. "Would she come to court to make that claim? For if she does, no one will believe her. The fact that she conceived proves that she enjoyed it."

Of all the lies men have fashioned around women, this is one of the most hateful.

Beast holds no patience for it either. "Some philosophers subscribe to that view, but the real world tells a far different story."

Cassel puts his hands behind his back and considers Beast. "So my son is the notorious Benebic de Waroch. The man they say can carry an ox in each hand and fight a dozen men at once. This sounds like a son I would be willing to call my own."

Beast's heart thuds against his chest so loudly it is all I can do not to cover my ears. "Whatever strengths I have do not come from you," he growls. "I have acquired most of them myself, while others are gifts from the saint who claimed me at birth."

"Claimed you?" Cassel snorts. "Who would claim such a child? Did you make an offering to him? A sacrifice on his altar?"

"No. You did when you forced yourself on my mother. I am the result of that offering, and Camulos claims all such offerings as his own."

"Is that all it took?" Cassel's voice holds a faint note of interest, as if he is intrigued by the idea of acquiring more such sons. "If you have no desire to prove this to anyone, why claim you're my son?"

"I would have gone happily to my deathbed never having met you. It was not I who informed the court."

"No." The single word is drawn out, thoughtful. "It was not you. What is the girl to you?"

"What girl?"

"Do not play the dumb beast with me. The Lady Sybella. She is the one who told the king."

"She is nothing to me." I nearly cheer that Beast does not rise to the bait.

"One of the queen's most trusted attendants, serving Her Majesty just as I do."

"That is a lie. She claimed you were connected to her sisters."

"That part is true. My sister was married to her father, years ago. I myself learned of it only recently, and it has naught to do with my service to the queen."

As silence falls between them, General Cassel begins to slowly pace in front of the cell door. "And yet she shared this knowledge with the court. Why is that, I wonder?"

"I have heard she has a great fondness for justice."

"But how would she come to know of this connection between us?"

"Captain Dunois told her."

Cassel stops walking. "Did you know Captain Dunois well?"

"We fought together in the Mad War, then served on the queen's council together. He was one of the most loyal, valiant, and honorable men I have ever known."

The general's bark of laughter raises my hackles. "Is that what he told you?"

"It is what I observed with my own eyes." The ire in Beast's voice would surely worry a less vainglorious man.

"He turned his back on his liege and threw in his fortunes with the dukes rebelling against the crown. When last I looked, that was the very definition of treason."

"That is where his honor shines brightest. His liege overstepped, moving without cause to usurp power, lands, and titles legitimately held by others. That he stood against those illegal ambitions when so few others did is a sign of great integrity. Even a king must obey the laws."

Cassel shrugs. "The king is the law. He can change them at will."

"But should he? If treaties have been signed, successions agreed upon, borders defined, is it right to change them on one man's — or woman's — whim?"

"You sound like Captain Dunois, and I will not tolerate such treason in my own son."

Beast laughs outright at that, a great rolling sound that fills the dungeons. "As you said, there is no proof that I am your son. You have no power over me."

"Don't I?" The general's musing question sends goose flesh down my arms. "I may not be able to question the queen, but it will be easy enough for me to question the girl. She lies more than most women, and is better at it. There are many answers I wish to have from her. And as she is an assassin trained, I suspect it will be a challenge to convince her to spill her secrets." He leans in closer to the window of Beast's door. "Have I mentioned how much I enjoy challenges?" My heart is now beating as rapidly as theirs. Not in fear, at least not for myself, but for Beast. Cassel is baiting him as surely as a hunter baits a bear.

A low growl rumbles through the dungeons, echoing off the stone walls, chasing away any memory of his former laughter. There is a clank of chains and a roar as Beast slams into the door of his cell.

Cassel steps back, watching with fascination and growing excitement. "Such power you possess," he murmurs.

Beast's enormous hands grasp the iron bars in the small window of the door, bulging and straining as they try to tear them from their moorings.

With taunting patience, Cassel turns to the small table behind him, looking carefully before picking up one of Beast's own knives from it. Does he think to hack at Beast's fingers?

"It appears anger awakens this strength of yours. Does pain make you angry? Would it allow you to break free of that cage?" The cool dispassion in his voice is more unnerving than any battle lust could ever be.

I was raised by a man such as he — a man who held cruelty and superior strength in high regard. A man who felt any matter was best settled by fists or swords or crushing force, and that peace came only after you had salted the earth or slain all who survived. I spent an entire lifetime being ever watchful in a household full of men precisely like this one. They are capricious, and that unpredictability makes them even more dangerous than their strength.

"Should we kill him?" Gen's whisper against my ear is naught but a slight movement in the air as she asks the very question I am struggling with. Would Beast care if I killed his father? I think not, but the complications would be nearly insurmountable. I shake my head and point at Gen.

She nods. "You wish me to do it?"

I put my lips to her ear. "No. The king would immediately suspect you, and in a choice between you and Cassel, I am not certain where the king's heart would fall."

Her nostrils flare in irritation — an irritation I share. In spite of my warning to her, I take a step, thinking to intervene in some way, but Gen's hand clamps down on the back of my gown.

"Is everything all right, General?"

I freeze, then shift to peer in the armor's reflection. It is one of the guards. Gen tugs my arm again, more frantically. Her eyes are wide and she thumps her hand silently against her chest, then points to her ears. She hears his heartbeat.

He's going to die.

"We heard a . . . a noise and thought we should check."

"It was nothing but this beast. We are about to see just how strong he is."

The guard's head rears back, clearly startled. "But, sir, the king gave the order that he wasn't to be —"

There is a whisper of movement, followed by a muted gurgle. In the silver reflection, it looks as if the general and the guard are embracing. Until the general shoves the other man from him and lets go, leaving a knife protruding from the guard's chest. Beast's roar of fury rattles the lanterns on their hooks as the guard slumps to the floor.

Cassel looks down at the dying man and nudges him with his boot. "It is too bad our prisoner's battle lust rages so out of control. How were you to know that the others failed to relieve him of all his weapons, or that he could reach through the bars of his cage and kill you?" When next he speaks, I can hear the smile in his voice. "And when he hears of it, the king is sure to let me question you the way I wish."

CHAPTER 64

s Cassel strides back toward the main part of the floor where the other guards are, I hear him call out, "It's nothing. The prisoner is simply earning his nickname. Your man will stay with him for the next few hours until he settles down. The rest of you remain here at your posts."

Before he has finished speaking, I hurry over to the fallen guard. Gen kneels beside me. "Can he be saved?"

I shake my head. "He was stabbed in the lung. Even now he is drowning in his own blood." There is another rattle and thud against the door as Beast, still in the grips of his battle fever, reacts to this news.

"That is horrible," Gen says. "And all for trying to follow the king's orders."

The guard moves his lips, trying to say something, but only red bubbles emerge. He begins to cough. I grab the end of his cloak and wipe away some of the blood. "Easy, now."

Gen's face is pinched white, her shoulders hunched slightly.

"Are you all right?"

She nods. "It is just so loud — the beating of his heart."

He coughs again, his heart beginning to race in panic even as it does not have enough blood to do so. "It is an ugly way to die," I murmur. And certainly not a death deserved by someone who tried to act so nobly.

My hand tingles with the memory of the fallen guard back in Rennes, so many months ago. He, too, had been handed an ugly death for equally noble deeds. Without pausing to think, I gently lay my hand on the man's chest, just over his heart. "Thank you," I whisper.

"Your honor saved one I love from great agony. Your spirit will live on with my enduring gratitude."

The beating of his heart eases somewhat, as if no longer terrified. *How?* I pray. *How may I ease this man's plight?*

Just as before, the answer comes from deep within, filling me with a presence that is not wholly my own. I do not question whose voice it is, know only that it is wiser than I and allow my hand to settle more firmly.

"Go," I whisper. "We will see that justice is done."

With my words, he gives one last, shuddering breath, then grows still. Gen stares at me open-mouthed, but before she can say anything, his soul clambers from his body, much like a man who has been buried alive might claw his way from the dirt. He is distraught. Angry. Outraged. The soul starts to flit down the hall, as if it means to go after Cassel, then changes its mind and heads for Beast's cell, pausing in confusion before whirling around and hurrying back to his body, rubbing against it like a cat, as if trying to put itself back in.

"Three days," Gen says, staring down at the man. With her face downcast, it is hard to tell, but I think there are tears shimmering in her eyes. "He must endure this for three days. All for trying to stop that rutting monster." Her fists clench. "I will tell the king. I will tell him what I saw with my own eyes."

I grab her arm and give it a gentle shake. "Stop and think. You will only put yourself at risk. He will likely not even listen to you. Not after your conversation yesterday."

"We must do something."

"We will."

"We cannot let Beast get blamed for this."

"We will not let that happen."

Her gaze falls back to the dead man and the soul that is thudding uselessly against its old body. "But none of that will help him."

It is her nature to act, I realize. She needs to act as most people need to breathe. "Here. Let us try something." I take her hand.

She resists. "What?"

I sigh. "I would show you a way to help him. We do not have much time if we want to keep Beast from being falsely accused, but the dead are also our responsibility. Do you remember you asked how I was able to make Fremin's soul disappear?" She nods. "I did not have time to tell you then, but I will tell you now. Blood and bone. Ours. The same stuff that gods were once made of. Let us see if it holds true for you as well."

"Show me."

When I have explained it to her, she takes one of her own knives, makes a tiny cut on the top of her wrist, then turns her arm over so the blood drips upon his forehead. As soon as the blood touches the body, the soul stops its desperate thumping and grows still, waiting.

As Gen smears the blood with her thumb, she murmurs, "May the Nine grant you peace." For the briefest of seconds, the quivering tension leaves the soul and then it is simply gone. Vanished.

Gen sits back on her knees, her eyes and mouth open wide with wonder.

I give her exactly one minute, then gently cuff her on her head. "There is no time for that. We must move this body before the blood soaks through his cloak and leaves a trail on the stone."

"What about one of the other cells?" she asks.

"It would be best if the body wasn't found for a few days."

She hops to her feet and disappears down the corridor while I place the dead man's arms upon his chest, then reach for his cloak. Fortunately, it is one of the long, wide cloaks of the palace guard, and I am able to wrap it twice around him, which will prevent any leakage for a while longer.

Gen reappears just then. "There's a large drain. Just around that second bend. There is a grate on it, but I think we can pry it loose."

I nod, then grab the shoulders of his cloak while she reaches for his booted feet, and together we drag the guard away from Beast's cell. It is farther than I had thought, and I am out of breath and sweating when we reach it at last. Gen drops his boots, pulls her knife, and uses it to pry the bolts from the stone. That, too, takes longer than I would like, but between the two of us, it is done.

"It feels wrong to stuff him into a hole like this."

"I know. But his soul is gone from here and will hopefully never know. Besides, it is not *unlike* a catacomb."

She nods stoically, then places her arms on his shoulders and shoves while I direct his body into the drain. "Wait!" I call out, and she stops. "We don't want to leave Beast's knife." I pull it out slowly, then wipe it upon the man's cloak until it is mostly clean, and tuck it into my boot. "Okay."

But now it is Gen's turn to pause. "What is he holding?" His left hand is closed tight around something. Gen gently pries it open, then brings the object out into the light.

It is a gold mantle brooch. She looks up at me. "This belongs to the general."

"The gods have not yet determined the ending to this story," I mutter. "Leave it. If the body is found, it will point to the general."

Once Gen has left, I check the area in front of Beast's cell one more time for any signs of what has transpired. When I am assured we have erased anything that can be used against Beast, I finally approach his door.

His heartbeat has returned to its slow, steady rhythm, but even though he was gripped by battle lust, I know he will be aware of all that transpired.

Be aware and feel the weight of it on his soul.

When I reach the door, I peer in through the small grate. Only the faintest bit of light reaches inside, and I can just make out his silhouette sitting on the lone wooden bench, his head in his hands.

"It is taken care of," I tell him.

He looks up at the sound of my voice but does not stand. "I thought you had left."

"We were simply hiding the body."

"The man is dead." The words feel like boulders dragged up from the depths of Beast's heart.

"Yes. And blessed, and his soul released with as much grace as two of Death's handmaidens possess. He knows how grateful we are to him."

"I did not ask him to sacrifice his life." It is anguish I hear in his voice, not anger.

"Of course not, but you are not the only one to whom honor means something. Other men are allowed to defend it as well."

He inhales sharply, then rises from the bench.

"We will find a way to use this against Cassel. At some point," I say. "But for now, with so much stacked against us, we must use this to our advantage. He plans to blame it on you, but there is no body to be found. No weapon. He cannot push too hard, or he will reveal his own hand in this."

Beast comes to peer out the grate, seeing with his own eyes that the horror that just transpired is nowhere in sight.

"He plans to blame it on the beast within you. So let us go with that. Do not come to the door when the guards approach. Make them shove your food inside. Do not talk with anyone. Roar or growl once in a while, if need be. Especially if the general approaches alone." I do not want the man near Beast, and if playing a beast helps ensure that, then we will embrace it.

"I am not afraid of him."

"Nor am I."

He reaches for the bars of his window. "You should be." His voice is low and thrumming with despair. "He all but threatened you. He knows I care for you and all but threatened you. He is not one to let a weakness go unprobed."

"I grew up around men like him and am well aware what he is capable of. Although I will forgive you for forgetting, given the day you've had."

He huffs out a half snort that could be laughter.

"The general's actions have just lit the cannon's fuse. We will have to move fast, and so we will. I don't know how yet, but we will get you out of here. And soon."

I grasp his fingers through the grate and give them a squeeze. "And, Beast? Do not ever — and I mean *ever* — claim that you are the monster your father

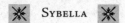

is. Surely even you can see how false that is now that he has exposed his true nature."

Then I force myself to let go and step away from the door. I will be of no use to him if I sit here weeping for all that he has had to endure.

CHAPTER 65

When I have finished telling the queen everything we have learned over the last two days, from the regent's ultimatum to General Cassel's horrifying fascination with Beast, she lifts a trembling hand to her brow, as if to rub away the weight of all these revelations. In truth, she has aged at least ten years during the telling of it.

She takes a deep breath before speaking, "Please tell me you have a plan for protecting Beast from any more interference from the general."

The question is like a thorn in my heart. "Not yet, Your Majesty. I have counseled Beast to remain deep within his cell and not come to the door unless they drag him bodily, but other than that, we are somewhat limited."

She looks hopefully at Gen, who glances down at her feet. "The king has already summoned me once, Your Majesty. It did not go well. Especially when I attempted to gently point out the flaws in both the general's and the regent's claims. I was, in effect, ordered to leave and not come back."

The queen closes her eyes. "My fool husband's pride is going to blind him to the attempted coup taking place under his nose."

"For whatever reason," I say slowly, "the regent is choosing to fashion this into a weapon against you rather than believe it is a credible threat. General Cassel is not inclined to believe any woman and has the king convinced that listening to you is somehow a weakness. It does not help that the truth of Beast's absence fits so nicely into the falsehood they are trying to build."

She snorts in disgust. "Well, it seems they've succeeded. If ever there was a case of cutting off one's nose to spite one's face, surely this is it."

"Of a certainty, I agree with you."

"But then what am I to do?"

"Do you think the king will be more receptive once he has absorbed it all?" Gen suggests tentatively. "Perhaps if you spoke with him in private, without the general or regent nearby."

She casts her a wry glance. "You mean in the marriage bed?"

"No! Just somewhere alone."

The queen gives a firm shake of her head. "He has already cast me as one of the villains in this. I do not think he will listen to reason, even if I clout him on the ear with it." She is quiet a long time. "It makes no sense. They have fought so long and so hard to possess my country, now they will let it slip so easily through their fingers." She reaches up to rub her forehead again, as if it has begun to ache. "So all we must do is remove Genevieve from court so she cannot be used as a weapon against the king, get you someplace where Pierre and the regent cannot find you, and free Beast from prison to get him far away from the general and his disturbing interest." She lets her hand fall into her lap.

"And find a way to clear you from these false allegations of treason," Gen adds.

The queen throws up her hands. "May as well ask me to turn water into wine." Then her face hardens into decisive lines. "Very well. We shall have to deal with all of this ourselves. I will tell the king that I have had Genevieve sent away from court, no longer wishing to bear the burden of her company."

"My lady," Gen says, stricken, "I would ask you not draw the king's wrath to yourself for my sake."

"It is too late for that now," she says dryly. "Although this is not of your doing."

"While I agree with the need to get Genevieve away from the regent," I say softly, "I do not think it is wise for me to leave you."

"We have no choice. And as wroth as the king might be with me, he will do nothing to harm the babe, so I am at least safe until it is born."

"But what if —"

"Furthermore, Heloise and Elsibet will both be here. I shall be safe. Far safer than my people who are about to have war brought down upon their heads."

I decide to put aside my arguments for the moment. "What are you proposing, exactly?"

She straightens and casts her gaze toward the fire in the hearth. "I am queen. In spite of my husband's obstinacy, by our marriage contract, I have authority over Brittany. I am proposing that I exercise it. We must prove the rebellion is real. We must show the king how blinded the regent is by her own scheming and dislike of me — so much so that she is willing to ignore a credible threat to France. If we can do that, we should be able to loosen the regent's renewed influence on the king, clear Beast of the accusations against him, and prove me innocent of this ridiculous idea that I have betrayed my husband." She pauses long enough to take a breath. "You are all going to Brittany to put down the rebellion. That is the only thing that will achieve all of those objectives."

The queen's plan is both brilliant in its audacity and terrifying in its risks, and my admiration for her has only grown.

She squares her shoulders and lifts her chin. "I trust you two can find a way to make that happen?"

"I think it's best if you leave the palace now," I tell Gen once we are back in her room.

"Tonight?"

"Yes. Collect your things. There is a good chance you will not see them again otherwise."

Gen looks as if she is being punished. "This is for your own safety," I gently point out. "I do not trust the regent to give you the full week. Do you still have your letter?"

"Yes."

"Give it to me, and I will see that it is delivered to the king, although not by my hand." When she has done that, I lead her outside to the servants' chapel. She sends me a questioning glance.

"It will be easier to get Beast out of the dungeon if we have people inside the palace. Father Effram can hide you for the next day or two until we are ready to make our move."

As we step inside the chapel, Father Effram is there, as if waiting for us. The smile he gives Gen is warm and full of compassion, although by the tilt of her chin, I am guessing she is refusing to accept either of those. I must fold my arms across my middle to avoid giving Gen a quick hug, and I cannot even say why. "I'll see you soon."

She nods, then follows Father Effram toward the south wall. For some reason I am put in mind of her arrival at the convent, when she was but seven years old. Instead of turning to leave, I wait. Just before she slips out of sight, she looks back over her shoulder. I give her my most confident grin. A flicker of surprise crosses her face, then she returns the smile before following Father Effram out of sight.

CHAPTER 66

Maraud

It wasn't until the fifth day on the road, when the rage had cooled to a simmering boil rather than a seething one, that Maraud asked where they were going.

Pierre d'Albret cut him a sly glance. "In good time, Crunard. In good time."

"And just who is this person you think I am so eager to see?"

"Also in good time."

Maraud gritted his teeth and considered whether or not he could kill d'Albret before being taken down by his men.

Luckily for d'Albret, Maraud heard a seventh thrush call just then, and the birds simply weren't that plentiful this time of year. Which meant that his friends were behind him.

That night, instead of imposing on the hospitality of a castle — there were none nearby — they spent the night in a town. It was small, and there were nearly fifty of them, filling the three inns to overflowing.

D'Albret made it a point to ensure that he — and six of his most brutal minions — were housed in the same inn as Maraud. Even sat at the same table. Maraud hunched over his dinner and tried to ignore them.

"More wine, m'lord?"

Why not? Maraud shoved his cup to the edge of the table and glanced up to nod his thanks, then froze, his heart thumping once in gladness before plummeting to his feet in cold dread when he recognized Valine. He glanced at d'Albret and his men, but their heads were close together as they hatched their evil plots.

She gave him a flirtatious smile as she poured his wine — just as any tavern wench might. "Will that be all, m'lord?" She cocked her hip out at a saucy angle and placed a hand on it, making her meaning clear.

Maraud choked. The noise drew the attention of Pierre, whose calculating eyes swept briefly over Valine. "Take her up on it, Crunard. Maybe bedding the wench will release some of the black humors plaguing you. They grow tiresome."

"You see? Even your friend agrees we should get to know each other better." Maraud had known Valine for over seven years and had never seen her like this.

"Well," he muttered grumpily into his cup, "if my lord insists."

Pierre looked at her again. "If you don't, I will." That spurred Maraud to his feet.

"And, Crunard." Pierre motioned for him to draw closer. When Maraud's ear was nearly to his mouth, Pierre said, "If you try to escape, I will take it out on the girl. Have no doubt."

"I don't," Maraud grumbled, then grabbed Valine's hand and allowed himself to be tugged toward the stairs.

"What in the name of the Nine are you doing here?" he hissed at her.

She leaned against the wall at the top of the stair landing. "Watching your back."

"I don't want you anywhere near these men. It's *d'Albret*, Valine."

"Have you turned into an old woman since we last fought together? I know who it is. That's why we're here."

"We?"

"Second table from the fireplace. Andry and Tassin. We thought it would be easy enough for them to insinuate themselves among d'Albret's other mercenaries."

"To what end?"

She looked at him as if he had grown simple. "So you will not be alone in an enemy camp. You'd wanted to know what he was up to. Now is our chance.

And while it's a shame he forced your hand, don't let that blind you to an opportunity."

"What about you and Jaspar?"

"We will follow behind but keep away from the main party."

Maraud nodded in approval. "How did you know where to find me?"

"At first I thought Lucinda had set the king's men upon you. But when I went to talk to her —"

Relief surged through Maraud, and he stepped forward to grab Valine's shoulders. "You saw her?"

She scowled. "Of course. How else was I to find out why you hadn't come back?"

He closed his eyes and allowed himself the first deeply drawn breath he'd had in over four days. "Praise Camulos."

When he opened them, it was to find Valine studying him with a speculative look. "She grew agitated when she saw me, and fearful. I hate to admit it, but she cares for you. Although saints only know why."

"Pierre claimed to have someone I would want to see. I was afraid it was her."

Valine's face cleared with understanding. "You can put aside that worry."

Maraud ran his hands through his hair. "Thank the saints for small blessings," he murmured. He then hurriedly told Valine what little he knew of d'Albret's plan, and how Andry and Tassin might best approach d'Albret to get hired on. When he had finished, Valine reached up, put her hands in his hair and messed it. He reared back. "What's that for?"

"D'Albret's no fool. You need to come back looking like you've just had a decent tumble." Her hands left his hair and came down to loosen the lacings of his doublet, then reached for his breeches.

He hopped back, quicker than a rabbit. "I can loosen my own breeches," he said shortly.

"Good." Then she stepped past his hand, rose up, and pressed her lips against his. It wasn't soft or romantic, but pure business. When she had smashed his lips good and hard, she took a moment to rub her own cheek against his stubble, reddening it. "There," she said at last. "I think that will be enough to convince him. Although if you want to stare at me from across the room occasionally looking like a lovesick fool, it couldn't hurt." She smirked.

And with that, she yanked her own bodice askew, twisted her skirts off center, and sauntered back down the stairs.

CHAPTER 67

Genevieve

t is, perhaps, the strangest gathering ever to have taken place in this chapel. For one, the chapel is different at night, with only the flickering votives to illuminate it. Without any light streaming through the stained-glass windows, it is darker and more mysterious feeling.

There is an Arduinnite, although she is dressed as a serving maid rather than in their traditional garb of leather breeches and fur tunic; a little man who resembles a gnome from a hearth tale; a slight, dark-haired charbonnerie who looks as sharp as a hunting knife; a soldier named after a chicken; and two of Death's daughters — all overseen by a priest who follows the patron saint of mistakes.

The knife-sharp man shoots me a dubious glance. "She doesn't look dangerous enough to threaten the king." A touch of humor softens his words.

"Come now, Lazare, that is what makes her such a good weapon," Sybella says. "Surely a charbonnerie would know that."

Father Effram waves us to the front, where everybody else is already seated on the hard wooden benches. We all look — more or less — like servants, although why we are in the chapel in the dead of night would require some explaining.

Father Effram raises his hands in a blessing, just as if he were conducting a true mass. "So how do we get our friend out of his predicament?" His voice is pitched low, as if reciting the liturgy.

"How do we get him out of it without anyone being the wiser or discovering he is gone, is the more relevant question," Sybella corrects him.

Father Effram reaches for a simple gold chalice, places it on the altar in front of him, and fills it with wine. "Well, the court will be leaving for Amboise in two weeks' time. Perhaps we need only fool them that long."

"Unless they're taking Beast with them." Sybella's face is calm, but for a moment, I would swear that I have her gift and can feel her heart racing.

"They're not." Everyone turns to look at me. "The king wants to leave him here to avoid upsetting the queen with his presence in Amboise and causing her to fret over him."

Sybella makes a sound of disgust. "More likely, if Beast is left here, the king can quickly dismiss whatever arguments she tries to bring up."

The Arduinnite shifts on the wooden bench, tugging at her skirt. "Does anyone know exactly where he is being held?"

"He is in one of the cells in the dungeon at the bottom of the central tower," Sybella says. "There are four guards in the guardhouse, but none in the dungeon itself. Some of the rooms are cages, but not Beast's. His door is thick oak bound with iron, with nothing but a small square opening. Even without the iron grate that covers it, it is too small for me or even Yannic to pass through. There are no windows, no drains. Nothing but twelve feet of thick stone wall. What about your favorite weapon?" she asks the charbonnerie.

"Fire won't work," he says. "Stone doesn't burn, and even a diversionary fire in that enclosed space would likely kill us all with its smoke before we could get him out. Not to mention that said smoke would likely draw too much attention our way."

"And if we disable the guards, we have just announced our presence and lost the advantage of surprise and stealth, and the hunt will be on," the Arduinnite says.

A melancholy silence engulfs us.

Father Effram sets the chalice of wine aside to make room for the ciborium. "So we must get past the guards, get Beast out of his cage, make sure no one sees us, get him out of the palace, and make sure no one discovers it." He looks up. "And get him out of the city."

"That will be the easy part," Lazare says. "Once he's out of the palace, we're free."

"It is not just the palace but the palace grounds," I point out. "The larger gate that connects the palace to the city will be heavily manned, even at that hour."

"You people and your gates," Lazare grumbles. "The river, then. A boat is easier to get ahold of than horses, anyway."

Aeva cuts him a glance. "But far less reliable. Or steady."

"And you still have to get everyone over two walls," I remind him.

The charbonnerie swears. "I'll figure something out." Sybella eyes him as if she is considering taking one of his kidneys as hostage on that promise. "I *will*," he says.

"Sybella and I can handle the guards," I tell the others. That pulls her attention from the charbonnerie. She — just barely — resists asking me how.

"Without killing them?" Lazare challenges. "Because that will alert every —"

"Without killing them."

Lazare blinks lazily, then is on to the next obstacle. "How do we get him out of the palace?"

I look at Sybella, almost embarrassed to ask the question, as it seems like something I should know. "Is it possible to use the shadows to cover him as well as us?"

"I . . . I don't know," she says, clearly never having considered it before.

"Try it." Aeva's suggestion comes out more like a command.

Sybella studies the small group, skipping Lazare, who has some command of shadows as a follower of the Dark Mother, and the Arduinnite, as they move more quietly than a shadow itself. And who knows what innate powers Father Effram possesses that he has yet to share with us. "Yannic? Would you come here?"

The little gnome grins and hops up from the pew, pleased to have a role to play. "Let's try over by the wall. The shadows are thicker there," I suggest.

Forcing myself to ignore all the others watching us, we retreat to the back of the chapel. "How would we do this with another person?" I murmur.

Sybella shrugs. "When you think of the shadows enveloping you, simply think of them bigger and wrap them around Yannic as well."

It is so simple, and yet it also tests the bounds of the gift itself. For the longest time I thought it merely an exhortation by the convent to use the shadows, work with what material we had. But since I returned to Plessis and met Sybella, the shadows have felt like they offer more protection than simple opportunity.

"One, two, three—" Sybella says, then the entire room gasps, letting us know that it has worked. When we release the shadows, the little man—Yannic —shivers. "Are you all right?" Sybella asks him. He nods and rubs his arms, as if chilled.

The lone soldier in the room, Poulet, clears his throat. "But just to be safe, we should also find a guard's uniform. That way if the magic fails, Beast won't be fully exposed."

Father Effram sets the Eucharist plate down. "I can take care of that."

"Will a uniform be enough to get him past the tower guards? Or the city gate, for that matter?" Aeva asks.

"Likely not."

"Would he have a better chance during daylight? When there are more people about?"

"If he were a normal person, yes," Sybella mutters. "But he stands out too much."

"Not to mention the rumors that have already circulated about him turning into an actual beast of some sort." Father Effram does not look at Sybella and me, but he might as well have.

I turn to Lazare. "What if we had someone at the gate? Someone who would let us pass?"

"Who?" Sybella demands.

"I'll tell you later," I murmur.

"That's all well and good," Lazare says. "Until the guards check on the prisoner the next day and see he's not there. Then the search is on."

The small chapel falls silent as we think. The only sound is the click of Father Effram's rosary beads as he runs them through his fingers.

Sybella says, "If I were to remain here for a few days after he is gone, it would prevent them from assuming we plotted together."

"You're not playing sacrificial lamb," Aeva says. "Beast would have all our heads."

Sybella scowls at her. "I wasn't planning on it." Although I suspect she would do exactly that if it came to it.

"With the rumors floating around," I murmur, "I think General Cassel is the only one who would venture down there to check on Beast. It would be ideal if he could be called away for a time. At least until the court left for Amboise."

"And who has the authority to order such a convenient thing?" Lazare asks.

"Not the queen, surely," Sybella murmurs.

I weigh the risks. "I might know someone," I say slowly.

Lazare studies me more carefully. "You have been a busy little thing here at court, haven't you?" His sharp humor reminds me of my aunt Fabienne. You could not help but smile, even as it cut you.

"Who?" Sybella asks, soft enough for my ears only.

"Do you trust me?" I murmur.

To her credit, her hesitation is so small as to be nearly invisible. She nods. "Then I will tell you, later."

"But even if Cassel is gone," Lazare points out, "the guards feed Beast once a day. Surely they'll notice."

"Not if we put someone else in there," Father Effram says.

"Who would go without a fight? Or wouldn't scream for help once we shut them in there?" Poulet asks, mildly appalled.

"Someone who couldn't talk."

All eyes turn to Yannic.

"Don't even think of sacrificing Yannic," Sybella tells Father Effram.

"Of course not. I was thinking of the bear."

The long moment of silence that follows this announcement reassures me that I am not the only one who is uncertain I've heard correctly. "What bear?" Poulet asks.

"The one in the courtyard," I murmur.

"That's absurd," Sybella says.

Lazare is a bit more respectful, but then it's not his lover who is imprisoned. "How do you see that working, Father?"

"We've already established that the guards are afraid of Beast, it is difficult to see into his cell, and his roars of fury have kept everyone away. I've heard they even draw straws to see who must bring his day's meal. No one will know — certainly not for two weeks, and possibly longer."

He looks to Sybella and smiles brightly. "If we were to place the poor bear inside, who would notice? Even if he were seen, there is a good chance everyone would just claim Benebic had finally turned into the beast he has always been."

Sybella remains unconvinced. "This is a ludicrous plan. There are too many ways it can go wrong."

Aeva, however, is stroking her chin, deep in thought. "I would have to speak with the bear first, to be certain he agreed."

"I think you will find him amenable," Father Effram says softly, then picks up the offering he's prepared and heads for the wall to the left side of the altar. That is when I see the nine niches — this chapel is old enough to have included the worship of the Nine, once upon a time. "It is worth considering." He sets the offering down and begins placing a small portion in each of the alcoves. When he has finished, he returns to stand before us. "There," he says. "We have asked God and the Nine for their blessing on this endeavor. Surely they will answer our prayers."

"Surely," Lazare mutters.

"I don't care what they answer, we are not using that bear," Sybella mumbles.

CHAPTER 68

he bear is surprisingly docile, no doubt because the Arduinnite has her hand firmly on the scruff of his neck. She speaks to him in soothing whispers as they amble across the causeway over the ditch that protects the west wing of the palace. Beside me, Sybella waits, tension humming through her body like musical notes through a harp string.

"Can't they hurry?" she mutters.

"The patrol just passed. We have a few minutes before they're within sight again."

"At this rate, it will take them every one of those minutes."

"I hope not," I say, even as I glance around for a hiding place should her words prove true.

When the bear is finally across the causeway, with four minutes to spare, he rises on his hind legs and snuffles the stone arch. Up close, I can see that he is old, with bald patches in his coat. Aeva had told us he was tired. Tired of crowds and performing, being surrounded by loud people who wanted to poke and dare him, tired of not being able to curl up and hibernate in the winter, as was his nature.

He had, according to her, consented to this idea, welcoming the reprieve it would bring him. Beast's dungeon cell, deep below the earth and dark, is as close as he can get to a cave, and he will take it gladly.

Or so he told Aeva.

Yannic is with them, ready to claim he is the bear's owner should he be discovered. The bored queen had seen them through the window and asked for a private performance. It is a feeble excuse, especially in the dead of night, but if we need it, we will have bigger problems to worry about. Lazare brings up the rear, looking every bit as impatient as Sybella.

Once inside the palace, the bear lumbers toward the donjon as if he knows right where to go. "He smells the water from the fountain," Aeva explains.

"He'd best forget the fountain and get out of sight," Sybella hisses, "before the next patrol comes along."

"Two minutes," I whisper.

Aeva tugs the bear back in the direction of the servants' chapel, where Father Effram and Poulet await. Our hiding place until the next passing of the sentries.

Father Effram has just closed the door when we hear the scrape of the patrol's boots upon the stone. I let out a sigh of relief while Sybella glares at me.

Inside the wings of the palace proper, we do not need to worry about patrolling sentries so much as the random wandering courtier or servant. But we do not get to linger long. We must get ourselves and the bear across the inner courtyard that surrounds the central tower.

"You ready?" I ask as I tug the bodice of my gown a little lower, then bite my lips to make them look fuller and riper. Sybella does not look ready to flirt and distract, but far more as if she is preparing to ride into battle. I nudge her playfully. "We will only flirt long enough to drink a cup of wine with them, long enough that when they wake in the morning, they will not think of sleeping drafts and wish only they had not drunk so much. They will also be too embarrassed to mention it to anyone."

"You seem to be enjoying this." She rakes me over with one of her penetrating looks that is supposed to unnerve me, but with the agitation I see there, it is not quite as effective as she wishes.

"Pinch your cheeks. Put a swing in your hips. I'll do the rest." I hoist the wine jug Father Effram put aside for us and head for the guardhouse.

Inside are four guards, somewhat sleepy and very bored. They perk up when they see us, all but one, who scowls like one of the king's hunting mastiffs. He is the one we will have to win over. Before he can say anything, I lean forward, making my eyes wide and excited. "Is it true?" I ask breathlessly. "Do you really hold"—I lower my voice—"the Beast of Waroch down there? Is he truly as savage as they say?"

The youngest of the four puffs up. "It's true. Every word of it. And yes, he is —"

"Shut your trap, pup, and don't go yammering to the first pretty face who pops her head in here. Afore you know it, we'll have flocks of maids wanting to know this or that about our guest." The older guard snickers, as if relishing the thought.

"And won't that make General Cassel happy," the bulldog growls.

"He'll never find out." I pour him some wine. "We'll certainly never tell. But if there is such a savage beast in our midst, surely we have a right to know so we may protect ourselves."

Sybella leans forward, intentionally allowing her décolletage near their long noses as she fills the other cups. "I hear he gnaws on the bars of his cage rather than eat the food he is brought."

The young guard warms to the subject. "I've never heard or seen anything like it, m'lady. And the stench!"

"She's no lady, you imbecile," the bulldog growls. Fortunately his doubt of her noble blood does not prevent him from drinking the wine I have poured.

That is all the encouragement the others need before they toss back their cups. Well, that and a flash of cleavage now and then. For all that Sybella claims I am good at this, she is no slouch either.

It takes less than half an hour before all of them finally succumb. The bulldog is the last, of course, and he is not sitting, but standing so that we must catch him.

"Feels like he had rocks for his supper," Sybella grunts as we lower him to the ground.

When he is laid out, I stand up and wipe my hands on my skirt. "Come on, then, let's get the others."

Crossing the inner courtyard to the dungeon is the most vulnerable part of the plan. We cannot even cling to the shadows, but must strike out into the open where anyone from any palace window might see. It is why we have chosen the darkest hour of the night, when even the most debauched have taken to their beds — if not sleep — and it is too early yet for even the most industrious of servants to be about.

It also leaves only two hours until daylight, when the main gates open and we can hide ourselves among the crowd.

"How many other prisoners are there?" Father Effram asks when we finally reach the stairs that lead down to the dungeon.

"None," Sybella tells him. Even so, she stops at the bottom of the stairs and checks for heartbeats. When she motions that all is clear, we proceed. Or try to. The bear picks that moment to balk, rising up on his hind legs and emitting an unholy moaning sound.

"He smells blood," Aeva says.

"That would be the corpse of the guard General Cassel killed," I explain.

Aeva rubs the creature's back and murmurs something near his ear, and he drops down on all fours again and begins shuffling forward.

We have not gone twenty steps when the bear stops again, this time fascinated by the shiny suit of armor. "For the love of the Dark Mother, tell the thing to hurry," Lazare says.

"It is his last taste of freedom, and he is doing us a great service," Aeva says. "Let him take his time."

Finally growing bored with the armor, the bear lumbers back toward the hallway, and we begin herding him toward Beast's cell. "You'd best go ahead and let him know what is coming," I tell Sybella.

"There is no way to prepare him for this daft plan," she says. Even so, I fall back and let her approach alone.

"Hello," she whispers. "I've brought you some company."

"Good. I am tired of speaking to the walls." The words rumble out of the depths of the chamber, sounding remarkably like a bear's growl.

I busy myself with picking the giant lock on the door — which is easier than stealing the guards' keys, then having to return them. When it is unlocked and opened, the bear makes as if to bolt into the dark cave, but Aeva holds him back — barely.

"Not just yet," she murmurs. "Beast might not be in the mood for surprises right now."

"He loves animals," Sybella says. "He would not mind."

Lazare looks at her like her head is stuffed with cabbage rather than brains. "It is a *bear*, not a hunting hound or horse."

The bear breaks out of Aeva's grasp just then and lopes into the cell. There is not even time to call out a warning.

A long beat of silence is followed by snuffling noises. Moments later, Beast appears, the bear at his side like a loyal hound. "May I keep him?" Beast asks, rubbing the creature's head.

Sybella closes her eyes, and I can see the wave of relief sweep through her. "Sadly, no. He's heard about your cozy den and wishes to have it for himself."

Beast's amused expression clouds over. "What do you mean?"

It is Aeva who steps forward to explain it to him.

"Where is this body you spoke of?" Lazare's question is so close to my ear it makes me jump. "Maybe there's something we can do with it so it won't stink up the place and alert everyone to the fact that there's something dead down here."

"This way." I direct Lazare and Poulet to the drain, then leave them to their task.

Beast is dressed by the time they've got the body more fully hidden.

"That is no guard's uniform," Sybella says flatly.

Father Effram shrugs apologetically. "They had none big enough for Beast. They are also closely guarded. Besides" — he brightens — "it is safer to maintain the pretense we began with than to switch partway through."

"How are we going to get a man wearing a bearskin out of the palace gate?"

"Beast will discard the skin for his peasant's garb and leave with the night soil farmers," Lazare says. "No one inspects those wagons."

"It will work," Beast says. "But first, I must say goodbye."

The bear is happily curled in the thin blanket on the pile of hay that served as Beast's bed. Aeva is talking with him and gives his nose a final scratch before standing up. "He is ready."

Beast nods, then kneels down before the bear, putting their faces close together. The words he utters are too low to hear, but something meaningful passes between them. When Beast stands up to leave, Father Effram slips into the cell, carrying a loaf of bread. "I have heard the food they serve the prisoners is unwholesome," he explains.

Now that Father Effram has made the first gesture, I feel less foolish as I take the small bag I've carried at my belt, remove three sweet yellow apples, and set them before the bear. "Even bears do not live by bread alone," I whisper. The bear lifts his head to eye me with faint curiosity.

Lazare pokes his head in. "We haven't got all day, people."

Sybella darts past Father Effram. "Go on," she tells me. "I'll be right there." But of course I stop to see what she is doing. She unwraps a large piece of honeycomb dripping with honey and places it in front of the bear. "Thank you," she whispers.

The bear leans forward and licks her face, and I must turn away, but whether to laugh or to cry I cannot say.

CHAPTER 69

east is much more cooperative than the bear, and we move quickly across the inner courtyard toward the east gate tower. "You are certain Angoulême will be there," Sybella murmurs in my ear.

"I am." I paid him a visit the night after we all met in the chapel. He was not amused when I stepped out of my hiding place in his chambers and demanded his help — at knifepoint.

Once I explained what we needed, he was more cooperative. "He is not just doing it for me, but because of his dislike of Cassel and his admiration of Beast."

Before Sybella can press me further, she tilts her head. "Someone is coming." She listens a moment longer, then swears. "The regent."

Shock pins me in place. "Here? Now?"

"Which direction?" Beast asks softly.

"From the spiral staircase. Get out of sight," she hisses at everyone, using her hands to motion them along.

Father Effram murmurs, "This is where I think I shall leave you. My presence will be better spent trying to divert Madame."

While we all scramble toward the shadows of the gatehouse, he backs up a number of paces so that he is adjacent with the central tower, then begins strolling toward the spiral staircase, hands folded and eyes cast down in thought. Just as we reach the safety of the jutting wall that will hide us from her view, Father Effram's voice rings out. "Madame Regent! What a pleasant surprise."

"Father Effram!" The lilt in her voice does not speak of pleasant surprise but a most unwelcome one. "What are you doing here?"

"One of the servants has taken ill, and I promised I would pray for him. Sometimes I find it helps my praying if I walk. Or mayhap it is not my praying it helps, but my wakefulness."

"Outside? In the dark of night?"

"I always feel closer to God outside, Madame — is it not so with you? And, I must admit, the cold helps keep me awake."

And what brings you out here, Madame? The question is there, hanging like a ripe plum ready to be picked, but he does not ask it. It would be too great an affront.

"I hope everything is well with you, Madame? I should be happy to add you to my prayers as well, if you'd like."

"I do not need your prayers, old man. And you'd best find your way to your bed before you catch a chill and others must take care of you."

Her words are followed by the sound of clipped footsteps as she crosses the courtyard. To our great relief, they do not veer in this direction, but move toward the opposite wing. Sybella puts her lips against my ear. "What is she doing up and about at this hour?"

"I have no idea."

"And where is the be-damned count?"

"Maybe he saw her coming and is hiding until she has passed?"

But long moments tick by, and he doesn't show. Beast joins Sybella and me. "If he is not coming, we'd best figure out another plan. Can you tell how many are in the gatehouse?"

She draws closer to the wall, places her hands against it, and closes her eyes. "One," she says, after a moment. "There is only one guard inside."

Just as Beast's face brightens at this unexpected good luck, the door to the gatehouse opens and out steps Count Angoulême.

Relief gushes through me, propelling me forward. "What are you doing here?" I try to peer around his shoulder. "Where are the guards?"

"Good evening to you, too."

"Do not play games right now. The regent just passed by here not moments ago."

"That is why I did not open the door sooner." His face grows sober. "I did not trust that the guards would keep their mouths shut. Instead, they received conflicting orders so that there was some confusion about who is on duty tonight, leaving the way clear for me to assist you."

I am momentarily stunned — it is far more than I would have expected of him. "Why?"

"As you so eloquently argued, I owe you. Not to mention, I abhor what the general is doing to some of the best young knights that have ever graced our battlefields. I am also hoping this will even the score between us."

I stare into his puffy, hooded eyes and wonder if the debt between us can ever be settled. But debts can also be forgiven. I nod. "As even as it can ever be." He looks disappointed, but resigned. "However, I must warn you, we will come for Margot's babe. She is of Mortain."

"She is also mine, and I care for her deeply."

As deeply as a man such as himself can care for a daughter. "Nevertheless, we reserve the right to claim her." I feel a whisper of movement at my back and know that Sybella is behind me.

"Is everything all right here?" she asks.

Angoulême stares at her, then back at me. "Yes. Now, would you all like to come in, or shall we stand here arguing until the regent decides to return?"

"Thought you'd never ask," Sybella mutters.

As the others file in, I linger behind for a moment, "Have you come up with a way to get General Cassel away from here for a few days?"

"There is good hunting north of Paris, and the king is growing both bored with court and disgusted with his advisors. A hunting trip will do him good."

"And what of the general?"

Angoulême laughs. "He will not need persuading. He lives for the hunt."

"Even when he has such an intriguing target as Beast before him?"

"Yes, but if he goes with the king, he gets to kill things — and that is always his first choice."

He steps away from the door. "This is goodbye, then." I am surprised by the note of sadness in his voice. He reaches out and runs a finger down my throat. Annoyance flares, but before I can give voice to it, he says, "Your stubborn chin has always been your most intriguing feature." He sighs. "And now I must go hunting with that man. Christ, I'm likely to end up with a spear in my back."

"Stay upwind," I tell him.

CHAPTER 70

Sybella

t the far side of the first room is yet another door. To our relief, it opens easily and holds a stack of torches, as well as stone sconces for setting them in.

"One portcullis and a drawbridge, then we're free." Beast glances around until he finds the narrow stairway tucked behind the door. "The mechanisms to raise both are likely up there. Poulet, come with me."

Once the portcullis is raised and the drawbridge lowered — with no guards or sentries alerted — Beast comes back down the stairs to join us. "We have a problem," he announces.

"What now?" Lazare asks.

"The drawbridge is raised using a winch and pulley." We all look at him blankly. "It will be too heavy for Sybella to operate on her own."

And just like that, our plan is felled not by our enemies, but by simple mechanics.

"Nonsense," I mutter indignantly. "It is only the pedestrian drawbridge, not even the main one."

"But it still weighs four hundred pounds."

Which is why there is a winch, I think but do not say. There is no point in arguing further until I know if I can do it. Wanting to prove Beast wrong, I mount the stairs to the room that holds the workings of the drawbridge.

"I'll stay," I hear Poulet say. "No one knows my face, and it will be easy enough to slip out of the palace yard in the morning."

"No one is staying," I call back down. I have operated winches before, and I'll be damned if I'll let this one foil our plans.

I place my hands on the spokes, then pull with all my might. It does not so much as budge. Resisting the urge to kick it in frustration, I come around to the other side, grip it again, and push, putting my entire body into it. Still nothing.

"It is too heavy." Beast leans against the wall by the stairs, arms folded as he watches me.

"Poulet is not staying behind," I say stubbornly. There is too great a chance they would find him and punish him for our escape.

"No, he's not."

Alarm leaps in my breast. "And you most definitely are not staying behind. Don't even think it."

He pushes away from the wall. "Would that be so very bad, to have me stay behind long enough to ensure you, too, got away safely?"

I tilt my head back to meet his eyes. "Yes," I whisper. "The entire point of this was to get you out of here." And away from your vile father.

He reaches for me then. "I do not like leaving you here."

"It is only for another day or two. Long enough to be certain no one discovers your absence or, if they do, connect it to me and thus the queen. And Pierre is not here," I add softly.

There is a flicker of something in his eyes before he gathers me close. "No," he whispers in my ear, "but the regent is, and she is every bit as venomous as he."

"I will be fine."

He slips his hands into my hair and cups my head, forcing me to meet his gaze, his dislike of this part of the plan clear in his face. "If you are not fine, I will come back and raze the palace to the ground with my bare hands and choke the life out of anyone who has harmed you. Are we clear?"

"It will not be necessary. I promise." I rise up on my toes and press my lips against his, trying to reassure him that this will all work out as we've planned.

"I hate to break up you two lovers, but are we going to leave tonight or just make camp?"

"Lazare," Beast growls, "tell everyone to get ready to cross the drawbridge." Once they are all across, he steps around me, then reaches for the winch. Although the muscles in his arms bunch and flex impressively, he does not even have to breathe hard. It is beyond annoying.

"You promised you would not stay behind," I remind him.

"I'm not." He grins. "There." He reaches for a nearby torch and jams it into the turnwheel. "Most of the weight is up and balanced on this side of the fulcrum. You should be able to get it up the rest of the way. Try it, but leave the brake in."

I reach for the spokes again, relieved that they do indeed move when I pull on them hard enough. "There. I can do it. Now how will you get down if the drawbridge is not —"

He grabs me once more, this time in a rib-cracking kiss meant to both silence me and reassure me that he does not bear a death wish. Then he releases me and trots down the stairs. I hurry after him in time to see him take a running start, then leap, reaching for the top of the drawbridge with both hands. With the length of his body pressed against the wood, he begins to pull himself up, his heart beating rapidly with the effort — no, wait. "Someone's coming!" I whisper. He nods, then hoists himself the rest of the way, balancing on the four-inch lip of the drawbridge, graceful as a cat. I race back upstairs to finish raising the bridge as soon as he is clear.

I hear a grunt as he launches himself across the moat. With no time to ensure he has not hurt himself, I place my foot against the spokes of the winch to remove the brake, then hoist the bridge all the way up. No sooner have I done so than the door to the gatehouse opens. With trembling arms, I step back against the wall, inching toward the corner where the shadows are the deepest.

"The regent said she saw the old priest wandering around down here. Wanted us to patrol the gates and make sure nothing was amiss."

"Everything looks fine," a second voice says, then grunts. "Except there ain't no guards in here, like there should be."

Their heartbeats grow louder as they cross the first room, then move into the second, where they stop. "Portcullis is down, bridge is up. Just the guards are missing."

"Do we tell her that?"

A long pause as they consider the price of displeasing the regent. "Not yet. You stay here while I go see who was supposed to be on duty. If I can't find out who and where they are, *then* we'll tell her."

I lean my head back against the wall as my own pulse begins to return to normal, not quite believing that they have gotten free.

CHAPTER 71

My head has scarcely touched my pillow when Elsibet is shaking my arm. "Wake up, my lady. The king has sent for you."

Alarm clangs against my ribs like a bell. Praise the Nine he did not send for me two hours ago. As I dress, I try to reassure myself that he cannot have discovered Beast's absence. If so, he would have sent an armed guard. The thought is not as reassuring as it should be.

Once I am presentable, I am ushered, not to the king's audience chamber, but to his private apartments, past the main salon, past the bedroom where his valet is overseeing the last-minute packing for his hunting trip, to an office of sorts. The king sits at his desk. A stack of correspondence is shoved to one side while a small white letter sits in the middle. He does not bother with a greeting.

"Do you know where she is?"

Not Beast, but Gen, and I am prepared for this. "No, Your Majesty. Her departure was a great surprise to me. While she and I have known each other only for a short time, I would have thought she would have informed me of her plans, but she did not."

That pleases him, although he tries not to show it. He splays one hand on the desk, straightening a corner of the letter with his finger. "Perhaps she did not trust you, just as I do not trust you." His fingers curl in on themselves. "Or perhaps you are lying. It would not be the first time you have lied to your king."

"I am sorry circumstances forced me to lie to you, but I would do so again to protect those I love."

He makes a dismissive gesture. "You only want your sisters for political gain, as does your brother. You are as ruthless and political a creature as he is."

His words probe roughly at a bruise that has not yet healed. "Only because life has forced me to be."

He reaches for one of the map weights and begins rubbing it with his fingers. "I am sick of your entire family."

Would that you were sick enough to banish me from court, I think, but the gods never make it that easy.

As if in rebuke, the small black pebble in my pocket grows warm. It is not too late to provoke him to such an act. I lift my chin in defiance. "I have done everything I can to meet your queen's needs. I do not know what else I can do to persuade you that I have only her best interests at heart."

He closes his hand around the map weight, capturing it. "Leave." The word bursts from him like an overripe fig from its skin and my heart fair dances a jig in my chest. He leans forward, warming to the idea. "The only way you will ever convince me you are not the political creature I believe you to be is to love the queen enough to leave court. The sooner, the better." His heart beats rapidly with the intensity of his emotions.

I bow my head. "If only I could be assured of the queen's safety, I would do so at once."

My words displease him. "Safe from what?"

"The regent. She is the only one who has moved against her."

He studies the map weight in his hand. "Then you will be most pleased to know that I have ordered her to remove herself from court for the time being. She has her own family to see to, after all."

It is hard, so hard, to keep my jubilation from my face. I incline my head in thanks. "You are correct, Your Majesty. I am comforted knowing that is the case."

"Then you will have no issue leaving as soon as possible? Although I suppose today is too much to hope for."

"Not impossible, no. Not if that is what you wish."

He carefully sets the map weight on the table. "It is. Now go."

That very afternoon, the same day the regent was to expose Gen, browbeat the king, and try to reclaim his power for her own, I leave the palace. Not, however, before I see her own entourage ride out. "We have not seen the last of her," the queen says, standing at my side as we watch the departure from her solar.

"No, but it is a reprieve, and I will gladly take it."

"As will I. Now be safe. And Godspeed to you all."

Of course, the king does not take my word that I will leave and has chosen to send an escort to accompany me to the Abbey of Saint Odile, the place recommended to us by Father Effram. I do not mind, for the hardest part is behind us. Now all we must do is warn the Breton barons of Rohan's plans, aid them as necessary, then return with the proof of his treason. While Rohan is one of the wealthiest land owners in Brittany, he is only one man, and his resources are limited.

The abbey is but an hour's ride from Paris. As we leave, the fear and tension is pulled from my body, as if the end of it has snagged on the walls of the palace gate. It slowly unravels until it is naught but a thin, frayed thread that snaps when we pass out of the city limits.

When we arrive at the abbey, the abbess herself greets me. She was born in Brittany, and her mother was a dedicand of Saint Brigantia. She does not offer any refreshment to my guards, but instead ushers me inside while they turn around and begin their ride back to the city. Once we are within the sturdy stone walls, she glances at me. "Would you like to rest and partake of some refreshment?"

"No thank you, Reverend Mother."

Her mouth twitches. "I did not think so. And it is just as well, as I think the larger one is going to chop all my trees into firewood to pass the waiting."

We proceed through the abbey to the grounds behind it where I spy the others. Beast looks up just then, drops his ax, and begins striding toward me. "It is done. We are free."

CHAPTER 72

How many do you think there are?" Poulet keeps his voice low so it does not carry down into the valley.

Lying on his belly with half his chest hanging over the edge of the ridge, Beast grunts, "Two hundred."

We are all on our bellies, spying on Rohan's troops that surround Marshal Rieux's holding at Châteaugiron, but Beast is the only one risking life and limb. I resist the urge to yank him back from the edge. As if I could budge his great bulk.

Lazare spits off to the side. "Are we sure he's not working with them?"

It is a fair question, given the marshal's fickle loyalties in the past. "I think the eight cannon pointed at his castle are a fair indication that he is not," I say.

Lazare shrugs. "Could be for show."

"To show whom? No one is coming as far as they know."

He lets it go, but not without muttering something under his breath. I ignore him and angle my body to better hear what Beast is saying.

"Two hundred men, eight cannon. No other siege engines, except a battering ram."

"Is that normal?" Gen asks.

Beast shakes his head. "They are trying to stay as nimble as possible."

Gen stares back down at the heavy cannon, each of them at least five times the weight of Beast. "Those are nimble?"

Beast grins. "Compared to other siege engines. And they can do far more damage in less time."

"How do a dozen of us overpower two hundred men and their

cannon?" Gen muses. To her credit, her voice gives no hint that she thinks the task impossible.

Beast scoots back from the edge. "Very strategically."

Lazare rolls over and stares up at the sky. "We will foul their powder."

Aeva frowns at him. "They will have more brought in. Why not simply aim their cannon at them?"

"Cannon aren't very effective against infantry," Beast explains. "They're too scattered to provide a solid target. You might take out a few, but you won't do any lasting damage."

Lazare sighs to make sure we all know how we try his patience. "Besides, then we wouldn't have the gunpowder."

"Wait. If we want the gunpowder, why not just steal it?" Gen asks.

"Because we don't want them to suspect anyone is out here working against them." Lazare shoots her a lopsided grin.

"What is the advantage to having fouled powder?"

He rolls his eyes. "They will send for more. And when they do, we'll ambush *that* shipment of powder, and we will have it and not them." His eyes take on a dreamy, faraway look. "Do you know what I can do with all that powder?

I smile. "I have a good idea."

Beast nods in approval. "Now we just need to get a message to Rieux to let him know what we're planning. If timed well, he could use the interval to turn his cannon on them and do some damage without risking his holding."

We all stare down in silence at the impenetrable fortress surrounded by two hundred foe and wonder how in the name of all the saints we are to get a message through that.

"It's impossible," Poulet finally says.

Aeva scoffs. "It's as easy as breathing." She motions to the castle. "I get close enough to shoot an arrow over the wall." I eye the distance dubiously, but if anyone can, it is she. "Unless he's of duller wit than I remember, he will recognize the fletching as belonging to Arduinna." She glances at me. "And he can read, can't he?"

It is decided, over Beast's protests, that Genevieve, Aeva, Lazare, and I will be the ones to sneak into Rohan's camp and foul the powder. The four of us were born to shadow or forest, and we are armed with knives and garrotes, arrows and wineskins.

"We will accompany you as far as the edge of the woods," Beast insists.

As we head out, Aeva gets close enough to mutter, "He wasn't nearly this fussy before you got here."

I shoot her a withering look. "That's because he doesn't care what happens to you."

"Or he knows I'm not as impulsive as some."

Lazare cuts us off. "Unless you are planning to alert the enemy to our approach, I suggest you all hush your flapping mouths." We are nowhere close enough for Rohan's men to hear us, yet we stop talking all the same.

Once we draw near the camp, we spread out. It is more difficult to notice one person moving in the dark than an entire troop. The sentries on night watch do not so much as cast a glance in our direction as we sneak past them. At the main camp, there are a dozen pitched tents — we are having a warm, early spring, so many of the men sleep out in the open.

The artillery wagon is with the rest of the supply train. While a number of men have laid their bedding around it, there are no additional posted guards. They are either certain of their watchmen or confident that they will meet no opposition. They are wrong on both counts.

Aeva stays back from the supplies, on the far side of the sleeping men, with her bow drawn in case any should wake and want to interfere. Lazare leads Genevieve and me toward the wagon. After peering at the contents for a few moments, he springs lightly up into the wagon bed and begins silently moving around.

He finds seven small wooden barrels and carries them to the back, where Gen and I wait. He removes a knife and pries the cork from the hole, then peers inside. "This is it." His voice is nearly indistinguishable from the soft night noises around us.

Using my knife, I pry the cork from the barrel closest to me, then lift the wineskin and pour all the water from it into the barrel, moving the stream around so as to soak as much of the powder as possible. Beside me, Gen does the same.

But we have only brought six wineskins, and there are seven barrels. Before I can ask Lazare what we should do for the seventh barrel, I hear a faint trickling sound. Beside me Gen makes a muffled noise. When I look up, Lazare grins over his shoulder as he pisses into the final barrel. From the twinkle in his eye, I cannot help but think he planned to do that, no matter how many barrels there were.

When we have finished with the powder, we return to the woods where Beast, Yannic, and Poulet are waiting. Aeva glances at the sky. "The wind has died down, and the camp is asleep. Now is the best time to send the message."

"Do you have a spot picked out?" Beast asks.

Aeva points.

"Very well. Lead us to it."

She stares at him. "I do not need an armed guard to shoot an arrow."

Beast shrugs. "Mayhap not, but we are going to provide one, nonetheless."

It is clear she wishes to argue, but having traveled with him for weeks must have taught her the uselessness of such effort. With a quiet huff, she heads toward her vantage point.

It is an impossible shot. A small wooden door facing our direction in the north tower. But she is an Arduinnite and makes it easily. Or mayhap Arduinna herself guides the arrow with our message wrapped around its shaft. Whatever is behind it, skill or luck, it sinks into the door and stays there.

"Will they find it, do you think?" Gen asks.

Aeva stares at her.

"I mean, we don't know how often they patrol this tower. It doesn't face the main conflict they have before them. What if no one wanders up here for two days?"

Aeva purses her mouth, takes another arrow from her quiver, and removes a small clay flask from one of the pouches at her belt. She dips the arrowhead into the pitch — for that is what it is, I can smell it once it is open — then holds the point out to Lazare.

He has already produced a flame from some flint or powder — or mayhap his be-damned fingers — and ignites the arrow.

In one deft movement, she raises the bow, sights down the shaft, then shoots. This one, too, lands in the door, but farther up. The flame is not hot enough to burn through the door — or our message — but it sends a thin stream of smoke into the air. Within a quarter hour, a guard comes to investigate.

Our message has been received. Now all we must do is wait.

CHAPTER 73

Genevieve

I come awake, my hand at my knife, as something nudges me in the ribs.

"Watch," Sybella says softly.

The sun has not only barely begun to rise, but the battlements of Châteaugiron have come to life. Men scramble along the ramparts, hurrying to and fro. Before my eyes can sort out what I'm seeing, a loud belch of thunder explodes nearby. I clap my hands to my ears, then shove to my feet and hurry to the ridge overlooking the valley. Just as I reach it, another explosion erupts from the castle cannon.

Rohan's encamped forces are in complete disarray. Men scurry in all directions — toward their cannon, for cover, and for the panicked horses. I can just make out their commander bellowing to ready their own cannon. I feel a tug on my arm and look to see I am the only one standing. I quickly drop to my belly so we will not be spotted, and watch with the others.

A third cannon goes off, fire disgorging over the rampart as the explosion shakes the ground and trembles through my body, causing my bones and innards to rattle. Wood splinters and metal screams as the projectile strikes one of Rohan's cannon. The men on the ramparts cheer, and it is all I can do not to join them.

A sense of happiness sneaks up on me, catching me unaware. All my life I have searched for happiness, but have never found it, or when I did, it was as fleeting as a glimpse of quicksilver.

But in this moment, I am the happiest I have ever been. It doesn't matter that what we do is dangerous, or that our lives are in peril. I am surrounded by a newly formed family, and it anchors me to this world as solidly as the roots of an oak tree. I wish to preserve this moment forever, like a stray leaf trapped in ice, but ice that will never melt.

If only Maraud were here.

As the reverberations of the cannon begin to fade, I realize I can feel the beating of a heart. It is faint and far away. Moments later, I feel a soul drift up into the sky buffeted on the wind. It does not rush or feel angry or even carry many images. Perhaps because of the distance. I have only a sense of surprise and disbelief and then it is gone.

Rohan's men — the ones not laid low by the cannon blast — hesitate for a moment before the commander bellows at them to light their own sodding cannon. As they scramble to do so, I hold my breath. Lazare is the expert and swore it would work, but I will not rest easy until I see with my own eyes that it has.

Two men load the heavy ball into the cannon, while another carefully pours powder from one of the kegs into the powder chamber. Or tries to. He shakes the small barrel, but nothing comes out. He gives a harder shake.

Another blast from the castle scatters them. Although I am growing more used to the sound now, it still feels as if the sky is being torn apart.

This, I think. This is precisely the sort of thing I imagined doing when I joined the convent. Not stealing powder or watching artillery fire, but things that mattered. Things that helped people. Things where I could make a difference. Turn the tides of war. Make desperate bids for victory. Sneak behind enemy lines. Not the endless waiting and making myself small and invisible.

The commander steps around the wounded to see what the matter is. The cannoneer gesticulates wildly, and the commander sends for another keg of the powder. The gunner wrenches it open and tries to pour, but the same thing happens — nothing comes out.

The commander casts it onto the ground, grabs a pike from a nearby infantryman, and stabs it into the barrel, then kneels to examine the black mess.

He looks up and begins shouting, and the cannoneers back away.

"It worked," I murmur.

Lazare looks wounded. "Did you doubt me?"

"Knowing a miracle will occur does not keep one from marveling when it does."

He turns away, a hint of a smile curling his lip.

The castle gets off a dozen more cannon shot, leaving the field below in disarray. Lazare pushes to his feet. "I'm going to get closer and see if I can catch wind of which way they will send for more powder. Then we'll know where to set our ambush. Anyone want to come?" He looks at all of us, but his gaze lingers a moment on me. Aeva, Poulet, and one of the queen's guards volunteer, but the rest of us stay at camp.

When they have gone, Sybella scoots closer to me, her eyes bright as she nudges me with her shoulder. "I think Lazare likes you."

"He is enjoyable company." I keep my eyes on the scene below.

"It would not take much to encourage him."

"It wouldn't."

She draws back to study me. "You aren't hesitating because he is a charcoal burner?"

I cannot help it. I laugh. "No!" As if I would ever hold anybody's beginnings against them. After she continues to stare at me in bemusement, I say, "My mother is a whore. All the aunts I told you about — they work in that same trade. I am in no position to throw stones at anyone else's beginnings."

She blinks once, the only reaction she allows to show. "I would never have guessed you were not noble born. You have mastered your training well."

I shrug, not sure what to say to that.

A considering look crosses her face. "Then why not dally with Lazare? I can't help but think that your dealings with the king have left a poor taste in your mouth. Perhaps a fun tumble would be just the thing to cast it from your mind?"

She is right. "A fun tumble would be just the thing. But my stupid body has decided there is only one person it wishes to tumble with, and saints know where he is."

"Who?" she asks gently.

I jerk my head around to look at her. "I did not say that aloud."

She smiles faintly. "You did, actually."

Rutting goats! I stare straight ahead, debating whether to tell her or not. "Maraud," I say finally. When she still looks puzzled, I clarify. "Crunard. Anton Crunard."

She stares at me a long moment, then gives out a whoop of laughter.

I scowl at her and start to rise to my feet. "No, no. It is not you. It is just that I think Father Effram is more correct than he knows when he tells us of the gods using us for their own amusement."

It is not her laughing that has me wanting to get up and move, but the concern that has lurked in my breast since Maraud disappeared. I have not told Sybella yet. The more I think upon it, the more I fear it is not coincidence that he went missing the same time as her brother. I do not want to place that burden on her shoulders.

"He is not dead," she says finally.

Hope quickly fills me. "Is it one of Mortain's gifts that tells you that?"

"No. It is me being hopeful. I refuse to believe the gods have woven all these threads together simply to snip one off too soon."

I stare down at the grass. "What if they have decided that is my punishment?"

"For what? Sleeping with the king? If that were the case, every courtesan, mistress, and favorite throughout history would've been struck dead."

It is more complicated than that, but before I can explain further, she continues. "As much as it pains me to sound precisely like Father Effram, I cannot help but believe it simply means his role in all of this — whatever this might encompass — is not over."

CHAPTER 74

Maraud

By the time they reached Limoges, Andry and Tassin were riding with the group, although Maraud had not spoken to them or even made eye contact. But knowing they were there was enough. D'Albret's holding was a teeming mass of soldiers and men-at-arms. There was only one thing so many men could be preparing for. "Having a jousting tourney, are you, d'Albret? I didn't think that was a sport you enjoyed."

D'Albret cut him a glance that told him just how unamused he was by Maraud's taunting. "We're preparing for war."

Just as he'd feared. "Against whom?"

Another sideways glance, this one sly. "You'll see."

Maraud turned his attention toward the keep, taking in the training yard, the stables, the looming manor that had a more oppressive air than most hulking piles of stone. "You keep saying that. I think you've got nothing but bluster."

The half-loaded supply wagons gave lie to that, but Maraud pretended he didn't see them. Whatever the man was planning, it was a thoroughly provisioned affair.

"You are dangerously close to calling me a liar, Crunard. Be a shame to have to cut that clever tongue of yours out. Think of all the ladies who'd be disappointed."

Maraud dropped the pretense. "Who are you planning to fight?"

"We. We will be fighting."

"You still haven't said against whom, and I am not inclined to sign up blindly for an ill-defined war against an unknown enemy."

Without warning, Pierre brought his horse to a stop, then tossed his reins to a nearby lackey who scrambled his way. "Come with me."

About damned time, Maraud thought as he dismounted and strode after Pierre. They reached the north tower of the keep, then waited for the guards to step aside.

"To answer your mewling question," Pierre said, "we're riding to Brittany. Day after tomorrow."

"Brittany? Why?" Maraud stepped into the gate tower, the sudden lack of sunlight causing him to blink rapidly. The door clanged shut behind him, and his mind screamed, *Trap!*

Pierre made for the staircase. "Because a foolish fourteen-year-old girl negotiated it away when it wasn't her right to do so."

"You're still mad she refused your father."

Pierre whirled around on the steps to face him. "She refused *us*. Refused to give us what had been promised, time and again. Refused to give us that which we have as legitimate a claim to as she does."

"There were other claims to the ducal throne with more legitimacy than yours."

Pierre grinned. "Yes. And one of them plans to seize it."

"With your help."

Pierre's smile widened. "And yours."

Maraud laughed. "You're daft. I've no interest in committing treason."

They'd finally reached the top of the stairs. "Are you so very certain?" Pierre put his hand on the door. "It is, after all, a family weakness," he said, then thrust it open.

A man stood at the window looking out over the courtyard. When he turned to face them, it was like a spurred boot to Maraud's gut.

He had aged at least fifteen years since Maraud last saw him, although it had been only three. His eyes held three lifetimes more pain, and even when he smiled, it did not reach his eyes. "My son."

CHAPTER 75

I'm sure you two have much to catch up on, and I've no wish to intrude." D'Albret shut the door, leaving Maraud alone with his father.

The father who'd reviled and rejected him for years, yet sacrificed everything he ever claimed was important — honor, loyalty, strength of purpose.

How was a man supposed to feel about a father who'd betrayed his country and cast away the family's honor for him? Maraud had been pondering that question for over a year now and still had no answer, only deeply worn ruts in his brain. He folded his arms over his chest and stared at the old man — for he was clearly that now. No longer the towering pillar of virtue that had dominated the first half of Maraud's life.

"I cannot fathom why d'Albret thinks I would be interested in seeing you."

"Perhaps because he knows that we are all we have left."

His father watched him as if drinking in his face, and Maraud wondered what he saw there. "We do not even have that. Why are you here?"

"Because they said they would help me find you if I aided their cause." He left the window for the small desk in the center of the room.

Wanting to put as much distance between them as possible, Maraud leaned back against the door. "I didn't need you to find me."

"You are my last son. I could not let you languish in prison. Not after what I paid for you."

Just the thought of what he'd paid still made Maraud sick. "It wasn't a price I was willing to pay."

His father placed his hands on the desk and leaned forward. "It wasn't your choice."

"So now that you've found me, you will betray your country again?" Maraud laughed at the sheer audacity of it. "I will have no part of this."

"Then they will kill us both. It is that simple."

"Whatever happened to death before dishonor? I seem to remember that was one of your favorite morality tales."

"That was before death had taken so very much from me."

Maraud could hear the pain in his voice, recognized it immediately. He folded his arms. "If only I had known all those years what a fraud you were. Although I am glad the others did not learn of it. They held in great value what you have tossed aside. It would pain them deeply."

"Do not dare judge me," his father said, coming out from behind the desk. "Not until you have stood and watched all your sons die. Then you can talk to me of honor."

"I have stood and watched men who fought under my command die. I have stood and watched my own brothers slain. And yet I did not offer up my honor to the first man who asked." Maraud swung around and pounded his fist on the door. "Let me out. We are done here."

"Wait!"

Maraud ignored the old man and strode past the guard. He found d'Albret just outside the tower, almost as if he'd been waiting for him. "Why am I here?"

"Because you were the price he insisted on for helping us."

"Well, he has seen me, your price has been paid, and now I will leave."

Pierre laughed. "I don't think so. While he has had much practice betraying his country, you are still a virgin at such things. We will keep you with us until Brittany is ours, lest you take it into your head to inform the king." He took a step closer, placing his hand on his sword. "The real question is, must I put you in chains, or will the promise of killing your father be enough to keep you in line?"

Maraud stared into Pierre's cruel face. He did not care about his father's safety, but he did care about his country. "Threats against my father will be enough. You have no need of chains." He would stay long enough to learn exactly what d'Albret was up to. Then he would do everything in his power to stop it.

CHAPTER 76

Sybella

e wait among the trees until Rohan's supply wagon comes into view. The cart has a driver and two mounted guards. A lark sounds nearby. A moment later, a small silent missile from Yannic's slingshot strikes the driver of the cart in the temple. He keels over, so quiet and sudden that the other horsemen keep riding before they realize he is no longer steering. Finally one of them glances over his shoulder. "Now what, Remy?"

When Remy doesn't answer, the man returns to the wagon and peers down at his slumped companion. "How much did Remy have to drink last night?"

As the guard stands there pondering how drunk Remy might be, another silent missile emerges from the trees, this one striking his horse in its flank. It rears up in startled surprise, nearly throwing its rider, as it kicks and bucks, then bolts down the road.

The second mounted soldier calls out after the other, then quickly swings his horse around, his hand going for his sword as he rides back to the cart to see what is going on. Yannic sends a third missile out, this time hitting the horse in the shoulder, eliciting a similar reaction.

The sharp pebbles were Aeva's idea. They surprise the horses, startle them much as a bee might, but do no lasting harm. We spent an hour debating the merits of hurting the horse or killing the man. In the end, Aeva assured us the effect on the horses would be both brief and forgettable. Since she knows more about horseflesh than the rest of us, we bowed to her judgment. It was much preferable to leaving a trail of bodies behind.

The rest of us emerge from our hiding places, each grabbing a small barrel and stuffing it into a sack, then we make a clumsy, obvious trail leading back to the castle. Better to let Rohan's men think Marshal Rieux stole his powder and ensure no thoughts of hidden resistance or sabotage enter their minds.

Once we have stashed the powder, Beast brushes off his hands. "And now," he says, "it's time we go see if anyone from Marshal Rieux's garrison has ventured out to meet with us."

Beast leaves nothing to chance and sends two of his men ahead to be certain the message hasn't gone astray and our proposed meeting place been compromised. They return shortly with news that all is clear and we proceed to the menhir that lies just south of the castle.

The menhir is one of the oldest sites in Brittany where standing stones mark the passages of the old nine gods. This one in particular is sacred to Arduinna. Small offerings are propped against the two vertical stones, small bundles of the last of the harvest's wheat, now dried and brown. A small egg, cracked and sucked dry by some wild creature, a green ribbon faded to almost yellow from its days out in the sun. There is no shortage of maids, young or old, beseeching Saint Arduinna for protection.

We dismount to go forward on foot, then hang back at the edge of the trees, waiting. Just as I am counting heartbeats to be certain we are still alone, a rustling reaches my ears.

"Hold! Do not move. Any of you." A voice comes from the trees off to the left.

I glance at Beast and reach for one of my rondelles.

"And, Arduinnite!" the voice calls again. "Do not even think of reaching for your bow. We have four arrows trained on you even as I speak."

Aeva cuts an annoyed look Beast's way. "I thought your scouts said it was clear."

He shrugs, embarrassed. "And I thought you could hear someone coming from twenty paces."

"Hush!" I tell them both. "That voice is —"

"Beast! Is that you?"

"Ismae!" Joy mingles with disbelief. "I'm turning around now, and if you shoot me, I will strangle you."

"Sybella?"

And then all thoughts of caution and formality are cast aside as she comes running out from behind the hillock of hay, her crossbow forgotten. I meet her halfway, throwing my arms around her, my throat tightening at the sight and feel of my oldest friend. "Oh, how I've missed you."

"We've been so worried," she says.

"It *is* you!" Duval drops his own weapon and rushes forward, he and Beast coming together with the force of boulders crashing. "What are you doing here?" Duval asks.

"Us? We were expecting Marshal Rieux's garrison commander, or maybe the marshal himself — and we find you. That is a most favorable trade."

Duval shakes his head. "I should have known it was you, you cunning bastard."

"You did know it was him," Ismae points out. "It was your first guess."

Beast's pleased grin nearly splits his face in two. Duval claps a hand on his back. "Let's go someplace less exposed so we may talk. I have a feeling this meeting does not bode well for our predicament."

Before we mount up, some introductions are in order. I pull Ismae over to where Genevieve waits with Aeva. "Ismae, I want you to meet your new sister, Genevieve."

Ismae rolls her eyes. "I wish she wouldn't do that," she tells Gen. "As if finding sisters lurking all over the country isn't awkward enough."

Her honesty surprises a smile from Gen. "I am finding it not such a terrible thing to discover unexpected sisters."

By the time we reach Rieux's holding, I have filled Ismae in on most of the events of the last months. As we are ushered into the keep, keeping my voice low, I ask, "Have you heard anything from Annith?"

"There have been no crows since you left Rennes. Although they would not know where to find me, as we had to leave shortly after you did."

Marshal Rieux comes out to greet us just then, thanking Beast for his timely intervention. "We're glad to be able to help, and had hoped to speak with you to find out what exactly Rohan is planning and whether you could tell me how to find Duval. To have accomplished both in one fell swoop feels lucky indeed," Beast says.

"Why are you both here?" I ask Duval and Ismae.

There is a moment of awkward silence before Rieux answers. "They came to accuse me of being involved in Rohan's plans," he says dryly. "At knifepoint."

Ismae rolls her eyes. "I did not pull my knife on him. I merely set it on the table."

"A fine distinction, indeed," Rieux says, clearly not over the affront.

"We were quickly disabused of our suspicions," Duval says, trying to smooth things over, "but Rohan's army arrived before we could take our leave. How many troops will the king be sending to combat Rohan's forces?"

Beast and I exchange glances. "None," Beast says quietly, then explains why.

When he has heard, Duval leaves the table where we are all gathered and heads for the window, to gain control of himself, I think. "It's even worse than I thought," he finally says.

"That's why we're here." Beast's voice is filled with such certainty, such assurance — as if he will make it happen through sheer will alone.

Marshal Rieux looks up from the map. "You are but a handful of men." It is not said unkindly, simply a recitation of the truth.

Beast grins. "We are a handful of men with six kegs of powder and your garrison. Those are better numbers than we had yesterday."

Duval's mouth quirks up at the corner, and he looks back to the map, as if seeing it with new eyes. "And what, pray tell, do you propose we do with such an overwhelming force?"

"From my time in Brittany three weeks ago, I know Rohan has troops here, here, here, here, and here." He points to Ancenis, Rochefort-en-Terre, Malestroit, Vannes, and Quimper.

Marshal Rieux's face turns gray. "He holds the south," he says.

"But not with a tight fist," Beast says. "His men are drawn thin. And each of those holdings and cities has a garrison that can fight, if they can get out. How many troops do you have here at Châteaugiron?"

"Four hundred."

"And here?"

"Eight hundred."

In all, Rieux has two thousand troops spread out among his holdings.

"Your holdings are our best crack in their defenses," Beast says. "You have men garrisoned there who are loyal to you. They need only a way out and your blessing. I can provide the former," Beast says solemnly.

"And I will gladly provide the latter." Rieux's color has returned somewhat. "But you can't mean for our success to rest on the few hundred men we can scrape up from my holdings."

Beast pushes away from the maps. "It will give Rohan several more fronts on which he must fight, spreading their numbers even thinner."

"Plus," Duval adds, "it will be a major thorn in his side, poking at him to know who is behind it."

"Not only that." Aeva speaks for the first time. "But the Arduinnites will join us."

"You can count on the charbonnerie as well." Lazare turns to spit, thinks better of it, then simply clears his throat. "We're not happy about France thinking we're their country now, but we'll be damned if this knob thinks he can come in here and undo everything we fought for."

"What can his endgame possibly be?" I wonder.

Duval looks at me. "He has always believed he had a greater right to the duchy than my sister. I think he has decided now is the time to press that claim."

"You mean, he'll fight for his own interests, but not his liege's when she needed him?"

"Precisely."

As he continues to look at the map, Marshal Rieux shakes his head, not in disagreement, but uncertainty. "The odds are not in our favor."

"By our estimations, Rohan can have no more than six thousand men," Beast reminds him.

The news we have brought of his sister, and her precarious position, has only hardened Duval's resolve. "Brittany has a long history of overcoming superior numbers with smaller forces," he reminds the marshal. "Besides, they're the only odds we've got."

CHAPTER 77

Genevieve

 he siege broken, Ismae and Duval leave for Rennes the next morning with half of Marshal Rieux's forces, using the south postern gate to avoid Rohan's decamping troops. Duval believes that the city garrison is loyal to the queen and needs only a spark of encouragement and a few extra hands to retake the city from Rohan's control. The rest of us move south. We give wide berth to Châteaubriant — a holding of Françoise de Dinan, the queen's former governess and a traitor besides. That she was once Count d'Albret's lover also ensures she will never be an ally of ours.

At Marshal Rieux's holding in Ancenis, our maneuver proves successful once more. Relieving the siege there goes off swiftly and smoothly as planned. Rieux's garrison is greatly heartened by their liege and, I think, Beast. Next, we travel to Nantes, but it is a Rohan stronghold, so we skirt it and strike out for Rochefort-en-Terre, another of the marshal's holdings, this one with a garrison of over seven hundred troops.

By the time we arrive, we are a much larger party. And while it is good to have the presence of solid troops at our backs, they are incapable of moving as silently. Fortunately, we time it so we arrive two days before Rieux's main force, giving us a chance to do our deeds well before Rohan's troops are aware of our presence.

As before, cloaked by the darkness of night, the four of us slip into camp to foul the powder. Just as before, we are able to evade the sleeping men — eight of them this time — to reach the wagon. I listen for any change in their breathing patterns, but hear only the faint rustle of the night — the call of an owl, followed by the faint scream of some small prey. I pry off the corks of the two barrels Lazare has set before me, empty the wineskins of water into them, and shove the corks back in. I grow faster each time — we all do — and am ready to go while Lazare is still pissing into the last keg.

When he finally jumps down off the wagon, I grab his arm. "You cannot mean to do that every time." My voice is pitched so low that it makes less noise than the soft night air blowing in from the river. "It takes too long. And it is dim-witted besides."

Lazare pulls his arm away, but slowly. "Someday I'm going to give you a lesson on gunpowder. Piss and wine make it more potent. As it turns out, I'm full of both."

"But this is the enemy's powder. Not ours."

"It will be once Rieux and his troops get here. They'll confiscate it, spread it out to dry, and it will be good as new." He winks. "Only better."

I roll my eyes, pull the shadows more firmly around me, then hurry to catch up to Sybella and Aeva, who have taken the lead. It is a good thing Lazare brings such a unique set of knowledge, because he is also uniquely annoying.

The moon is only half full, enough to see by but not so much that I do not have to pick my path carefully to avoid stepping on a branch that could give us away. That is why I do not see the man until I am nearly upon him. He sits on a fallen log looking out at the night around him. Behind me, a boot crunch on the forest floor has me pressing back against the nearest tree and reaching for my knife.

Sybella is six steps ahead of me, her knife already in her hand. Our eyes meet, and a silent question passes between us.

"You're late," the man on the log says.

The approaching sentry — for that is who he is, the changing of the guard — says, "Christ, I haven't slept more than half a night in I don't know how long."

"When are those other troops Rohan promised going to arrive? We're spread too thin. That's the only reason them loyalists have been able to get through."

"How many attacks did the messenger say there were?"

"Two."

It has been three, so their news is old.

"Told us the relief troops would be here mid-March. Still nothing."

"You don't think he lied to us, do you?"

More silence, as neither wants to answer that question. "Could be worse. At least we're not still dragging all them cannon to Vannes."

"Hard, slow work, that."

"It'll be worth it. That'll convince Lord Montauban to surrender the city."

"Then we'll be able to move on the city. Can't wait to get let loose among them pigeons."

Sybella does not even have to wake the others, as Beast will not sleep until she is safely back, and Yannic will not sleep until Beast does. "We have news," she says.

Beast motions to Yannic, who wakes up the rest of our party. When we have shared with them what we learned, Beast scratches his chin thoughtfully. "We knew our good fortune couldn't last."

"Who says this isn't a stroke of good fortune?" Lazare asks as he leans against a tree.

"I've never known you to be an optimist," Sybella says.

He shrugs. "I'll admit, troop reinforcements are not good news. They didn't happen to mention how many reinforcements or where they were coming from, did they?"

"If they had, I would've mentioned it."

Lazare grunts before continuing. "Well, they're not here yet. And we have a chance to strike a hard blow."

"The cannon train," Beast says.

The smile that spreads across Lazare's thin face makes him look like a feral fox. "Exactly."

CHAPTER 78

hroughout the morning as we ride, we are joined by Arduinnites, in small groups of two and three at a time. They are easy enough to recognize — they all dress like Aeva, with their legs and arms covered in brown leather and their vests made out of fur. There is also a wildness about them, a sense of living close to both the forest and the gods. They are not threatening, they simply slip out from the trees and join our party. I have never seen so many before — nearly thirty.

"Why are they here?" I ask Aeva.

She regards me a long moment. "They are offering their aid in this venture."

"I am glad of it, but why? This does not seem like their fight."

She glances at the Arduinnites trailing behind us. "Our mission is to protect the innocent. That mission does not stop with a Frenchman sitting atop the throne. That is still our work. And," she adds after a moment, "what better way to protect innocents than avert war?"

I cannot argue with her reasoning, so do not.

We spend nearly the entire day talking about the cannon train and how best to approach it.

"We could simply free their horses," Aeva points out. "Then they would have nothing to pull them with."

"But they could still be used at a later date. Would it not be better to destroy them?" Poulet suggests.

"You mean destroy the powder like we have been? Won't they just get more?" Aeva asks.

"No. I mean destroy the cannon themselves."

"Easier said than done, I think," Beast says. "It takes eight pounds of powder to launch a cannonball. I can't imagine how much it would take to destroy a whole cannon."

"Not as much as you'd think," Lazare says. "They're all made of metal, but most have been pieced together so they're vulnerable at the joints. It only takes a little more powder, loaded in a slightly different way, to make the entire thing explode."

Beast steers his horse away before it nips at Lazare's. "I have seen that happen in the field. One minute the cannoneer is putting the flame to the powder, the next everyone within spitting distance has been killed by the explosion." He shakes his head. "It is always tragic."

"Except when it is our enemy," Lazare points out.

"What if we do both?" I suggest. "What if we cut the horses loose and ensure they are far away by the time we set off an explosion?"

Lazare picks up where I leave off. "Which we will do by picking a few cannon in strategic positions. When they go off, they will destroy not only themselves, but those close to them. If nothing else, they will incinerate the wagons and carts they're carried on and will be unable to be moved until new ones are built. But once we do this, it will become too dangerous for us to remain nearby. The explosion will be seen for miles."

"So we go north," Beast says. "To where Duval and Ismae are. Rohan will keep looking for us here, but we will move on. And if we stay ahead of those expected reinforcements, we can do some damage up there. At the very least, we can harry the supply trains, disrupt the food sources, take out bridges — generally slow them down and make it harder so the garrisons we have freed will have a chance to fight back."

One by one, we all nod.

"The cannon train," Beast says. "Then north."

CHAPTER 79

e spend two nights following the cannon train, paying close attention to how it settles itself for the night. There are twenty cannon, each pulled by ten horses. Two drivers are assigned to each transport, and one man to follow alongside to shout out a warning should anything start to slip or go wrong. That is sixty men and two hundred horses, plus grooms and handlers and an additional twenty armed guards. This will not be easy.

On the second night, Lazare and two other charbonnerie sneak into the camp to test both their alertness and, more important, to see what kind of powder they have brought. The sleeping guards stir not at all, which answers one question.

When Lazare and the others return, he is rubbing his hands in glee. "It is corned powder, not serpentine."

"Good," Beast says, although it is clear that it means little to him. "What kind of watch did they post?"

"A dozen guards camped near the horses, but only two that are awake. They change every four hours. There are another two posted on watch at the main camp, just outside the perimeter."

"Perfect," Sybella says.

On the third night, we make our move. "Horses first," Aeva reminds us. "Once they are free, the other Arduinnites will encourage them to scatter before the explosion goes off. But first we must deal with their guards."

"Do we kill them?" I ask.

Aeva gives me a mocking look. "They are transporting weapons to destroy hundreds of innocents in the city. Of course we kill them."

"It just seems different when they're asleep," I point out.

"Yeah, it's easier," says Lazare.

I spread out with the others. When Lazare reaches the closest guard, a second heart starts up inside my chest, stopping as Lazare coshes him on the head — killing him instantly and releasing his soul.

As we move through the camp dispatching the sleeping sentries, my chest feels as if it contains a dozen blacksmiths, all hammering at my ribs. Even though I try to ignore it, the force of it causes my hands to shake so that when I slit the first throat, it is an ugly, crooked cut. Seconds later I am greeted by the frantic soul as it rushes from the body, trying to understand what has happened.

When all of those who guard the paddock have been killed, the Arduinnites, silent as a night breeze, begin moving through the horses, speaking to them in voices that are naught but whispers, keeping them quiet and slowly herding them away from the camp.

"Are you okay?" Sybella asks.

I keep my eyes on the horses. "So many souls. And heartbeats." If she must endure this around the living, I cannot fathom how she does it.

She gives my arm a brisk rub, which helps ground me in the world of bodies and cannon rather than souls.

As we make our way back to the cannon train's main camp, Sybella and I slip away from the others long enough to kill the two posted watchmen. When we return, there are small groups of charbonnerie clustered around six of the cannon. At some invisible signal, they all shove a wooden rod into the powder chamber and tamp down, the faint crunch of the powder no louder than the sleepy stomp of a horse's hoof.

Then Lazare gives the signal, and we all scramble back, all except the six charbonnerie who will light the cannon. We retrace our steps, stopping when we are about half a mile away.

But it is not far enough. When the explosion comes, it feels as if it rips the very world in two. Brilliant orange light erupts from the camp, so bright we must look away as it shatters the silence and pulls the ground out from underneath our feet. The sound of it slams into our ears with such force that they ring like bells.

Beast looks at Sybella. "They will have heard that from Vannes to Guingamp."

"Then we'd best be on our way."

The Arduinnites have our horses saddled and ready to go when we reach camp, the charbonnerie close on our heels. They are fair humming with a nearly frenetic energy, wide grins splitting their soot-and-grime-covered faces.

"Come on," Beast says, climbing onto his horse. "You can congratulate yourselves once we're far enough away."

Although we have decided to head north, we strike out in an easterly direction in order to cut a wide berth around Rohan's lands. Beast is right. The explosion was likely heard for miles, and those who didn't hear it will see the smoke soon enough.

Perhaps it is that thought that has my nerves strung tight, but the farther away we ride, the faster my heart races. At first I think it is merely the shock of it all — so many deaths, all the souls, the heartbeats. Not to mention the thunder of the explosion. I cannot tell if my ears are still throbbing from that or if — no. Are those hoofbeats in the distance? I tighten my hand on the reins to stop the jingling of my horse's bridle, and listen. There are no hoofbeats. All is quiet.

Too quiet.

That is when I realize I'm not *hearing* anything, but *feeling* hearts beating in my chest again. More death is coming. I only have time to call out, "Ambush!" before a volley of arrows flies out of the trees. Pale glints of silver and flashes of movement lurk just beyond the forest's edge — but they stay back for now, letting their archers do the work. I draw my sword and raise my cloak, although it is thin protection against arrows. The swell of heartbeats thudding in my chest grows.

I do not know how — some new gift from my god or simply from having lived together these last few weeks, but I recognize two of the heartbeats.

"Beast! Poulet!" I scream. "Get down!"

Both men throw themselves from their horses, tucking and rolling as they hit the ground, coming up with their swords raised as two arrows arc over their saddles.

Another familiar heartbeat. I whip around, trying to locate —"Lazare!" He flings himself to the ground in time to avoid the arrow aimed at his back. Quiet as smoke, the other charbonnerie slip from their horses onto the ground, staying low as they crawl toward the cover of the trees.

There is a shift among our attackers then, and I can almost feel the unseen archers aiming for me. My warnings have made me a target.

As the Arduinnite next to me takes an arrow in the arm, I yank my leg from its stirrup, then leap to the ground, the faint whistling of an arrow nearly parting my hair as I land. The injured Arduinnite and her sisters wheel their horses around and ride into the trees at the opposite side of the clearing. Within moments, they begin returning fire, shooting at an angle to avoid us and direct their fire into the trees. Soon, the arrows raining down on us begin to diminish.

As they slow, I hear the incongruent note of a thrush, then the mounted knights emerge from their hiding places into the clearing. "The rest are coming!" I shout.

The charge of the attack frightens the riderless horses, who bolt. But Beast already has a hand on his panicking mount and manages to leap onto its back. A maniacal gleam shines in his eyes as he rises up in his stirrups, battle-ax in one hand, sword in the other.

The pounding of hooves and clashing of blades is so loud it nearly drowns out the score of heartbeats thundering in my chest. I draw my sword and try to pick out any familiar beats, but there are too many.

A mounted knight sees me, changes direction, and heads for me, his sword raised high. Just as he is upon me, I drop to the ground and roll away. He shouts in frustration, then wheels around to try again, but is stopped by one of the Arduinnites' arrows going straight through his eye.

There is no time to be grateful. A foot soldier charges me, and suddenly I am back in the oubliette with Maraud. Everything he taught me falling into place. I take my stance and block his blow, letting the force of it run up my arm. While he is still processing his surprise, I swing my blade down, then up again, driving it into the small sliver of exposed neck right above his breastplate.

Souls begin bursting from the fallen bodies as their wounds claim their mortal lives. The battering of the new souls along with the beating of the hearts in danger make it nearly impossible to do anything but keep my weapon in front of my face. I consider blocking my mind against the souls, but fear I will miss the instant's warning of a familiar heartbeat.

The souls are particularly thick around Beast, whose ax swings through men as if he were back at the abbey chopping wood for the fire.

Just as I manage to fend off a second attacker, another one surges toward me. He is taller than the last, his shoulders broader. I fear his greater size will prove too big an advantage. As I get my blade up to meet his, a new heartbeat slams against my ribs, this one as familiar to me as breathing.

"Sybella!" I scream.

As quick as a man cut from a gibbet, she drops to the ground, bright silver arcing through the air where her head has just been. It is then I remember my own opponent. But too late. There is a sharp explosion of pain in my head, and everything goes black.

CHAPTER 80

hen I open my eyes, my first thought is that I have been sent to hell. It is dark, and there are no stars, the blackness overhead relieved only by the flickering of orange flames.

"There she is," a melodious voice says. That is not the voice of hell. "Sybella?"

"Don't get up! Stay where you are. You took a blow to the head."

"Because she was busy saving you." Beast's voice is as solemn as I've ever heard it, as if he still cannot believe how close Sybella came. "Saving all of us," he amends. His gravelly voice echoes faintly. We are in a cave.

"Did we lose anyone?" I ask.

"No," Sybella assures me. "How in the name of the Nine did you do that?" The awe in her voice makes me acutely uncomfortable.

"By accident, mostly. I felt the heartbeats in my chest, and this time I was able to recognize them."

"Do not ever again tell me how useless your gift is," she says with a smile. "I will know it for a lie. There are a couple of cuts and scrapes. But no casualties."

"Because of you." I turn at the sound of Aeva's voice, wincing at the pain the movement causes. She crosses her hands upon her heart and bows at the waist. "Thank you."

Not knowing what to do with all this gratitude and thanks, I reach up to tenderly feel at my head. "I hope one of you managed to kill the rutting bastard who hit me."

A moment of complete silence follows. "What?" I ask, uneasy.

Sybella glances behind me. I am desperate to look but afraid if

I turn my head the pain will resume its hammering. In that same moment, I become aware that my head is being *cradled* — on something softer than a dirt-packed floor. And warm. A hand reaches out to brush the hair from my brow, and my body starts to tremble, knowing that touch before my mind has pieced it together.

"I did not mean to hit you so very hard," Maraud says softly.

As my mind scrambles to reshape the world — a world that once again includes Maraud — Beast leans closer to Sybella. "See?" he mutters. "I am not the only one," then grunts as her elbow connects with something tender.

Maraud ignores them. "The man you were fighting was about to skewer you, and you stepped back just as I swung."

I try to push into a sitting position, needing to see with my own eyes that it is truly him, but his arms around me tighten. "Don't move."

I smile. "It *is* you." He is here. Holding me in his arms. My body is so flooded with relief — both at his safety and how things are between us — that it almost washes away the pain.

My heart has never been this full. With the wonder of my gift, the deep satisfaction at saving so many, and now Maraud . . .

"Did you take a blow to the chest?" Maraud asks as he takes my hand from where it was rubbing at my heart.

"No. Just . . . happy."

He grins down at me. "Me too."

Sybella clears her throat just then. "Genevieve should rest after her ordeal," she announces to the others. "There will be time to hear Maraud's full report soon enough. Have we collected any stray horses? Ensured there are no survivors who could report our identities back to Rohan?"

Beast doesn't move. "But we have only just found him," he protests.

Sybella takes his arm. "Others have missed him as well," she explains gently. "He and Gen have some catching up to do."

Once we are alone, I become viscerally aware of each breath Maraud takes, which awakens all the nerve endings in my body.

He sweeps my hair back from my face. "Did you think I'd abandoned you?"

"It briefly occurred to me, although I didn't truly think you would do that. And then Valine found me, and I knew something had gone horribly wrong."

He tenderly cups my cheek. "Thank you for your faith in me."

I revel in the feel of his palm against my cheek — the strength of his fingers, the calluses, and the warmth. "I had planned to go with you," I confess. "That day. When you came."

His hand tightens briefly. "You had?"

I nod.

His eyes grow darker, filled with shadows of frustration and regret. "I am sorry I let you down. Shall I explain it to you now or when I tell the others?"

"Later," I say, unwilling to spend what little privacy we have been granted on the tale. He is here now, and that is what matters. "What of the others? Valine? Jaspar?"

He leans down to kiss the tip of my nose. "That, too, is part of the tale, but they are here and safe." He rubs a thumb along my bottom lip once, twice, and then I open my mouth and gently place my teeth around it. "You are not well enough for this," he murmurs, but does not withdraw his hand.

"Perhaps it is what will cure me."

He removes his thumb from my mouth, then brings his lips down on mine, so tender and loving that I nearly weep. "Later," he promises.

Almost as if he had been waiting for us to finish, Beast reappears at our side and sends me an apologetic look. "I have known him for fourteen years, my lady."

"By all means," I say. "I do not mean to keep him to myself." But I do. At least once the others have had their fill.

The look the two men exchange is so eloquent that it causes my eyes to sting. "Come to tag along, have you?" Beast asks.

"If you'll have me."

Beast grins that infectious grin of his. "Always." Then he sobers. "Through Genevieve, I have learned of your time in prison and the oubliette in Cognac, as well as your subsequent escape. I am eager to learn how you ended up with Rohan's forces."

Maraud's smile is tight and humorless. "Not Rohan. I'm here with Pierre d'Albret."

Silence fills the cave. Sybella grows pale and briefly closes her eyes, then opens them again before Beast's gaze lingers too long upon her. She gives him a cocky grin, but it fools none of us. "So that's why he never showed up for his second audience with the king," she muses. Then she frowns. "Although I still don't understand why he chose to leave that day."

"That I do not know, my lady," Maraud says.

Beast stares up at the ceiling so innocently that Sybella grows immediately suspicious. "You wouldn't happen to know anything about this, would you?"

"Wait," Aeva says. "Have you not told her yet?"

"Told me what?" Sybella asks.

Beast shrugs his massive shoulders. "There hasn't been time."

"We were on the road for *eight days*, and have been here in Brittany for three weeks. There was plenty of time."

Sybella looks from Aeva to Beast. "I'm not going to like this, am I?"

Beast glares at Aeva. "That was why I was not going to tell her."

"She deserves to know," the Arduinnite insists.

Beast heaves a great sigh. "The night before Pierre left, I *may* have paid him a visit."

"*Alone?*"

"No," he scoffs. "I had Aeva with me."

Sybella directs a heated glare at the other woman, who simply shrugs. "He is about as easy to dissuade as you are."

Beast reaches up to scratch his chin. "And I may have held a knife to his balls. Explained that if he left peacefully, he could keep one of them, but if he did not leave immediately, he would lose both."

Sybella looks torn between humor, horror, and disbelief. "I wish I thought you were jesting, but I am fairly sure you aren't."

"So how many balls did he end up with?" By the grin on Maraud's face, I can tell this escapade is not the first of its sort.

"Both," Beast says morosely. "His lightskirt returned from the garderobe just then, and I didn't want to frighten her."

"What about frightening me, you lackwit?" Sybella places her hand firmly around Beast's collar. "You and I must have a talk."

"But we haven't heard the rest of Maraud's story yet." She sighs and lets go of him.

"My time with d'Albret wasn't by choice," Maraud continues. "He said he was holding someone I would want to see." His gaze darts briefly my way, and I realize he feared Pierre had taken me. "It was my father." His voice is utterly flat, dead. "My father is working with them."

"But you are not," Beast reminds him.

"No." Maraud does not so much smile as grimace. "I'm not."

Beast steps in to the brittle silence. "Well, this answers one question. Where Rohan's reinforcements were coming from. How many?"

"Over three thousand. When I realized I was stuck there, I learned everything I could, then as soon as the opportunity presented itself, I left, intending to get the information to where it would do the most good. Little did I realize that meant delivering it directly into your hands."

His eyes grow grim. "Rohan had caught wind of the resistance and ordered a contingent of Pierre's troops to go after them. Tried to anticipate your next move."

"He almost did. We were only two days ahead of you."

"When the commander heard of the cannon train, he assumed that would be a likely target."

"And so he turned it into a trap."

"That very nearly worked."

Everyone's glance flits over to me again. I close my eyes and gently nudge Maraud to keep talking. "When I heard of their plans to try to take out the resistance, I arranged to go with them and give warning. The resistance is the one thing that is giving Brittany hope. The one weapon that is successfully gnawing away at Rohan's carefully laid plans. But they have no idea it is you," he adds.

"They think it is just a couple of hotheaded local barons. Or a small group of loyalists."

"Does he not realize everyone is loyal to the queen?" Sybella asks. "For having averted yet another war. Does he not remember the hundred long years of war our people have already endured? They want peace. They want their lives back."

Maraud shifts. "I wish that were the only news I carry."

Some of the light fades from Beast's eyes. "There's more?"

"They have allied with England. Four thousand English troops will be landing in two weeks."

CHAPTER 81

as Rohan lost his mind? Why bring England into this?" Beast rubs his hands over his head, as if in pain. "Doesn't he realize that with one foot in the door, the English will likely not leave? The duchess tried to walk that fine line when accepting their aid last year, but this . . . ?" He shakes his head.

Jaspar, Valine, Andry, and Tassin have joined the others in the center of the cave, while I listen from my spot against the wall.

Maraud stretches his long legs out in front of him. "It appears they really didn't want Brittany in the hands of the French."

"Then they could have damned well sent more troops the first time we asked," Beast says.

"Why didn't they?" Poulet asks. "Why would the English give Rohan that many troops when they could only spare the duchess half as many?"

Sybella cuts him a glance. "Do I really need to answer that question for you?"

"If you would, yes."

Sybella's irritation has her leaning forward. "Because he is a *man*. A commander in his own right, a leader of armies. Whereas the duchess was merely a young girl trying to defend what was hers."

"More the fool Rohan if he thinks he can control them," Beast grumbles.

"We already know he is a fool," Sybella says. "But now we have learned he is a traitor, too."

"I suspect Rohan is confident he can manage them," Maraud says. "Especially with d'Albret's help."

"But can he?" Beast asks.

"We will find out."

Silence ensues as we contemplate the horrors of the war that ran for a hundred years between France and England. The people of our country will not survive another such campaign.

"The regent blamed the queen for starting false rumors of this rebellion to serve her own ends," Sybella says. "But if England is involved, the king will have to believe us now. This is no longer a squabble over a duchy but a foreign invasion."

"But how do we get the king to see this new truth?" I ask.

"We win," Beast says, at the same time Maraud says, "We present him with proof."

"How many men did d'Albret bring with him?" Beast asks Maraud.

"Fifteen hundred mounted knights and another two thousand infantry."

Beast swears. "With the English, that is nearly eight thousand more men than we planned for."

"Your defensive positions are the key here," Maraud points out. "If we can hold them, and depending upon how long Rohan's coalition will persist."

"It's spring. Plenty of time for a long siege."

"Marshal Rieux still commands all the holdings that you retook in the south," Maraud says. "And now, with the cannon out of the picture, I imagine Montauban will be able to keep Vannes, as well."

"Where will these English troops be landing?"

"Morlaix. Providing the weather breaks."

Aeva steps forward then. "I will get word to the Arduinnites."

"Thank you," Beast says. "There are no archers I would rather have at my back."

Lazare, who has been surprisingly silent, speaks. "I cannot make promises for them, but it is possible the charbonnerie can help, but we will have to put it to a vote."

"We could certainly use the charbonnerie's resourcefulness."

Lazare smiles. "You don't even know the half of it."

Some of the sense of doom leaves Beast's face. "How do we go about getting that permission?"

Sybella glances at Maraud. "It would be wise if you all stayed hidden a while longer. And I think Gen needs another day of rest before she can travel."

I start to protest, but she silences me with a wave of her hand. "The more thoroughly we stay hidden, the better our chances."

We remain in the cave for two nights, Sybella staying by my side to ensure my head injury does not trouble me overmuch. On the second night, Maraud approaches as we are getting ready for sleep. "I will keep watch over her tonight," he offers.

Sybella arches one graceful brow. "Will you, now? How very thoughtful of you."

Maraud keeps his face sober, but I can see it is a struggle. "She is much better today. I think the danger has passed."

Sybella looks down at me, her mouth twisting in amusement. "I think you are correct. And thank you, I will take you up on your offer." With one last smirk at me, she drifts away in the direction of Beast's voice.

Maraud stretches out on the floor next to me, propping himself on his elbow. "You will never know how glad I was when I saw you yesterday."

"Oh, I've a fair idea."

"Standing there," he continues, "in the midst of battle, calling out warnings left and right with no heed to your own safety." He takes my hand in his.

"I'd put my cloak up!"

"Yes, wool has always been the shield of choice against arrows and swords." He reaches out and strokes my cheek, touching something deep inside my heart — something I have only recently learned not to be terrified of.

I was given the gift of Maraud too soon. I realize that now. Just like a starving man must begin to eat slowly lest the too-rich food make him ill, so it was with me. It would have been too easy to sicken myself with the richness of what he offered.

But that hole in my heart has been filled — by Sybella, the queen, by Beast and Lazare and Poulet. Even Valine has had a hand in making my heart feel whole again. Every time one of them accepts me for who I am, with no scorn or contempt or hidden manipulation, that wound heals even more. I am no longer starving. Well, mayhap in a different way, I think as Maraud lowers his head and brings his lips to mine.

CHAPTER 82

Sybella

e set off first thing in the morning, while the mist hovers over the forest floor still damp from last week's rain. The Arduinnites recovered enough of our horses after the battle that we do not have to walk. They even managed to recapture Beast's vile mount — who tosses his head, then tries to bite Beast's fingers. Beast merely chuckles, and soon the creature is pliant, if not tame.

The farther north we ride, the deeper we venture into the forest, the trees doubling in size, their thick roots reaching deep underground, their broad canopy filtering out much of the light. It feels as if a cloak of safety has been drawn around us. No one lives this deep in the forest but the charbonnerie and a crofter or two, neither of whom is likely to offer word of our passing to Rohan or d'Albret.

Just thinking of my brother casts a pall over the morning. Pierre is here. In Brittany. He has taken up arms against the crown — even if the crown is too stupid to know it yet — and is marching in our direction. I would not wish his troops on anyone — let alone the country of my birth. The people we worked so hard to spare from the horrors of war with the French.

The French would have been far kinder to them than he will.

As the sun dips lower in the sky, we pass one of the large standing stones jutting out of the earth like the bone of some long-dead giant. "Not too much farther now," Lazare says.

He turns right at the standing stone, leaving the hint of trail we'd been following and picking his way straight through the trees, which feel as thick and ancient as time itself. The sharp scent of wood sap mingles with the rich smell of the forest floor.

When we reach the clearing, I recognize the dozen mounds of earth, each with piles of wood slowly baking deep within until it is the charcoal the charbonnerie are known for.

There are also nearly two dozen rough tents and cooking fires whose smoke lazily drifts upward toward the trees, where children scamper among the branches like squirrels. Everyone grows still at our approach. It becomes so quiet I would swear I can hear the smoke moving through the leaves.

One of the men tending the nearest smoldering mound steps forward, his gaze skipping over Gen and me, pausing briefly on Beast, then landing solidly on Lazare, who bows from his saddle. "Greetings, Kerrigan. I hope the Dark Mother is being good to you and your families."

Kerrigan finishes surveying our not insignificant numbers. "She has been, yes." His tone makes it clear he suspects that is about to change.

"May I speak with you?" Lazare asks.

The man waves his arm — wrapped in thick bandages — in permission. Lazare dismounts, then he and Kerrigan step away, speaking softly. Whatever Lazare is saying, the man looks unconvinced.

"Mayhap we will spend the night under the trees," Beast murmurs.

"Might be better than this place," Poulet says, gazing around at the clearing.

"Poulet." The single word from Beast is enough. Neither Gen nor Maraud look particularly perturbed, but from what Gen's told me, they've had interesting travels of their own.

"I'll have to consult with the others," the older charbonnerie finally says. "This is not a decision for me alone."

"I know, Kerrigan. That is why I came here first."

The other man nods. "For tonight, they may spend the night in our forest, under our protection, but I cannot guarantee you any more than that."

By the time we have set up our small camps and bedrolls, nearly fifty charbonnerie have drifted out of the woods — far more, I'm guessing, than live in these two dozen tents.

We are invited to dine with them and share our meals — they their acorn mash, bitter but filling, and we our dried meat and hard cheese. As before, I am fascinated by the faces of those around me, their colorless drab clothes and nearly invisible appearance belying a fierce, proud nature. Many of the women's gazes dart my way, and I wonder what they see.

When the rituals of hospitality have been observed, Kerrigan leans back against his log. "Lazare tells me that you wish our cooperation," he says to Beast.

Beast cuts a sideways glance at Lazare, for it was Lazare's idea to seek help from the charbonnerie. "I welcome any and all aid we can get to put down Rohan's rebellion."

"You will forgive me if I point out that it hardly matters to us. We already fought this war once. Or Erwan did on our behalf. If I remember correctly, that was to maintain Brittany's independence, which has been lost to France. For us, the war is already over."

"While that is true, this is what I would point out. The queen is your ally. Rohan is not. She has done much to raise the status of the charbonnerie, including appointing one to her personal guard. She will continue to defend your rights."

"If the king will let her," a voice calls out from the back. I cannot help but wonder if rumors have spread this far or if it is simply the age-old disbelief that a man will honor a woman's wishes.

"Furthermore," Beast continues, "war is never good for the people. Not the charbonnerie, not the farmers, nor the merchants, nor the crofters. That is what the duchess was trying to avoid by marrying the French king. They would have looted our holdings, razed our fields, and burned our forests to win what she has brought them by marriage."

Kerrigan shrugs. "She would have had to marry anyway."

"And lastly," Beast leans forward, the light from the fire reflected in his eyes, "Rohan has sought the aid of the English, and knowing the English, they see this as an opportunity not to aid a Breton noble, but to stake a claim to Brittany — perhaps even France. We have seen what the British do to our land when they cannot have it."

Silence falls over the group as everyone remembers the horrors of the war between France and England that lasted a full hundred years. "And England has even stricter regulations surrounding the collection and use of wildwood, some jurisdictions viewing it akin to poaching."

Kerrigan slowly lifts his eyes from the fire. "While that is most unwelcome news, how can a handful of men repel such an invasion?"

"We know where they are landing and when. And we are far more than a handful." Beast goes on to tell him of our activity in the south and the near four thousand loyal troops that have joined in our fight.

Murmurs go up among the men who sit just beyond the light of the fire. Kerrigan thinks another moment. "We must discuss this among ourselves."

Lazare opens his mouth to speak on our behalf, but Kerrigan waves him still. "I know Erwan trusted this man and the duchess, and was willing to join their cause. But he is the leader in the east, where the charbonnerie have more interaction with other folk than we do. I must weigh the risks to our future alongside the risks we will face in the present if we join you. Besides, you don't just wish us to help. You wish to share our secrets, which is another thing altogether."

Lazare lifts his chin. "I believe the woman has a right to those secrets, as she serves the Dark Mother."

I grow perfectly still, having had no idea Lazare planned to use me as a bargaining piece. By the echoing silence around the fire pit, the charbonnerie are equally surprised.

"Which woman?" Kerrigan asks, but I can already feel over half of the eyes staring at me.

"The Lady Sybella," Lazare says, pointing at me.

The leader stares at me with flinty eyes. "How do you come to serve the Dark Mother?" he demands.

The silence in the clearing is nearly deafening. Even the small creatures lurking among the trees and bracken have ceased their rustling. "I do not know if I serve the Dark Mother as much as I honor her," I say, picking my way through my words. "I am a daughter of Death who is learning how to use her skills in a new world where my father is no more. That is all."

"But they say he's no longer —"

"They are right. He has given up his godhead and now walks the earth as a mortal. The god of death's time on earth has come to an end." Saying those words out loud causes the emptiness inside me to swell. I shrug helplessly. "So who was I to serve? Who was I to pray to? Especially since my gifts from him are dark. That is when I remembered the stories of the Dark Mother, how when one is out of hope, it is she who leads us out of despair. She had done this for me before, and there are times when I feel as if she is doing this for me again."

"In other words," one of them says, "you are undergoing your own rebirth."

The words hang in the space between us, and I wish to snatch them out of the air, but I can't, for there is truth in them as well.

Lazare leans forward again. "She not only honors the Dark Mother, but serves her as well. I have seen the power she holds, and it is akin to the Dark Mother's own. I have seen her kill, countless times, but for a daughter of Death, that is nothing. What I have also seen her do is to call death from the body, as if coaxing a fox to eat out of her hand. I have seen her own blood work magic on the souls who linger. I have seen her, time and again, wrest hope from the darkest of hours. I tell you, she is the Dark Mother's, even if she does not know it yet."

As he speaks, the black pebble inside my pocket grows hotter and hotter, pressing its heat into my leg so that it runs through my entire body, causing me to tremble. Lazare's words terrify me, even as they feed something deep inside me that is hungry for such nourishment. I didn't just lose a father when Mortain passed, but my very identity — if I am not my father's daughter, who am I? Perhaps the Dark Mother is answering.

Beast finds me later, leaning against one of the trees, staring out into the dark forest. He silently slips his arm around my waist, pulling me closer, and I allow myself to lean against him instead, soaking up the comfort and solace he offers.

"He is not wrong, you know," he murmurs. "What is it you have always claimed? That you take Fortune's wheel and give it a spin to turn disaster into triumph? Is that not the very essence of what the Dark Mother does?"

"Yes, but that is an entirely different thing from being compared to the Dark Mother herself."

He heaves a great, dramatic sigh. "Not to mention that now I'm going to have to do something truly spectacular to deserve you."

When the charcoal burners have finished discussing the matter, they return to the fire pit, this time with an older woman accompanying them. Her gown is the color of leaf mulch, as are her eyes, and while they are old, they are not clouded with age. On the leather cord around her neck hang three acorns. A mark of some high office?

"Let me see the girl," she says, and the charbonnerie open a path among themselves. Beast gives me a reassuring nudge, and I make my way past all the soot-covered faces and curious gazes to the woman. As I draw closer, I see that Kerrigan holds a giant oak gall in his hands.

"Come here, child," the woman says, "so I may look at you."

I angle my face closer to the fire so she can better find whatever it is she is searching for. As she studies me, her gnarled fingers gently trace the bones of my face. "You have lived long in the darkness," she murmurs, then presses her parchment-like hand to my brow. "But the fire burns bright." She nods, then looks at the rest of our party, who sit just inside the light of the flames. "The fire burns bright in the ugly one as well. And in that girl there" — she nods in Gen's direction — "it has recently begun to burn." She steps away. "They have the Dark Mother's blessings upon them. Let us consult Brother Oak."

Kerrigan sets the oak gall upon a stone near the fire, then removes the ax he wears — like every charcoal burner — at his waist. He holds the blade over the flames and murmurs a prayer, or blessing. When he stops, he lifts the ax up and brings it down, splitting the oak gall open.

At first, I think it is empty of either grub or moth, but then a piece of the darkness itself dislodges and flutters into the air, like black ash from the fire. When Kerrigan looks at me, there is new respect in his eyes. "The Dark Mother has spoken. You will have our full support in all that you ask."

CHAPTER 83

he next morning when we resume our travels, our party includes a number of charbonnerie. Now that he's received permission to help us, Lazare's plans practically spill out of him. "Fire," he says. "Fire is the great equalizer, and the best way for a small force to take on a larger one."

"Yes," Beast says, "but far better to prevent the forces from landing in the first place and avoid having to fight them at all."

"So we use the fire against their ships."

Beast mulls that over as he ducks a low-hanging branch. "There will be a wide expanse of water between us. How exactly do you suggest we do that?"

Lazare's enthusiasm is undampened. "We take the fire to them."

Beast fixes his gaze upon the smaller man. "Why are you being so helpful with this? The charbonnerie are not normally this involved."

Lazare turns his gaze to the trees around us, eyes darting among the shadows for saints know what. "Powder artillery is the way of the future and something the charbonnerie know well. It seems a good time to demonstrate that to the king."

That is well thought out, as it will give his people a way forward if or when their rights to the wildwood that has been their livelihood for so long are compromised.

Beast scratches his ear. "And I presume you have suggestions on how we may do this?"

"I wondered when you'd ask."

Toward the end of the day, we come to another menhir, this one a giant slab of stone laid over two smaller ones, like a table. Lazare turns right at the ancient stone and leads us into a section of the woods so populated by trees, I fear Beast's wide shoulders will prevent him from passing.

After nearly half a mile through that — accompanied by a number of curses and grumbles from some of the men — the trees thin out abruptly and we spill into a clearing.

This one also contains a handful of the charcoal burning mounds and as many tents. It looks smaller and far less prosperous than Kerrigan's.

A long, thin man steps from behind one of the trees. By the number of heartbeats surrounding us, I am guessing the others hide there as well.

"Greetings, Burdic," Lazare says. "I am here with Kerrigan's permission."

Burdic's eyebrows rise higher in his dome-like forehead, staring at the rest of our party. "And the others?"

"Also have Kerrigan's permission."

Ignoring us, Lazare dismounts and ambles over to the other charcoal burner. As they talk, Burdic's eyes keep returning to us, his frown growing deeper.

"You don't have to like it," Lazare finally says. "You just have to let me do what Kerrigan ordered."

Claiming Kerrigan ordered rather than gave permission seems a stretch of the truth, but clearly this is charbonnerie business.

"I'm surprised he doesn't just say that the Dark Mother is with him," Beast murmurs in my ear. "That ought to settle it once and for all."

"Hush. It's probably your terrifying visage that is giving him pause." We fall silent as the two men stop talking and head toward us.

Burdic doesn't bow, but does incline his head, which is something. "I will honor Kerrigan's promise of hospitality," he says. "But as you can see, we have little enough to spare, so all I can truly offer you is a place to camp." His glance keeps flickering to me as he talks, and I wonder what exactly Lazare told him.

"That is all the hospitality we require," Beast says.

Burdic nods again. "Got work to do. You're welcome to join us around the fire tonight." And with that, he returns to his business, the others finally emerging from their hiding places behind the trees. Two, I notice, hold long crossbows, which they lower.

"You five, come with me," Lazare says, pointing at Beast, me, Maraud, Aeva, and Gen. "The rest can get started making camp. Dark comes early to this part of the forest."

I find myself wondering if it ever leaves.

Lazare leads us through the thick leaf mulch to a brownish mound, also covered in leaf mulch. As we draw to the other side, I see a long, narrow opening across the front of it, like some ancient mouth. "Here we are," Lazare announces. "Ladies first."

I stare at him. "Am I to climb into that hole in the ground like some badger?"

"It's not a hole, you half-wit. It's a cave."

"With no room to do anything but crawl! I don't think Beast can even fit through it."

"I can." Beast's voice is muffled as he slips through the opening into the cave beyond.

"Do you require assistance, my lady?" Lazare asks with mocking politeness.

"Of course not, you insufferable goose." With as much grace as I can muster, I drop to my knees and slither through the opening to find myself in a strange new world unlike anything I have ever seen before. The cave stretches back as far as my eye can see, the ceiling opening up so that there is plenty of room to stand upright. The smell of rich earth is nearly overpowered by a bitter, acrid odor that burns the inside of my nose. Against the walls of the cave are every size and shape of barrel, sacks, shallow cauldrons full of metal shavings, small ceramic pots stacked upon each other, arrow shafts of all thicknesses and lengths, some longer than my leg.

In the very back is an enormous metal table with three round holes in its surface. Hanging over them are wooden poles attached to some kind of a spring. Pestles, I realize. It is a giant mortar and pestle. "For grinding the powder," Lazare says from beside me.

"You have an entire artillery in here," Beast marvels.

"Not just any artillery, but the finest in all of France. Or one of the finest," Lazare amends. "There are two more like it. But this one is a mere day's ride from Morlaix."

"Wagons," Maraud says. "We'll need wagons."

Lazare snorts. "If there is anything charcoal burners have, it's wagons."

For the first time since hearing Maraud's news about the English forces, Beast gives one of his slow, feral grins.

Lazare smiles back. "I think we can manage a handful of English with this, don't you?"

CHAPTER 84

The water at the mouth of Morlaix bay is a brilliant deep blue, the sun sparkling off the small, wind-tipped waves. It does not look like the staging ground for a vision from hell, although that is precisely what Lazare is describing.

"Here." He points gleefully. "If we put the cannon here, they will have enough range to reach the ships as they enter the bay."

We have not yet gone to the town itself, but decided to see if Lazare's plan was even feasible before proposing it to the city leaders.

"But how do we lure the ships into the bay?" Beast asks. "Surely they will wait for a signal from Rohan that the city is secure?"

Maraud motions to Andry, who reaches for a packet in his saddle. From it he pulls the red and yellow standard of the house of Rohan. "Got it," he says.

Beast nods in approval, then half closes his eyes, picturing the plan Lazare is suggesting. "Let's say they have sixty ships. High tide, the flag goes up. They begin sailing into the bay." He opens his eyes. "Do we have enough artillery to take out a fleet of sixty ships? They could practically fill the entire bay from the coast down to the city itself."

Lazare has clearly thought of this. "We position some of our weapons farther down, where the chain used to be. Which we'll need to replace, by the way. We'll wait until the last of the ships enter, then begin coordinated firing from both sites."

"Won't the others turn and run when they see the bottleneck? Once they're out of the bay, they can simply sail down the coast and find mooring elsewhere." Maraud echoes my own concerns.

"Yes," Beast says. "So we will have a small force on either side of the bay to alert us if they do."

"They could even sail east and pull in at Lannion or Tréguier," Maraud says. "They might be willing to try taking another port so they can disgorge their entire fighting force."

"True, but we will have two or three days to finish off the first ships and be ready to meet them by the time they get here. Or we could take the fight to them and set up at a strategic spot to fight on our own terms when they are not expecting it."

Beast looks at Maraud. "Is Rohan sending a welcome force to ensure Morlaix is open to them?"

"No. He sent a half a dozen men to lie low in the city. When they spot the fleet off the coast, they're to send a message. That's when he'll send troops north to hold the city so the British can disembark."

"It seems to me we need to find those men first," I muse. "Gen and I will take care of that."

Beast nods his agreement. "Our plan still leaves a lot of land fighting, and I don't like our numbers."

"What if we could reduce their numbers even more?" Lazare's eyes shine bright as flames.

"I would like that very much."

"Then we get a boat of our own," Lazare says.

"One boat against sixty? Or thirty if our first attack is exceptionally lucky?"

"Not just any boat, a fire boat."

In the silence that follows, all that can be heard is the sound of the waves crashing on the rocks below.

"A boat loaded with flammables, set on fire," Lazare explains. "Then set to sail right into their fleet."

We all exchange glances. "It is an intriguing idea," Beast says slowly. "Except for the part that someone would have to man such a boat. There would be no hope of escape, would there?"

Lazare shrugs and looks away. "Wouldn't need more than five or six volunteers."

"Volunteers to be burned alive?"

He shrugs again. "We already know some of us are going to die. Maybe some can wrap their minds around it early and be of use."

"There will be few volunteers willing to burn to death," Maraud mutters.

"Maybe," I say slowly, "they won't have to."

"Please saints." Beast scrubs his face. "Tell me you have a solution."

"Not me, but the abbess of Saint Mer. What if we use her initiates? They are as comfortable in the ocean as otters. Is it possible that enough of them could steer the ship from the water?"

"Like human rudders," Maraud says thoughtfully.

"Not so sure about the human part," one of the queen's guard mumbles. He was with us the last time we came to Morlaix and has seen the Mer maids for himself.

"That would work," Lazare says, and Beast looks as if he might weep with relief.

"Now all we must do is see if the abbess of Saint Mer is willing to help."

"And find Rohan's men. If we eliminate them before they get a message to Rohan's larger forces, we can be in and out of here without Rohan even knowing it."

Or Pierre, I think. I glance at Maraud. Pierre will not forgive Maraud's betrayal.

CHAPTER 85

en casts her gaze to the rocky shore and the sparkling blue sea just beyond. "I have never seen anyone who serves Saint Mer."

I smile, remembering how I worshiped Saint Mer as a girl, reveling in her wildish nature, her command of storms, her disregard of men. "You will not forget once you have."

As we draw closer to the ancient stone abbey, the tang of the sea and smell of fish and rotting seaweed grow stronger. Before we can dismount, the door opens and two of Saint Mer's initiates come out to greet us. I glance at Gen, who is working hard to keep her mouth from hanging open. Even I, who have seen them before, must make an effort not to stare. The most noticeable thing about them is their skin, its almost translucent quality. The second is their webbed hands and feet. Gen is so busy staring at those that it takes her a full moment to finally look up into the face of the girl greeting her and see her slightly pointed teeth.

The abbess's office is spare and barren, with clean, whitewashed stone walls. She sits behind a desk in the room's single chair. She is as old as I remember, small and wizened. Around her neck are strands of cockleshells, and she holds her sacred trident in her left hand. She does not rise, but coolly looks us up and down, her eyes as shifting as the sea.

As is her due, we all bow and wait for her to speak first.

"What brings you here?" She addresses her question to Beast.

Beast bows again. "I regret if we have displeased you by coming."

"Displeased me," she snorts. "As if you have chosen not to invite me to some ball, when what you have actually done is place us in the hands of a foreign power."

Merde. She is unhappy with the queen's marriage. She rises to her feet and thumps the butt of her trident on the stone floor. "No one asked me what I thought of such a union. No one asked Saint Mer if she wished to be part of France."

"Forgive us, Reverend Mother. There was little time to consult with anyone, with war at the gates."

"You consulted with her." She points her trident at Aeva.

Aeva inclines her head in polite greeting. "They consulted us on the one weapon — one that belonged to Saint Arduinna, herself — they had that could prevent the needless loss of life. And we agreed. What choice did the duchess have?"

The abbess sniffs and looks out the window toward the sea. "War does not distress us as it does the landlocked." She shifts her sharp gaze to me. "And you? Of a surety, death is partial to war, they often go hand in hand. Was it a difficult choice for you?" Her smile borders on cruel. She knows Mortain fell that day.

"Indeed not, Reverend Mother. As you have no doubt heard, my god set aside his godhood rather than see death take so many for so little reason."

Her smile grows mocking. "That is not why he set aside his godhood. It was the girl, not some noble wish to save lives."

"Can it not be both?"

She shrugs, setting her seashells tinkling. "For some, mayhap, but not us. Ships that founder and sink, sailors and soldiers who cannot swim, these are riches to us. Offerings, if you will." She turns her turbulent eyes back on us and, for a moment, they do not look like human eyes, but as if the sea lives inside her. "For those of us who serve Saint Mer, there is much to be gained."

Beast folds his thick arms across his chest and smiles. "Then you will be most interested to hear of our latest venture. Lazare?"

The charbonnerie steps forward and bows respectfully before telling her of our plans.

"A fire ship," she breathes when he has finished. "Won't that be an extraordinary sight. We want the right to whatever falls into the sea," she demands. "Dead or alive."

Maraud looks uneasy. "What would you do with the men? The live ones?"

"They are your enemies, what do you care?"

"It is because they are my enemies that I care. I do not wish to have to kill them twice."

The abbess laughs, a gushing sound from deep inside her chest. "I like this one. Don't worry. We will only amuse ourselves with them for our own enjoyment. Saint Mer's daughters grow tired of poor fishermen."

It takes a moment for Maraud to grasp her meaning, then a faint tinge of pink colors his cheeks.

"That has always been the law of the sea, has it not?" I ask.

Her gaze shifts to me. "Yes."

"We do not have any intention of changing the laws that have governed Saint Mer since time out of mind," I assure her.

She smiles and some of the tension leaves her. "Then yes." She thumps her trident once more. "Whatever you need from us you shall have."

The next thing Beast does is speak to Morlaix's garrison commander. While the man is unhappy to hear about the approaching English ships, he is eager for a chance to strike back at them. It sat poorly with him that we welcomed them on our last visit. He is only too glad to show us the town armory, and Beast is eager to see what — if any — weapons we will have at our disposal.

We are in luck. Morlaix's armory has all manner of firing weapons and a surprising number of siege weapons as well. At Beast's questioning look, the garrison commander shrugs. "They're most effective against the English pirates constantly trying to raid our coast. Can't use a sword — or even a pike — on a bloody ship."

Beast chortles with glee when he sees the rows and rows of pikes. At Lazare's questioning glance, he tosses him an amused grin. "Because pikes are simple to use and effective, even in an untrained man's hand. It takes years to make a competent archer or skilled swordsman, but give me half an hour with a willing man, and he can wield a pike with devastating effect."

While he composes love poetry to the simple pike, I go to examine the firing weapons, many of which are small, shorter than my arm. "Hook guns," Lazare explains, picking one up. "You rest the end of it against a wall, like this. Then light the powder inside here."

"It looks much like a crossbow."

He gifts me with an approving smile. "It's built on a similar frame." He sets that down and goes to examine a longer iron tube, this one longer than my arm by half. "Culverins," he says, his face alight. "These, now, these are a rare find."

"Are they not just bigger hook guns?"

He shakes his head. "They are more like handheld cannon. But they can also be engineered to fire arrows."

"And what good would arrows do against a boat?"

"We will make these arrows with shafts of iron. And if we fill that shaft with our powder, we can fire it at the ships and —" He makes an exploding noise.

That afternoon, preparations begin in earnest. Beast sets two lines of men digging trenches two hundred paces in front of the city walls. "I'm telling you," Lazare says, "the English won't make it this far when we are done with their ships."

"I'm not worried about them. I'm worried about Rohan getting impatient when he doesn't hear from the scouts he had in place to alert them to England's arrival."

The charbonnerie wagons begin arriving the very next day, cordoning off the armory and artillery to set up their shop as they begin preparing their weapons for their *feu de Mère Noire* — the Dark Mother's fire.

CHAPTER 86

I stand next to Lazare, waiting. Rohan's banner was raised nearly an hour ago. The tide is high, and the wind is at their backs. Why aren't they coming?

At first, we fear they have somehow managed to sniff out the trap and will not enter the bay. But at last two of the smaller ships draw anchor and head toward us. The cannon at the mouth of the bay remain silent, the charbonnerie positioned behind them hidden, as the ships come through. Once Lazare confirms that the rest of the fleet is following, we get on our horses and gallop the four miles down the coast to where we have set the trap.

Along both shores, the charbonnerie have set up all manner of siege engines and artillery. The cannon with the longest ranges are positioned at the widest points of the river, but are hidden for now with branches and other bracken.

None of these hold cannonballs or stones, but the specially made projectiles and fire pots filled with the Dark Mother's fire.

Behind the artillery, fire pits roar, their flames crackling, eager and hungry for their work.

Across the water, just within sight, are the machines of the second group of charbonnerie. By the time the ships see us, it will already be too late. The passage is too narrow here, and the way forward blocked by the chain, which the initiates of Saint Mer, along with six teams of oxen, helped retrieve from the deep.

My blood fair bubbles with — I do not even know what I am feeling. The tension and apprehension before any fight, yes, but also a sense of standing on some precipice beside the Dark Mother herself.

When the first of the ships finally reaches our location, my heart begins to beat faster, and a murmur of excitement runs through the charbonnerie. "Not yet!" Lazare says, his voice loud enough to reach them, but not so loud as to carry over the water.

I keep my eyes glued to the ships. Men scramble on deck, trimming their sails, manning the rudder, and readying the anchor. Do they have any inkling or premonition of what is about to rain down on their heads?

More ships come into view, filling the wide bay with their wooden hulls, canvas sails flapping in the wind. There are more here now than came to the duchess's aid over a year ago.

"Steady, steady," Lazare says. We have set the artillery up behind a thin screen of trees and bushes so that the English will not catch sight of it, but with wide enough openings that our missiles can get through.

At last, the first ship reaches the chain, which stops its progress altogether. The crew appears confused, growing more active as they try to see what the problem is. Then their confusion becomes alarm as the following ships draw ever closer. But still our signal has not come. The last of the ships has not yet entered the bay.

"My lady?" I turn at the sound of Lazare's voice. He holds up a burning torch. "Would you do the honors?"

He means for me to light the incendiaries. "Have you forgotten how?"

He does not rise to the bait. "The men would prefer that you light the first fire."

I draw in a sharp breath, but do not refuse. Instead, I take the torch from Lazare and wait for the three flaming arrows to arc up into the sky — our signal.

May the Dark Mother bless this fire, I pray. *And me*, I add, *for lighting it*. I set my torch to the tightly bound and weighted explosives in the bucket of the catapult. The men bow, then Lazare takes the torch from me, and in the same time it took for me to light one weapon, they have lit them all.

"Now!" Lazare orders.

The wooden frame creaks as it lurches forward, followed by a ground-shaking *whomp* as a ball of flame is launched at one of the ships. The sailors barely have time to see it coming before the incendiary crashes onto the deck and explodes into a mass of thunderous flames. Screams quickly follow.

A second incendiary is launched, then a third, each one striking a ship with deadly precision. Within moments the first six ships are consumed in flames. Behind them the crews on the other ships panic, but there is no room to maneuver, no room to tack or order the ships to turn around. In the distance we hear the boom of cannon as they launch similar loads into the last of the ships at the mouth of the bay.

With the first dozen ships nearly engulfed in flames, it is time to move to the second stage of our plan.

Once Lazare checks to make sure the charbonnerie have everything they will need for the second launch, we mount and, along with two dozen knights, begin riding north again. As Beast said, the bay is five miles long, and while our fires will take out the majority of the men, it is inevitable that some will escape. We must be ready for them.

Along each shore, we have placed Arduinnite archers at quarter-mile intervals. Between their extraordinary hearing and their uncanny accuracy with their bows, they should be able to pick off individual sailors as they come stumbling out of the water. Beast and Maraud ride along the opposite shore, each with a force of fighting men. The direction of the wind will push any disabled ships in that direction rather than ours.

For even as skilled as the charbonnerie are, it is impossible that they will hit each of the ships. Especially those in the middle, where the bay widens to its greatest distance. We have no way to get projectiles that far. And so we ride for the fire ship.

Halfway between the chain and the coast, we pull in our horses and head toward the craggy outcropping. There is a small cove where the old ship has been waiting. It has been packed to the rafters with every flammable material imaginable: oil, pitch, straw, kindling, and resin. Two dozen of Saint Mer's maids stand on the beach next to the charbonnerie. As Lazare rides into view, he raises his arm. Making no sound, the maids slip into the water while the charbonnerie use three culverins to launch three burning spears at the ship.

It ignites immediately, the flames catching greedily. Slowly the ship moves away from the cove, the Mer maids in the water pushing it inexorably toward the English sitting in the middle of the bay.

It is the stuff of sailors' nightmares, a ship of fire heading straight for them. It does not take much for a ship to ignite. They are held together by pitch — a most eager fuel. One brush against flame, a falling ember, that is all it takes.

The fire ship works even better than I could've imagined, careening through the bay like a drunken sailor, igniting each ship it touches.

The crews do their best to put it out, but the Dark Mother's fire is impervious to their efforts. Even when they pour water on it, the fire simply spreads faster.

"How do you do that?" I ask Lazare.

His eyes never leave the flames. "A charbonnerie secret."

"I thought I was allowed access to those?"

He smiles. "Not all."

As we talk, we scan the shore, looking for any stray soldiers who may have slipped over the railing of the flaming decks and decided to take their chances in the water.

We had thought my ability to detect heartbeats would help with locating survivors, but the noise of all the panicked heartbeats on the burning ships, combined with those of us attacking it, the roaring of the flames, and the mass exodus of souls leaving their bodies renders that skill useless. I join the Arduinnites in patrolling the shore, quietly slitting a throat here, or breaking a neck there. I feel no guilt, for this is war, after all, and this seems a far easier way to die than by fire.

CHAPTER 87

Genevieve

It is a sea of flame. Of roiling, bubbling fire and the charnel of charred ships. The heat coming off the bay is hot enough to peel skin, so I wrap my scarf around the lower half of my face. The water churns — with falling timber, flailing men, and the eager arms of the Saint Mer's maids who greet them. Those in armor do not even put up a fight, the weight of their breastplates and chain mail ensuring their fate. I hope the Mer maids at least make it more pleasant.

Others leap into the water and strike out toward shore, struggling to avoid the flaming debris. The charbonnerie fire does not extinguish in water, but spreads.

I watch one man dodge a flaming mast, go under it, then come up on the other side, only to be met by a Mer maid. He shoves away from her and swims hard for the shore.

The relief he feels when he reaches land is palpable. Such odds he has overcome. But I can still feel his heart beating. One of Arduinna's arrows, so swift and silent that he must look down at his chest to understand what is happening, claims him. His soul does not hover or return to his body, but is caught in the massive updraft of the fire and carried aloft like ashes on the wind.

This happens time and time again, too many for me to count. When enough come ashore at once or are out of the archers' range, I am there to greet them as they crawl from the wreckage. They are surprised at first, relieved it is a woman, mayhap with a tender heart come to bestow mercy.

And in a way that is true, although the mercy I grant them is not what they are hoping for. I smile at them, always a smile, to acknowledge their valiant struggle, to acknowledge their humanity, to grant them a welcome as death claims them with a swipe of my knife across their throats.

I try also to bless their souls, but the updraft of the fire is so great they are gone before I can utter the words. I like to think they can hear them anyway.

I do not know how long this grisly task takes. It feels as if we have been at it forever, but by the faint glow of the sun behind the thick haze of smoke, it has been no more than a few hours.

A few hours to create such devastation.

A few hours to prevent an enemy force from bringing more war to our land.

As Aeva and I follow the curve of the shore, there is a lull in the chaos, the roar of the ships' fires finally diminishes somewhat, or mayhap the wind simply shifts, carrying the sound to the far shore instead. But in that lull my heart begins to beat so frantically that I can barely hear the sound of clashing metal, thudding blades, and shouts of men. And then, as if it were the gentle stroke of his finger against my cheek, Maraud's heart rises above the others. *No!*

"Aeva!"

We scramble over a rocky outcropping covered with scrub brush. Two ships — untouched by fire — have drifted aground in the shallows. On the shore below is a narrow path from the river bank blocked by Maraud, who is cutting the enemies down as soon as they appear. So why the heartbeat?

"There!" Aeva points.

Slightly upriver, one of their captains has pulled the bedraggled remnants of his army into a decent fighting force. They are approaching from the north, hidden by the trees. And while they are on foot, they are armed, and there are nearly a hundred of them.

"Behind you!" I scream, trying to get their attention over the noise of the fighting.

Led by Jaspar, most of Maraud's small force wheel their mounts around and charge toward the coming attack. Andry stays back to cover Maraud and Tassin as they try to finish off the encroaching stragglers. I unhook the crossbow I have been carrying all morning.

Aeva reaches for her bow as well. "It will be hard to avoid our own men, so stick to the fringes where the bulk of the enemy are."

"That shouldn't be hard," I mutter, "as there are six times as many of them." Maraud's heart is still beating frantically, as are dozens of others. Just inside the trees, the commander motions with his hand. Twenty archers run forward.

"Archers!" I bellow down at the others. As if spurred by my words, Maraud administers two final sweeping blows, then wheels his horse around and rides directly for the bowmen, cutting through them like kindling.

Aeva is far faster and more accurate with her bow, but I manage to pick off close to twenty. Maraud's force — though small — is a wonder to behold. Maraud stands in his stirrups, his sword swinging first to his left and then to his right. Seeing him thus, it is hard not to squirm with embarrassment, remembering my bold proposition that he spar with me.

Whether because the English are weary, or seasick, or simply disheartened by the turn of events, the fight does not last long, in spite of the uneven numbers.

When it is over, the men begin loading the fallen English back into the skiffs they used to come ashore. As the first boat is filled, pale, slender arms reach out of the water to claim it, but for what, I do not know.

I climb down from the outcropping to find Maraud. He is doubled over, breathing hard, sweat dripping down his face. His knife flashes near one of the bodies — not doubled over, then — the captain, I think.

"Is he dead?"

Maraud slips something into the leather pouch at his waist. "Yes."

I glance back at the body and see it is missing two fingers.

"His signet rings," Maraud says shortly. "I'll be damned if I'll stand before the king and make two accusations with nothing to back up my words. The Earl of Northumberland's seal should convince him."

A horse on the gallop calls our attention, and Maraud reaches for his sword.

A messenger from the city garrison rides into the clearing, his horse lathered. "They're here!" he yells.

Maraud heads for his horse. "Rohan's troops?"

"No," the messenger says. "Pierre d'Albret's. Over three thousand of them. They will reach the city within the hour."

CHAPTER 88

Sybella

The charbonnerie and I barely make it back to the city before they close the gates. "How far out are they?" I ask as I dismount, my gaze searching the courtyard for Beast.

"Half an hour, my lady," the groom says. "Maybe more."

"And Captain Waroch?"

"In the gatehouse."

Inside the gatehouse, I shoo away the incompetent squire fussing with Beast's armor and take over the task myself. "None of this armor is big enough for you," I complain as I tug on the straps of the largest breastplate we could find. There is still too much room for a sharp blade or well-shot arrow to get through. Hopefully, the chain mail hauberk he wears will stop them.

Beast grins, that part feral, part holy light that appears during battle already beginning to glow from him like a newly lit candle. "It will be fine."

He cannot know that. It is only his indomitable will, his optimistic nature, and the love of battle that is his gift from Saint Camulos that has him thinking so. I reach for his gauntlet and slip it over his left hand.

"My squire can do this," he says softly.

I tug harder. "I want to do it, you thick-witted goose." I want to assure myself that every gap is sealed, every strap tightened, and every moment we have together savored, in case — no. I will not let myself think it. To have Beast die on any battlefield will shred my heart to tatters, but to die while fighting Pierre will turn those tatters into the bitterest of thorns.

"Sybella." He lifts his ungauntleted hand to my face. So much love shines there that it hurts. I cannot have that snatched from me. Do not want to live without that in my life. He brings his head down and kisses me, aching and tender at first, then slowly filling with more passion as his exuberance for life rises up.

I break the kiss. "Give me your other hand, you lummox. We've not much time." Focused on the buckles at his wrist, I say, "If you get us out of this, I'll marry you."

His heart pauses before thudding twice against his ribs. "I thought you said no."

I did, because I am an imbecile. "I changed my mind."

"And now is the time to discuss this?"

"What better time? Besides," I say lightly, "I know you like an incentive."

"That I do." He flashes that feral grin of his, even more determined to vanquish this foe.

"I must go."

"I know. Have a care for yourself. If not for your sake, then for mine."

He grins again. Truly, he is worse than a court jester. "How can I not after what you have promised me?"

And with that, he is gone, disappearing into the barely contained chaos of our defenses making ready in the courtyard. There are one hundred fifty mounted knights, including Beast and the queen's guard and Maraud and his men. Four hundred soldiers from the city garrison, and another two hundred conscripted from the locals and armed with Beast's beloved pikes. It is not nearly enough. Not against the forces Pierre brings.

I make my way to the ramparts, determined to make myself useful.

On the battlements I can see Pierre's forces in the distance, his standard-bearer riding ahead of the party. A cloud of dust swirls on the horizon from the pounding of their horses' hooves.

Our knights have positioned themselves two hundred paces in front of the city gate, just behind the central ditch they spent nearly a week digging. Their horses snort and paw at the ground, as eager to fight as the men they carry. In front of them is a line of thirty Arduinnite archers.

Beast and Maraud hang back closer to the gate, making final adjustments to their strategy, their deep voices carrying up to me. "If your father is with them, he will know this maneuver. He is the one who drilled it into our heads time and again."

"I know." Maraud's voice is devoid of emotion.

"Will he warn d'Albret?"

"I am hoping his willingness to sacrifice so much for me will include his saying nothing."

"He does not need to say anything — he need only veer away to alert them to the trap."

"If he starts to veer, we shoot him first." Then Maraud steers his horse away from Beast out of the gate to the waiting troops.

Gen appears beside me, her face so pale I fear she will faint. "There are too many," she says.

"Don't think about the odds," I tell her as I take her hand.

"Where are we going? I will not sit safely in some guarded room to spare myself the discomfort of what is happening."

I stop walking to look at her. "Is that what Maraud wanted you to do?"

"No, but the garrison commander did."

I snort and continue walking. "We are going to do all in our power to increase their odds."

CHAPTER 89

Genevieve

The ramparts are frantic with preparation for our approaching enemy. Sybella picks Lazare out of the crowd and heads directly for him. We weave our way through scores of charbonnerie readying their weapons for the coming battle. "There." Sybella points at two dozen hook guns and arquebuses propped against the crenelated wall as we go by. "That is how we will help them. Lazare will show us how. And I want to see if he was able to prepare the fire rain."

Lazare does not look up at our approach. "If you say I told you so, I will hit you, even if you are a lady."

Looking nearly angelic, Sybella says, "I would never be so tactless. Besides, it was not my idea — Beast insisted on having a third and fourth plan in place."

Lazare's fingers on the hand cannon he is hefting into position grow still, and for one minute I fear he will strike her. "I thought you weren't going to say it?"

She smiles sweetly. "I didn't. I gave Beast all the credit." That is how she bears it, I realize. She harries others to relieve the tension I know is coursing through her. "Is it ready?"

Lazare points behind him down into the gateyard. Beast had not wanted to leave the city without defenses and insisted we keep two of the catapults within its walls. Just behind their lowered buckets, wide, shallow metal bowls as large as wagon wheels sit over charcoal braziers.

"Excellent," Sybella says. "But we are to save it for the infantry. Do not launch it too soon."

Lazare rolls his eyes. "Yes, Your Majesty."

"Do you have time to show us how to fire the hook guns?"

A long, slow smile spreads across his face. "That's what I like about you — always willing to try something new." He leads us back to the guns placed against the wall. They are not small. Some look like miniature cannon, while others are more complex. Lazare picks up one of the complex ones.

"The others take longer to load and are less reliable, so use these until you can't. All in all, it's fairly simple," he says.

But it's not remotely simple. He holds up one flask of powder. "This goes into the barrel, then the wad, followed by the ball. Then ram it all in nice and tight with this rod here. Next, take this powder" — he holds up a second flask — "and place it in the primer pan. This here hook holds a small piece of slow-burning cord — we call it a match. When you pull this lever, the cord touches the powder in the primer pan and then *boom!* Got it?" There is a challenge in his eyes — as if he knows it is far more complicated than that and wants Sybella to ask him to explain it again.

"We've got it," Sybella says, grabbing the weapon from him.

"Oh, and this hook here is so you can prop it on the wall. They're only good for about two hundred paces, so don't waste it on targets farther away than that. And for the love of the Dark Mother, don't go shooting our own men."

Sybella looks as if she would like to use him for target practice, but sets the gun down against the wall and reaches for another one — to practice on.

By the time we have five of them loaded, a cry goes up from the eastern watchtower. I glance up from my work to see the standard-bearer. Behind his yellow and blue flag ride four knights in full suits of armor. Behind them ride more mounted knights, as far as the eye can see. Their visors are down, their horses lathered, as they gallop toward us. Any hint of humanity is hidden by the heavy metal that protects their bodies and those of their horses.

"Sweet Jesu," I mutter.

"They will not expect to have to fight so quickly," Sybella says. "The dance of chivalry allows for both sides to take their positions on the field before engaging, but Beast has chosen to force the fight on his timing."

Down below us, Beast calls out, "Archers! Take your positions!" The Arduinnites disappear into the nearby trees, except for the thirty who will remain before our defensive line.

"Steady," Beast reminds everyone. "Do not move until I give the order."

The silence grows heavy as we wait for Pierre. One of the horsemen detaches from the rest of the unit and rides forward, Pierre's lathered horse prancing as he catches the scent of the other stallions.

"You cannot think to fight with so few men," Pierre calls out for all to hear. "Here are my terms. If Anton Crunard is among you, send him out and I will accept your unconditional surrender with no retaliation."

"He does not recognize Beast," Sybella whispers. "Or know about the destruction of the English fleet."

"Or he is lying."

No one makes any move to accept his offer. Perhaps they too know he is lying. Maraud's horse paws at the ground, bringing him one pace forward. "If you are too afraid to fight," he says, "simply say so."

Pierre's helmet swivels in Maraud's direction. "You will pay for this. You have betrayed me, destroyed our can —"

"That was no betrayal — I never agreed to fight for you."

Sensing his rider's temper, Pierre's horse rises up, pawing at the air. "I will cut out your heart myself," Pierre says.

Maraud raps his gauntlet on his breastplate. "If you can find it."

As Pierre swings his horse around to ride back to his waiting forces, Maraud calls out, "Hey, Pierre! Exactly how many balls do you have left?"

Guffaws of laughter erupt from our line as Pierre puts his spurs to his horse and gallops away.

Sybella nods in appreciation. "Invoke his intemperate fury. This boy of yours has some wits."

Stupidly, I feel a glow of pride.

Pierre does not lead the charge himself, but gives the signal by bringing his gauntlet down in a swiping motion. His first assault surges forward, the three knights that rode with him in the lead. I wonder which — if any of them — is Maraud's father, or if he is already dead, killed by Pierre for Maraud's escape.

The five hundred knights riding toward us do not slow down, or fall back, or veer to the left or right. Indeed, as they draw closer, the knight in the center stands in his stirrups and raises his helmet's visor. From the ramparts, it appears as if he is looking directly at Maraud. With their gazes locked, he rides forward, never checking his stride. He is the first to reach the ditch hidden by branches and brambles, the first to pitch forward into it, his limbs flailing and his horse's legs tangling with his own.

The other knights are too close to turn back. They, too, ride forward, plunging into the ditch and the sharpened spikes that wait there. Shouts of surprise, screams of terror, the crunch of bone and metal fill the air as scores of knights go pouring in after them, like water over a cliff.

Those in the vanguard take the worst of it. Behind them, the riders veer to the left and the right, hoping to avoid the ditch. But Beast and Maraud have thought of that and have more waiting for them on either side. More screams, more clashing and crunching as the first line of attack is swallowed. I can no longer tell if the thudding that reverberates through my body is the thunder of the assault or the heartbeats of all the dying.

A few are lucky. Their horses throw their riders over their heads so the men avoid being crushed by their own mounts' bodies in the fall. Others are luckier still and are tossed completely over the ditch, landing on the far side — but are met by Arduinna's arrows.

It takes mere minutes, but by the time it is over, the casualties of the first assault are horrific.

The second line of assault approaches much as the first, riding toward us at full speed. Beast calls out, "Pikesmen!" The two hundred conscripts step out from behind the mounted knights and take up position just behind the Ardu-inna archers. They jam their pikes into the ground and brace their bodies. As the second assault draws closer, the riders try to veer around the ditches but are met with hundreds of arrows pouring out of the trees, forcing them toward the trenches. The half that manage to avoid the ditches and arrows are met by the pikesmen. The force of the cavalry's impact drives them at least six feet back, but the pikes do their work.

While the second line of cavalry is nearly finished off, Lazare mounts the culverins to the ramparts. By the time the third wave of cavalry comes galloping toward us, they are ready. "Now!" Lazare calls out. Down the line, four charbon-nerie touch their hot wires to the hole in the powder chambers. Within seconds, four explosions erupt in rapid succession, clouds of white smoke rising up. The cannonballs hurtle into the oncoming cavalry, knocking a dozen men from their horses but creating additional chaos as the horses bolt, men rear back, and the ground shakes beneath their feet.

It takes them a moment to regroup. Whether because their ears are still ringing from the blast or because they are reluctant to continue forward, I don't know.

When they do, a second round of culverins goes off, creating as much dam-age as the first, reducing the number of charging knights by half. And then they are too close for us to use the cannon without risking our own men.

With his cavalry in ruins, Pierre signals to his infantry. They shout out their battle cry and charge. Our own infantry starts to regroup in order to meet them.

"Get back!" Beast shouts.

"Ready, ready, *now!*" Sybella says.

Lazare shouts to the charbonnerie below. *"Now!"* There's a whack and a thump, followed by the ringing of metal as two bowls of burning sand and bits of metal go arcing over the wall, over our own men, who have drawn back against it, and straight into the oncoming infantry. Earsplitting screams follow as a molten barrage of metal and sand rains down upon them, searing their skin and finding its way down their clothes.

Our own men cheer. Between the pits, the culverins, the arrows, and the catapults, we have reduced their numbers by at least half, possibly more.

A wiser commander would draw back, regroup, take some time to find a tactical way around the defensive position Beast has set up. But Pierre is not that commander. With every field assault, his temper and determination grow more entrenched.

But once there are no more tricks up our sleeve, Pierre's forces advance again, and although their numbers are greatly reduced, it is still more than two to one.

The clash is deafening.

Beast charges into the fray with a bloodcurdling battle cry, the sound of it surely sending a chill through all who hear. As he rides, he swings his longsword in one hand and his battle-ax in the other. He surges forward to the closest knight, his great sword nearly severing the man in two. Another knight tries to approach from behind, but Beast swings his battle-ax blindly, connecting with a sickening blow that sends the man tumbling from his horse.

The battle lust has fully come over Beast. He not only moves fast, but his blows look like they have the force of three men. Although he is faced with a wall of knights, he goes doggedly forward, leaving devastation in his wake. Within minutes, he is surrounded by the bodies of the fallen and is in danger of being boxed in by their corpses. He does something with his knees, his horse rearing and then leaping over the fallen, trampling a few to get clear of the mound.

Beside me, Sybella says, "Ready?"

"Ready." I place my hands over my ears as she triggers the latch to bring the cord down to the priming pan. There is a hiss and a sizzle as the small round bullet is discharged in a thick cloud of white smoke. It strikes one of Pierre's knights, punching through his armor and knocking him from his horse.

"It's a hit!" I turn to congratulate Sybella just as she rises to her feet, rubbing her rump. "That poxy bastard did not tell me the powder would kick so hard," she grumbles.

And so we enter the next stage of the battle. We bombard the enemy with everything we have: Arduinna's arrows, the arquebuses and the older hook guns, and the knights and soldiers, always the soldiers fighting and hacking and slicing, falling and getting up again. The grunting cries of pain, the screams.

And that does not even factor in the souls. So many souls escaping their bodies, like a murmuration of starlings against the smoke-filled sky.

As the sun finally begins to lower toward the horizon, Pierre finally signals a retreat, calling back less than a quarter of the men he started with.

A rousing cheer goes up, starting in the battlefield, then quickly taken up by the city.

CHAPTER 90

We stand, gasping for breath, muscles trembling, too exhausted to move as we watch Pierre and his troops flee.

Our men are bone-weary. They have been fighting in one form or another since early this morning. It is Beast who rouses himself first. He is blood splattered, his breastplate dented in numerous places, and two arrows protrude from his left arm. "We've wounded to see to." His deep voice booms through the haggard silence.

Slowly, townspeople begin to venture forward, coming out of the gate. A handful of them are the priests from the local abbey, and another handful are the Brigantian nuns. Beast waves them over to where the majority of our wounded lie. Instead of following them, he heads for the first pit.

Sword still in his hand, Maraud limps over to Beast. "You are not tending their wounded before our own."

"Your father is in there. Your father who chose to ride into the pit rather than alert Pierre to our gambit. We both owe it to him to see if he is still alive."

Maraud's expression is unreadable as he shoves his sword in its scabbard. When they reach the pit, the Arduinnites are already there, quieting the injured horses and gently putting them out of their misery.

Maraud places his hand on the rim of the pit, then hops down into it, followed by Beast. I hold my breath, barely able to imagine what a grisly scene must await them. Moments later, Maraud's muffled voice calls out, "He's alive."

Beast emerges from the pit, carrying Maraud's father carefully in his arms, not wishing to make his wounds worse, but unable to get him out any other way. By the time he has laid him on the makeshift stretcher two of the priests have produced, Maraud has climbed out of the pit as well. Instead of following his father into the city, he heads for our own wounded.

Beast puts a hand on his arm to stop him. "There are plenty of others to take care of the men. Go with your father. Although you did not want it, he gave much for you — both his honor and most likely his life."

The men's eyes meet, and the weight of what passes between them squeezes my throat. Finally, Maraud turns to follow the priests. When I fall into step beside him, he says nothing. At first, I think he will ignore me, but he takes my hand instead, holding it tightly the entire way.

The infirmary is clean and spare, and smells of dried herbs and human bodies. The floors are stone, the walls bare and lined with beds. We wait while they clean Crunard and get him settled, wanting, I think, to spare us the pain of his discomfort. Maraud's jaw is clenched the entire time, his eyes staring straight ahead.

"Would you rather be alone?" I ask.

His grip on my hand tightens. "I would rather not be here at all, but if I must, better with you at my side."

One of the nuns appears and motions us into the room. I have never seen Maraud's father before, but instantly recognize the lines of his face, the plane of his jaw, the arch of his nose. That is where the similarity ends, however. This man's flesh hangs loose from his face, his hair has gone gray, his lips thin and bloodless.

"It is a gut wound," the priest says quietly. "He is still alive, and may be for days, but it is fatal, make no mistake."

"Thank you," I tell the priest. When Maraud makes no move, I gently lead him to the bed.

As if sensing his son's presence, the older man opens his eyes.

"You knew." Maraud's hand on mine tightens. "You knew it was a trap."

Crunard gives an imperceptible nod.

"And yet you rode into it anyway."

"To veer would have given it away." The words come out ragged.

Maraud's emotions bubble through him. Confusion and anger, bitterness and disbelief, and buried beneath all of that, grief. "Why?"

Crunard's lips draw back in an echo of a smile. "Did you ever think —" He stops to breathe. "Had come to make amends?"

The look on Maraud's face makes it plain he had never considered such a thing.

"Besides" — another ghostly grin — "couldn't let them take you twice."

CHAPTER 91

Sybella

ou are injured as well," I remind Beast as we leave the infirmary.

"You are being daft."

"I am not the one with two arrows in my arm, a gash across my forehead, and, I suspect, a broken rib."

Beast glances down, breaks the shafts off the arrowheads, then tosses them aside. "All taken care of."

"And your arm?"

He grins. "Don't tell me you're afraid of a little blood."

I snort.

"You are mistaken," he continues in a more sober tone, "if you think I will rest while there are men to see to."

Of course I knew that, but had hoped he would at least allow his wounds to be tended first.

As it turns out, there are not that many wounded. Two of the queen's guard have broken legs from falling from their horses, but they are not bad breaks and will mend well. Valine has a cut on her arm, almost a near match to Beast's, although she has the good sense to have at least wrapped it. Three charbonnerie received burns — which they consider as sacred as medals of honor — and the Arduinnites have only a half dozen arrow wounds among them.

That is not to say there were no casualties. A man was crushed by his own horse, another took a pike to the chest, and a dozen pikesmen died of wounds sustained during the battle.

"See that their families are taken care of," Beast tells the priest who tallied the dead.

When the priest has left, I cannot help but ask, "How did you bring so many men through unscathed?"

He scowls at the sea of bodies. "I would not call this unscathed. And I had help. Maraud, the Arduinnites, you, Gen, the charbonnerie, the men's own fighting spirits."

But it is more than that. I have seen it time and again. It is as if his battle lust, his own will and determination and sheer stubbornness pull his men along in his wake, casting a veil of protection over them.

"Well, it is a small miracle," I say, knowing he will be uncomfortable if I tell him how big a miracle it truly is.

When I finally get Beast to the infirmary, it tries him sorely to lie still with so much to be done. And although he claims his saint allows him to heal quickly, I have seen him delirious with wounds that very nearly killed him. "Wouldn't you be embarrassed if the mighty Beast of Waroch was brought low by an infection of the blood or a gangrenous limb?"

"It would never happen," he says stubbornly, picking at the blanket the nuns have placed over him. "Although," he concedes, "it would be most ignoble."

"Besides" — I settle myself next to him on the narrow bed — "think of me. I need a day or two to rest. I have been lighting fires, arguing with Lazare, and worrying about you. It is a wonder my hair is not full gray by now."

"Ah. When you put it like that, how can I say no?" He removes his hand from the blanket and begins playing with my fingers instead. "Why did you change your mind?" he asks softly.

I do not pretend not to know what he is talking about. "Things have changed. I have changed."

He is quiet, hoping I will say more. I prop my head in my hand so I may better see his face: the pockmarks, the lump of a nose, the scar that graces one cheek — he will have a matching one on his forehead now — and among all that cheerful ugliness, two eyes of nearly unnaturally light blue framed with spiky lashes.

"I have decided," I say, lightly tracing the scar on his cheek, "that you want me only for my body and thus will be easily managed."

Humor shines in his eyes, but also regret that I will not be serious. "But mostly," I continue, "I have learned how to wrestle with my own fears so they do not destroy my future chances at happiness. Being with you will make me very happy."

Those eyes of his — how they glow! Not with feral light, but with joy and love and all the things I once thought I would never experience. I lean down and press my lips on his. "Besides," I murmur, "if you become too demanding, I can always slit your throat while you sleep."

"Then at least I will die happy," he says, pulling me back down.

When Beast awakes the next morning and is told he still may not use his arm or strain his torso, he decides we should leave for Amboise. "If I am forced to do nothing," he grumbles, "I may as well do it on a horse." It is as inactive as he can be, so I agree to it. "Besides, we must get word to the king and queen. We do not know if the English will try to return now that Rohan has given them an invitation. The king will need to meet force with force." His face brightens. "And, since we have rid him of this pesky rebellion, perhaps he will grant us permission to marry."

That is the difference between Beast and me — he is a dogged optimist, while I am a dyed-in-the-wool cynic and cannot accept that it will be so easy.

CHAPTER 92

Genevieve

n the morning, Beast and Sybella come to check on us. "How is he?" Beast asks.

"He is still alive," Maraud says. "But will not be for long."

"I am sorry."

"He said he agreed to d'Albret's plan in order to make amends."

"He succeeded."

As Beast and Maraud continue talking softly, Sybella pulls me aside. "Beast and I need to return to court," she says. "We need to get news of the English attack to the king and queen. It has gone far beyond a squabble among French nobles."

"Will he believe you?"

"I have to hope so, especially now that we have won and the queen has nothing to gain from the situation."

"As if she ever did. Shall I come with you?" I do not wish to abandon Maraud, but convincing the king is too important to leave to chance.

Sybella's eyes soften. She knows Crunard is not long for this world. "No. Your place is here. You can follow in a couple of days."

Even though Maraud's father does not waken again, we stay with him through the night. Maraud slumps against the wall, and I curl up on a spare blanket, giving him some room to come to grips with the shift in the nature of his father.

He lifts his head and stares up at the ceiling. "If not for my anger with him, I am not sure I would've survived my time in the oubliette."

"Sometimes anger is all there is to live for," I tell him.

He falls silent, unable to reconcile himself to his father's attempt at atonement.

"What price would you have paid when you thought Pierre d'Albret had me?" I ask softly.

"Any price. Although I would like to think I would not have betrayed my country." I can see him think back to that moment, the terror that gripped him. "But I do not *know* that. Not for certain."

I rise from my own spot and go sit next to him, pressing my shoulder against his. I cannot help but think of my mother and her small bag of gold. "Our parents are merely human, for all they would have us believe otherwise."

"But his actions hurt so many."

"And his recent actions saved many. It seems to me, the scales have been tipped toward justice."

He pulls me closer and buries his head in the crook of my neck. I say nothing, but offer what little comfort I can.

After two more days and nights of his father's worsening condition, I tell Maraud, "If he is ready to die, and you wish it, I can ease his suffering."

Maraud stares at me in amazement. "How?"

"It is something Sybella showed me." Each day has brought more fever and putrefaction. "He is rarely conscious for more than a handful of minutes at a time, and I think he has suffered enough."

"He has," Maraud says bleakly. "If you could do that for him, I would be grateful."

His answer pleases me, his willingness to grant his father mercy indicating he is on his way to forgiveness.

I have never done this on a living mortal, but his soul has already been in agony for three days — surely that is enough penance. And as Sybella has said, we are moving in uncharted waters and are allowed to make some of these decisions for ourselves.

Ignoring the stench of his father's wounds, I cross to the bed and gently place my hand upon Crunard's chest, right over his heart. To my surprise, I can feel its thready beating, thin and tenuous. As I close my eyes, I feel his soul detach itself from the body, as the wheat separates itself from the chaff when it is ripened, almost as if it knows what I intend to do. *Come*, I tell the soul. *It is time for you to go. You have done your work here.*

Like some timid creature emerging from the underbrush, the soul slowly eases from Crunard's body. It is cloaked in regret and remorse so thick I can almost see it with my physical eyes. It is also filled with love and cannot resist drifting to Maraud and wrapping itself around him. He shivers, as if chilled.

"Is that him?" he whispers.

"Yes," I say around the lump in my throat. "He is telling you goodbye."

Maraud closes his eyes and opens himself, I think, to the soul — allowing some final understanding to pass between them. It is a moment of not only divine grace, but human as well.

CHAPTER 93

Sybella

s the great spires of the city of Nantes come into view, the sudden onslaught of sordid memories takes me by surprise. Unwelcome images — Count d'Albret slaying innocent servants, pressing his lips to mine when he learned I was not his true daughter, Julian lying in a pool of blood — fill my vision, causing the late spring day to darken. I am overcome with a deep reluctance to continue. "Will Lord Montauban meet us out here, or must we enter the city?"

"We do not have to enter the palace." Beast's softly spoken words are laced with understanding.

"Did you already arrange a place to meet?"

"No. I was to send word once we returned." He watches me quietly as I sort through our options.

Marshal Rieux had said he would send letters to Nantes from the other noble houses in Brittany for us to deliver to the king. Their confirmation of the rebellion — and the news that it has successfully been contained — will carry the most weight.

The main gate and its two round towers come into view, the light-colored stone nearly blinding in the bright sun. Beast holds up his hand and raises his voice so those behind us can hear. "We'll rest the horses here before entering the city," he tells the rest of our party, giving me more time to think.

Aeva sends him a look of disbelief that disappears when she sees my face. This is beyond idiotic, I berate myself. I am not some child to be haunted by nightmares. Nevertheless, she, Lazare, Yannic, and the others fall back into the shade of the nearby trees.

After a short silence, Beast says, "It is natural to grieve. And be afraid."

"You are never afraid," I point out.

"Of course I am. All the time." He squirms faintly in his saddle. "Well, mayhap not all the time."

"When?"

"Whenever your safety or the girls' is in question, I am terrified."

Our gazes hold for a long moment before I take a deep breath. My old enemies cannot hurt me now. The disloyal Jamette, the brutal Captain de Lur, the duplicitous Madame Dinan, even Lord d'Albret have been vanquished. Only Pierre remains, and he is far away from here. I take a second breath, letting this one force the ghosts of the past from my mind. "We shall enter the city, although I would prefer we stay at an inn. You can arrange for the letters to be sent there."

"We may not need to," Beast says. "The marshal appears to have been alerted to our arrival and has sent an escort." He motions toward an approaching group of riders.

My heart lifts at the thought that I will not have to enter the city after all.

But as we wait, I notice the party is well armed, and there are nearly a dozen of them, which seems too many for a simple escort. Furthermore, they are not wearing Rieux's colors. "Those are the king's colors," I say softly.

His face impassive, Beast calls back to the others. "Stay where you are and do not come out." Behind us, there is a rustle of movement as they slip deeper into the trees for cover.

"Do you think he has heard of our success in putting down the rebellion?" I ask.

"It is possible." Beast does not sound convinced.

When they are close enough that we can see their faces, I recognize Captain Stuart riding at the head, and a wave of foreboding washes over me.

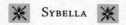

They do not slow their approach, but ride to encircle us, Captain Stuart's voice ringing out. "Benebic de Waroch and Lady Sybella d'Albret, you are under arrest for raising arms against the crown. I have orders to take you directly to the king."

CHAPTER 94

nside the palace, the guards do not grab us by the arms, but maintain a tight formation around us. While my heart beats faster, Beast's continues its slow, steady rhythm.

We are not taken to the main hall, but to the smaller, more private chambers attached to the ducal rooms that the king has taken for his own. One of the men opens the door, and Captain Stuart very nearly shoves us inside. Beast does not even notice, but I must struggle to keep my footing.

As I look up, every fear I have had since first seeing the escort crystallizes at the familiar faces around me. Not only is the king here, but also the regent, the Bishop of Albi, and General Cassel, as well as two advisors I do not know. The Bishop of Narbonne is not in attendance.

The king sits rigidly in his chair, his face hard, as he watches us approach. Captain Stuart bows. "The traitors, Your Majesty."

The word is like a slap, and I must fight to keep my temper in check. I sink into a deep curtsy as Beast goes down on one knee.

"Read the charges against them," the king says.

General Cassel steps forward. "The two of you are charged with acting against the crown and trying to incite a rebellion among the barons and commoners against their true liege, escaping the king's lawful imprisonment, and murdering one of the king's guards."

I do not dare look at Cassel for fear he will see that I know he was behind the murdered guard. I do not want to show my hand just yet.

"What say you to these charges?"

Beast's voice rumbles into the chamber. "I have killed no one but your enemies, Your Majesty. I do not know what tale has reached your ears or been reported to you, but we rode here to put down the rebellion that was already underway. And while I did escape from the dungeon in order to do so, my only aim was to see that Rohan did not succeed in raising nobles to his cause."

"And what cause was that?" The regent's voice fair curdles my stomach.

"Asserting his right to the duchy over the queen's and claiming she did not have the authority to sign a treaty on his behalf."

"You lie." The regent impugns Beast's honor as casually as swatting at a fly.

"With all due respect, Madame," I say. "He does not lie. If you were to speak with Lord Montauban, or Lord Châlons or Marshal Rieux, they would all support our claim."

It is the king who answers. "All those men have been loyal to the queen. I cannot trust them in this. Besides, your actions speak louder than any words." I can hear a faint thrum of fury in his voice.

"What we need you to tell us," the regent interjects smoothly, "is how involved the queen has been with this plan."

I meet her gaze, allowing all my righteous outrage to spill out. "She has only acted with honor, to ensure the dowry she brought to this marriage was not stolen out from under the king."

"So she was involved."

There is but the briefest moment to make a choice. "Only to the degree you saw in Paris, when she presented her arguments in front of you."

"Is that true?" she asks Beast.

He does not hesitate. "Yes." I allow myself a small, internal sigh of relief. We will at least be able to shield her.

"Yet another lie, I'm afraid," she says lightly, before her face grows hard and smug. "English soldiers were among the dead at Morlaix."

"They were not fighting *for* Her Majesty," Beast explains, "but against her. Not only did Rohan initiate the rebellion, he invited France's enemies to move against the queen as well."

"Your Majesty." I direct my words to the king. "If you do not trust us, all you must do is locate Viscount Rohan and put the questions to him. Find out where he was, who he was corresponding with. It will prove that we tell the truth."

There is another long pause. "We have already done so," the regent says. "And he has testified that he was approached by the queen to participate in such a scheme, but refused."

She has gotten to him. The regent has gotten to Rohan and convinced him to implicate the queen to save his own hide.

"Take them away," the king says with a wave of his hand.

Soldiers step forward then, holding chains and manacles as they approach Beast. I want to scream at them, but will not give them the satisfaction. I look at Beast, wondering if we should make a break for it. We could — easily. We have fought twice this many before and won.

He gives a faint shake of his head. It is a different thing altogether to raise one's hand against the king.

And so I must watch in silence as the man who risked his life time and time again to secure this fickle kingling's lands is chained and led away. He does not fight, and his head does not bow. His innocence shines like a beacon — for those not too blinded by their own political scheming to see it.

I am escorted by six armed guards to a small room in the north tower. Four of them remain at my door. I immediately cross to the window and look down in time to see the entire palace courtyard below come to a standstill as Beast is led to the dungeon housed in the old tower. I feel, rather than hear, the clang of the door as it shuts behind them, imagine them leading him lower and lower to that dark pit. I clench my fists. I have gotten him out of there before, I can do so again.

But such thoughts feel like empty promises and bring me little comfort.

Sometime later, my door opens, and much to my shock, the king enters. "Your Majesty."

He says nothing, but simply circles me, watching. At last he says, "Rise," then turns to stare into the fire.

When minutes pass and he still has not spoken, I decide I have had enough of games. "What will you do with Sir Waroch?"

He glances over his shoulder. "What we normally do with traitors."

Cold, piercing fear takes over my body. "You cannot kill him! He was only trying to protect what was yours."

"I am king. I can do whatever I like."

I clench my fists and try to calm myself. "Will you not at least consult with the men he named to see if their stories match his?"

"We have Viscount Rohan's sworn oath already."

"And if Rohan were behind this, as we claim, do you not see how convenient that would be for him to sign such a thing?"

A small frown creases his brow. "He gave his word."

"I can swear my oath as well."

"Yes, but we already know you are a proven liar, spy, and assassin. Your word is worthless."

"Sir Waroch's is not."

"You would not be the first woman to have corrupted a man." He pauses a moment, placing a hand on the mantel to stare into the fire. My mind whirs, striving to think of something to say, something I can do that will open his eyes to the truth.

Before any such thing comes to me, he whirls from the fireplace, fury contorting his face. "You lied to me. You said you were going to a convent. You freed Beast from my dungeon and left a . . . *bear* in his place!"

"I did not lie. I did leave the palace, and I did spend some time at the abbey. And the bear was too old and tired to hurt anyone. Truly, for an assassin, I have worked hard to ensure that nobody died."

He takes a step toward me. "You are a dangerous influence on the queen. Ever since you have attended upon her, she has changed. You poison her mind with your thoughts of power. You push her to disobey me. It was a mistake to ever indulge her and allow you at court."

"You are mistaken if you think your queen is so malleable as all that. She has ever been strong and resolute."

"I will have to set her straight on that, but will wait until the babe has come so as not to risk anything happening to it. However, I can at least rid myself of you now."

"Shall I be executed as well?"

"I have no stomach for killing women. You shall be permanently banished from court. I am returning you to your family and will let them deal with you."

My family. He means —

"Your brother Pierre will be here by nightfall. You will be given into his custody, and I will wash my hands of you."

No. I have not gone through so much, come so very far only to end up back where I started. "Your Majesty, one of the things we discovered while here was that Pierre was also involved in the rebellion. His troops fought alongside Rohan's. He is not loyal to you. He cares only for his own interests."

The king gives me a withering look. "You will say anything, grasp at any straws to save yourself, won't you, demoiselle?"

I give Fortune's wheel one last spin. "The guard that was killed — what did you do with his body?"

"I don't know. Gave it to his family."

"Send someone to contact that family and retrieve whatever personal belongings were on him, Your Majesty. In them you will find a gold brooch that will tell you precisely who killed the man. It was not Beast, who was locked behind a thick wooden door."

"You, then?"

"No. General Cassel."

He stares at me a long moment, his face unreadable. "Farewell, Demoiselle d'Albret. I sincerely hope our paths never cross again."

Needing to move, I cross once more to the window and look out. I am still five floors up, the stone is still too smooth to climb. There are no ledges or molding or even crumbling mortar I could use as a foothold.

Even worse, they have posted a half dozen armed guards at the base of the old tower. Even if I were to get out, I could not get Beast free.

With no path for escape, the king's words finally sink in. If I had thought returning to Nantes was difficult, how much worse will it be to reside in a d'Albret household again?

And if I am not here, who will free Beast before he is executed?

Each realization is like a stone being laid upon my chest until it is nearly impossible to breathe. Old remembered pain comes hurtling out of its hiding place, infecting me like a plague, causing my hands to shake and my knees to weaken. It is like having gnawed one's arm off to escape a trap, only to find oneself back in the very same trap.

The ghosts come then, not just my own, but the castle's as well. Their cold presence seeps out of the stone into my very soul, chilling me to the bone, and saps my spirits even more. I thrust them aside, feeling them scatter like pigeons who have spied a cat, then begin to pace the small room, wishing a servant would come and light the fire in the hearth.

Then I laugh. As if I do not know how to light my own fire.

I cross to the fireplace, take wood from the stand, and lay it upon the hearth. I search for the tinderbox, my hands fumbling with cold — or fear — as I strike the flint. A spark catches. I set it to the kindling and watch the flame come to life. The faint heat eases something inside me.

It is the Dark Mother to whom I have prayed these last months. It is she who brings hope out of darkness. And though this moment feels hopeless, that doesn't mean I must give in to despair. Hope need not shine brightly. It need only be a dogged refusal to give up.

The king — and his be-damned advisors — may be playing a game of chess, but I do not have to agree to be their pawn. I can turn this game into one of my own making. I need only figure out what that might be.

The king does not wish to make a public spectacle of my brother dragging me off in front of the entire court, so they wait until dusk. When Pierre arrives, it is clear he is taking no chances.

Even though we are accompanied by nearly forty men, every one of them cut from the same rough cloth as Maldon and le Poisson, he ties my wrists and my ankles. But not before he searches me, looking for weapons, quickly removing my five knives and my anlace. He did not find, or mayhap did not recognize, my rondelles or my garrote bracelet. To my great relief, he did not linger or tarry at the task, but executed it with quick efficiency.

Panic tries to beat its hot, fluttering wings against the inside of my chest, but I refuse to acknowledge it. It would have been easy enough to flee, that moment when the king announced my fate, but I did not. Nor did I flee when I was escorted from the palace, still within the king's view, and had not yet been bound.

If I had I known I was going to be bound, I might have. But now I focus on the questions that plague me: How did the regent know that the English were in Morlaix? They landed but a week ago. If she had spies in place, then surely they would also have reported how valiantly we fought?

Unless . . . I remember the look the regent and Pierre exchanged, as if a debt had been settled. I know that Rohan and Pierre were allies in the rebellion, and had hoped that once I was at Pierre's holding, I could find proof of that. But now I wonder if I might catch a much larger prize.

CHAPTER 95

Genevieve

atching Maraud say goodbye to his father has put me in mind of my own family. How are they faring? Are they all still alive? It seems as if I would know if they weren't. Surely someone would have sent word to the convent — but with what Sybella told me about the former abbess, who is to say the news would have reached me?

That is why, as we draw closer to Nantes — and the village where I grew up — I decide I must see them. Besides, I know all about Maraud's family, including its secrets. It is only fair that he know about mine. I want honesty between us, and if he cannot accept the nature of my family, then I must know.

My village has grown since I left ten years ago. And even while it is different — six more houses, a larger smithy, a market square we did not have before — it feels the same as well.

My family's inn has not changed. The roof still needs fresh thatch, although the walls have been recently washed with lime, and smoke chugs from the square chimney. My palms grow damp with anticipation. What if they hoped to never see me again?

And what shall I tell them when they ask what great things I have done with the life they so selflessly guided me to?

The pit of my stomach feels hollow as I realize this was a most poorly thought out idea. I glance over at Maraud, who is watching me.

"Let me go in first, lest we shock them all." I wipe my hands on my skirts and step inside.

After the bright light of midday, the inside of the tavern is so dark I must let my eyes adjust. The low, dark-beamed ceiling seems to suck up whatever light gets in through the wooden shutters and door. Once I can see more clearly, the first thing that greets my eyes is the thick, sturdy figure of Sanson, standing behind the counter, his meaty arms wielding a knife with precision as he prepares two chickens for the soup pot. Is that gray hair peppering his beard?

He lifts his head. "May I help you?"

Panic runs along my spine. He does not recognize me. "That depends," I say, my voice unsteady. "Do you have any stray cats that need feeding?"

He looks at me again — really looks — the knife growing still in his hand. "Genevieve?" My name is uncertain on his tongue.

"In the flesh!" I intend the words to sound saucy, as my aunts might say such a thing, but it comes out in a wobble. Then he is wiping his hands and coming out from behind the counter, his beefy arms opening wide just before he clasps me in a massive hug that is like being swallowed by a tree trunk.

"We thought never to see you again." He turns away from me and bellows, "Bertine! Come see what the cat's dragged in!"

And then she is there, my mother. The woman who invited Death to her bed on a dare. She is the same, but different. Softer in some places, harder in others. Her warm brown eyes have more wrinkles at the corner, but from laughter rather than hardship.

She knows me instantly, clapping a hand over her mouth in surprise before running to me and gathering me in her arms — even though I am now nearly half a head taller than she is. Her arms feel the same as they always have, warm and welcoming. The most accepting place in all the world.

"I was not sure you would ever return to us," she says at last.

"I have not had a chance to before now. My work has had me in France for the last five years." By this time, my aunts have gathered round, every one of them needing to hug me and pat me with their own hands.

"Come." My mother pulls me to one of the tables. "Tell us of your adventures."

"I will, Maman, but first I have someone I'd like you to meet."

Hours later, my mother finds me sitting outside in the back of the tavern, leaving Maraud to fend for himself among my adoring aunts. As she sits down next to me, she nudges my shoulder with her own. "Don't leave him alone with them too long. You never know what they might try."

I smile down at the twig I am playing with. "I am glad they like him. He is honorable and has a most generous spirit."

She nudges me again. "It does not hurt that he is well-built and strong, and looks as if he knows how to please a wom —"

"Maman." I smile and shake my head.

"Do you like your life, Genevieve?"

The question catches me off-guard, her gaze intense as it tries to peer into my very soul. "It has many advantages," I say. "Although there have been periods that were harder than I imagined they would be."

She gives a little shrug of her shoulders. "That is true of all lives." Then she reaches for my hand, tugs it. "Come." She rises, pulling me along with her toward the back corner of the garden, where she plants the turnips and carrots and onions every year. She glances around, as if to ensure there is no one to see.

She counts off twelve paces from the east corner of the hen house, then takes the stick I still carry in my hand. She kneels on the ground and counts out four hand lengths and begins to dig. When she is done, she looks around once more, then pulls something from the ground. As I kneel down beside her, she brushes it off, and thrusts it into my hand. "Here."

Dirt still clings to the small cloth bag, the leather cord nearly eaten away by worms and the damp. My hand shakes a little as I open it. Shiny gold coins wink out at me.

"What is this?" My voice trembles.

"It is for you," she says, pleased with herself. "I have always told you I wanted you to have choices. I have kept this so if you did not like the life you were living, you would have something to start over with."

She did *not* take the coins for herself. She took them for me. Even then, determined that I should have not just one more choice than she did, but several.

"Maman, you and Sanson could use this. The tavern still needs a new roof."

My mother waves her hand. "The tavern will always need a new roof, the beds new mattresses, and the pot more mending. But you, you are my only daughter, and I have always wanted more for you."

"The day you left me at the convent, why did you not turn back to bid me goodbye?"

She cups one hand, still gritty with dirt, around my cheek. "You were having a hard enough time parting ways. I did not want you to see me weeping."

I throw my arms around her and allow myself, allow us, to have the hug we denied ourselves that day. And just like that, the entire world shifts, casting itself in a new light. Her words have removed the bandages from a wound I never had, but carefully guarded and protected nonetheless.

I wipe the dampness from my face and give the bag back to her. "Keep it for me. I'll come back when I have need." And I mean it. That small bag has opened up yet another road on my horizon, and it will be there should I need to take it.

CHAPTER 96

Sybella

hateau Givrand sits on a small finger of land that thrusts aggressively into the sea, the waves lapping at the base of the west wall of the castle. It is made of thick, rough gray stone with narrow arrow slits for windows. One wall of the main tower is still reddened and blackened by a centuries-old fire. It is old, and the chateau is of little strategic value now that silt has reduced the usefulness of the nearby port. Everyone will assume that Pierre has returned to his stronghold in Limoges. Few — if any — even know of my family's holding south of Givrand. It is the last place anyone will think to look — if they even remember it at all.

There is only one approach, a long narrow road that leads to the square courtyard built upon the rock. When we are safely inside the keep, they remove my shackles and Pierre leads me to the wide spiral stairway that leads from the castle yard to the main hall.

The first floor of the keep is used for storage, the second is the guards' room, and the two upper floors have been given over to the family apartments.

Pierre leads me to the fourth floor. As he escorts me down the dark cramped gallery, one of the doors opens and a woman steps out carrying a cloth-covered bowl. She is tall and thin, and was once elegant, but no longer. When she sees us, she grows motionless, waiting for us to pass. Our eyes meet, and with a shock, I recognize Madame

Dinan. Her face is pale, not fashionably so, but drawn with it. Hatred shines bright in her eyes, animating an otherwise lifeless face.

"What is she doing here?" Her harsh words thrust into the silence of the hallway.

"The king has finally given me custody of her," Pierre calls over his shoulder. "This was the closest holding."

"She cannot stay," she calls after his retreating back.

He stops walking so suddenly that I nearly plow into him, stepping nimbly aside just in time. Ignoring me, he slowly strides back toward Madame Dinan. "What did you say?" His words are couched in polite tones that do nothing to hide the threat lurking there.

Madame raises her head, gaze flitting briefly to his before fluttering away again. "I said she cannot stay."

He takes a step closer, crowding her. "You do not give the orders here."

She does not look at him, but at me, taking her strength from the hatred she harbors. "It is not your holding," she says, and I cannot help but admire her foolish bravery. "It is still your father's. Until he is dead, it is his, and he would not want her here."

"But as he cannot tell me that, I shall be the one to decide, and I say she stays."

Madame Dinan's mouth works, twisting and pursing with all the words she wishes to say, but dares not. I think of all the sharp, witty, biting responses I have heard over the years, unsurprised that my family has finally driven them from her tongue.

"Now get rid of that slop," he says, and stalks back down the hall to where I wait in silence. He sends one malevolent gaze my way, then resumes walking. My mind can hardly wrap itself around Madame. Her sharp, brittle elegance worn down to naught but a drudge.

Pierre stops again, this time opening a door. "Here is your room. There will be two guards posted outside. Be wise, sister dearest, and do not make this any harder than it has to be."

I smile prettily at him. "I am certain I shall enjoy your generous hospitality, my lord." He grabs my shoulder and shoves me into the room. As he steps outside, he motions the two guards forward and closes the door behind him.

I do not move, but stand perfectly still, willing my heart and my lungs to calm themselves. Force myself to feel my feet still anchored to the floor. My body that is not — yet — in any pain or danger. Finally, when I can draw a full breath and my hands do not shake, I allow myself to take stock of my room.

It is small and dark, dank and damp from the ocean outside. There is but one window, too high and narrow to climb out of. Nevertheless, I cross over to it and peer out, straight down to the sea hurling itself at the rocks below. Perhaps a mouse could scale that wall, but he would have to become a fish once he reached the bottom.

There is an unlit fireplace, and a bed with faded green curtains, and two thick, dusty tapestries. I shiver, wrapping my arms around myself. I am not a prisoner, I remind myself. I am here by choice. I am hoping that Pierre has something that will prove Rohan's — and the regent's — involvement in the rebellion. Once I have that, I shall leave. I glance back at the window. Somehow.

As I am considering yanking one of the curtains from the bed to use as an extra cloak, the door opens and two servants come in bearing my trunk, a woman close on their heels. As they set my trunk down, she tells them, "Light the fire, and find some candles."

The familiarity of that voice has me reeling. "Jamette?" I ask, half fearing my mind has given in to panic in spite of my resolve.

The fire catches, casting a glow into the room. Moments later, three candles flare to life, and I see that it is, indeed, Jamette and that she is watching me.

"You may leave," she tells the servants, who hastily do as instructed.

Once they have gone, I take a step toward her. "What are you doing here? You were supposed to leave when you had the chance!" While I have never borne her any love, it was her love for Julian that ultimately allowed me to live, and I would not wish my worst enemy a place in this household.

Her pretty pink lip curls. "Where was I to go? You killed my father. I had no one else."

"There are other places you could have gone. Nantes alone has scores of convents that would have granted you sanctuary —"

"A nunnery!" she scoffs.

"Or the Arduinnites!"

"A pack of wild women who live in the forest? Surely you jest."

I want to shake her shoulders till her teeth rattle. "Surely anyplace would be better than here. Julian would not want you to —"

"Do not dare speak his name! I gave you that knife to save him. Not you. You were supposed to offer yourself up on your father's sword so he could live."

"I tried." My voice is as bleak as the memory. Oh, how I tried. "But Julian would have none of it."

And then she is gone, and I am left standing in an ice-cold room, feeling as if I have stepped back through time, my past determined to follow me, no matter how far I run or how much I change.

CHAPTER 97

That night, the guards escort me down to the great chamber for supper. It is a large room with a raw-beamed ceiling and a carved wooden screen that separates the kitchen from the chamber itself. The fireplace, which takes up one entire wall, does little to warm the cavernous space. Iron chandeliers fashioned in the shapes of stag antlers hang from the ceiling, thick yellow candles impaled on the points. The effect makes the entire holding feel like one large dungeon.

I am given a seat at the far end of the high table, the only person other than Pierre to be given a place there. I am surprised that he does me this much honor.

I take a sip of wine from the heavy wooden goblet and cast my gaze over the men. Most of these faces are new to me, with only a handful that I recognize. They are not as unruly and belligerent as the men I am used to serving my family. Mayhap they are tired. Or wary.

When the first course is set before us and the men turn their attention to their dinners rather than the high table, I ask Pierre, "How long will we stay here?"

He spears a piece of the fish with the tip of his knife and places it in his mouth. "Until you tell me where our sisters are."

I hold his gaze a beat longer, then apply my own knife to my meal. "We shall be here a long time, brother."

He smiles as he spears another chunk of sole. "We'll see."

I do not like that smile, not at all, but he is also very good at bluffing and boasting when he has no reason. I change the subject. "Will your other estates be able to manage without your oversight?"

He laughs, and I vow, a good-natured Pierre is far more unnerving than a foul-humored one. "Are you so very eager to get on the road so you may try to escape?" He wags his knife at me. "I would advise against it. My men have orders to shoot if you dare to break out of the riding line." He takes a drink of wine. "To maim, not kill," he clarifies. "Sadly, you are too valuable to kill, although it would give me great pleasure."

"Let the girls remain where they are." I pitch my voice low so he must lean closer to hear it. "They are too young to marry, nor do you even need them to sign the betrothal contracts."

"I need them to control you."

Keeping my eyes on my trencher, I smile, making full use of my dimples. "Ah, but you're wrong. I came here of my own accord. I could have escaped many times and chose not to." When he looks at me in disbelief, I quickly name half a dozen places on the road I could have gotten away.

"You lie." But there is no heat — or conviction — behind the words.

I wag my knife at him, copying his earlier gesture. "You're hoping I lie, but regardless, the queen has burned her bridge with the king. She will not be able to offer the protection I wanted for the girls. So now, once more, it is down to you and me. My sisters stay where they are, but you get me." I pop the fish in my mouth and pray I will be able to swallow the greasy lump of revulsion that accompanies it.

"You will have all my many skills at your disposal. You've simply to point me in the direction you want, and I will be your diplomat, your spy, or your knife in the dark. As you told me, brother, my skills hold great value for you. But only if they are willfully given. Otherwise, you can never trust that I will do as you command and not betray your own interests."

"That is why I need your sisters."

Your sisters, not our sisters. "That is where you are wrong. If you force them to come here, I will be so concerned — and involved — in their safety and upbringing I will be unable to serve you in the manner you wish."

His eyes glint with both interest and wariness. "We shall see."

"Yes, we shall."

When the interminable meal is finally over, we rise from the table. I grab my goblet, still half full of wine, then take a sip. "Can you give me a tour of the holding? I have not been here in over ten years and fear I have forgotten much of it."

He pauses, considering, then nods once, motioning for my guards to follow at a distance. As we leave the great chamber, I smile again. "Did you think to bring the hawks?"

He glances at me. "Yes, but it will be a while before I trust you enough with such freedom."

My heart sinks. We are to stay longer than I'd hoped. "I look forward to earning that trust," I say over the rim of my goblet, then take another sip.

He takes me through the third floor, where his rooms are situated. It is far more richly appointed than the fourth. When I have seen all I need to, I make a point of yawning. "Thank you, dear brother. I find I am growing fatigued." I turn to the guards then. "Come along, fellows. I'm off to bed. And no use fighting over who will join me tonight, for I am too tired after our long journey."

Once back in my room, I begin pacing, tired though I am. The castle layout holds no surprises, but no answers either. There are no visible exits but the ones I passed through on my arrival. No stairway out the back, no private inner courtyard that I can access. It is not much to work with, but it is more than I had three hours ago.

I have also learned the location of Pierre's strongbox — the one that every lord carries with him from holding to holding that contains all his important legal documents.

And correspondence.

Now I must simply find a way to evade my guards, sneak to his office on the floor below — without being detected — and search the box that is secured with not one, but two locks.

Unable to sleep, I rise from the bed, slip into my cloak and shoes, and head for the door. The guards come to attention as I emerge from my room. "Are you to prevent me from leaving or merely follow me if I do?" I inquire politely.

They exchange an uncertain glance. "Depends on where you're going," one of them says.

"Just down the hall. I wish to pay my respects to my father."

After a moment's indecision, they agree and follow me to d'Albret's chamber.

I scratch at the door lightly, braced for Madame Dinan to launch herself at me, but it is only a somber maidservant, who quickly steps back and lets me in. I pause at the threshold, not sure what is driving my desire to see this man. Mayhap to assure myself that he is still incapacitated.

As I draw near the bed, I search for his heartbeat and feel . . . something. It is not a truly beating heart, but more of a stirring, much as a pebble is stirred by the flow of a stream.

Slowly, half afraid that if I look at him he will miraculously recover and leap from the bed, ready to wreak havoc on my world once more, I draw back the bed curtain.

Shock is my first reaction, for I would not have recognized him if I had not known who he was. D'Albret le Grand has shrunk to naught but loose skin on overlarge bones, his face gaunt and drooling. It is nearly impossible to reconcile this man with the one who made my life a waking nightmare.

He should be dead from the blow I dealt him — would be if not for the promise Mortain made my mother. I wonder at the person she was, a woman who not only invited Death into her bed, but extracted two promises from him as well: that I would live and that her husband would never be allowed near her again, not even in the realm of death.

Chapter 98

Genevieve

ince there is no word from Beast or Sybella waiting for us as we draw near Nantes, Maraud and I decide to approach separately, especially given my history with the king, although I do not share that part of it with him. Unlike most men I have known, he has not brought up the subject of former lovers. Yet another mark in his favor.

As I dismount in the palace's sprawling stable yard, I find myself surrounded by guards. Although not completely unexpected, it is most unwelcome.

"That was fast," I say lightly to Captain Stuart, whose face tells me nothing.

"We have been told to watch for you." The captain does not take me to the grand salon, but to the royal apartments, where a fuming king waits for me.

"Your Majesty." Not knowing how much trouble I am in, I give my deepest curtsy. He leaves me with my nose nearly touching the floor as he slowly circles me, my gaze fixed on the tips of his cordovan leather boots.

"Where have you been?"

"In Brittany, sire. Helping to put down Rohan's rebellious uprising."

"You mean the queen's."

"No, Your Majesty. The queen was not involved, although Rohan had seen fit to ally with the English. If not for our actions, you would even now have four thousand English troops marching on French soil."

"Why should I trust what you say? You have not only spurned my favor and aligned yourself with the queen, but taken up arms against me, adding salt to the wound. Of all those who betrayed me, your cut is the deepest." His mind is more closed to me than it has ever been.

"Did Your Majesty not find the note I left you?"

He stops his circling. "The note that accused me of not being able to protect you? The note that doubted I possessed the wit to best my own sister?"

And there it is — the true source of the pain he is feeling.

"Why, Genevieve?" The harsh words are tinged with despair. "Why is your loyalty to the queen and not me?"

I risk looking up into his face, wanting him to see the truth it holds. "My loyalty is to both of you, sire. I thought that in securing Brittany, I was serving you as well as the queen. The regent made it impossible to continue serving you at court, so I sought to do so in another way."

"Which meant running away without so much as begging my leave?"

"I did it to protect what was rightfully yours."

"Get up. I grow tired of your groveling. You did it to serve the queen, not me."

Once I am on my feet, it is all I can do to keep from giving him a bracing slap to restore his wits. "You loved her enough to turn the tides of war away from her. Why can you not find that love in your heart once more?"

"Because she wishes to take what is mine."

He is not talking about Brittany, but power. "Sire, you are not a child to have his favorite toy snatched from his hand. You are a king, it is in your blood. No one can take that from you. Not even the queen, if she'd a mind to, but she doesn't. She has no wish to wear the crown of France. That was only ever your sister's dream — one she could never have. Bitterness and jealousy clouded her judgment and reason. In her head, she twisted everything the queen did into a power play because that was what she would do.

"The queen never played those games. She has no desire to do anything other than follow through on the promises she made to her people, and serve as your dutiful queen. It is what she was raised from birth to do."

"Then why does she keep sticking her nose into the crown's affairs?"

"Only when it is her business as well." He starts to protest, but I stop him. "Think upon it! Every time she has become involved, it has revolved around Brittany or the safety of those who served her. Would you have your queen be less loyal? Less caring? Less giving of her Christian charity?"

He closes his mouth with a snap.

"She is as different from your mother as you are from your father. She does not have the mind to do nothing but sit and sew with her ladies. She is fiercely intelligent and intensely loyal. She went nose to nose with your sister and held her at bay. She turned a sure defeat into a victory. Why would you not want your children to possess such virtues as she possesses?"

The tightness around his mouth softens.

"My lord, her father is dead. Her mother, too. As well as her younger sister. She has no family but the one you create together. She has so much to give. As do you."

"But she created this rebellion in order to . . ."

"In order to what? For therein lies the true flaw of your argument. She gains nothing by any of this. It was the general's and your sister's doing. Whether they engineered it or simply grasped the opportunity once it presented itself, they used her as a scapegoat to hide their own desire to influence you. All they needed to say was that she wished it, and you did the opposite. It was no more difficult to steer your thoughts and inclinations than it was to steer a cart."

His nostrils flare in irritation.

"A very royal, magnificent cart, Your Majesty."

"Do not lob empty flattery at me."

"It was but a jest. I know how hard it can be to look at our mistakes, made with the best of intentions, but mistakes nonetheless. For me, jesting softens the sting of it."

"Yes, let's talk of your mistakes," he says. "Your note." His lips curl in a sneer. "I could have protected you. The council would not have listened to her."

"Are you so very certain, Your Majesty? The Bishop of Albi is her creature, bought and paid for. General Cassel wishes to punish everyone — most brutally — at the slightest provocation. And I am still not convinced that he is not working in close concert with your sister. What if they *hadn't* listened to you? It was not a risk I was prepared to take.

"I had to go where she could not find me or else be used against you. I could not live with that possibility and did not want you to have to live with that threat."

"You think me too weak to stand against her."

I fear a pitched army of ten thousand is too weak to stand against her, but do not share that with him. "No, but she is cunning and devious enough to weave a web that ensured standing up to her cost you dearly. That is what I wished to spare you."

He stares at me, unmoved.

I take a step toward him. "She threatened to expose you to the council if I could not convince you to hand Sybella over into her brother's custody. She gave me the choice of betraying you or betraying my sister. I chose neither."

"Lady Sybella is as important to you as your king?"

"She is my sister."

"She is a fellow initiate of the convent!"

He does not believe it was a true choice. He thinks we are nothing but friends. "Which means she is my sister," I say gently. "We are all of us sired by the patron saint of death. That is how we come to his service."

"Saints do not lie with women!" For a man who has lain with more than his fair share, he sounds scandalized.

"Saints who once walked the earth as gods do. It is how we are made. Why we are trained in his arts."

He stares at me a moment — belief warring with doubt. "That is precisely why my advisors wish to have you renounce your faith — it is heretical."

"It is not, sire. Surely the Church keeps detailed records of its decisions and councils. There was exactly such a council that created the Nine. Your Majesty, it is not my intent to argue theology with you, but to show you that Sybella is, for all intents and purposes, my sister, and I could not betray her in such a way."

His head snaps up. "And how would putting her in her brother's custody, where she rightfully belongs, betray her?"

No matter how hard I try to extricate myself, I only get caught further in the net. "He does not have her best interests at heart. Where is she now?"

He angles his body away from me, as if disgusted. "She is being detained for her part in the rebellion."

"She was not rebelling, she was fighting against it."

"And so we're back to that." He averts his head, unwilling or unable to look at me.

"Why are you so convinced the queen was behind it?"

"Viscount Rohan has come forward and told the entire truth."

I frown. If that were the case, he and I would not be having this conversation. "And what truth was that?"

He rounds on me, eyes glinting. "That she approached him and he pretended to go along with it only to lull her into a false sense of security until he could get word to me."

I cannot help it, I laugh. The entire story is so twisted and absurd. "Until he could get word to you? Has he never heard of messengers?"

The king's reply is stiff. "He could not risk it being intercepted."

"Come now, Your Majesty. You receive messages every day, from far more important dignitaries, and none of them has ever been intercepted."

He frowns slightly, considering. I press my advantage. "Furthermore, what could the queen possibly hope to gain by such a move against you?"

"Power."

"What witnesses could I produce that you would believe? Tell me, and I will find them."

He turns to stare into the fire. "No one," he says. "I am surrounded by lies."

I have done my best to plant the seeds of doubt. Now I can only pray I will be given time to coax those seeds into full-blown misgivings.

CHAPTER 99

Sybella

The next morning, Pierre himself shows up at my door. At first, I fear he has heard of my visit to his father's chambers, but he is not angry enough for that. Instead he crosses over to the fire and rubs his hands almost gleefully. A gleeful Pierre is one who is about to spring a trap.

"To what do I owe this most unexpected pleasure?" I ask.

"Now that you have settled in, we will be having a formal welcoming dinner in the great chamber tonight."

"A welcoming dinner," I repeat warily. "Was that not what we did last night?"

He waves a hand. "That was but a casual supper." He rises up on his toes. "You have been gone so very long. When was the last time we were all together in one of our own holdings?"

"Two years and eight months, but I did not know that was something to be celebrated." Not to mention that we will not "all" be together. A number of us are missing: Julian, Charlotte, Louise.

He grows more somber. "Our family is always more powerful when we are together."

I nod, as if in agreement, but as far as I'm concerned, the d'Albrets need to be scattered far and wide so that they can never find their way back to one another again.

"I've even managed to convince Madame Dinan to join us."

"You do know she loathes me and is looking for a chance to kill me."

His eyes gleam with anticipation. "Yes."

While he may have begun to grasp the art of nuance and subtlety, he is as brutish and cruel as he ever was. "Am I allowed to defend myself?"

He grins widely. "It will not come to that." His smile disappears as he takes a step closer. "You will be there, and you will be dressed for the occasion. Do not make me come looking for you, or you will regret it deeply."

And then he is gone, the foul taint of him still lingering in the room.

I do not let myself think of Beast locked away in a dungeon, nor let myself wonder how he will possibly get free without me. Instead, I go to the narrow window and rest my chin upon the sill, looking out into the turbulent waters swirling against the rocks. But the window has not grown wider, nor the drop less steep, nor the landing any more forgiving.

When the guard raps on my door to announce that it is suppertime, I emerge from my room. I have taken great care with my appearance, no hair out of place, every bit of finery I possess strewn about my person. While my golden hair net only has a half dozen pearls left, I have arranged them artfully and within easy reach. I feel naked with no knives, but am wearing the thick gold cuff that holds my thin garrote and have fashioned my rondelles into brooches and affixed them to the waist of my gown. The guards' eyes widen in appreciation, but to my surprise, say nothing. Those who serve the d'Albret household are not known for their restraint.

As I descend the staircase to the grand chamber, my heart sounds so loud to my own ears that it nearly drowns out all the other heartbeats within the holding. I berate myself for letting a simple dinner, even one Pierre is so smug about, unnerve me so, and yet it has.

When I am ushered into the grand chamber, my senses are assaulted by the press of scores upon scores of bodies, their scents, and the cacophony of their hearts. The warm light thrown off by the fire and the candles in the stags' antlers, the snarling wolf-head andirons, the sea of hardened cruel faces, all feel as if I have wandered into a nightmare.

Pierre himself comes to escort me to the high table. I give him my most charming smile, as if I have been waiting for this moment all day and not considering dashing myself on the rocks below.

"How elegant you look." He lifts my hand to his lips and presses a kiss upon it. "Not only am I pleased with your unique convent skills, I find I am also glad you are not truly my sister."

It takes every particle of will I possess to keep from slamming my fist into his face. Instead, I focus my gaze above his eyebrow. "You are a brave and persistent man," I say lightly, "considering how that ended the first time."

He lets go of my hand to lift a finger and rub the white scar there, the one I gave him ten years ago. "It is a good thing your mouth is so lovely, else I would be tempted to strike it," he says, matching his tone to mine.

"And so we find ourselves at checkmate," I murmur.

He smiles again, this one the most disturbing I have seen yet. "Oh, far from that. Come." He tucks my arm firmly in his and pulls me past the milling retainers toward the high table. When we are halfway there, he pats my arm. "Lest you grow lonely, I have brought someone to keep you company. Someone I know is dear to you."

My heart gives one painful beat of dread as he pulls me past the retainers so that I have a clear view of the high table. In the chair to the right of Pierre's sits a young girl dressed in a blazing scarlet silk and velvet gown, her thin neck adorned with pearls and gold, her fingers flashing rubies and sapphire rings. The sight of her small, pale face causes the bottom to drop out of my stomach.

"Charlotte."

She turns her haughty gaze to me, looking down her nose as if I am some serving woman come to take her plate.

"What are you doing here?" Panic squeezes my throat so tight I can scarce get the question out.

"I ran away," she says coolly. "I left with one of the night rowers once he had made his delivery."

Her words reverberate along my bones as if they have been struck by a mallet. She chose to come back. She *chose* to leave the safety of the convent and return to Pierre. I was too late.

The revelation makes me so ill that I fear I will retch. If I had not been so absorbed in my own problems. If I had left the convent earlier. If . . . if . . . if. So many places where I could have made another choice that would possibly have saved this child from making hers.

"She's a smart girl," Pierre says close to my ear. "She made her way to Tonquédec."

My head whips around. "Tonquédec?" That d'Albret holding is but a few miles from Morlaix.

Pierre sips his wine. "Which is where I found her."

The convent was never meant to be a prison to keep us in, but a fortress to keep others out while we willingly learned the lessons they taught us. "Where you just happened to be for the rebellion."

He clutches the goblet he is holding. "How do you know about that?"

He does not know I was there — that I saw him with my own eyes. "Some of the queen's men returned to Nantes just before I did, and they spoke of it."

"Does the king know?"

I shrug as casually as I can. "He would not believe it, even if he'd heard. He is convinced the queen was behind it all."

Pierre's face relaxes, and he takes a sip of wine. "That was always the plan. Now, come. Take your seat over there, and Madame Dinan will sit opposite you. I think dear Charlotte deserves the place of honor at my side for her cleverness, don't you?"

I say nothing, but move numbly to take my place at the table. I want nothing more than to snatch Charlotte from her chair and steal her from the room, but there are far too many of d'Albret's men here to do that.

And she would just run back.

Truly, he has won. And before we'd even begun the game.

CHAPTER 100

Genevieve

The first indication that something is amiss is General Cassel's face growing pale. It is the closest I have ever seen to him showing fear.

I cast a quick peek over my shoulder to find Maraud standing in the doorway of the king's audience chamber. His height, the confident set of his shoulders, the proud tilt of his head all cause him to stand out among the other nobles and courtiers who have come for a chance to petition the king. He is dressed as finely as any of them, if more somberly.

The steward approaches, intending to show him out, but Maraud leans close to confer with him. Seeing this, General Cassel steps from behind the throne and begins striding to the door.

No. He will not silence him again. The knives against my wrists and left ankle are solid and reassuring as I quickly make my way toward Maraud. He looks up just then and sees Cassel. He utters something else to the steward, who nods, then escorts Maraud toward the king, careful not to cross paths with the approaching general. I switch directions and aim for the throng of people between them, an added buffer if needed.

When they reach the throne, the steward introduces Sir Anton Crunard, and the room grows hushed.

"Your Majesty." Maraud's bow is low and courteous.

"Sir Crunard." Bewilderment lurks behind the king's courteous welcome.

"I have come to bring your attention to General Cassel's deceitful and false conduct on the battlefield and petition that he be made to answer for his crimes."

The regent pushes her companion out of the way to better see what is happening.

"Crimes? That is a very harsh word."

"Murder and dishonor are very harsh things, Your Majesty."

The king's expression darkens. "Are you not a member of the family responsible for betraying my lady wife?"

"I am the son who was held hostage in order to force the late chancellor to commit such an act."

Like a hound catching a scent, the king searches out the regent. "I thought you said the queen's claim was false? Her version sounded remarkably like this man's."

Maraud does not give the regent a chance to spew more lies. "I do not know what claim the queen made," he says. "But my captors were fond of reminding me that my father betrayed the duchess because of the sword the regent held over my head."

The king's face grows sharp with interest. "That is precisely as the queen tells it."

"What the queen could not have known was that even when my father complied with the regent's demands, she did not release me as promised. She gave the crown's word and did not honor it."

The king's hand grips the arm of his chair.

"If that is true," the regent challenges, "then how do you come to be here?" It is hard to say whether she truly wishes to know or is merely stalling for time to plot out her response.

"I will gladly tell you, although I don't believe it is something you will wish to share with the entire court."

"Leave!" the king commands the assembled courtiers.

As the room clears, he glances at me, his eyes unreadable. I lift my chin, but he does not order me to go. Mayhap he is remembering my own recounting of similar events.

The king's council remains. "Now." The king gestures to Maraud. "The room is yours."

General Cassel steps forward, no longer able to remain silent. "Your Majesty should not indulge this man's lies."

"But surely he should hear of crimes his own general has committed in his name," Maraud counters.

The general's face grows red, and he takes another step forward.

"General!" the king says sharply. "If you cannot get ahold of yourself, you may wait outside."

Maraud returns his attention to the king. "The story starts on the battlefield of Saint-Aubin-du-Cormier, where my brothers and I fought alongside Duke Francis. It was" — Maraud's lips twist in a wry smile — "a rout, clear to all of us on the field that Your Majesty's forces had won and the best course of action was to surrender and save further bloodshed."

"Which the duke did." The king sits with his elbow on the arm of his chair, listening intently.

"As we all did. Including my brother. He surrendered and laid down his sword, as noble knights have done since the time of Charlemagne, expecting quarter and ransom. Instead" — Maraud shoots Cassel a look heated enough to melt iron — "the general accepted his surrender and his sword, then beheaded him there on the field."

A collective gasp goes up among the king's advisors, and the bishops cross themselves.

The king turns cold eyes on his general. "Is this true?"

General Cassel stands rigidly straight, shoulders back. "It is true that I slayed enemy combatants, Your Majesty. Traitors who had taken up arms against their rightful sovereign. My instructions were to put down the duke's insurrection at any cost."

"I meant spare no effort and explore all tactics. I did not mean to spit on the accepted form of honorable surrender and kill in cold blood."

The general's hands twitch ever so slightly, and he shifts his gaze to the wall behind the king.

"Ives was my last surviving brother. When the general learned who I was, he devised a different fate for me."

"A hostage," the king says.

"Yes. A message was sent to my father, informing him that the price of returning his last remaining son was preventing the marriage of Anne of Brittany to Count d'Albret and arranging for the duchy to fall into French hands."

"He lies!" The words explode from the general. "He was dressed as a common mercenary. I did not know he was Crunard's son."

"Is this true?"

"I was dressed as a mercenary, sire, but it was well known that as a fourth son, I fought with the mercenaries who served Brittany rather than under my father's banner."

The king leans forward, his face almost hungry. "You defied your father?"

"We had different ideas on how a man should live his life, what loyalty looked like, and where our duties lay."

The king carefully banks all the questions burning within him and instead asks, "What happened then?"

"I was imprisoned at Baugé, then taken to Cognac and placed in Angoulême's dungeon." The king's glance darts briefly in my direction. "I was held for nearly a year before being placed in the oubliette."

The king unleashes his full anger on the general. "You took a man of noble birth who was deserving of every honor and courtesy, not to mention ransom, and put him in one of those rat holes?"

Cassel gives a sharp shake of his head. "That was not on my order, Your Majesty."

"Then whose?"

Maraud lets the silence draw out before saying, "I believe it was the regent's."

Chapter 101

"**Y**et more lies, Your Majesty!" The regent shoves her way through the small wall of advisors between her and the king.

"He does not lie, Madame." My own voice echoes into the room, surprising everyone. It is also the first time Maraud sees me. A brief measure of warmth crosses his face, then is gone, nothing in his expression indicating that we are acquainted. "You forget that I, too, resided at Cognac and can confirm the order you sent Count Angoulême."

For a moment, I half fear the regent will launch herself at me and strangle me with her bare hands. "How do you know?"

I say nothing — she knows I am convent sent, and she can guess how I acquired such information. Feeling the room turn against her, she glares at me a moment longer, then collects herself before returning her attention to the king. "If he was placed in such a fetid rat hole, how does he come to be here at court in front of us?"

"Would you care to enlighten us?" the king asks Maraud.

"After I had been in the pit for weeks — possibly months, time has no meaning there — I heard a voice." His own has fallen into the rhythm of the mummers when they tell stories. The king, the bishops, even the general and regent hang on every word. "Since I was certain I was dying, I thought it an angel, but no. It was a lady, a lady who served the convent of Saint Mortain —"

The bishops take in a collective gasp, and the king's gaze darts to me once again, but briefly.

"She brought me water, fed me. Spoke with me and pulled me back from the darkness that had encircled me for so long." I am struck by how he tells the story, making me out to be the hero of it. "I trusted her enough to share my tale." How easily he polishes over all the distrust between us. "When it was time for her to leave Cognac, she freed me from my prison out of fear I would die there."

"She did not attempt to murder you?" the Bishop of Albi asks.

"Never," Maraud answers, his face the very picture of innocence and truth. Truly, he has missed his calling. "It was her convent skills that allowed us to escape."

"How many did she kill, then?" the bishop presses.

"None. The only time she killed was when we were attacked by brigands, and then she simply fought back — as any man would and with equal skill." A faint heat suffuses my cheeks, and pleasure warms my gut at his description.

"When was that?" the regent demands.

"Near Christmastime."

"That was five months ago. Where have you been since?"

"First I went to Flanders looking for General Cassel, but he was no longer there. Next I came to Paris to bring my case before the king. Alas, before I could do that, I was detained and forced to go elsewhere."

"Forced," the regent scoffs, her eyes taking in the height and breadth of Maraud.

"You do not believe men can be forced, Madame Regent?" he asks.

"Not men who are as skilled as you claim to be."

"Well," he concedes, "it was not merely one man, but a dozen of them."

The king leans forward in his chair. "Do you know who they were?"

"It was Pierre d'Albret."

Though the regent maintains her composure, I sense the faint spark of panic she is trying so desperately to hide. "Why would he force you to go with him? It makes no sense."

"D'Albret was holding my father hostage in an attempt to lure me to his side."

"But why?" the king asks.

"He wished me to participate in the rebellion in Brittany, along with him and Viscount Rohan. Pierre felt my father could be of help, and that he would cooperate more freely if I was there to threaten him with."

The king's gaze grows sharp enough to cut glass as he looks at his sister. "This corroborates what the others have said, that Viscount Rohan was behind the rebellion, not the queen."

Maraud shakes his head. "The queen had no part in the rebellion. If not for the aid she sent, Rohan would have succeeded in his attempt."

"Have Viscount Rohan returned to court immediately," the king orders. "I find I have a number of questions for him."

"Sire." The regent steps forward. "This has already been proved. What this man spouts is nothing but pure lies."

"I grow bored with that excuse, sister. What he says fits too neatly with what Lady Sybella and Sir Waroch have claimed. What does he have to gain by lying?"

With her mouth pinched tight, the regent thrusts her arms out in my direction. "Because she was the assassin who helped him." A faint buzz of muttering rises from the bishops.

"I am aware of that," the king says.

His public admission of that knowledge gives the regent pause. She has one less weapon to use against him now. "Then can you not see? They are lovers! He is lying to protect his lover from her involvement in the rebellion."

In the silence that follows, I do not look at Maraud, nor does he look at me. I keep my attention focused on the regent and force my heart to keep beating, my lungs to keep breathing. Slowly, as if it pains him greatly, the king turns to me. "Is this true?"

"Do you really wish to have this conversation here, Your Majesty?"

"Answer." If I thought him hard and impassive when he learned of my participation in quelling the rebellion, it is nothing compared to the sense of deep, personal betrayal lurking in his eyes right now.

I look over at Maraud. His face is devoid of expression, as if bracing for what he already knows I must say. If I wish to keep the king's favor, I must deny him again. But I have already denied him three times and caused him to doubt his own sanity with my lies.

I am done with lies. "Yes, Your Majesty. Sir Crunard and I were lovers." I stare at the king, willing him to understand there is more to the story than that. That I knew Maraud before I knew him. I want to explain to him the hundreds of nuances to the entire situation, but his mind — and his heart — are closed to me.

Breathy whispers race around the room, and General Cassel looks as victorious as if he'd just reconquered the Holy Land. While I expect to see anger writ raw upon the king's face, instead I see disinterest, almost boredom. "Take her away," he orders.

"And if they would lie about *that*, Your Majesty, it surely proves that they would also lie about what he claims he saw on the battlefield."

"While I have no proof of what happened on the battlefield that day," Maraud's voice rings out, "I do have proof of who was behind the rebellion." He takes a pouch from his belt and withdraws a piece of red and yellow fabric from it. He unrolls the banner Andry stole from Rohan, then tosses the grisly contents onto the floor before the regent's feet. Everyone pauses, even the guards escorting me from the room.

"These are the signet rings of the two English barons leading the troops Rohan invited to join him."

The king's gaze remains fixed on the two fingers. "How many troops?"

"Four thousand."

"Where are they now?"

"Dead."

The regent gasps, drawing the king's attention.

"And Rohan was not the one who killed them," Maraud adds.

Then the guards remember their duty, and I am led away.

CHAPTER 102

Sybella

nce I am finally alone in my chamber, all the pain and horror I have been feeling comes over me in a wave. *Too late, too late, too late.*

No. I shove the panic away. This disaster will not break me, although *disaster* seems far too tame a word. Surely it is a tragedy. A tragedy that the d'Albret family insists on eating its young. How many more will be destroyed by its foul legacy? So far, only Louise has escaped.

Unless Charlotte has told Pierre where Louise is. I clutch at my stomach. No, if she had, he would have crowed about that as well.

Unless he is waiting to spring it on me as yet another surprise. Sweet Jesu.

Too late, too late, too late.

The words gnaw on my heart, wearing it ragged.

Cold. I am so cold. I cross over to the fire and place my hands before the flames, rubbing them over the heat, using the sensation to find a way back into my body and away from my turbulent thoughts.

The heat of the flames licks my skin, and I close my eyes to pray. As the warmth begins coursing through me, I realize I am not too late. I was farther gone than Charlotte when I came to the convent, and they did not give up on me. They did not leave me to my fate, no matter how much I, in my panicked unreason, kept trying to escape.

They did not give up on me, and I will not give up on Charlotte.

I will drag her away, again and again and again, until she finds herself ready to be reborn. Not through the same flames I endured, but there are other ways to begin anew.

My panic falls away from me, and I clench my hands and stare into the fire. I will find the proof I need to clear the queen's name, collect my sister, and destroy Pierre.

But how? Especially without getting Charlotte or myself killed in the process?

With flame, the fire whispers. Or mayhap it is the memory of Lazare's voice when he told us fire was the best way for a few to take down many. Either way, once the idea has formed, I know it is the right one. It is the instrument of the Dark Mother herself, after all. Now I must simply find the means to apply it.

The next night at supper, I spend most of my meal looking out over the hall full of men gorging themselves on food and wine. I can feel Charlotte watching me, feel Pierre watching us both, but I ignore them and act as if I am considering which stud to add to my stable.

When the food is cleared away, the men move to other entertainments — dicing, arm wrestling, and loud arguments over nothing. I sip my wine, my face a mask of ennui.

Charlotte's eyes are still on me, and the desire to go to her, to shake her small shoulders then whisk her from the room is so overpowering that I must stand up and move lest I give in. I saunter toward the towering fireplace to watch the dice game, boredom and indifference dripping from every pore, which only makes the men compete harder to capture my interest.

Under the guise of allowing one of my servants to refill my wine, I glance up at the high table, relieved to see that both Madame Dinan and Charlotte have left. Good. Now I may set my plan into motion.

On the next bet placed, I raise my eyebrow and murmur into my cup, "Such an unadventurous bet, Sir Knight." His face flushes at my words, but it is too late to change it, for the other man rolls. He wins, then doubles his bet for the next roll. As does his opponent. In no time at all, the mood around the game grows heated. The stakes have been raised. They are not just playing for coin, but for their pride.

And, they think, my attention. Possibly even my favor. It takes less than a half an hour for a fight to break out, one men bellowing "Cheater!" before launching himself at another. Around them, the crowd cheers and urges them on as they crash into one of the tables. Before they have finished, two of Pierre's burliest guards wade in and pull them apart.

Pierre comes to stand just behind me, seething. "What do you think you are doing?"

I glance up at him with innocent eyes. "Watching the entertainment."

He grabs my elbow and hauls me away from the flying fists. "You started this."

"How? I wasn't even playing."

He glares at me. "Would you be happier confined to your chamber?"

"Of course not. I should go even more mad with boredom. You must know I am not the sort who can be cooped up for days and nights on end, stitching."

His eyes narrow. "What would you prefer?"

"To go riding—"

"Not on your life."

"Or hawking?"

"How stupid do you think I am, to let you out of the keep for even a minute?"

"You cannot expect me to sit here like an andiron. You said it yourself, I am not made to be a lapdog. I grow too restless, and it is not healthy for me. Besides, you don't want me to grow soft and lazy before you even have a chance to use my skills, do you?"

His hands are balled into fists as he glares at me. "You may walk the yard. As much as you'd like. But not alone."

"Yes, yes. My guards, I know."

"Not only them, for I can see how easily you can twist them around your

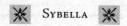

finger. Jamette will go with you." He leans in close, bringing his lips to my ear. "No one knows where you are. No one is coming to save you, and there is no way out of this holding. Best get that through your beautiful skull."

I reward him with an amused grin. "My, how you do go on about a demoiselle just wanting some fresh air."

CHAPTER 103

Genevieve

It takes three days, three days of pacing my small room, with no word or news of anyone — not so much as a pitcher of water to wash with — before the king decides to seek me out. Of course I have not been idle. I have spent the nights — when the hallways are thick with darkness — searching for Sybella's room. To my immense frustration, it is not in one of the towers, which means the king has put her in the dungeon.

When I hear the latch thrown back, I think it is the guard getting ready to toss the midday meal at me. Instead, the king strides in and closes the door behind him.

His immaculate dress makes me immediately conscious of how grubby I am — it is all I can do not to fidget or tuck my unraveling braid behind my ear. Instead I square my shoulders and curtsy. He says nothing, drawing closer, his gaze roaming over me.

"You may stand," he says at last. "I do not wish to talk to the top of your head."

As I rise to my feet, a small sliver of hope also rises with me.

"I will tell them to bring you a bath."

"That would be most appreciated."

He puts his hands behind his back and saunters to the window. "It has been an interesting three days. Sir Crunard has made some very serious claims against both General Cassel and my sister. Much of what he says lines up nicely with what you have told me. But then, it would if you were lovers, would it not?"

I want to ask him about Maraud's proof — if it was enough for him — but instead say, "I would not lie for a lover. Surely I have proved that to you at least."

My response provokes a wry twist of his mouth. "Touché." His mouth twists again, only this time not with humor, but with sadness. "What I would like to know is why you took him for a lover when you refused me."

My heart drops. I knew it was inevitable that we should talk about this, but I do not relish the task. "Your Majesty, he and I were lovers before I ever came to your bed. Were lovers, and then parted, as lovers often do. I did not think I would see him again. When we came upon each other" — in Paris — "in Brittany, we realized we had unfinished business between us."

He fingers the tapestry that covers the wall. "I thought we meant something to each other."

"We do. We are friends."

He grimaces. "Is that what we've become over the last months?"

"A friend is nothing to scoff at, Your Majesty. Indeed, our friendship is one of the truest things between us. You have had so very many lovers, and a veritable army of advisors and councilors and courtiers seeking something from you. Influence, favors, table scraps of your power. But I, ever since our first night together, have asked nothing of you, only listened and offered my insight where I thought it could help."

He turns from the tapestry to stare back out the window.

"I like to think we understand each other better than most. We have seen each other at our most private, unguarded moments. Not of passion, but of temper and melancholy, uncertainty and remorse. And through all of that, we have maintained our connection, our mutual respect." I pray that it is so, even as I utter the words. I still respect what I know him to be deep down, and will respect him even more when he finally embraces it. "Which is something no mere lover can provide. Surely you can see the truth in that?"

His face holds equal measures of contemplation and sadness. "That is one thing you have always done, Genevieve — tell me the truth. At least such truth as is convenient for you to tell."

It is hard not to wince. "That is a personal failing, sire, and not something I reserve exclusively for you."

"And so I will call on the friendship you offer and ask you to tell me the truth once more. Do you know if General Cassel did what Sir Crunard accuses him of?"

"I was not on the battlefield that day, so cannot give you an accounting of what transpired. What I can tell you is that when I first came across Sir Crunard, he was chained in an oubliette and left for dead. Even then, the one thing that shone brightest in his mind was the injustice visited upon his brother. It was his thirst for justice that kept him alive those long, dark months. It was one of the first things he spoke of to me, well before he knew who I was."

"And how did you come to know him?"

I shrug. "I was bored. Lonely. Grieving for Margot." I recognize now that I was grieving for her even before she was dead. Mourning the loss of our friendship, mourning that it was never what I thought it to be. "I came upon him —"

"In the oubliette?"

"Yes, and we began to talk."

"Of what?"

"At first, he thought I was the ghost of his brother. Bringing him food cured him of that notion. The more we talked, the more I began to wonder if he had been unjustly imprisoned, as he asserted. When Count Angoulême was away, I went through his correspondence."

The king scowls.

"It is what I was trained to do," I remind him. "And in that correspondence was a note from the regent, ordering Angoulême to make him disappear."

"You are certain it was the regent?"

"She was not so foolish as to sign it, but I have seen her writing many times and recognized it instantly."

"But why?"

"Because she did not want you to know she had blackmailed the chancellor of Brittany into betraying the duchess. Because once she had, she did not want you to know that she reneged on her promise to return his only son. Whether that was to protect General Cassel from his crimes or for her own political gain, I do not know."

The king's mouth flattens into a hard line. "It is near impossible to recognize the truth among all the lies."

"Who has lied to you the most in the past, Your Majesty?"

He jerks his head up at that. "You know from your own experience with him that Viscount Rohan's loyalties are more fleeting than the wind. General Cassel has been accused of acting dishonorably on more than one occasion, by knights who are held in high regard. And your sister lies to you as easily as she breathes."

He clenches his fist and returns to the window, his eyes staring unseeing at the courtyard below. "But my father trusted her. I cannot believe she would betray *him*."

"I'm sure she believes she is serving him."

He frowns in confusion.

"She is fashioned from the same cloth as he is."

"And I am not." The despondency in his voice cuts deeply at me.

"Your Majesty. Parents, good parents, don't want us to be miniature versions of themselves, but hope for us to have a better life —"

"But I am a king!"

"A better life isn't just measured in the titles we hold, but in how we feel while living it. Your father may have been a great king, but he did you a disservice by constantly railing against the things you value."

His eyes shift to the wall, almost by instinct, and I am glad that rutting picture is hundreds of miles away. "Your ambitions, which were different than his, were still a way to keep the crown of France thriving," I continue. "And while I've no love for the regent, for the last twelve years, she's held the reins of power. If not for the misfortune of her sex, she would have been king."

He shoots me a glance. "And this is supposed to cheer me?"

"She clearly has the sharp wits and bold cunning to be an efficient ruler, but would she have been a good one? Who is to say what horrors she might have wrought if not required by law and custom to twist and contort in order to hide the power she wielded. Or perhaps such open power would have allowed her to be less devious. But that was not the case." My voice hardens with my own anger and bitterness. "She not only clung to power once it was rightfully yours, but has gone out of her way to undermine you and the rightful queen. She is like a pauper who, once starved, will never be full again. No matter how much she eats, that deep hunger will always haunt her."

"Are you saying my sister deserves mercy?"

"No more than she has shown others."

His eyes glimmer with appreciation. "A neatly issued sentence."

I shrug. "She tried to use me as a weapon against you. Though I am not a sword, the cut would have been deep. I am not so generous a person as to be able to forgive that. Are you?"

Chapter 104

s instructed by the steward, I present myself outside the king's audience chamber and await further instructions. Moments later, the king approaches, deep in conversation with General Cassel.

No, not conversation but an argument. I keep my attention focused on the audience chamber even as I strain to listen. "But your father —"

"My father is no longer king. France is mine now to rule as I see fit." It is all I can do not to cheer at the king's words. Now if only he will rule as I hope he will. "The sooner both you and my sister come to accept that, the better." When they reach the door where I wait, General Cassel gives the king a brusque bow and enters the chamber.

"You sent for me, Your Majesty?"

"Yes. The queen should be here to witness this, but since she is still in Amboise, I thought you should do so on her behalf."

"Or mayhap Lady Sybella?" I suggest, frustrated by his continued disrespect for her.

But he is in no mood to hear suggestions. "Do you wish to bear witness for your queen or not?"

"Of course." He nods once, then strides toward the front of the audience chamber. I hang back, close enough to hear but not so close as to draw unwelcome attention.

In addition to his Privy Council, I am surprised to see both the Duke of Orléans and Madame Regent's husband, the Duke of Bourbon. A door opens off to the side, and the regent herself is escorted in by Captain Stuart. He leads her, not to where the other council members are gathered, but to stand in front of the king. As if she is on trial. My pulse quickens.

"Anne de Beaujeu," the king intones.

The regent's nostrils flare, and she tilts her chin in defiance.

"In the last two years, you have engaged in a number of activities without the approval of myself or the council at large. Many of these activities — in spite of your assurances otherwise — go directly against the wishes of the crown. In light of recent testimony, I believe that the queen was only involved in the rebellion in an effort to stop it. I will be releasing the prisoners, believing them innocent until I have demonstrable proof otherwise." It is all I can do not to raise my arms in the air and cheer. "I have called Rohan back to court to question further."

She opens her mouth to argue, but he puts his hand up to silence her. "You are to listen today, not speak." Her mouth snaps shut and for all that she tries to hide it, she looks truly concerned for the first time since I have known her.

"To ensure that such unsupported claims are not made in the future, you will be signing an agreement declaring your aid and support of our queen and swearing that you will not set your allies upon her. The agreement will also be entered into and signed by the Duke of Orléans and your husband. Nod if you understand."

She hesitates, drawing the moment out, longing to defy him, calculating. Concluding that she does not have any rope left, she nods once.

"I want to be most clear on this. If you move against my queen again, it will be treason." The king motions to his steward, who hurries forward with a small table. Next the Bishop of Narbonne steps forward and lays several sheets of parchment on the table. "If you will please read the document so you understand all that you are agreeing to, then sign it."

Again the regent hesitates. This time, she looks to her husband, but he merely stares back at her, appearing more than a little repulsed. With no other options before her, she turns to the document, making a show of reading it carefully. At last she signs with a flourish. "This is not necessary, you know. I have nothing but your best int —"

"Sir Beaujeu, you may now sign the agreement."

The Duke of Bourbon steps forward and signs, not bothering to read it, which makes me think that he has seen it before. This is confirmed when the

Duke of Orléans signs, for he does not read it either. As the men step back, the king looks once more to his sister. "I thank you for guiding the crown when I was too young to do so, but that is no longer the case. Further, it is past time for you to look to your own holding and family. You have a daughter — turn your attention to her upbringing. Are we clear?"

The regent's face is starkly white as she realizes she is being stripped of all power. I can see her mind churning, trying to find a way to make one last convincing argument, but the stony set of the king's face makes it clear he will not listen. "Yes, Your Majesty."

"Good. Captain Stuart will escort you and your husband from the palace and see you on the road to home. General Cassel? I will speak with you next."

When he does not come forward, it takes everyone a moment to realize he is no longer here.

CHAPTER 105

Sybella

 takes me two days of restlessly walking the castle yard and two trips to the chapel, Jamette sniveling at my heels, to collect most of the information I need. I contrive a visit to the stables to check on my horse, who I told her I feared was lame after our long ride here, but as I draw near the mews to see the falcons, she balks, worried I will try to send a message. I shrug and let her steer me away.

I am not after the hawks or messages, but wanting to understand every nook and cranny this holding possesses. I now know who comes and goes, what gate they use, how carefully those gates are watched. I know the patterns of the household, how many of them attend chapel and when, and how often they change the guard. I have learned the impassable barriers and the more vulnerable spots — the drains, the culverts, the shortest points on the wall, as well as the parts of it that cannot be seen by the posted sentries. All in all, I am pleased with what I have learned, although it is discouraging as well, for there are few options. However there is still one prize I seek, one that I cannot explore without raising her suspicions.

That is why I have kept us out until nearly dark. She is tired and cold and cranky and half ready to shove me into the well and be done with it. "Here, let's go look at the handsome guards. That ought to cheer you up." Some of the ire smooths from her face as I steer her toward the garrison.

I lean in close. "I think that tall one with the nicely shaped beard has been watching you," I murmur in her ear, my heart twisting with guilt when I see the way her face lights up. *Merde*, having a conscience is tiresome. But what is her small vanity compared to Charlotte's and Louise's safety? While she sends flirtatious looks to the guard, I take two steps back and press myself against the wall where the shadows have lengthened. With no eyes on me, it is easy enough to cloak myself in their darkness as I hurry back across the courtyard to the artillery. That — and what it might contain — is at the heart of my plan.

I scuttle around to the backside of the building, where no one can see. This building is newer than the keep, and the windows lower and wider. When working with cannon and gunpowder, one needs all the light one can find in order to avoid a fatal mistake.

Using my elbow, I scrub the glass clean of dust and peer in, my heart giving a skip of joy. The light does not penetrate far into the room, and the keep has not been garrisoned for battle in at least fifty years, but through the gloom I see a number of large, lumpy shapes covered with canvas — at least three of which I recognize as cannon. A pile of squat iron pots teeters haphazardly in one corner. They are similar to the ones the charbonnerie filled with gunpowder and used to create explosions. There are a number of long iron tubes that could be culverins. Oh! And ribauldequins! I can only pray the small kegs hold the gunpowder the ancient cannon require.

And that it has not gotten wet. Or separated. Or any number of things that would make it useless. Even so, my plan is viable.

Heartened by this, I pull the shadows close once more, then skirt the outer wall over toward the mews, where Jamette was so determined I not visit. When I am but fifteen feet away, I let the shadows drop.

A moment later, Jamette calls at me from across the yard. "Sybella!"

I pause.

"It is time to go in now." Her voice is sharp, as if she has caught a naughty child and cannot wait to scold him. I toss my head, as if defiant, and saunter over to her. When I reach her side, she grabs my arm and gives it a painful squeeze. "Do you want me to have to report you to Pierre?"

"Of course not," I say sharply, because it is what she expects. But I also wonder why she would hesitate.

CHAPTER 106

Genevieve

nce Captain Stuart has been sent off to find the general, and the regent and her husband have been escorted from the chamber, the rest of the king's advisors begin to drift away, talking softly among themselves. I wonder how they feel about this turn of events. When the king is nearly alone, I risk coming forward, then wait for him to indicate I may approach.

When he gives me permission to speak, I ask, "When will you release Sir Waroch and Lady Sybella, Your Majesty?"

He does not meet my eye, but instead focuses on the group of men leaving the room. "Captain Stuart is on his way to release Captain Waroch as soon as he has found the general. As for Sybella, she has already been released."

"What?" I take a step forward without thinking. "Why have I not seen her?"

He finally looks at me then. "Because she was released into Pierre d'Albret's custody three days before you arrived."

His words stun me as thoroughly as any blow, and for a moment, I think I will be sick.

If only I had never come to court.

If only I hadn't spoken to the king about the convent.

If only I had returned to Nantes with Sybella and Beast instead of lingering in Brittany.

But regrets will not help anyone now. Instead, I take those feelings and shift them into something darker and more useful. Anger. I bob an abrupt curtsy at the king, then stride from the audience chamber, racing back to my room.

She has been in his custody for over a week. My body starts to tremble, not with fear, I tell myself, but with a need to fix this.

If only my foolish heart had stayed in the iron box I so carefully fashioned for it. For this, I realize, is precisely the reason I have hidden it so deeply. This is why I have always preferred my dealings with others to be negotiations or trades to be worked out. One would never give a piece of one's heart away in a mere trade. Or worse, with nothing to show for it but pain and a nearly suffocating remorse.

But, a small voice reminds me, *you have found joy and laugher, love and grace, as well.*

And while that is true, when placed on a scale that tips so heavily toward tragedy, I fear it will break my heart beyond repair.

When I reach my room, I cross to the cupboard against the wall, yank open the bottom drawer, and take out my pack — the very one I carried with me from Cognac. I quickly collect all my various knives and other weapons from their hiding places about the room and am just shoving the last of them into it when the king arrives.

I barely glance up from my packing.

He closes the door behind him. "Where are you going?" He tries to sound peremptory, but the words come out vaguely uneasy instead.

"I must get to Sybella."

"I have not given you leave to go anywhere," he replies.

I stop long enough to give him my full attention. "Then you will have to imprison me again — or kill me — for I will not rest until I have gotten her out of there."

"You are so certain she is in danger?"

I clench my fists so I will not throw my pack at him. "Yes, Your Majesty. I am completely certain of it. As are you."

He makes a noise of disagreement.

It is only the brief flicker of shame that I see in his eyes that stops me from getting angrier. "Sire, ask yourself why d'Albret used so many extreme and underhanded methods to retrieve his sisters. Why not simply petition the king and be satisfied with his answer?"

"Because under the law they are his to —"

"They are his. That's all he believes. He views them not just as his responsibility, as you believe, but as his possessions. He believes he owes them less consideration than he does his horse or hunting hound. That they are his to do with as he wants. To use in any way he sees fit to advance his power, form an alliance, slake his lust, or punish simply because he is angry.

"You are governed by honor and chivalry, Your Majesty, but he is not. I have seen it with my own eyes."

"You have seen him this way with his sisters?"

"No. I have seen him this way with Sir Crunard, a man who by all measures is his equal both by virtue of his sex and lineage. When Crunard would not do as he bid, he set a half dozen men with swords upon him in answer to such perceived disrespect. When Crunard survived that, d'Albret sent an entire battalion of men to kill him or bring him back. When that failed, d'Albret then seized Crunard — from your own palace in Paris! — and forced him to take part in a rebellion. He held Sir Crunard's own father hostage to force his cooperation."

"You have made it clear that the man is a brute, but that is not against the law."

I close my eyes so I will not fly at him in a murderous rage. "Isn't it? Is not what General Cassel did against the law? Is not what your own sister did against the law? You were willing enough to punish her. You were willing enough to punish Sir Waroch when you thought he'd simply left his post without your leave. Is a woman's safety so much less deserving of the law's protection?"

"But Viscount d'Albret has done nothing to me —"

"To you. Is that what the standard is? If so, how easily you forget what both Crunard and I have told you — that he was involved in the rebellion. That he has allied with your sister time and time again to move against you. However, that is your choice to ignore, for it only endangers your own power and authority. What you have done with Sybella endangers her very life."

"He would not harm her. She is his sister!"

I do not even try to mask my scorn. "Mayhap we have a very different definition of harm, Your Majesty. Or mayhap I have been wrong about you all this time."

He looks so confused, so conflicted, that it touches some deep patience I did not know I possess. Or mayhap the saints themselves lend me theirs in this moment. I take a deep breath. "May we sit for a moment?" I motion to one of the low couches near the back wall.

I can see the relief in his eyes as he gives a brief nod and follows me to the couch.

"Thank you." I settle into the seat. "May I tell you a story, sire?"

"Yes, but why are you taking my arm?"

In truth, I do not know. I am moving on pure instinct now. "I need a friend to journey with me on this particular story." And while that is not true, I think that he will need one.

With his hand in mine, I begin. "What if I told you the story of a girl whose father was one of the richest lords in the land. He had everything, castles, money, children. He wanted for nothing."

He looks at me in wonder. "Your father?"

I squeeze his hand. "No, sire. It is only a story." When I resume talking, I brush my thumb gently over the top of his hand. "But no matter that this man had everything. He wanted more. And what he could not have, he wanted to destroy. He cared so little for his liege, that even though he promised troops, he held them back at the last moment. Even though his children were loyal to him, he abused them terribly, with cruel blows and even crueler torments. The girls were not spared, I fear, but received the most wicked treatment."

His face pinches in distaste. "You cannot mean —"

"But I do, sire. The world is a cruel place, not only for poor girls with no one to protect their interests, but noble ones as well, when those who should protect them choose not to.

"And in this kingdom, in the house of this lord, there lived three daughters. One was nearly a woman grown, and had already suffered more than a man so nobly raised as yourself could believe. But she had two small sisters, girls who were young enough to have escaped such cruel intentions. So far."

Against my palm, his pulse quickens. He does not like this story. Good. "And what if that oldest sister wanted to protect them from the same abuses she had suffered? What if that was the only thing that made all her pain and agony worthwhile?"

"I would say it was a noble aim. Did she have no brothers or other men to help her?"

"No. She did not. The one brother who could have helped her was no better than her father." I hear his quick intake of breath then, feel the moment he understands who and what this story is about. "So she did the one thing she could do — through dedicated and loyal service to her liege, she gained protection for her sisters."

He pulls his hand out of mine then and shoves to his feet, distraught. "And what has this story to do with me?"

I do not need to answer — he already knows. "Collect what evidence you need, search for proof among people who are highly skilled at ensuring that there is none. Ignore what your own heart is telling you. But I will ride today to retrieve Sybella."

"My heart?"

Unable to sit still a moment longer, I rise to collect my riding boots. "You know, deep inside, that what I say is true, but either you do not care, which I do not want to believe, or you feel you need proof, which I may never have. Or by the time we find it, it will be too late."

My words find their target, and he blanches. He pushes away from the mantel and runs his hands through his hair. "What would you have me do, Genevieve? Ride out with sword in hand and slay this dragon? That is the stuff of tales and legends, not something that kings do."

"Perhaps your father did not do it, and his father did not, but kings have done precisely that. Knights — such as Sir Crunard and Sir Waroch — do it all the time." I take a step closer, either anger or clarity burning through my caution. "Mayhap that is precisely what you should do. Ride out with me and see for yourself what happens in your kingdom under your own nose." My breath is heavy when I finish, my anger mixing with fear at how completely I have overstepped my bounds.

His brow is creased in thought. "Perhaps I will speak to Sir Crunard again and hear his thoughts."

"Yes!" I throw up my hands. "By all means! Speak to him. But also ask yourself why you will not listen to *me*. Why you will not believe *me*."

He looks slightly perplexed. "Because you are a woman."

It is the very answer I expected, yet it infuriates me all the same. "And women do not understand chivalry? What, in the name of the saints, do you call leaping on a horse and riding after my sister? What do you call gathering arms and putting down a rebellion for our queen when she was not allowed to do so herself? What do you call moving heaven and earth to try to protect innocent children? Men who have done those things have had tales told about them for hundreds of years, but when I do it, you must consult with someone over the proper chivalrous response?"

"That is not what I meant." He looks extremely uncomfortable.

"It may not be what you meant, but it is true nonetheless."

He opens his mouth, closes it, then opens it again. "I . . . You make a good point. But what I mean by you being a woman is that you have a staked interest in whether or not I believe you. You are not impartial. It is like asking a thief whether or not he stole. I feel others will be able to discuss this issue without the prejudice of your sex."

I turn from him, biting my own tongue for fear what anger will cause me to say. I begin shoving my plainest gowns into my pack. When I am finally able to speak, my voice has lost its sharpness. "You asked earlier if I was suggesting that you ride out with me. The answer to that is yes. I am suggesting precisely that. You were unfairly sheltered as a boy and young man, given no chance to see the world, with all its warts and muck, as others were. You have not experienced firsthand the injustices that exist beyond the palace walls. Perhaps it is time to fix that."

"You wish me to accompany you on this rescue you are planning?"

"Yes. But only if you hurry. I am leaving within the hour."

CHAPTER 107

Sybella

ortune smiles on me again on the third day as the skies open up and release a torrent of rain, forcing us to stay inside. Since I have learned all I can about the outer defenses, it is time to turn my attention to what the keep itself has to offer up.

"But *why* do you want to be down in the storerooms?" Jamette asks in a plaintive whine.

"What else have you got to do?"

"I don't know. Drink wine. Play draughts. Embroider. Anything that involves being in front of a fire and warm."

I glance at her over my shoulder. "The exercise will do you good. You have grown soft and pasty-looking."

Her mouth snaps shut, and she looks down at her bodice. It is not true. If anything, she has grown sharp and brittle, as if a single blow could turn her into fragments. But arguing with me gives her an outlet for all the bilious humor that is eating away at her.

"Besides," I say more gently, "the keep is old and drafty, and I wanted to see if there were any tapestries or bedding or carpets we could use to help keep out the cold air." That reasoning appeases her somewhat. "You take that side, I'll take this one."

She nods and moves off toward the right, while I veer left to where the stored items look distinctly unlike bedding or tapestries.

"You should leave," I tell her.

She snorts. "My life is worth nothing if I leave you alone."

"I don't mean this minute. I mean leave the holding."

"I already told you, I've nowhere to go," she says as she wrestles with a large roll of heavy fabric.

"And I have told you that you are wrong about that. There is only death for you here, Jamette, be it a fast one or a slow one. You are too young to resign yourself to this fate." I see a stack of barrels and draw closer.

"Is that not our lot in life? To resign ourselves to fate?"

"No. We must fight and push and shove. Put our hand on Fortune's wheel to give it our own spin."

Her mulish gaze is joined by something else — something too feeble to be called hope, but interest, mayhap. "And how does one do that?"

"By leaping." The barrels hold wine and cooking oil. Beside them are vats of tallow. In short, a wealth of substances that will cheerfully catch fire.

She glances to where I've been staring. "You have grown mad again."

I casually turn to my right and examine whatever is in front of my nose. It is a stack of old straw mattresses. More flammable materials. "I don't mean leaping out the window, you foolish goose. I mean taking a chance. Risk. Stepping outside what you know and hoping it will be better than what you're used to. It cannot be worse."

"And where am I to go?" She flings her hands out to her side. "I do not have a duchess who will take me in or a knight who will run away with me. I am not brave or skilled like you are. I am just a girl who has nothing — no family, no future, no one to turn to. I do not wish to sell myself on the streets to any man who fancies me."

"I do not wish that for you either, but there are other choices. None of them anything like the future you once hoped for. But they can lead to a good life, a solid one with moments of happiness and contentment." I do not just want her away from the fire when it starts, but from Pierre as well. She can survive a burn, but I am not convinced she can survive Pierre.

She folds her arms. "Like what?"

"I think the convent of Saint Brigantia is your best choice."

She barks out a laugh. "So whore or nun? Those are my choices?"

"Many Brigantians do not take a vow of celibacy. Convents are also places of learning, of second chances, places where girls like you may find respite from the world while you decide what path to take." I take a step closer to her, marveling at what a sapskull I've become to care about her. "I promise you, it will be better than this one that you're on."

The guardedness finally falls away from her eyes. "Even if I were to want that, how would I possibly get free of here?" she asks in a small voice.

It has worked — I have piqued her interest. "You watch for a chance to escape. We are surrounded by chance and happenstance every day. We've only to watch for it."

"Is that what you were looking for yesterday? Happenstance?"

I steadily meet her gaze. "No. I was hoping to see if they had any messenger pigeons in the mews."

She huffs out a sigh. "They don't. Now, stop all this talking and snooping, else you get us both in trouble."

There. I have said all I can without risking giving away my entire plan. I will have to hope that it will be enough.

CHAPTER 108

Genevieve

nce I am packed, I change into my plainest, most serviceable gown. Hopefully, Beast will have been freed from his prison by now. He will want to know of Sybella's fate — and will likely wish to come with me.

His help would be most welcome.

I slip out of my room intending to find Maraud and let him know what has happened. I will not simply disappear on him again. Besides, like Beast, he may wish to come with me, and I would not mind the backup. Although, if the king accepts my challenge, that could prove awkward.

But he won't. That would require setting aside a worldview he has too heavy a stake in.

The palace at Nantes is big, and I have no idea which of the many rooms Maraud has been given. I spend a quarter hour searching, wishing, for the dozenth time, that my gift was more like Sybella's and I could sense heartbeats of the living.

In the end, there are simply too many rooms, and I do not wish to delay my departure any longer. Mayhap I can find Jaspar or Valine and leave a message with them.

Outside in the palace courtyard, a handful of courtiers linger near the dovecote, and servants scurry to and from the well, but there is no sign of Maraud. I hitch the pack higher on my shoulder and begin making my way to the stables at the end of the yard. Just as I pass the old round tower whose stones are roughened with age, the door flies open and Maraud steps out, his face holding all the furies of a winter storm.

"What is wrong?" I ask.

It takes him a moment to register it is me. "Genevieve!" He grabs my arm and pulls me to the south end of the tower, away from the palace windows that glitter like so many eyes. "He is gone." The words nearly explode out of him.

My head is so full of my concern for Sybella that I can't process his words. "Who is gone?"

Anger sparks in his eyes. "Beast. That rutting pig Cassel left the palace and took Beast with him."

I swear violently as Sybella's chance for rescue grows slimmer. "How? The man is bigger than an ox and cannot have gone willingly."

Maraud glares at the tower, as if trying to discern the answer from its walls. "I don't know. But I will find out." For the first time, he notices my gown and the pack slung over my shoulder. "Where are you going?" Then he looks at my face. "What's wrong? You look pale as a corpse."

"The king handed Sybella over to Pierre three days before I got here. I am going after her. I was trying to find you and Beast before I left."

It is Maraud's turn to swear most foully. "Two people we must rescue."

"And no idea where either of them are."

In frustration, Maraud puts his hand on his head and stares up at the sky. "D'Albret might have taken Sybella to Givrand. It is much nearer than Limoges and is where he staged the troops and supplies he needed for the rebellion. At the very least, he will have stopped there on his way to another holding. He won't risk taking such an unwilling prisoner to an inn."

I nod and veer toward the stables. "I will start there. I had hoped you could come with me, but you must go after Beast, and I will find Sybella."

Maraud looks at me as if I have sprouted horns. "You cannot wander into that viper pit alone. We will come with you."

"We?"

"Jaspar and the others are here in Nantes, awaiting my instructions."

"They need to go with you. Given Cassel's penchant for both brutality and cruelty, we cannot just leave Beast to his care. There is no knowing what he intends to do."

"As you said, Beast is strong as an ox, and I know he would rather we spend our efforts on Sybella before coming for him. In truth, he would likely have my bones for breakfast if I were to do anything else. I'll send Andry and Tassin after Beast."

I cut him a glance. "And how will they find him? Besides, you have your own unfinished business with the man."

"It is not as important as your safety. Or Sybella's." In spite of the direness of our circumstances, I cannot stop the warmth his words cause in my chest any more than I can stop the rising of the sun.

As we draw near the stables, I feel rather than see a shift in the shadows on the left side of the barn. My hand flies to the dagger at my waist as a short, lithe figure detaches itself just enough to be visible. Lazare spits to the side. "Thought you'd never show up."

"You're here!" I say.

"Came with the others." Lazare tilts his head toward the shadows, where I see Aeva, Yannic, and Poulet. "Been waiting for you. Although I've had the Dark Mother's own time keeping Yannic from riding off after Beast."

Maraud's hand drops from his sword. "You know where they went?"

Yannic nods emphatically, and Lazare says, "He'll show you, and I'll go with her."

"See?" I tell Maraud, my heart surging. "I won't be going alone. I'll have Lazare with me. And Yannic will lead you to Beast."

His face is pure anguish. "Beast would want me to go after Sybella with you."

"If you do not go after him, he may not live to kill you," I point out. "Besides," I remind him gently, "Sybella is worth four men at least. Between the two of us, Lazare, and the others, we shall be fine."

He has opened his mouth to argue more when Lazare emits a low sharp whistle of warning. Yannic slips out of sight just as the sound of booted feet reaches my ears. I turn on my heel and, to my utter shock, find the king and eight of his men standing there, dressed as if they are going hunting.

The king glances at Maraud. "Is he coming too?"

"No." I turn to Maraud. "See? Even the king will be at my side."

Maraud's eyes widen in a moment of shock, then he simply raises an eyebrow, his brown eyes touched with humor. "Very well, then." He bows to the king. "Your Majesty. I know that you will keep her safe."

It is the perfect thing to say, and the king's manner relaxes ever so slightly. "I will, Sir Crunard. Why are you not joining us?"

Maraud's mouth hardens. "Because it seems General Cassel has left the premises and taken Sir Waroch with him."

Lazare starts to spit again, then stops himself — out of consideration for the king, I imagine. "If you've all talked enough, we'd best be off if we want to get started today, else we won't have enough daylight to even bother."

The king scowls at me. "Who's this?"

"This, Your Majesty, is Lazare, one of the queen's most trusted guardsmen, the mastermind behind our stunning artillery display at Morlaix, and to my great relief, the man who will lead us to d'Albret's holding."

CHAPTER 109

Sybella

ate that night, when everyone else has been asleep for hours, I sprinkle a pinch of night whispers into my hand, close my palm around it, and cross to the door. Once there, I kneel down and blow the fine powder out toward the two guards whose heartbeats are my constant companions.

I am not trying to kill them, only ensure they sleep — soundly — for the next few hours.

It does not take long. By the time I stand up, brush off my hands, and grab my cloak, their hearts have slowed to a deep, steady rhythm. I hear a faint thud as one of them slumps to the ground, then a second. I slip the small metal box containing the night whispers into the hidden pocket of my gown and open the door.

Stepping over the guards' inert bodies, I call the shadows to me and make my way from the fourth floor down to the first. Outside it is like child's play to stick with the shadows and avoid any of the patrolling guards' attention. When I reach the armory, I wait until the sentry makes his pass, then once he is out of sight, hurry to the door. Using a thin knife, it takes mere seconds to pick the lock, slip it from the latch, and let myself in.

Once my eyes have adjusted, I move directly to the pile of small iron pots that I saw from the window. Ever since that moment, a plan has been taking shape in my mind.

I squat down and examine them. Nearby is a discarded and

equally ancient stack of arrowlike bolts, the leather wrapped around them old and fraying, but not rotting. They will be perfect for setting off small explosions throughout the keep to move everybody toward the exit and get the innocents away from the coming conflagration.

In front of them sit the ribauldequins, looking like a giant's broom with the twelve iron barrels pointing out from the wooden platform. While they are old weapons, more popular a hundred years ago, they will serve my purposes well enough. They do not need to destroy the castle or take down armies, they need only to start a fire.

One too big to be put out.

I approach the cannon. The first will blast a hole through the armory wall. The second, the castle wall itself. Then the ribauldequins will launch a succession of smaller shot and arrows that will deter Pierre's men from approaching the armory before all the other explosions have gone off.

I stand there a long moment, envisioning the sequence. It could work. It *will* work. But it all boils down to timing. Precise, precise timing. And the gunpowder. Please, Dark Mother, do not have brought me so close only to have my plans die for want of black powder.

But my concerns are alleviated. A quick search reveals it is all there, the corned powder and even the flax cord I will need as a fuse. If this is not an indication of the Dark Mother's blessing on my plan, I do not know what is.

I am so giddy with my good fortune that I float back to my room, nearly as weightless as one of the shadows I am pretending to be.

CHAPTER 110

he king accepted my challenge. My mind can scarce wrap around that truth. Oh, it was couched in an invitation, but it was a challenge nonetheless. One made out of anger and frustration. He has surprised me when I had despaired of ever getting through that thick skull of his.

But now that he has finally heard me, will it be too late for the person I've come to love more than any sister?

Mayhap that is why my heart is pounding so fast and will not stop.

Or perhaps it pounds because I wish it were Maraud beside me and not the king, although I know it is selfish, as Beast cannot be left to Cassel's ministrations.

But Maraud has fought Pierre — many times — and won. He has demonstrated he is worth a dozen of Pierre's soldiers, while the king . . . I sneak a quick glance his way. I cannot imagine him withstanding even one of Pierre's hardened knights. Guilt pokes at me, knowing this is precisely what the king fears when others look at him. I tell myself that it requires even more bravery to go up against a foe when you are not as skilled as those around you, but rutting goats, I hope I do not end up getting His Majesty killed.

No. Not even Pierre would do such a thing.

But the king is in disguise, wearing the clothes of a minor nobleman, accompanied by only eight of his king's guard. Pierre could easily strike him down before realizing who he is.

And that is only one of the ways this can all go wrong. Indeed, having any of this go right will be harder than threading a needle with a length of straw.

I have come so close to fixing what I broke. The queen's innocence has been proved. The regent neutralized. And the king is here, with me, willing to open his eyes to the world and see the truth about Sybella. Truly, it is a mountain I thought I would never reach the top of. Please Mortain and all the saints, do not let it be too late.

We reach Pierre's holding late on the second day, just as night is falling. The gate is locked for the night, and all is quiet. I want to pound on it and demand they show us Sybella, but the king and Lazare convince me that is unwise. Best not to approach until we have formed a plan. If we had an army at our back, the king's presence would be all that we need, but we do not.

Lazare slips off to reconnoiter the area while the rest of us make camp. There is little talk — we are too tired, and I, for one, am too on edge.

Sleep eludes me. My body holds such a sense of foreboding, a sense of building pressure that is so overwhelming I can no longer lie still.

I rise and collect my weapons. If Lazare can scout in the dark, so can I.

No sooner have I taken half a dozen steps from camp than I hear an explosion from the castle. Lazare? But he comes bursting into the clearing. "What was that?" I ask.

"Hopefully, Sybella. Wake the others. We'll need to be ready."

Another explosion goes off just then, saving me the trouble of waking them.

CHAPTER III

Sybella

 had hoped to have more time. Two more nights, at least. One to search Pierre's study for the papers I know are there and the second to set up the explosions. But Pierre spent the entire time at dinner badgering Charlotte to tell him where Louise was. He was most aggrieved when she claimed she could not remember. The look in his eyes as he sent her from the table stirred an alarm deep within me. Now I will have to do it all tonight.

I use the second-to-last pinch of night whispers on my guards, waiting once more until I hear their heartbeats slow, then the accompanying thuds as they slump to the ground.

Moving quickly, I hurry from the holding to the armory. There is a cold wind whipping, and even fewer guards are about than last night. But the sky is clear, not a cloud in sight. Rain is the one thing that could ruin this plan.

It takes four trips from the armory back to the castle to carry the iron pots and set them in place. I spend the next couple of hours painstakingly laying out the fuse I will need, doing my best to estimate the time it will take to ignite the cannon and ribauldequins. As Lazare so often told us, it is an inexact art, even more so in my hands than his.

When everything is in place, I do not light the fuse, but return to the castle and make my way to Charlotte's room.

I stare down at her, noting how young her face looks, the brittle, annoyed edges smoothed away by sleep. She is the most difficult part of this entire undertaking. I do not know how much she will fight my attempts to get her away from the danger, or how hard she will fight to warn Pierre. Nevertheless, she is at the heart of this, and I will not leave her to the fate she thinks she has chosen.

I gently place my hand on her arm. "Charlotte," I whisper. "Wake up. We must go."

She comes awake in an instant, her eyes clear as she sits up. When she sees it is me, her face relaxes. "What are you doing here?"

"We do not have much time. You must get dressed."

I pull the covers from her and begin helping her into her gown. "Where are we going?" she asks. "Where is Pierre?"

"The castle will soon be under attack," I tell her. "Pierre and I both want you safe." While it is not a lie, it is a roughly patched bit of truth, but it seems to appease her. Once she is dressed, I help her into her shoes, settle her cloak around her shoulders, and draw her toward the door.

I peer out into the hallway. All is clear. As we step outside her room, she looks up at me, a question in her eyes. I hold a finger to my lips and draw her as close as possible so the shadows will hide her as well.

When we reach the chapel, she finally asks the question that has been gnawing at her. "If Pierre wants me to be safe, why are we sneaking around?"

I kneel down to face her. "Because not all in the castle are as concerned with your safety as Pierre and I are. Charlotte, this will be hard, but you must wait here until I return. Or" — as much as I hope it does not happen — "if you see smoke, not just from a kitchen or hearth fire, but thick, roiling smoke or flames, you must go as fast as you can to the gate. There will be confusion, but the guards should not prevent you from passing through."

"Will I not be walking into the enemy?"

I stare at her a long moment. "No. The enemy has already breached the castle. They are inside. Promise you will do as I ask."

After another long moment, she finally nods. And with that, I steer her to

the confessional booth, plant a quick kiss on the top of her head, then shove her in and shut the door. As I pass by the cross hanging over the altar, I pray to God and every saint in His army to watch over her until this is over.

Now it is time to light the fuse.

Chapter 112

As I return from my final trip to the armory, I can almost hear the hiss and sputter of the flame as it travels the length of the thin line of powder I have left, leading it to the first cannon. While the fuse is long, it leaves me barely enough time to do what I must.

I race up to the fourth floor, light the equally long fuses on the hidden iron pots, then grab the two hidden culverins. They are heavy and cumbersome, but I do not have far to go.

When I reach the third floor, I place the culverins in one of the niches behind a rusted suit of armor, then head for Pierre's chamber. The guards do not catch me by surprise this time. I step briefly into their line of view, but before they can ask my business, I bring my hand up and blow the last of the night whispers into their faces. Just as the first guard's sneer of disdain has twisted his lips, they both hit the ground. My muscles are already screaming in fatigue from all the hauling I have done, but with a sigh of resignation, I reach down and drag the guards down the hall and into Charlotte's room so they will not be discovered.

I race back to the niche, grab the culverins, then slowly lift the latch and ease myself into Pierre's apartments. I cross hurriedly to the door that leads to his bedchamber and listen. He is still asleep, his heart beating slowly and rhythmically. I draw a much-needed deep breath, then stash the weapons over by the main door.

I did not have enough night whispers for both Pierre's guards and Pierre himself, so I will have to do this another way. I crouch down to hide behind his desk and wait.

It does not take long. The first iron pot explodes in the distance, shortly followed by shouts of alarm. I count to fifty before the second one goes off. Dammit. It was supposed to be a count of thirty. But the second explosion is louder, the shouts more frantic. A guard bursts into the room and heads for Pierre's bedchamber. Before he can reach it, Pierre flings open the door, pulling his dressing gown around him and calling for the guards. "What is going on?"

"We don't know, my lord. Explosions from the fourth floor."

He swears, grabs his sword, then races out of the room with the guards.

I wait until I can no longer hear their heartbeats, then spring up, my attention on the large trunk that sits behind the enormous wooden desk.

With no time for subtlety, I grab the small kindling ax propped against the hearth, then head for the trunk.

As I raise the ax, the third pot explodes, the noise of it covering the sound of my blow. The lock shatters. I toss the ax aside and yank open the lid. So many papers! I do not have room to carry them all. The last of the iron pots goes off, and I pick up a handful of papers — I am running out of time.

Scanning the words on the pages for anything that could be from the regent or Viscount Rohan, I mutter, "Got you," when I find a letter asking Pierre to join Rohan in his Breton campaign. It is dated one week after the duchess was betrothed to the king. Victory surges against my ribs. Now to find proof of the regent's involvement.

An enormous explosion rockets through the holding just then. *Merde!* The first cannon! I have tarried too long. I shove the letters into my bodice as a second massive explosion goes off, and I curse the timing of the fuses. That one was too soon. But it is followed by a third, far louder explosion that rocks the very ground under my feet, and I hear the sound of screams. As the tower sways slightly, I realize the second cannonball must have reached the storeroom — with all the oil and wine and tallow.

The entire keep is about to go up like a torch.

I pick up the culverins and head for the door. When I reach it, I set them on the floor then snag a sturdy twig of kindling from the fireplace to use as a match. I return to the guns, leaving one leaning against my leg, and lift the second, touch the ember to the powder hole, then hang on as it belches flames at the curtains behind Pierre's desk.

The explosion causes my ears to ring, but the curtains catch fire immediately. I toss the empty culverin aside, and pick up the second one. As the noise from the explosion clears, I become aware of a heartbeat off to my left. I jerk my head in that direction to see Pierre blocking the path to the door, his face alight with the red and yellow glow of the flames.

"What have you done?" he asks, stepping more fully into the room. He holds his sword in his right hand and a crossbow in his left.

"I am ending this."

"This?"

"Our family's legacy. *Your* family's legacy," I correct myself. "You have ruined enough lives."

"You are mad! Killing a hundred innocent people to get your revenge on me?"

"Not all of them are innocent," I remind him sharply. "But that was what the first explosions were for — to give them time to get out. Even now they're choking the halls and doorways, pouring out into the courtyard, heading for the gate tower. If worst comes to worst, they can heave themselves over the wall into the sea. The fire cannot reach them there."

The flames have consumed the curtain behind me. I am out of time. I raise the culverin. He stumbles backwards, eyes fixed on the weapon. "You cannot mean to kill me."

I laugh. "I have waited years to kill you." Except, the driving hunger to kill him, to kill his father, has left me. I just want them out of my life and unable to ruin others'. Surely death is the only way to accomplish that.

Even if I must die to do it? For Pierre's crossbow is aimed at me, and he will have time to release his bolt before the culverin's finds his black heart.

As we stand at our impasse, I become aware of a small heartbeat behind Pierre. No. Please no, do not let it be Charlotte.

"Surely you are not afraid to die," I taunt, to distract him. "You who have meted out death as casually as an almoner hands out scraps?"

But he is. Fear overshadows the hate and fury in his eyes as they shift between me and the flames. Finally, he drops his sword and grabs his crossbow with both hands. I touch the ember to the culverin just as a shout of pain escapes him and he drops the crossbow.

"Down!" I bellow at Charlotte as the flames explode across the room. She throws herself to the ground, rolls out of Pierre's reach, then springs back to her feet with her knife in her hand as the wall behind Pierre erupts into flame.

True panic flares through him then, softening his face somehow, and in that moment, I remember a younger Pierre and the first time he felt such pain. He was not more than six, and it was the second time he had fallen on his father's bad side.

He panicked because he remembered the first time all too clearly, the scars only having just healed a fortnight before — the shame and the humiliation had not yet healed at all.

How could he have grown up to be other than who he was? Who was to have served as his guide?

The flames draw closer, and he screams, "Sybella!" It is the voice of the younger Pierre, the one terrified of our father, the one who used to hide with Julian and me before our father had taught them to hate one another. I am happy to let the current Pierre be destroyed in the flames of his own making, but I am not certain I can let that younger Pierre burn.

And that is when I realize that I have truly become one of the Dark Mother's own. That I am as enthralled with others' potential for rebirth as I was my own, and that I will always give them that choice.

"It is not too late!" I call to Pierre. "You have a choice."

He glances from the flames to me, eyes wide with terror. "What choice?"

"You can die by flames, by leaping into the sea below, or you can walk through the flames and live, but only if you let them burn away the ugliness of who you've become."

"I cannot walk through flames!"

"You can, though. They have not fully caught over here. But you must know this: I have the proof of your treason against the king. If you choose to live, you will start anew, without your father's ghost to haunt or shape you. Without hate to warp you. It is your chance to shed that skin and be someone new. It is not a painless choice, but it is a choice."

He looks desperately from the wall of flames that nearly engulfs the room, then over his shoulder at the window that leads to the long drop to the shore below, then back at the quickly narrowing opening, where flames only lick along the floor.

"Your window is closing. I would not tarry too long."

Behind me, Charlotte waits in silence, and I do not know how much she can hear over the roar of the fire. I must get her out of here. Now.

A strangled sob stops me long enough to glance over my shoulder, my heart inexplicably lifting to see Pierre take a step toward the flames. "The faster you go, the less it will hurt," I call out, then grab Charlotte's hand.

"I thought I told you to stay in the chapel!" I tell her as I drag her out the door.

She looks up at me, vexed beyond belief.

I give her hand a squeeze. "I am very glad you did not," I say, and her face clears as I pull her toward the stairs. Seconds later, the floor above us comes crashing down in a rain of crimson and gold fire.

Chapter 113

Once we are free of the flames, I stop running and pause, turning to face her, my hands on her shoulders. "Are you all right?" I examine her, frantically looking for any signs of burns or singe marks, but her face is unblemished. "Pierre did not hurt you?"

Her eyes study me with equal intensity. "No. Not the way he hurt you."

Her words are like a blow, setting me back on my heels. "Why did you do that?" she asks.

"Do what?"

"Give him a choice?"

I want to tell her because of the same reason I gave her one. Instead I ask, "Why did you give me a choice? Why did you come back?"

She gives me a ferocious scowl. "I didn't give you a choice. I didn't want him to come after us and needed to protect Louise."

"But you did. When you came back and stabbed him. While it may have been due to your feelings for Louise, it also gave me a choice — a space in which to save myself."

She is quiet then. I glance down at the knife. "Where did you get that?"

She glances at me in scorn. "It is the knife you gave me."

The words cause my throat to thicken. I gave her the knife.

I taught her to fight, then set Aeva to teaching her when I couldn't.

I placed her with women who are warriors at heart.

I showed her the path and, like a flame set to kindling, she took it. She has already begun her rebirth, and I want to weep for the joy of it.

Outside, the courtyard is like a vision from hell. Red flames cast their glow, reaching up to the dark sky. People are running, horses fleeing, cows mooing in alarm. I hold Charlotte's hand tightly and look to the stables, but the entire household has turned out to grab a mount for themselves and flee. The main gate is choked with people, backed up toward the armory, which blazes like a torch against the night sky.

I do not know if they will all make it out in time.

I do not know if *we* will make it out in time. I had not planned on lingering so long in Pierre's study. Even if we can fight our way to the stables and there are any horses left, it will be impossible to wrest them from the panicked grip of others.

"The wall," I mutter to Charlotte.

She gives me a look of disbelief. "How are we to get through a wall?"

"Not through it, over it. I have a rope."

But no sooner do I have the grappling hook out and over the wall than we are spotted by frantic servants, who come running our way. Big and burly, they shove and push, and I must let go of the rope else risk being separated from Charlotte or trampled.

Merde. I have not come this far to be trampled to death by the very people I was so intent should not be harmed.

I pause in the shadows to think — the heat of the flames pressing against my back — trying to remember how far away the drainpipe that leads to the ocean is, and if Charlotte can swim. Before I can ask her, there is a small explosion off to the left. It is the opposite end of the courtyard from the armory, and I did not set any bombs there. As the bright flash recedes from my eyes, I see someone, no, two someones, pushing their way through a hole they have blasted through the wall. The first figure clears the rubble, sword raised, long braid whipping back and forth as she scans the chaos.

"Genevieve!" Relief gushes through me, making me giddy.

Her head swivels in our direction, and she motions us toward her. Beside her another head pokes through, and I nearly laugh as I recognize Lazare. They have come! Beast has come! I dared not hope, and yet here they are.

I tighten my hold on Charlotte's hand, and we sprint the short distance toward the others. When I reach them, much to my surprise, Genevieve throws her arms around me in a fierce hug.

"Are you all right?"

I nod, ignoring the lump in my throat.

"If you two have finished your lovemaking," Lazare drawls, "we'd best get out of here before the entire thing's engulfed."

I elbow him in the ribs. "Watch your language. There's a young lady present."

Genevieve grabs my arm, my other still attached to Charlotte's hand, and drags me toward the hole in the wall. "And who is this?"

"My sister."

Her steps come to a sudden stop, and she gapes at me. "It is a long story."

"Which you will tell her some other time so as we don't all catch on fire or get trampled," Lazare says, then puts his hand to my back and shoves.

As I step through the hole, I look for Beast but only see Aeva, Poulet, and a few men I do not recognize. I whirl around. "Did Beast go in there to find me? We must let him know I am out."

My words are met with silence. Genevieve and Lazare exchange a glance. "Beast is not here," she says at last.

"Where is he?"

"General Cassel has him. Maraud has gone on ahead. We are to meet up with him as soon as we have you."

Before I can order everyone to mount up, I hear Charlotte ask, "Who are you?" When I turn to see who Charlotte's question is addressed to, I gasp and drop into a deep curtsy, hissing at Charlotte to do the same.

"I am the king, demoiselle."

"What are you doing here?"

He looks at me, then at her. "I have come to rescue you."

She meets his gaze steadily. "My sister already did that."

The king looks at me again with a smile that is both rueful and nonplussed. "So I see."

Nevertheless, he came. He himself rode out to see to our safety. The greatest man in all the kingdom has — finally — bestirred himself on our behalf.

I let the gratitude and thanks that fill my heart show upon my face. He grows flustered, mayhap even blushes, before giving a quick nod.

It is time to go find Beast.

CHAPTER 114

Maraud

Waroch is going to be battered to mincemeat before he even gets where they're going," Jaspar said.

"A normal man, maybe. Not him." Maraud needed to believe that. "It'll just piss him off even more." It was late afternoon, and they'd been following Cassel's party for three days. The poxy bastard of a general carried Beast in a rutting cart. Trussed up like a goose. In a chain.

Of course, there was no way else they could have dragged him anywhere unwillingly, but still it rankled Maraud.

"Have you figured out where they're going yet?" Valine asked.

"Near as I can figure, it's got to be Cassel's holding near Luçon. Unless he's got more I don't know about." Which was entirely possible. He'd been imprisoned for over a year — who knew how handsomely the general had been rewarded during that time.

An hour later when they came around the next bend in the road, a single stone tower thrust up into the sky like an obscene gesture. A scattering of buildings clustered nearby, but not too near, as if they didn't want to get any closer than absolutely necessary.

"Jaspar, you stay with me. The rest of you, hit the village and see what the locals think of the lord returning. Also see what you can find in way of lodgings."

"We're not going to just sleep on the road tonight?"

Maraud glanced around at the empty fields. "We'll be too easily spotted if they post any kind of lookout at the keep. And an inn in the village will be the most likely place to hear word of when Gen and the others arrive."

There is a long moment of silence. "You think the king is still going to be with them?"

"Unless he gave up halfway and went home, he'll be here." But of course, the king wouldn't give up. Not with Gen there. He wouldn't want to do anything that might weaken him in her eyes.

Maraud still couldn't believe she'd stood straight and proud, looked the king in the eye, then admitted they were lovers. The woman had stones, he'd give her that. And apparently, the king had some as well if he was willing to accept her challenge.

The road forked here, one stretch ambling down toward the village and the other leading to the keep. Maraud slowed his horse and lifted a hand in farewell as the others headed for the village.

"We'd best not come in too close on their tails," he told Jaspar.

Jaspar slowed his pace. Maraud wished there was a scrap of forest or a tree or two alongside the road to skulk among, but there wasn't. "We'll go as far on horseback as that last copse of trees, then tie the horses up there and go the rest of the way on foot."

Much to his regret, it turned out to be their bellies. They were simply too easily spotted otherwise. After crawling half a mile through rye grass and weeds, they were finally in position to see the main gate. Cassel and his party had just reached it.

A lone figure came scurrying out, bowing and scraping, then another long delay as he returned to the gate tower to raise the portcullis.

"Not expected, then," Jaspar said.

"No. Looks to be mostly empty. Wonder how long since he's stayed here." It was a lesser holding. Once it had held strategic importance, but that was three hundred years ago, when it was first built and long before the ocean waters that had lapped at its base had receded.

Once the general, his men, and the cart hauling Beast had gone inside, Maraud said, "Let's go see just how secure this holding is."

CHAPTER 115

Genevieve

id Maraud tell you where to meet him?" Sybella stares at General Cassel's keep in front of us so intently that I wonder if she is trying to burn a hole through it. For all that she holds her body relaxed, I can feel the tension in her thrumming like a plucked bowstring.

"We didn't have time enough to make those plans. Nor, I think, did he know what to expect."

"Will he have charged in ahead of our arrival?"

I lift my shoulders. "It is possible, but he is only one day ahead of us, and all is quiet. Hard to believe that if he'd already acted, there wouldn't be more activity." Or dead bodies hanging from the battlements.

Sybella glances down at Charlotte, asleep in the saddle in front of her. "I would be glad if she could pass the night at an inn. She's been through much and is exhausted. Do you think we dare risk it?"

I survey the village spread out around the keep like a thin petticoat. "I don't see why not." I lower my voice. "No doubt the king would not mind some more comfortable accommodations."

Just then a young boy darts into our path, and I must rein in my horse to avoid trampling him. "What in the name of the saints do you think you're doing?" I shout.

He doffs his cap, then flexes his knee. "Beg pardon, m'lady. I'm to tell you that—" He screws up his face as if trying to remember the words he was told to memorize. "That Rollo's wolf is waiting for you at the White Hart Inn." His face relaxes. "Can't miss it. It's the only one in the village." He bobs again, then turns and scampers away.

Sybella shoots me an amused glance. "It appears your friend has posted a lookout for us, which is most considerate of him. Let us go avail ourselves of the White Hart's hospitality. And see if we can find this — Rollo's wolf."

It turns out we do not need to look for him at all — he is seated in the great room of the inn, along with a number of familiar faces.

"You made good time," Maraud says.

I glance at Sybella. "It was mostly over before we got there."

"Except for the me-getting-out-alive part," she says wryly.

Her praise — for that is what such words coming from her amount to — makes me squirm, and I turn the conversation back to Maraud. "How do you propose we get in? It's as solid a fortress as I've ever seen, and the general does not scrimp on security."

"You've had a chance to observe the layout?" Lazare asks.

"Yes." Maraud proceeds to tell us all that he has learned about Cassel's holding. "And we had to kill two guards to get that much," he says under his breath when the king's attention is elsewhere.

Sybella studies the lines he's drawn on the table. "How many portcullises did you say there were?"

"Three. One at the main gate, then each of the postern gates has one as well."

It is hard not to get discouraged, but I keep my face neutral. "How like the general to be so mistrustful."

Sybella taps her finger on the left side of the drawing. "In this case, that works to our advantage."

"How?" Maraud asks. Andry and Tassin look at her like she is daft. No, I realize, they have simply lost possession of their wits around her.

"It is made of wood, yes?"

"True, but solid beams, and not something we could hack our way through. Not before calling the attention of the guards."

When she smiles, it is both beautiful and terrifying. "So we burn it."

The king looks up sharply. "You can't mean to simply march around the country burning down everything in your path?"

Sybella does not flinch. "If I need to."

The king looks away first. "We could just announce our presence. Tell him that their king is here."

I wince and try to remember he means well. Before I can intervene, Maraud snorts. "And give Cassel a chance to kill Beast and destroy the evidence of what he's done or slip out one of the back gates?"

Affronted, the king opens his mouth. "He would not —" He stops.

Mayhap because the king is here at my invitation, I feel obligated to cover for him. "It need only be a small fire, correct?" I glance at Sybella, who does little to hide her amusement.

"But of course. Just a small fire."

Maraud warms to the idea. "One that would cause a distraction and call the guards from the other gates long enough for us to sneak in."

"And create a way out that isn't through eight feet of solid stone," Andry says.

Sybella looks over at Lazare, who sits off by himself, leaning against the wall. "Well?"

In one smooth movement, he rises to his feet. "In the time it took you all to argue about it, I got it all planned out."

"Who will stay with the girl?" Maraud's question stops us cold.

Before Sybella can answer, Charlotte asks, "Why can't I go too?"

Sybella hurries over to kneel before her so they are eye to eye. "Because it will be very dangerous. These men are every bit as cruel and brutal as Pierre, but you will not have Pierre's protection here."

"Will you be safe?" Her calm composed face does not hide the faint note of fear.

"I believe so. Else I would not be going and leaving you."

"But you don't know. Not for certain."

"No, I don't. But then again, nothing is certain. There is always a chance."

"What will happen to me if you don't come back?"

"What would you like to have happen to you?"

She is pleased to be asked, her face serious as she considers. "I should like to go back to the convent. That would be the best place for me to finish growing up."

Sybella blinks a few times before she manages to speak. "Very well."

Aeva, who has said little for the entire trip, volunteers, "I will stay with her."

"You are the best shot of all of us," Maraud says. "We may well have need of that skill."

"I will watch her," Valine offers.

Charlotte turns to look at her, somewhat unconvinced. Valine leans forward. "I can teach you how to dice," she says in a low voice.

Charlotte's eyes brighten, then she glances at Sybella. "She can stay with me."

Sybella turns to Valine. "Do you know where the convent of Saint Mortain is?"

"Yes. I was raised in Brittany."

"Then if I do not come back, see that she is taken there. Ask for Annith."

She meets Sybella's solemn gaze. "You have my word."

CHAPTER 116

Sybella

s it turns out, there is no need to burn down the portcullis. The guards at the gate tower of General Cassel's holding are few and far between. Aeva is able to shoot them both before they even realize a bow has been fired.

With no guards to sound an alarm, we rush to the wall. When we reach it, Tassin stands close to the smooth gray stone in a wide stance. Like performers at a fair, Maraud scrambles up onto his shoulders, then Jaspar, lighter than the others, climbs up them as if they were a ladder. He carefully stands on Maraud's shoulders, which enables him to reach the top of the wall and pull himself up.

"We're in," Maraud says as he leaps off Tassin's shoulders. Once inside, he comes around to open the gate for the rest of us.

The courtyard is eerily empty and quiet. There is one lone groom at the stables who, if he sees us, decides to ignore us as we creep along the wall toward the main keep.

Inside, it is much the same. "Where is everyone?" Gen asks.

"Don't know, don't care," Tassin says. "They're not here getting in our way."

When we reach the stairs, Maraud mutters, "Up or down?"

I cock my head, not listening so much as feeling for other heartbeats. "Down." I take the lead. As we descend, sounds begin to reach us. One voice in particular grows louder the closer we get: "I am impressed that throughout all of the trials I have put you through, you have not given up the girls' location." Cassel.

At the landing, there is a doorway that leads onto a gallery overlooking a large open room — either an empty storeroom or a training room of some sort. I motion for everyone to fan out and take up positions along the gallery.

"Your fortitude and loyalty are most admirable." There is no anger in Cassel's manner, no bitterness, simply admiration. I cannot even begin to guess what his motive is.

I peer down into the room in time to see Beast wipe his mouth with the back of his chained hand. He is battered and bruised, with marks along his naked back and chest, and one eye swollen shut. My heart twists in fury.

"What manner of men serve you that they are so willing to throw their lives away in this malevolent game of yours?" he asks.

Cassel's nostrils flare. "These are not mere soldiers, but men who have been honed and fashioned into the most elite fighting force on the continent. Each one is worth ten of the king's soldiers. They know no fear, no hunger. They do not tire, nor will they stop fighting for any reason unless I give the command. That is part of why you fascinate me. They welcome war because it is how I have shaped them. You share their commitment even though I have not trained you. It is our shared blood."

"That is my saint's influence," Beast's voice grinds out. "Not yours."

Cassel's smile discounting Beast's explanation causes my fists to clench. Someone needs to wipe that be-damned smirk from his face. "You and the king claim these types of men are no longer needed, our wars are being fought with different tactics, different weapons. But he is wrong. These men are always needed. No crown, no country, no city-state can rest secure without this sort of strength at its core."

I glance over at the king, who stands beside Gen. His face is drawn into hard lines.

"So that is the nature of *my* men. I have yet to see the full potential of your own mettle. So far, I have given you easy choices. Kill or be killed."

It is hard — so hard — for me not to just end this now. But we are greatly outnumbered, and it is not my fight. Even so, I hold my weapon at the ready.

Beast says nothing, but simply stares straight ahead, his eyes alight with the fury he will not give voice to.

Cassel steps closer — but not close enough to be within reach of Beast should he escape his chains. "Let us make this a more valuable test." The note of anticipation in his voice makes the fine hairs on the nape of my neck stand up. "I will give you a truly difficult choice. Sacrifice yourself to save others. For that is what is at the core of your honor, is it not? I sent a company of men riding to the convent where I believe your sisters are being held."

As I bite back a gasp, Beast's head whips around to glare at the general, his jaw clenched so tight I can see the muscles bunching. "I have also sent a company of men to d'Albret's holding, where the king has sent the Lady Sybella." That is when I know he is lying.

"Both are important to you. You may stop one of them. Which shall it be?"

"I will destroy you," Beast growls, his eyes taking on that feral light.

"You will need to. If you want to save one of them, you will have to fight through me first. Once you have done that, you may ride after whichever is dearest to your heart."

Before Cassel has finished speaking, the battle fever begins to descend upon Beast. His eyes stop seeing anything but the general, his arms bunch and strain against the chains that hold him, his face contorting in agonized effort as the links slowly begin to stretch, their strength no match for Beast, until they finally give way and snap apart.

Before the men in the room can register what he has done, Beast jams his elbow into the closest one's gut, knocking the wind out of him. While the man is doubled over, Beast wraps his hand around his neck and breaks it, then grabs the dying man's sword just as his soul breaks free from his body.

I hear Gen gasp and slam down my defenses against this newest soul. As two more men rush Beast, I glance at General Cassel, the small twist of satisfaction on his face piercing me like an arrow as realization dawns. If Beast kills them all while in the throes of his battle lust, then Cassel will win. If Beast gives in to this, he will have become the thing that Cassel values above all.

I step forward from my hiding place on the gallery. "Beast!" My voice rings out above the noise below.

CHAPTER 117

he fighting ceases as everyone looks to me. Beast's body stills. "He lies. I am here. Safe. He has not sent anyone for the girls. We let loose all the horses in the stable. His men have nothing to ride on to this errand."

General Cassel's face twists with anger. Out of the corner of my eye, I see him gesture in my direction, ordering his men to seize me. Surely the stupid man does not think I've come alone. I motion with my hand, and the others step forward, bows drawn, arrows aimed below. But I only have eyes for Beast, who finally looks up at me. When our gazes meet, I take all the will I possess and shove it down at him, like I would thrust a rope to a drowning man. *Come back to me. Do not give in.*

Some of the eerie light leaves his eyes, and I take a deep breath. In any other circumstance, I would tease him, ask if he needs me to save him again. But not in front of Cassel. Instead, I call down, "May I play too, or is this a game for one?"

The feral light recedes further, and he even grins a little. "It is a game for one, my lady, but you can play next time."

Sensing the battle lust leaving Beast, Cassel grows incensed. "You cannot leave without fighting me."

"I will not stoop so low as to fight the likes of you."

"Do not stand so high on your honor. You do not understand the choices the world leaves people like us."

"People who are ugly? Brutish? Monsters?" Beast laughs. "Do you truly think I do not understand? I, whose own mother tried to kill me when I was not even two years old?" The laughter falls from his voice. "I understand perfectly," he says softly. "But I had too much stubborn pride to consider proving them right."

"Pride?" Cassel snorts. "What honor is there in letting a lady turn you from your deadly purpose?"

Beast laughs again, infuriating the general even more. "You mistake my lady if you think she ever shies from death."

"Foolish pride is not honor."

"No, but foolish pride gave me time to experience honor, to understand it was what I wanted. To know that no matter what I looked like, I could choose how I acted.

"I am uglier than you, bigger than you, stronger as well. They have called me Beast rather than General, but we both know who the true monster is."

Cassel raises his sword. "Fight or have the world know you as a coward."

Beast leaves his own weapon lowered. "This is not a war, and I do not care enough about you to commit patricide." I hear in his voice that it is true. Whatever horrors this day has brought, it has also brought him that peace. "Besides, there are other men with more claim to your life than I have." His gaze shifts to Maraud, who has come down the stairs into the room while the two men were talking. "Sir Crunard, with the king's permission, I leave him to you."

Surprise flashes across Cassel's face, and he swings his body around to find Maraud's sword raised in readiness, his easygoing manner replaced by something dangerous and lethal. Gen's eyes widen in alarm, her hand flying to her chest. She has heard one of the hearts in the room begin to beat. Understands that one of them will die. She looks at me, lifting her shoulders in a gesture of helplessness. She does not know which one.

Beast walks away from his father.

With a roar of outrage, Cassel pivots from Maraud, raises his sword, and rushes toward Beast.

Trying to recapture Cassel's attention, Maraud bellows, "Face me, you coward!" But the general's world has narrowed to Beast.

Determined resignation settles over Beast at the choice being forced on him. He stops walking, turns around, and simply stands there, as immovable as a mountain. I can only wonder what thoughts are going through his head as he lifts his sword. The general does not check his momentum — surely a man as battle seasoned as he is recognizes that Beast's blade is longer than his. Or mayhap he thinks Beast will give in and spar with him.

But Beast does not. He would not willingly make this choice, but he will not run from it either. He does not flinch and only grunts a little from the effort of holding his ground as Cassel skewers himself on the sword.

Silence spreads across the room like the blood spreading across the general's chest. Beast shoves his sword — and the general — from him, his father's body sliding to the floor and taking the sword with him. Beast looks up at Maraud. "That should have been your kill."

"He's not dead yet," I tell them, for while his heart is slow and feeble, it still beats.

Maraud nudges Cassel's shoulder with the toe of his boot. "Dead enough."

The fallen general tries to speak. After a moment's hesitation, Beast kneels down to hear, even as my mind screams, *Trap!*

"Honor is a fool's game," the general mutters.

"And yet it is you on the floor dying, with your past glorious deeds congealing around you like old blood."

"Honor is a fool's game," Cassel mutters again. "And yet you played it well." His fingers grasp Beast's knee, but Beast stands, causing the general's hand to fall back to the floor.

I scramble down the stairs, nimbly avoiding the stunned and grumbling remains of Cassel's garrison. Beast is battered, bruised, bleeding, and that is not even counting the damage to his heart this day. Not caring who sees, I throw myself at him, forcing him to hold on to me lest we both tumble to the ground.

"Thank you," he murmurs against my hair, his arms forming a protective shield around me.

"You did not even need our help," I say, dangerously close to weeping in front of all these vile men. I now understand precisely how Genevieve felt, standing outside Givrand.

"Now who has straw for brains?" He takes my face in his hands, forcing me to look him in the eyes. "Just seeing you — knowing you were here and not locked away in Pierre's holding — heartened me. If not for the sound of your voice calling me back, I would have lost myself, and he would have won." He places his forehead against mine. Then he sniffs. "You smell like the inside of a chimney."

"You're a fine one to talk." I close my eyes and wallow in relief like a hog in mud. I want to roll my entire body in it and splash it all around, but instead, I thank every one of the saints who had a hand in bringing us through this.

In the next moment, General Cassel ceases his struggle against the inevitability of his wound and passes into death, his soul erupting from his body, a hurtling projectile of force and velocity looking for a target.

It seizes on me. I have only a moment to reinforce my mental shields before I feel its impact. Beast grips my hands, as if he can physically protect me from Cassel's avenging soul.

After a moment of withstanding the battering, I realize it is not anger that propels the soul, but vigor. As he was in life, so he is in death. Once he has swirled around me with fierce curiosity, the soul shifts its attention to Beast, and its entire manner changes.

"What is happening?" Beast's voice is naught but a rumble that I feel in my chest.

"Your father's soul," I whisper. "It . . . he . . ." I cannot keep the amazement from my voice. "Was proud of you."

Beast looks at me as if I've offered Cassel's liver to him for supper.

I shake my head — in wonder, in disbelief, in order to keep Beast from pulling away. "In his own brutally twisted way, he was. You were everything he refused to believe in, but in the end you proved him wrong." I pause, trying to understand the rest of the sensations coming from the soul as they nearly overwhelm me. It is as if every feeling he denied himself in life has been let loose upon his death.

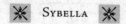

"He was glad," I say at last. "Glad that honor existed. And that you wielded it more gloriously than most."

The general is filled with pride that his son has more honor than any man he has ever met, feels that it exonerates him in some way. I do not share that with Beast. I will save it for some less fraught day. Say, when he is nearing his dotage.

CHAPTER 118

Genevieve

I watch Maraud staring down at the general's body. He looks like one of the statues the Church is so fond of, both beautiful and terrible in the same moment. The righteousness of his anger, the pain of his loss, the depth of his grief, the solemnity of what he has just witnessed all writ plainly on his face. In truth, he and Beast could not have given the king a better showing of honor.

Would that the king could have a painting of that to hang on his wall to guide him.

It seems to even have impressed the souls of the dead, who have been hovering and pulsing along the upper reaches of the room. Seeing Sybella in Beast's arms, jealousy courses through me. I long to run to Maraud. Throw myself in his arms, laughing and weeping with relief that his long nightmare is over. But I am not willing to trust the limits of the king's newfound tolerance. His face is a pale mask of horrified revulsion, and so I must stand here like a lump, my own paltry gifts of no help at all.

When the general's men begin to move, making ominous rumbling noises, I brighten. Mayhap I will get to skewer one of them.

The king finally bestirs himself. "I have seen all I need to see." He clears his eyes of the horror he has just witnessed, lifts his chin to a royal angle, and squares his shoulders. "Hold," he calls out as he steps to the edge of the gallery.

The men freeze. All of them have had occasion to see the king before and easily recognize him. "Although General Cassel is dead, he is being charged with treason. You may lay down your weapons and come peacefully, or I will send in the three hundred troops I have waiting just outside the holding."

After a moment's hesitation and a look around the room at Beast, Maraud, Andry, Tassin, Jaspar, and the others, Cassel's men do as commanded.

I shoot the king a sideways glance. "That was quite a gamble," I murmur. "You don't have three hundred troops."

The corner of his mouth lifts in the faintest hint of a smile. "I'd like to think that I've learned a thing or two from you."

I nearly laugh then, for surely I have brought the greatest weapon in our arsenal — the king's justice.

CHAPTER 119

Five days later, we arrive in Nantes to the shocked stares of the people of the city, as well as the palace guard, who had not realized the king was not within the palace.

Once we are ushered inside, the king calls his council to him and disappears while the rest of us are treated with utmost respect and given every courtesy. Most of that honor is lost on us, for we are all so exhausted from our travels that we sleep for the next four days. Well, I do. Sybella spends much of that time tending to Beast's wounds while Maraud watches and teases the stoic Beast about making such a fuss.

On the fifth day, I am summoned to the king's privy chamber. I arrive at the same time as Sybella. "Do you have any idea what this is about?" she asks.

"None."

Then we are ushered inside. The king is alone except for — I hear Sybella gasp — "Your Majesties!" She drops into a curtsy. I do the same, peering up through my lashes at the queen.

"You may rise," the king says.

"Since I can see you nearly choking on all the questions you are dying to ask," the queen says, "let me assure you I am fine. My health is good, and no, I did not risk it traveling to Nantes, as I came by boat, which was a most restful way to travel."

"I am relieved to hear it, Your Majesty."

The king silently drums his fingers on the arm of his chair. "You have both shown me the rot in my kingdom, as well as in your families and in my own. You have saved France, you have saved yourselves, you prevented war — and put down a rebellion!" He pauses a moment, as if overcome. "You managed to sneak a bear into my dungeon and exchange it for one of my prisoners. *A bear!*"

The queen bites her cheeks to keep from smiling.

Heartened by that, Sybella dares to speak. "Your Majesty, if I could be so bold as to ask, what became of the bear?"

The king gapes at her, then shakes his head. "The master of the hounds took a liking to him. He is now housed in the Louvre's menagerie and treated like a royal pet."

My heart lifts, for both the bear and also the further sign of the king's true nature.

"You are forces of nature," he continues. "Like a — a storm raging through the sky. Or — or waves, churning upon the sea." He waves his hand, as if agitated. "You are like the demigods of Rome, when the gods walked among mortals and fathered children with them."

I glance at Sybella, for that is exactly what we are, and though I have told him time and again, he cannot quite accept that I am speaking truth.

"You are outside every convention of society, and I have no idea what to do with you."

As he falls silent, the queen leans forward. "Use them," she says. "They serve us now. They have skills and talents that no one else in the kingdom possesses. Let them use those talents on our behalf."

A week later, Sybella and I are told that our presence is required in a formal audience with the king in his throne room.

The first thing I notice when I enter is that the king — and queen — are in full court dress. A most formal occasion, indeed. The second thing I notice is that we are not the only ones who have been summoned. Standing off to the side, as if waiting for us, are Beast, Maraud, Aeva, Father Effram, Lazare, and an older man I have never seen before. The air of solemnity is thick enough to cut with a knife and serve on a slab of bread.

When we are before the dais, both Sybella and I sink into deep curtsies.

"I have invited you all to this private meeting for reasons that shall soon become clear. All that I am about to explain has been written down, ratified by my seal, and witnessed by four members of my council. It is," he continues, "real and enduring. It shall outlast even me."

Unease begins to work its way inside me, for if a law or proclamation has been fashioned to live beyond the king who signed it, it is near impossible to have undone.

"This has been a year of learning for all of us." The queen shoots him a brief but bemused glance. "And that includes me most of all." He stops, takes a deep breath, and then says, "Let's dispense with the formality, shall we? In essence, my lady wife was correct. The crown should use you — your skills and talents. The crown *will* use you. I have created an Order of the Nine, a select cadre of individuals who have been chosen due to their skill, cunning, bravery, courage in the face of obstacles, and anything else I find worthy of rewarding. But," he continues, "these nine shall also honor the nine old saints of Brittany. I think they — and their duchess — have demonstrated beyond a shadow of a doubt their loyalty and commitment to the greater good of the people of the land. Because two of the nine are not able to serve, I have adjusted the numbers accordingly so that there will be nine of you — always nine."

He rises then and reaches for a black embossed box that lies on a small table between him and the queen. He carefully takes from it a simple gold chain with a nine-pointed star fashioned of three interlaced triangles. Each point of the star holds a different gemstone favored by one of the Nine. He crosses over to Maraud. "Sir Crunard, in thanks for your honor and loyalty, risks taken, and horrors endured. I am honored to offer you this seal of office."

Maraud bows his head and accepts the chain.

The king moves to Beast next. "Sir Waroch, for being the embodiment of honor in a world that tried so hard to strip it from you, and for serving your queen no matter the cost."

Aeva is next, for her skill in battle and knowledge and power of the earth with which she lives so closely, as well as her loyalty to the crown.

"And for you, charbonnerie, for using your most extraordinary knowledge on our behalf and for coming to the queen's aid when few else would." Lazare's face when the king places the chain around his neck is such a mixture of surprise, disgust, and pleasure that it is all I can do not to laugh.

When the king stops in front of Father Effram, a wry smile plays about his mouth. "Father Effram. You serve a trickster of a saint and always manage to be where you have not been invited, yet your advice is worth its weight in gold. Thank you for being the voice of reason when so many others could not find it in their hearts."

Next he comes to the older man I do not know, who turns out to be one of the mendicant priests who serve the patron saint of travelers. "As this is a cross-roads, it is right that we have one who serves Saint Cissonius on this council, to advise us on all the crossroads to come."

When he removes the next chain, he crosses the room to the queen, who sits in her chair looking faintly surprised. "And who better to represent Saint Brigantia than my own queen, who was dedicated to her at birth and has shown that saint's wisdom throughout the entirety of her life."

A knot forms in my throat then, for I can only imagine how much this means to the queen after how hard she has worked to get the king to consider her counsel. She quietly murmurs her thanks.

The king moves to Sybella next, and the knot in my throat grows so large that I can hardly swallow. "Lady Sybella." His voice is low and filled with sorrow and remorse. "No matter how ill you had been served, by this crown or others, you have consistently given your loyalty to your queen and gone far above your duty in all things, but especially in your most exemplary concern for your sisters. All children should be so lucky to have such an advocate on their behalf."

Sybella closes her eyes as she dips her head to receive the chain, but not before I see how brightly they shine.

And then he is before me, his face filled with warmth and pride and a faint glimmer of regret. "And, Lady Genevieve. Your service has perhaps been the hardest of them all. To stay quiet and hidden in the shadows, patiently and inexorably exerting your will on those who should already know what you worked so hard to teach them. For your loyalty, and your friendship."

I blink rapidly, but do not fool anyone as I bow my head. The gold chain is cool about my neck, the king's fingers warm as he allows them to brush against my skin. It is a touch that says goodbye to our past, but welcomes our future. Then he steps back and faces all of us. "As the founding members of the Order of the Nine, I charge you all with telling me — all of France's kings — the truth. And" — he glances briefly at me — "finding ways to help us hear it when we cannot." He sighs. "In short, you are to continue doing what you have done to keep our lands and people safe. There is a bit more to it than that, but I think that will suffice for now. I have had all of the ceremony I can stomach for one day. You are dismissed."

I am so stunned that it takes me a moment to find my feet, and when I do, my steps feel as if they do not touch the ground.

"Lady Sybella," the king's voice calls out. "If you and Sir Waroch would be so kind as to remain for a moment, I would like to speak to you about your sisters."

"But of course, Your Majesty."

I allow myself to continue walking out of the room, knowing she will tell me what transpires.

CHAPTER 120

Sybella

en is the last one out of the council room, leaving Beast and me alone with the king and queen.

"Regarding the matter of your sisters, Lady Sybella," he says without preamble. "I have come to a decision. Since Louise is Sir Waroch's sister's daughter, I felt he should hear what I have to say."

I glance at the queen, but if she has any notion what the king's decision entails, it does not show on her face.

"Given your brother's multiple acts of treason and his careless disregard for the lives of both those who serve under him and his own family, I cannot in good conscience grant custody to him. Indeed, I have still not decided if I shall pardon him for his crimes, although I think it will ultimately be his future behavior that determines that." Although we have heard nothing from him, Pierre's body was not found in the rubble at Givrand.

The king is generous with his pardons, having already granted one to Viscount Rohan in exchange for his sworn, true testimony to the events in Brittany as well as the exchange of some private holdings the crown has long wished for.

"But," the king continues, "there is no legal precedent for a woman, an unwed woman, no less, to have custody of children. Not only is there no precedent, I am not certain it would be legal, even if I decreed such a thing. For I would, my lady." His countenance grows earnest.

"If ever anyone has proved their care and devotion to their siblings, it is you. However, even a king cannot change every law to his own liking." My sinking heart must show on my face. "Do not despair. I think I have come up with what I hope is an agreeable solution."

I wait, relatively certain the king's perception of agreeable and mine will differ greatly.

"If you were married, my lady, I could then grant custody to your husband. And if, say, your husband was also related to one of the children, the legal claim would be even stronger."

Because it is precisely what Beast and I wish for, I must clarify. "So you are saying if I marry, my husband will be granted custody of my sisters."

"Which," the king hurries to add, "if you choose your husband wisely, he will in turn trust you in those matters."

I glance over at the queen who, instead of watching the proceedings with her usual sharp interest, is studying the rings on her fingers as if they have suddenly sprouted wings. I take a deep breath and look at Beast. "I do seem to remember making a promise to you along those lines, did I not, Sir Waroch?"

He nods solemnly. "You did, my lady. All it wanted was permission from our liege for us to proceed."

"You did not put him up to this, did you?" I murmur.

He gives a quick shake of his head. "Not I."

The queen clears her throat just then. "Is there a problem, Lady Sybella?" Although her face tries to arrange itself in stern lines, the twinkle in her eyes gives her away.

"No, Your Majesty. There is no problem at all." I turn back to the king. "I will gladly accept these terms of custody, Your Majesty. And thank you for finding a way to maneuver such a decision through the twists of the law."

"It is truly the least I could do," he says, most graciously.

Beast's smile of joy shifts suddenly to one tinged with faint horror. As I arch an inquiring eyebrow at him, he says, "This means I will have to ask your *father* for your hand in marriage."

CHAPTER 121

Genevieve

araud is waiting for me outside the chamber, his tall, broad form outlined by the light of the oriel window. He turns at my approach, his fingers playing with the gold chain about his neck, his eyes filled with admiration and warmth. "It appears you and I are to be stuck with chains around our necks for all our lives."

"I am sure we will manage," I say as I draw alongside him.

He looks back outside, at the Loire river that runs by and the fields of green grass beyond that. "So now what?" he asks. "Are those of us who serve in the Order of the Nine allowed to . . . consort . . . with one another?"

"I should hope so. I am hoping it gives us the right to do whatever we please. Besides, I should like to see the king try to keep Beast and Sybella apart. Not to mention that he consorts with the queen."

"And what would you do, Gen, with the right to do whatever you pleased?"

"I don't know," I admit. "I want . . . to live, and explore, and see new things. I want to line the world up before me, examine what it has to offer, and choose."

He continues to stare out the window. "Choice is a wonderful thing," he says. "As is exploring. Would you care for company on these explorations of yours?"

And of course, he is the first one to offer me a choice in this new life of mine. I reach out and take his hand, surprising him. "I would love company. Most especially your company, if you are offering it."

"I wouldn't say so much offering it as throwing it at your feet," he murmurs.

"However it comes, I welcome it gladly."

He grins then, and I smile back. He makes a sweeping bow before extending his arm. As we begin walking away from the council chamber, he bumps my shoulder lightly with his own. "So, I must ask. Did you ever end up saving those you set out to save when you left Cognac?"

The warmth that has been building in my chest since I first heard the king speak of the Order of the Nine swells so fully that I fear my heart will burst. I turn to him and smile, smile that he would remember to ask, and smile at the answer I have to give. "Yes. Yes, I did."

EPILOGUE

Sybella

I remember very little of my first trip to the convent, half mad with grief as I was. I was told they had to tie me down for fear I would hurt myself or hurl myself out of the cart.

Beast is quiet too, although for a different reason. I check to make sure the rest of our party isn't within earshot. "He's not going to tell you no," I reassure him.

He shifts in his saddle, an uncomfortable gesture that is wholly unlike him. "I don't imagine he will, but that does not make it any less harrowing — having to ask Death for his daughter's hand in marriage."

"Except that he is no longer Death, but Balthazaar, Annith's consort. Or is she his consort? I'm not sure how that works. But if he gives you any trouble, you can remind him that he must ask Maraud for Annith's hand in marriage, since he is her sole surviving male relative. Tell him you'll put in a good word for him."

Beast scrubs his hand over his face. "This is all too strange for me to wrap my turnip-sized brain around."

Ismae steers her horse closer to ours. "Has anyone thought to tell Annith of her father's death?" she asks. "Or that we are bringing her brother to her?" She does not think to lower her voice.

"No. Some things are better relayed in person."

"Wait." Maraud looks around our small traveling party. "Who is Annith's brother?"

I give Gen an accusing look. "You didn't tell him."

"I didn't know!" Gen protests. "Well, barely knew, and certainly not enough to explain it to him. Besides, we did have quite a lot we were dealing with at the time."

"Tell me what?" Maraud's voice is guarded.

Gen draws closer to him. "That you are not the only Crunard left. You have a half sister."

His face grows pale with emotion before he looks away.

"She was the former abbess's daughter," Gen explains softly.

"A handmaiden of Death? But my moth —"

"No. Your father's daughter," I explain. "Although neither your father nor your sister knew of it until recently."

Since poor Maraud looks as if he has taken a pike to the head, Gen leads him away from the rest of us. He will want to process without an audience.

"Do you realize," Father Effram says, "just how many lost and broken pieces have been put back together because of Genevieve?"

"She has done a masterful job of fixing her mistake," I agree.

"No. I mean that if she had not made that mistake, most of this would not have happened. Maraud would still be languishing in his oubliette, you would still be locked in a custody battle with your brother, the Nine would not be openly accepted at the French court, and war would even now be raging over our land."

"She did not stop the war," I point out.

"No, but if she hadn't known Maraud, freed him, we would have been caught unaware and likely lost."

And while it is true that he might have gotten free anyway, it is hard to see how he would have ended up in a position that helped turn everything to our favor. It is miraculous how the many pieces came together, making the sum of them stronger.

"So perhaps it was never a mistake," Father Effram continues. "But a necessary step on a long, arduous path that none of the rest of us could see."

"Except you," I mutter.

"Not me, but perhaps Saint Salonius had some idea."

The road curves just then, bringing the westernmost shore into view. A half dozen figures are gathered on the beach, with three black-sailed galleys bobbing in the ocean behind them. I had forgotten the convent even had such large boats.

"You can relax," I tell Beast. "Balthazaar is not among them."

"I'm not nervous," he mutters.

As we draw closer, I see that the figure in the middle has a long blond braid resting over her shoulder. "Annith!"

Behind me, I hear a little sniff of disdain — Charlotte.

"Do you have something you wish to say?" Aeva asks her.

"No. It just seems like a big fuss over seeing each other again. That is all."

"Are you not excited to see Louise?"

When Charlotte does not answer, Aeva continues, "And have you prepared your apology to Annith and the others for abusing their hospitality and running away?"

Leaving Charlotte to Aeva for the moment, I put my heels to my horse and race Ismae to the shore. I reach them first and leap from my mount to run to Annith, who is already moving toward me. I throw my arms around her and savor the feel of her close against my chest.

"I am sorry," she whispers into my ear. "I am so sorry we let Charlotte slip out of our sight. Sorry there was no way to contact you."

I hug her harder, letting her know I do not hold her responsible. "All is well now. And she has learned much and made some decisions. She wishes to stay here, if she may."

"But of course!"

Before I have a chance to ask how she is faring, Ismae arrives and pulls Annith from me for her own hug. As I watch, I realize that Annith has put on weight — no. "You are with child!"

Annith's cheeks pinken. "Yes. Ridiculous, is it not?"

"When?" I ask.

"We're not sure," Annith says. "I suppose we will know when it arrives." There is something in her face, the way she says that, that makes me think she knows — or suspects — and is not willing to say.

Father Effram dismounts from his mule and beams at her. "Then you are carrying either the last of Death's handmaidens or his first mortal child."

Whether because she does not wish to discuss this any longer or due to her innate kindness, Annith turns from us to where Genevieve waits a few feet away. "Genevieve." She moves forward, holding out her hand, her face full of remorse and regret. "I am truly sorry for the loss of your sister Margot and hope you will be able to forgive the convent's utter failure in its duty to you."

Gen looks stunned, as if the last thing she expected was an apology, sympathy, or compassion. She smiles faintly. "As I understand it, you had little to do with such matters, except in trying to locate us. I do not hold you responsible in the slightest." She means it, I realize, happy to remove one knot of worry from the string I carry inside me.

Two more figures emerge from the stables just then, no three. Tola, Tephanie, and — "Louise!"

She lets go of Tephanie's hand and runs toward me. "You're back!"

I catch her up in a giant hug, my arms wrapped around that small, frail body, and breathe in her familiar scent. She is safe, and her nightmare is truly over. I whirl her around and around until she is laughing and begging me to put her down.

As I set her feet on the ground, I look to Tola and Tephanie. "I can never thank you both enough."

Tephanie, dear sweet Tephanie, rolls her eyes at me. "We were happy to do it, my lady."

"Where's Charlotte?" Louise asks, her little face twisted with worry.

"Over there, sweeting." Before I have finished speaking, she is off, running toward her sister.

When she reaches her, instead of the hug we are all expecting, she hauls her arm back and punches Charlotte. We all stare in open-mouthed amazement, Charlotte most of all.

"You left! You scared me! I thought you were never coming back!" She pauses to catch her breath. "You were supposed to stay here — with me. And the nuns were worried, too. Annith even *cried*."

As proud as I am of Louise, I ache for Charlotte as well. She thought she was going to ensure Louise's safety — or at least that was what she told herself — and having that thrown in her face is painful.

"I didn't just run away," Charlotte says, rubbing her arm. "I was . . ." Her words trail off, and she glances up at me.

Aeva crouches down beside her. "It is not comfortable having your good intentions stomped on and misunderstood, is it?"

"No," she grumbles.

Louise sighs. "You're forgiven. Just don't do it again."

After Annith has greeted Beast and Duval, she explains, "Balthazaar remained on the island, but is ready to speak with you whenever you wish it." Then her eyes move to Maraud. "Who is this?"

There is a moment of silence as we all wonder who should tell her. Finally, Father Effram steps forward. "This is Anton Crunard, your long-lost brother."

Annith's face lights up. "You found him!"

Maraud shakes his head in wonder. "I have a sister. This is a boon I had not expected." He is not wholly without family — surely welcome news in spite of the shock.

"Nor I," Annith says. "We have much to talk about."

The happiness in Maraud's eyes dims somewhat. "Yes, we do."

She squeezes his hand. "When you are ready to speak of it, I will be most eager to hear. Now come," she says to the rest of us. "The boats are waiting."

The next morning, I find Balthazaar behind the convent, beyond the low stone wall that lies between Sister Serafina's poison workshop and the backside of the island.

As I approach, he stops what he is doing and rises to his feet. From this distance, he looks precisely as he did the first time I saw him. Tall, cloaked in black, impossibly still. But not truly the same. There is no frost beneath his feet and none of the terrible beauty of his divinity shines in his face.

He still smells of richly turned earth. Or mayhap that is the soil that clings to his hands. He smiles — in welcome, in joy, and, I think, in some way, in sadness. "Daughter." His voice is no longer the rustle of winter leaves, but a deeply pleasant human voice.

When he came to me as Death, I could feel that he was my father. But with this man, Balthazaar, I do not feel that same connection. "What shall I call you?"

"I am still your father, but if you are more comfortable with Balthazaar, use that."

Because I do not know the answer to that question, I ask, "Are you happy?" truly wanting to know. We spent last night feasting, all of the convent gathering to share stories and hear of the latest adventures. He seemed happy beside Annith, but now I am less sure.

He looks down at the earth under his feet, the faint breeze ruffling his hair, his face no longer unearthly white, but touched by days spent in the sun and the blood that now flows under his skin.

"Yes." It is such a simple word, but there is much behind it. He looks at me. "I am happy."

"You don't miss being Death? The power you held then?"

A hint of a smile. "I miss not needing food. I tend to forget that I need it, and remember at inconvenient times."

I cannot help it, I laugh. "Is that why you are out here digging in the dirt?"

It is hard to tell, but I think he blushes faintly. "I am planting something. See?" He squats down and points to a row of seedlings at the base of the stone wall. "Belladonna."

"Are we running low?" I had wondered if the convent would still make poisons.

"No, I just like the flowers. Like being able to touch the soil and bring life from it rather than death. Although" — he stares ruefully down at the seedlings — "I am not very good at it." He points to the second row, which has begun to wilt.

"They need water," I say gently.

His forehead creases. "Water. That's right. Serafina told me that."

"Here, I'll get some for you."

When I return with a bucket and ladle, I show him how to water the young plants. As we work together, I dare to say, "What can you tell me of the Dark Mother?"

He shows no surprise at my question and begins gently tapping another seedling into the ground. "I see her mark upon you. It has grown stronger since we last saw each other."

The black pebble that I still carry hums with warmth. "Is that why my power seems to be growing, expanding in some way?"

Finished with his seedling, he looks up at me again. "Is it?"

"I am able to do things — Gen is able to do things — we've never done before."

He shifts his gaze to stare at the ocean, his gray eyes the exact same color as the sea. "I wonder if it is your powers that have changed or you? From what the others have told me, you were broken and wounded when you first arrived here." He looks at me with pain in his eyes. "And I am deeply sorry for that. But as you grow stronger now, so do your powers. Or rather, your willingness to explore your own powers."

That makes sense, and yet. "Sometimes, it feels as if the power is . . . loose . . . in the world, now that . . . now that it is not held by you."

"Oh, that is also possible."

"How can you not know? You are — were — Death?"

He rests his arm on his knee. "And you are human. Do you understand all that being human entails? Why some are strong and others weak? Why some seek joy and others seek to destroy it?"

Now it is I who look away. I do not like that he doesn't have all the answers.

Or mayhap he no longer has them — they have slipped away with his godhood. "Father Effram said something once about the original covenant between the Church and the Nine."

Balthazaar smiles. "Gods, we were young. And the Church so full of hubris."

"Well, that part has not changed much."

"When we first entered into the agreement with the Church, they wanted to keep our powers contained. The covenant stated we could not bear sons, because the Church was so blinded it only saw men as threats to its power." He smiles. "Of course it was Salonius who discovered that loophole, and once we found it, we took full advantage. Gods do not like being restricted, even when they must agree to it." He falls silent again as he stares out at the thick green grass rolling its way down to the shore. "But I have now seen how much the convent has forgotten. How many powers they have stopped using. How many they did not know they possessed."

"But why? Why would they not hang on to those with both hands?"

He shrugs, a most human gesture. "I cannot say. Annith wants to search back through the records and see if she can find more information on what they were."

"Don't you know?"

"Each of my daughters is unique, my powers manifesting in each of you in different ways. I cannot guess all the possibilities and how they might reveal themselves." After a moment, he bends down to pick up another one of the green seedlings in his basket. With his attention still on the seedlings, I reach into my pocket, my fingers closing around the sprig of holly I still carry there. I take it out and gently plant it in the rich earth at the base of the wall. I do not know if it will take root, but feel it belongs here now.

"And you, Sybella?" Balthazaar asks. "Are you happy?"

He has never called me by my name before. I reach for the bucket and carefully pour some of the water on the holly, then sit back on my heels. I had intended to tell him of the hole he left in my life and the struggle I have had to fill it, but that no longer feels as important as it once did.

"Beast has asked for your hand," he continues.

"What did you say?"

"That it was your decision, not mine. He is a good man. One of the best I have met in this form or my other, but it must be your choice."

"Yes, I love him."

He stares at me then, his gaze nearly as penetrating and all-seeing as when he was Death. "I am glad you have found love."

We fall into a comfortable silence, happy to return to our work. It is enjoyable, this quiet companionship. Certainly not something I could have done with Death. When we have finished with all the seedlings — and watered them — he says, "Annith will want to know where you would like to get married. In the church or the —"

"Here," I say, looking out at the endless sea, the salt-kissed grass, the ancient standing stones, and the row of seedlings we have just planted together. "I wish to marry here."

It is the perfect place to start anew.

AUTHOR'S NOTE

So often, stories end with the wedding, or the promise of a wedding, but history tells us that such events are more commonly the beginning of a new chapter. So it was with Anne of Brittany. In truth, she is hard to discern through history — her story having been written by countless men with political agendas, conflicting alliances, stilted views of women, or simply an ax to grind.

To some, she was a schemer. To others, a proud symbol of Breton independence. Some saw her as a hapless pawn, while still others saw her as exerting her influence behind the scenes, as was so often the case with women of her time. From amongst all these accounts, a sense of Anne herself began to come through for me: a fully dimensional person who possessed a bit of all those attributes and motivations ascribed to her. But what I mostly saw was a young girl thrust into an impossible situation who used every resource she possessed to do the best she could for the country she was responsible for.

There is not much written about her after her marriage to Charles, other than to record various pregnancies and financial extravagances. But there were enough tantalizing bits that a picture of what life would have been like for Anne of Brittany in those first days of marriage began to take shape.

By all historical accounts, the regent, Anne of France, was a most formidable young woman as well, not especially willing to concede her power to the young queen. It was hard for me to keep in mind that she was only twenty-eight years old when the events in this book took place. In truth, she deserves to be the hero of her own story: having taken on the regency for her young brother at the tender age of twenty-two, she managed to fend off numerous revolts and attempts to usurp her power, as well as expand the holdings and power of the crown of France.

However, there was so much plotting and conspiring in those first days of Anne's queenship that the king did indeed have the regent swear to an alliance of mutual aid and agree to desist from agitating unnecessary intrigue within the kingdom.

As for the Breton uprising, I found approximately six lines in three separate sources about an attempted revolt led by Viscount Rohan, which was quickly put down. In that revolt, he invited England to assist him, which provided them the foothold they'd long been seeking. King Henry VII did invade French soil, landing at Boulogne in the autumn of 1492. King Charles of France quickly repelled the advance, resulting in the signing of the Treaty of Étaples. Those few lines were all my imagination needed to construct the bones of the story and thus be able to get to the part I love best — the human drama that lies at the heart of it all.

Once again, I have taken the greatest liberties with the timing of events and the d'Albret family, shamelessly manipulating both to serve the needs of the narrative.

Throughout the centuries, religious orders and houses sanctioned by the Catholic Church have come and gone, some lost to indifference or dying out, and others actively persecuted by the Church itself. It has also been a longstanding prerogative of kings and queens to establish military or religious orders to defend their interests and maintain the standards of chivalry within their kingdom. I like to believe that, over time, the Nine managed to weave their way into the larger tapestry of the Church's hagiography and remain with us today under different names that are, if we squint back through the lens of time, faintly recognizable.

It is often said that history is written by the victor and it is clear that for centuries women's stories have been excluded from the annals of history — their contributions diminished, overlooked, or erased altogether. That is one of the joys of writing historical fantasy — getting to reimagine the past with women at the center of their own stories. After being forced to be silent for so long, I feel certain that some of them would, indeed, like to burn it all.

ACKNOWLEDGMENTS

Once again, I find myself reaching the end of a book only by the grace and support of dozens of patron saints along the way. First among these is my editor, Kate O'Sullivan, the perennial shepherdess, guiding me ever closer to a book I'll be proud of.

My agent, Erin Murphy, has been unwavering in her support, not just for this book, but for all my books.

I hold deep gratitude for the entire team at Houghton Mifflin Harcourt, who continue to amaze me with their skill, professionalism, and passion. I am incredibly lucky to be the recipient of the talents of Mary Magrisso, Ana Deboo, Erika West, Mary Hurley, Margaret Rosewitz, Emily Andrukaitis, and Ellen Fast.

Special thanks to Whitney Leader-Picone and Billelis, who have outdone themselves again, encompassing the theme of this book with yet another stunning visual.

And, of course, no one would even know about the book if not for the talent and support of John Sellers, Nadia Almahdi, Lisa DiSarro, Amanda Acevedo, Matt Schweitzer, Colleen Murphy, Ed Spade, and their entire sales team.

Thank you also to my poor, long-suffering family, who, once again, were understanding and cheerfully supportive as I disappeared into an alternate world that consumed me wholly until I hit "The End."

Since this book ended up having a lot to do with fathers, a special thank-you goes out to my own — for being there for his family in so many ways and for loving me unconditionally, even when I shocked him by writing about assassin nuns.

But, most of all, I owe the biggest thanks to you, dear readers, those who have embraced my assassin nuns and their world and let me know it in so very many ways. I appreciate all that you have done: reading, handselling, putting the books into the hands of your students, emailing, DMing, tweeting, Bookstagramming, blogging, reviewing, rating, and YouTubing. Thank you so much for allowing my books into your life for a short while. My hope is that they have made it richer in some small way. I know you have made my life richer by far.